Beams of brilliant green light.

A spray of mist.

And suddenly a different view. A close-up in a flash of grainy light: a second creature, like the first, jerky movements, legs that ended in lobster claws, thrashing.

Then, "Oh, God!" Plath cried. "I saw its face."

For Katherine, Jake and Julia

The author wishes to thank two amazing bands,
The Methadones and Shot Baker, for permission to reprint some of their lyrics

First published in Great Britain 2012
by Electric Monkey – an imprint of Egmont UK Limited
239 Kensington High Street
London W8 6SA

·THE SHADOW GANG·

The digital experience that accompanies this book was created by
The Shadow Gang in conjunction with the author (www.theshadowgang.com)

ISBN 978 1 4052 5994 1

1 3 5 7 9 10 8 6 4 2

www.egmont.co.uk

A CIP catalogue record for this title is available from the British Library

Typeset by Avon DataSet Ltd, Bidford on Avon, Warwickshire
Printed and bound by CPI Group (UK) Ltd, Croydon, CR0 4YY

49879/2

BZRK

MICHAEL GRANT

Oh, that way madness lies;
let me shun that.

King Lear

ONE

A girl sat just three chairs down from Noah talking to her hand. To the back of her hand, actually, as she spread her fingers wide. Her fingertips were painted alternately red and gold, but not with fingernail polish, and not strictly on the fingernails. Rather, it looked as if she had used a can of spray paint.

She explained to the back of her hand that she was, "Perfectly all right. Perfectly all right."

Noah thought she might have been pretty, but it was hard to really assess her face or body when his glance was drawn so irresistibly to the rope burn around her neck.

She started screaming when the orderlies came for her. They had to lift her up bodily, one on each rigid arm. Her mother, or perhaps older sister, stood with her hand over her mouth, wept and echoed the girl's own speech.

"It'll be all right," said the sane one.

"I'm perfectly all right!" cried the crazy one.

The girl kicked her chair across the floor, and shot Noah a savage look from eyes edged red.

Noah Cotton. Sixteen years old. He had brown hair that defaulted to bed head without any effort on his part. His lips were full and downturned just a little, as if prepared for sadness. The nose was strong and sharp, a damned-near-perfect nose. But of course it was those blue eyes that drew you in. Where had he gotten eyes that blue? They looked unnatural. Like someone wearing tinted contact lenses. And Noah would turn those bright, unnatural blue eyes on you, and you wouldn't know whether you were looking into profound depths or maybe just into a very crazy place.

Well, if the answer was, "A very crazy place," then he would fit in perfectly with his location, which was the waiting room in the central hall of The Brick.

This place weighed down on him. Maybe it was the history. In the eighteenth century it had been called the Lord Japheth LeMay Asylum for the Incurably Mad. By the mid-nineteenth century that had been softened a bit to become the East London Asylum for the Insane.

Today it was officially called the East London Hospital for the Treatment of Serious Mental Illness.

But no one called it that, at least not outside the facility itself. Out in the world it was called The Brick.

It was a redbrick architectural monstrosity that had grown— metastasized, maybe—over the course of more than two hundred years. It wasn't all brick. Some of the towers and wings

2

were stone. Some outbuildings were flaking, painted plaster over ancient half-timbered walls. But the massive hall, with its fraternal twin towers, the Bishop and the Rook—one tall and pointed, the other squat and intimidating—were all in soot-encrusted red brick.

Noah was doing his best not to feel the echoes of the mad girl's cries, but the waiting room was about as schizophrenic as many of the patients: ancient oil paintings, a vaguely off-kilter black-and-white tile floor, yellow walls that were probably someone's idea of cheerful, and furniture from a rummage sale. Then, to top it all off, there was the chandelier, which had to have been plundered from some gaudy palace during a long-ago colonial war. It cast a light that was excellent at creating shadows, so that even the space under the chairs looked as if it might be the dark lair of tiny monsters.

Noah was here to visit his brother, Alex. His much older brother, Alex. Age twenty-five, ex-army veteran of Afghanistan, Royal Highland Fusiliers. (Motto: *Nemo Me Impugn Lacessit*— No One Assails Me with Impunity. Or the alternative version—Do Not Fuck with Us or We Will Hurt You.) Shoulders you could break a cinder block on, disciplined, up every morning to run ten kilometers in whatever weather London had on offer.

Alex Cotton, who had earned the Conspicuous Gallantry Cross for basically having balls so big he had taken out three

3

Hajis in a machine-gun nest while literally carrying a wounded comrade on his back.

And now . . .

Noah's name was called. An attendant, a swaggering thug with fat legs, a Taser in one pocket and a leather-covered sap sticking out of the other, led the way. Past office doorways. Through a reinforced glass and steel security door.

Through a second security door.

Past the control center where bored guards watched flickering screens and discussed sports with their feet up.

Through a third door. This one had to be buzzed open by an attendant on the other side.

And here the screams and wails and sudden shrill, rising cries and gut-wrenching sobs began. The sounds leaked through steel doors of individual rooms: cells, in reality.

Noah didn't want to feel those screams inside himself, but he wasn't armored, he wasn't impervious. Each wild trill of mad laughter made him flinch as if he was being whipped.

A nurse and two scruffy attendants were making their way from door to door. One of the attendants pushed a squeaky cart loaded with little plastic cups, each designated with a code number and containing no fewer than half a dozen and sometimes a baker's dozen brightly colored pills.

The pill crew came to a door, knocked, warned the inmate to stand back, waited, then unlocked and opened the door. One attendant—no, let's cut the bull, they were guards, turnkeys, screws, but not attendants—went inside with the nurse while the remaining guard stood ready with a Taser.

Noah reached Alex's cell. Number ninety-one.

"Don't worry, he's shackled," the guard said. "Just don't try to touch him. He don't like people touching him." The guard grinned ruefully and shook his head in a way that suggested Noah knew what he meant.

The door opened on a room five feet wide, eight feet deep. The only furnishing was a steel bunk. Fat steel bolts fixed the cot to the cracked tile floor. There was a radio on a high shelf, too high for a person to reach. The BBC was on, soft, some politician being grilled.

Alex Cotton sat on the edge of the bunk. His wrists were handcuffed to steel rings on either end. The effect was to stretch his arms out and limit his ability to move anything but his head.

The ghost of Alex Cotton turned hollow, vacant eyes on his little brother.

Noah couldn't speak for a moment. Because what he wanted to say was, "This is the wrong room. That's not my brother."

Then a low growl that at first sounded as if it might be coming from the radio. An animal sound. Alex Cotton's mouth snapped suddenly, like a shark missing the bait.

"Alex," Noah said. "It's me. It's just me, Noah."

The guttural sound again. Alex's eyes suddenly focused. He

stared at Noah, shook his head as if the vision caused him pain.

Noah made just the slightest move to touch his brother's strained arm. Alex yanked his whole body as far away as he could, which was no more than a few inches. He strained so hard that the handcuffs drew blood.

Noah backed away, held up his hands reassuringly.

"Told you, don't try and touch him, he'll start screaming about his little spiders and shit," the guard said.

"Alex, it's just me. It's Noah."

"Nano nano nano nano," Alex said in a singsong voice, and then giggled. He wiggled his fingertips like he was acting something out.

"Nano? What is that, Alex?" He whispered it, speaking as he would to a frightened child. Gentle.

"Heh heh heh, no. No. No no no nano nano nano. No."

Noah waited until he was done. He refused to look away. This was his brother. What was left of his brother.

"Alex, no one can figure this out. No one can figure out what happened to you. You know what I mean, to have you end up here."

Explain your craziness, crazy man. Tell me what happened to my brother.

"Nano, macro, nano, macro," Alex muttered.

"He says that a lot," the guard offered. "Mostly nano."

"Is this from the war?" Noah asked, ignoring the guard. He

wanted an explanation. None of the doctors had been very convincing. Everyone said it was probably the war, but Alex had been examined for post-traumatic stress when he came home, and everything had seemed fine with him. He and Noah had taken in some sports, gone on a road trip to the Cornish coast for the beach and for some girl Alex knew. His brother had been a little distracted, but that was all. Distracted.

The guard hadn't answered.

"I mean, is it memories and all that?" Noah pressed. "Is that what he goes on about? Afghanistan?"

To his surprise, it was Alex who answered.

"Haji?" Alex laughed a crooked-mouth laugh, like half his face was paralyzed. "Not Haji. Bug Man," Alex said. "The Buuug Man. One, two, three. All dead. Poof!"

"That's pretty good for him," the guard opined approvingly.

And for a few seconds it almost seemed as if the crazy had cleared away. Like Alex was straining to make his mouth say words. His voice went down into a whisper. He nodded, like he was saying, *Pay attention to this; this is important.*

This. Is. Important.

Then he said, "Berserk."

Alex nodded, satisfied with himself, then kept nodding harder and harder, until his whole body was vibrating almost like some kind of seizure. The shackles rattled the bed. The whole cell seemed to vibrate in sympathy.

7

"Berserk!" Alex said, louder now and louder still until he was shouting it.

"Berserk! Berserk!"

"Jesus," Noah said, hating himself for reacting, for letting his horror show.

"Once he starts on this, it's over for the day," the guard said wearily. He grabbed Noah's arm, not unkindly. "Goes on for hours with this 'Berserk' shite of his."

"Berserk! Berserk!"

Noah let himself be led from the cell.

"Berserk!"

When he heard the door locked behind him, he felt a wave of sickness and relief. But it didn't stop the sound of his mad brother's cries, which followed him down the hallway, drilling holes into Noah's reeling mind.

"Berserk!"

"BERSERK!"

TWO

Stone McLure wasn't model handsome. Not one of those guys who looked pretty. Even though he was just seventeen, Stone wasn't really for girls. He was for women.

Women would look at him and let their eyes slide over his face and those shoulders, because, you know, women don't stare the way men do. They just need a glance. And then, having memorized him with a glance, they would regret their marriage, regret their age, regret their sweatpants and faded Abercrombie T-shirts, regret that they were carrying a plastic bag of groceries in one hand and a twenty-four pack of Pampers in the other.

Stone pulled his earbuds out.

"Where are we stopping first?" he asked his father.

"We'll refuel in San Francisco and pick up a second pilot. Then I have a brief meeting in Hokkaido, and it's on to Singapore." He said it without looking up from his work.

Earbuds back in.

Stone had curly dark hair and eyes like polished green marble with golden threads woven through. He had a brow that seemed designed by God to mark him as honest, a strong nose, a complexion that had surely never been marred by so much as a freckle, let alone a pimple—what pimple would dare?

He looked a bit like his father, Grey McLure—and most of the world knew Grey's face—but Grey had the signs of weariness and wariness that came with being a billionaire of the better sort. A billionaire who had made his money with science and innovation and in all the ways you'd hope a billionaire would make his money.

They were sitting just a couple of feet apart in the back of a Cessna Citation X, Grey facing aft, Stone facing forward. It was a private jet, yes, but no more ostentatious than was absolutely necessary in a private jet. There was no hot flight attendant in a teasing uniform. No flowing Champagne. None of that. Grey's jet was about business. And his son was learning that business.

Grey was drinking coffee from a mug that said fairly decent dad. See, a mug that said world's best dad would have violated the Grey family's style, which was self-deprecating, wry, and utterly devoted.

Grey was tapping away at his pad and sipping and tapping and frowning a bit from time to time.

Stone was reading a book on his own pad, not maybe paying as much attention as he should, because in his ears were the buds and through them came the raw, hoarse voice of Tony Kovacs.

Being here with my surroundings,
Seeing all I'm looking at,
Evolution winking at me,
My face forms a smile.

Earbuds out.

"So this would be a flight measured more in days than in mere hours," Stone said, and stretched his legs.

"Long flight," his father acknowledged. "You could have spent the time with your grandmother in Maryland."

Stone held up mock-surrender hands. "Did I sound like I was complaining?"

"Your grandmother loves you."

"My grandmother loves painting ceramic figurines of First Ladies."

"Historically accurate figurines," Grey said and grinned. "You could have helped her decorate Abigail Fillmore's bonnet."

Stone pretended to weigh the alternatives. "Abigail's bonnet . . . Singapore girls in formfitting saris. Hmm. Tough one."

Earbuds back in.

Here am I living in it,
Here am I in everything.

His sister, Sadie, had gotten him started on punk, probably thinking he needed something less, well, insipid than what he came up with by following his usual pattern: downloading whatever his friends were listening to. Sadie was like that, one of those people untouched by trend or fashion, comfortable building her own world out of what she liked, from tunes and styles and reads that could be so ancient they were cobwebbed, up through to things so new they barely existed yet. Sometimes it was like she imagined something and conjured it into reality.

Sadie could be a prickly little witch, but at sixteen she was who she was in a way that Stone could not quite equal. Didn't bother him, not really. Stone had a defined role to play. He was the heir, the scion, the eldest. There'd been lots of times he envied Sadie's freedom—man, who wouldn't?—but he was okay with his destiny. Someone had to do it. Might as well be him.

Spent so much of my time thinking,
Feeling like I'm under attack.
Overlooking the reality in front of me,
Wandering down so many paths.

And for his mother, whose ashes had settled into the Atlantic at the midpoint between her native London and her adopted New York.

He looked out of the window, veering his thoughts away from that last image. Not right now, not right now, not that memory.

Stone and his father had taken off from Teterboro and now were flying over the Meadowlands. Down below, a game. Football, American style.

Stone's life had been split more or less evenly between New York and London, so he could appreciate both sets of sport obsession: football and baseball in the States, soccer and cricket in the UK. Still couldn't imagine what anyone saw in hockey, because . . .

Then he remembered.

Earbuds out.

"Hey, isn't Sadie at that game?"

Grey looked up and smiled, a conspiratorial look. "And I'm sure she's loving every minute of it."

Stone laughed. "Yeah. Nothing Sadie likes better than being outside in the cold and part of some big, cheering crowd." He shook his head. "I hope the dude is worth it. Is it that Tony guy I met?"

Grey nodded. "I think highly of his father. Tony himself . . . well, I suppose I could offer Sadie some fatherly advice on that kid."

They both burst out laughing. The idea of Sadie listening to advice from anyone. On any topic. Let alone her love life.

"You're not that brave," Stone teased.

"I'm not that stupid," Grey countered with a look of mock fear. Then, in a softer tone, turning his eyes away, looking out and down, "She's got your mother in her."

Which just veered Stone back to a place he didn't want to go. He nodded and didn't trust his voice to answer. Not even a 'Yeah." Even one syllable could break his voice.

Earbuds in.

Shot Baker was done. Someone else was singing, another song Sadie had put on his playlist. Come to think of it, was there anything on it that Sadie hadn't chosen for him?

Down below, the dome was a huge, oblong cereal bowl filled with eighty thousand Jets fans. The Jets actually had eighty thousand fans this year, because it was early December and damned if they weren't still in contention.

The dome's cover had been drawn back to let fans take advantage of the clear, weak, low-slung sun of fall. The sleet and the cold wind would come soon enough; a last sunny Sunday, even a chilly one, was not to be wasted.

A blimp turned lazily above the dome. It looked like some leisurely version of sperm and egg from up here. The image brought a smile to Stone's lips. He totally had to work that into his next English comp paper. Freak out his teacher with a sudden display of analogy. Or was it simile?

Earbuds out, reluctantly.

"Hey, I see her head. That's her, on the left," Stone said. "End zone." Making conversation so Grey wouldn't think he was upset about the mention of Mom. From this height the tops of heads were a mere suggestion of a dot.

"No," Grey said, "She's closer to midfield."

Like he knew right where she was sitting. Playing along, Stone thought. Although, sometimes it seemed to Stone that their father knew Sadie's every move. They had something, those two.

Sadie and Grey fought—word battles with all kinds of subtext Stone could hear but not understand. Word ninjas, those two. Fortunately Stone had always gotten along with his sister, because he'd be the first to admit he could not throw down in a verbal battle with her. The girl could put a knife right into your ego.

Sometimes it made him jealous that Sadie and their father could yell at each other. He and Grey never did.

The jet banked a sharp left. Like the pilot had read Grey's mind and wanted to give the boss a chance to peer down and make out the top of his daughter's head. Or like—

The turn was too sharp.

Way too sharp, hard and sudden. The right wing was arcing downward.

Stone was pulled against the bulkhead by gravity. The pad fell from his father's lap. Grey's fairly decent dad mug scooted across the table and toppled over to roll down the aisle.

"What the hell?" Grey demanded.

There was an intercom in Grey's armrest. He punched the button. "Kelly. What's the matter?" Kelly, the pilot. She'd flown the jet for six years. Like a member of the family.

No answer.

"Strap in," Grey told Stone. He stood up, but the g-forces threw him off-balance so that he had to sort of twist around his seat. He fell against a bulkhead and then pushed himself back up and lurched toward the cockpit door, moving like a drunk in a strong wind.

Now the jet was tilting not just to the right but downward. A definite dive. Like way too steep. Through the window Stone saw the field below already closer, and tilted crazily. Big men on a green rectangle seeming somehow to run uphill. He saw the Jumbotron screens showing a replay.

"Kelly!" Grey had reached the cockpit door, barely holding himself up. "Are you okay in there? What's happening?"

Grey rattled the little door handle. The door did not open.

That's when Grey looked back at his son. Their eyes met.

Weird how much a two-second glance could convey. Fear. Sadness. Regret.

Defeat.

Grey banged on the cockpit door. "Open up, Kelly! Open the door!"

Stone unbuckled and lurched to his feet. But the floor was falling away from him. It was as if he couldn't fall fast enough to keep his feet on the floor. Like when a roller coaster crosses that first big crest and suddenly you are gravity's toy. The ceiling came down and hit him. Not hard, but the ceiling had no business hitting him at all.

Stone didn't walk to the cockpit door, he tumbled. He snatched at seat backs and missed, fingers slapping tan leather, feet scooting uselessly on carpet. He plowed hard into his father.

Grey was slamming himself as well as he could against the cockpit door. Yelling. Cursing, which was not something Grey McLure did.

The plane was tilted so sharply now that it was more vertical than horizontal. Stone lay on his back on the carpeted floor and kicked against the cockpit door beneath him, while his father lay pressed against the bulkhead and slammed himself against it.

"Dad! What's happening?"

Stone kicked again and again.

A sudden give. The doorjamb cracked. One more hit would do it.

Stone hauled himself back up, using the seats to climb, like a slippery ladder, then dropped, feet punching out with every bit of power he had to give, and with a sound like a breaking branch the door gave way.

17

Stone fell through in a tangle with his father. The two of them hit Kelly's seat and crashed into the instrument panel, smashed into the windshield. Pain shot through Stone's knees, his elbow, his shoulder. Didn't matter because now the green field was so near. Zooming up at him.

A flash of Kelly's face, eyes blank, mouth bleeding from hitting the instrument panel, short-cut gray hair matted, staring hard in horror. Staring at something maybe only she could see.

A flash of the stands full of people.

His father flailing, legs tangling, something broken, head hanging the wrong way, too confused to . . .

"Dad!" A sob, not a shout.

Stone pushed himself back from the instrument panel and somehow found the stick with his right hand and pulled hard.

Kelly turned to look at him. Like Stone's action was puzzling to her. Like she was amazed to find him there. With dreamy slowness she reached for the stick.

The three of them tangled together in a heap and the field rushing up at them. So fast.

Way too fast.

And Stone knew it.

But he pulled back on the stick and yelled, "Dad!" for no reason because there wasn't anything Stone could do but look at him with eyes full of horror and so sad; so, so sad.

"Dad!"

The jet began to respond. The nose started to come up. The stadium seats looked like they were falling away, and now the top of the stadium, the upper rim was in view.

And some remote, still-functioning part of Stone's brain realized they were actually inside the stadium. A jet. Inside a bowl. Climbing toward safety.

Faces. Stone could see thousands of faces staring up at him and so close now he could see the expressions of horror and see the eyes and open mouths and drinks being spilled, legs tripping as they tried to run away.

He saw team shirts.

A redheaded kid.

A mother pulling her baby close.

An old guy making the sign of the cross, like he was doing it in slow motion.

"Dad."

Then the jet flipped. Up was down.

The jet was moving very fast. But not quite the speed of sound. Not quite the speed of sound, so the crunch of the aluminium nose hitting bodies and seats and concrete did reach Stone's ears.

But before his brain could register the sound, Stone's honest brow and strong nose and broad shoulders and his brain and ears, too, were smashed to jelly.

Stone was instantly dead, so he did not see that his

father's body was cut in two as it blew through the split side of the cockpit.

He did not see that a section of Grey's shattered-melon head flew clear, bits of gray-and-pink matter falling away, a trail of brain.

A small piece—no bigger than a baby's fist—of one of the great minds of modern times landed in a paper cup of Coors Light and sank into the foam.

Then the explosion.

THREE

Sadie McLure didn't see the jet until it was far too late.

The boy she was with—Tony—was not a boyfriend. Not really. But maybe. If he grew up a little. If he got past being weird about the fact that his father was just a department manager at McLure Industries. That he lived in a house half the size of the McLure home's garage.

"Sorry about these seats," Tony said for, oh, about the tenth time. "I thought I might get access to my buddy's skybox, but . . ."

Yeah, that was the problem for Sadie: not being in a skybox while she watched a game she didn't understand or like.

Until Tony had brought it up, Sadie had had no idea what a skybox was.

So *not* the most important thing in the world, that disparity in income. If she limited herself to dating the kids of other billionaires, she wasn't going to have much to choose from.

"I enjoy mixing with the common people," Sadie said.

He looked startled.

"That was a joke," she said. Then, when he didn't smile, she added, "Kidding."

Try to be nice, she told herself.

Try to be more flexible.

Sure, why not a football game? Maybe it would be fun. Unless of course it involved some otherwise perfectly attractive and intelligent boy apologizing for his five-year-old Toyota and his jacket, which was just . . . she didn't even remember what brand, but he seemed to think it wasn't the *right* brand.

If there was a downside to being well-off—and there weren't many—it was that people assumed you must be a snob. And no amount of behaving normally could change some people's mind.

"Have a nacho," Sadie said, and offered him the cardboard tray.

"They're pretty awful, aren't they?" he replied. "Not exactly caviar."

"Yeah, well, I've already had my caviar for the day," Sadie said. And this time she didn't bother to explain that that was a joke. Instead she just scooped up a jalapeño and popped a chip in her mouth and munched it gloomily.

This was going to be a long date.

Sadie could be described as a series of averages that added up to something not even slightly average. She was of average height and average weight. But she had a way of seeming far larger when she was determined or angry.

She was of average beauty. Unless she was flirting or wanted to be noticed by a guy, and then, so very much not average. She had the ability to go from, "Yeah, she's kinda hot," to "Oh my God, my heart just stopped," simply by deciding to turn it on. Like a switch. She could aim her brown eyes and part her full lips and yes, right then, she could cause heart attacks.

And five minutes later be just a good-looking but not particularly noticeable girl.

At the moment she was not in heart-attack-causing mode. But she was getting to the point where she was starting to seem larger than she was. Intelligent, perceptive people knew this was dangerous. Tony was intelligent—she'd never have gone out with him otherwise—but he was not perceptive.

Jesus, Sadie wondered, probably under her breath, *how long did these football games last?* She felt as if it was entering its seventy-fifth hour.

She couldn't just walk away, grab a cab, and go home; Tony would think it was some reflection on his lack of a diamond-encased phone or whatever.

Could she sneak a single earbud into the ear away from Tony? Would he notice? This would all go so much better with some music or an audiobook. Or maybe just white noise. Or maybe a beer to dull the dullness of it all.

"Clearly, I need a fake ID," Sadie said, but too quietly for Tony to hear it over a load groan as a pass went sailing over the head of the receiver.

Sadie noticed the jet only after it had already started its too-sharp turn.

She didn't recognize it as her father's. Not at first. Grey wasn't the kind of guy who would paint his plane with some company logo.

"That plane," she said to Tony. She poked his arm to get his attention.

"What?"

"Look at it. Look what it's doing."

And the engine noise was wrong. Too loud. Too close.

A frozen moment for her brain to accept the impossible as the inevitable.

The jet would hit the stands. There was no stopping it. It was starting to pull up but way too late.

Sadie grabbed Tony's shoulder. Not for comfort but to get him moving. "Tony. Run!"

Tony dug in his heels, scowled at her. Sadie was already moving and she plowed into him, knocked him over, skinned her knee right through her jeans as she tripped, but levered one foot beneath herself, stepped on Tony's most excellent abs, pushed off, and leapt away.

The jet roared over her head, a sound like the end of the

world, except that the next sound was louder still.

The impact buckled her knees as it earthquaked the stands.

Then, a beat. Not silence, just a little dip in the sound storm.

Then a new sound as tons of jet fuel ignited. A clap of thunder from a cloud not fifty feet away.

Fire.

Things flying through the air. Big foam fingers and the hands that had been waving them. Paper cups and popcorn and hot dogs and body parts, so many of those, tumbling missiles of gore flying through the air.

The blast wave so overwhelming, so irresistible, that she wouldn't even realize for several minutes that she had been thrown thirty feet, tossed like a leaf before a leaf blower, to land on her back against a seat, the impact softened by the body of a little girl. Thrown away like a doll God was tired of playing with.

She felt the heat, like someone had opened a pizza oven inches from her face. And set off a hand grenade amid the cheese and pepperoni. The first inch of hair caught fire but was quickly extinguished as air rushed back to the vacuum of the explosion.

The next minutes passed in a sort of loud silence. She heard none of the cries. Could no longer hear the sounds of falling debris all around her. Could hear only the world's loudest car alarm screaming in her brain, a siren that came not from outside her head but from inside.

Sadie rolled off the crushed form of the girl. On hands and knees between rows of seats. Something sticky squishing up through her fingers. Something red and white: bloody fat. Just a chunk of it, the size of a ham.

Should do something, should do something, her brain kept saying. But what? Run away? Scream?

Now she noticed that her left arm was turned in a direction arms didn't turn. There was no pain, just the sight of bones— her own bones—sticking through the skin of her forearm. Thin white sticks jutting from a gash filled with raw hamburger.

She screamed. Probably. She couldn't hear, but she felt her mouth stretch wide.

She stood up.

The fire was uphill from her in the stands, maybe thirty rows up. A tail fin was intact but being swiftly consumed by the oily fire. A pillar of thick, greasy smoke swirled and filled her nostrils with the stench of gas stations and barbecued meat before finding its upward path.

The main fire burned without much color to the flame.

Bodies burned yellow and orange.

Unless he had been blown clear, Tony's would be one of them.

A fat man crawled away, pulling himself along on his elbows as fire crawled up his legs.

A boy, maybe ten, squatted beside his mother's head.

Sadie realized a different scene of madness was going on behind her. She turned and saw a panicked crowd shoving and pushing like a herd of buffalo on the run from a lion.

But others weren't running away but walking warily toward the carnage.

A man reached her and mouthed words at her. She touched her ear, and he seemed to get it. He looked at her broken arm and did an odd thing. He kissed his fingertips and touched them to her shoulder and moved along. Later it would seem strange. At that moment, no.

The tail of the plane was collapsing into the fire. Through the smoke Sadie just made out the registration number. She'd already known, somewhere down in her shocked brain. The number just confirmed it.

She wanted to believe something different. She wanted to believe her father and brother were not in that hell of fire and smoke. She wanted to believe that she was breathing something that was not the smoke of their roasted bodies. But it was hard to pretend. That took an effort she couldn't muster, not just yet.

Right now she could believe that everyone, everywhere was dead. She could believe she was dead.

She looked down then and saw blood all down one trouser leg. Saturated denim. She stared at this, stupid, something going very wrong with her brain.

And then the stadium spun like a top and she fell.

*

"Good twitch," the Bug Man whispered to himself, a quiet congratulations. Satisfaction at a victory. Not that it was much of one. However dramatic the end result might be in the macro, in the nano it had just been a long wire job. There'd been no bug-on-bug fighting. Just wiring, connecting image to action.

Anyone could have done it. But could they have done it as fast? Could they have wired the pilot's brain in three days? And set her up to have a switch thrown as dramatically as this?

Hell, no.

He pulled his left hand from the glove. Then his right hand. They came free with a slight sucking sound. And with his hands freed he reached up and worked the tight helmet off his head.

Had to get that back strap adjusted right. It was still digging into the back of his head where the flesh of his neck met the close-cropped skull.

He was alone. There were larger rooms here on the fifty-ninth floor, and other twitcher stations with as many as four consoles. But the Bug Man rated a private space. Had he pressed the button for the motorized shade, he'd have seen the spire of the Chrysler Building a block to the west. No other twitcher had that view—not that he looked at it much. It wasn't about the view, it was about having the right to it.

The room was simple, scarcely furnished aside from the console. The light was low, just a glow coming from the Peace

28

Pearl aromatherapy candles in their elegant crystal dish. And the gray light of static on the monitor.

The Bug Man breathed.

A win. Take it, rack it, add it to the total.

He had known it was done when all eighteen nanobots—two fighters and sixteen frantic spinners—in the pilot had gone dark at the same instant.

Could anyone else have run eighteen bugs at once, with sixteen actively laying wire? Even platooned? No. No one. Let them try.

Still, just a wire job. Now if Vincent had been coming at him, yeah, then it would have been mythic. Could he have pulled that off? Maybe. No good would come from underestimating Vincent. Vincent had twitch.

The Bug Man glanced at the display panel, checking a readout from the telemetry off the lone 'sneaker' nanobot on Sadie McLure's date, hiding out up in his hair where no one would look. The readout showed a sudden spike from ambient temperature of twelve Celsius to sixty-three Celsius.

Fireball.

But not enough to kill the kid. Not enough to kill Sadie unless she was a lot closer to the explosion or else took some shrapnel.

Success. But not total. In all likelihood there was still a McLure.

Bug Man knew they'd all be waiting outside his room to congratulate him. He dreaded it because they would have the

TV on and they'd be watching it all in lurid color, hanging on the tension-pitched voices of reporters in helicopters.

Bug Man didn't like postmortems. It was enough to succeed. There was no point in wallowing in it and high-fiving and all the rest.

He wished he didn't have to go out at all. But he needed to pee in the worst way.

He fumbled for his phone and stuffed the earbuds in. He found the music he was looking for.

When enemies start posing as friends,
To keep you even closer in the end,
The rooms turn to black.
A kitchen knife is twisting in my back.

Bug Man had no friends. Not in this life. Not in this job. And plenty of people would put a knife in his back. Paranoia? Hah. Paranoia was common sense.

He pulled the hood of his sweatshirt over his head and, with a deep, bracing breath, opened the door.

Sure enough, Jindal was waiting with a high-five. Jindal was . . . well, what was he, exactly? A sort of office manager for twitchers? He saw himself as being in some kind of position of authority. The twitchers saw him as the guy who made sure the fridge had plenty of Red Bull.

Thirty-five years old, grinning ingratiatingly at a sixteen-year-old kid in a hoodie. Sucking up. Even doing a little dance move, like he was trying to impress the Bug Man with a flash of ghetto. Bug Man was from Knightsbridge, a pricey neighborhood in London. He was not from the Bronx. But what did Jindal know? Any black face had to be ghetto.

"The damn signal repeater on the blimp went weak on me, Jindal," Bug Man said, a little too loud over the music in his ears. "I was down to eighty percent."

Let's see if Jindal wanted to dance about a glitchy repeater. Bug Man pushed past him.

But Burnofsky was a different thing. Couldn't really just blow off Burnofsky. He might be a sixty-year-old burnout with a six-day growth of white whiskers and a drunk's chewed-up nose, but Burnofsky had game. No one was a better twitcher than Anthony Elder aka Bug Man, but if there was a close number two it was Burnofsky.

After all, he had created the game.

Bug Man pulled out one earbud. The band was going on about watching the company that you keep. Burnofsky was making that twisted, sneering face that was his most pleasant expression.

"S'matter, Bug? You don't want to see the video?"

"Bugger off, Burnofsky. I need a slash."

Burnofsky must have already been hitting the Thermos

where he kept his chilled vodka. He grabbed Bug Man's shoulder and spun him around. "Come on, kid. Don't you want to see the macro? This is an accomplishment. A great moment for all of us."

Bug Man knocked the old drunk's hand away, but not before being exposed to a high-def visual of devastation. Looked like a camera angle from that same blimp, too steady to be a helicopter. Smoke and bodies.

Bug Man turned away. Not because it was too terrible to see, but because it was irrelevant. "I just play the game, old man."

"The Twins will want to thank you," Burnofsky taunted. "You going to tell them to 'bugger off', too? I mean, you struck a major blow today, kid. Grey McLure and his boy are charcoal briquettes. You've stepped up to the big times, Anthony: you're a mass murderer now, up in the macro, not just shooting spiders down in the meat. And we're all one step closer to a world of perfect peace, happiness, and universal brotherhood."

"I just want to be one step closer to the loo, man," Bug Man said.

"It's called the restroom in this country, you little British bastard."

He started to move away, but Burnofsky stepped suddenly closer, put his bloodless, papery-fleshed hands on Bug Man's neck, pulled him close, and breathed eighty-proof fumes into his ear. "You'll grow up some day, Anthony. You'll know what you did." He lowered his voice to a whisper. "And it will eat you alive."

Bug Man shoved him back, but not so hard as to knock him down. "How stupid are you, Burnofsky?" Bug Man grinned and shook his head. He pointed a finger at his own temple. "I just rewired that pilot's brain. You think I won't rewire my own? You know, if I ever feel the need?"

That shut Burnofsky up. The old man took a step back, frowned, and waved his hand like he was trying to block the sight of Bug Man's smooth face.

"The macro is all micro, old man. You drown your conscience in booze or whatever it is you smoke that makes you smell like roadkill . . ." He saw Burnofsky glance nervously back at Jindal. So: Burnofsky thought that was a secret, did he? Old fool. "You do what you have to do, Burnofsky. It's not my business, is it? But I have a better way. Snip snip, wire wire. I mean, you know, if I ever get old and soft in the head like you. Now: I either go to the toilet or pee on your leg."

FOUR

Sadie McLure had passed out in the ambulance on the way to the ER.

She'd awakened in bits and pieces, in flashes of light, and hovering faces, and tiled ceilings and fluorescent fixtures rushing by overhead. Images of green scrubs, masks, tubes, and shiny metal instruments.

Like a dream. Not a good dream.

Sharp, breathtaking pain from her arm when someone jostled it.

And with the scrubs came the black suits. Security. Protect the McLure. That was her now: *the* McLure.

A stab of pain that was not from any nerve ending, a stab like a cold knife wielded by her own soul.

Then muzzy relief flowed through her veins as the opiates arrived to take the edge off.

Sleep. And terrible nightmares of falling into an oozing mass of burning flesh. Like overcooked marshmallow. And it wasn't her father or brother burning but her mother, who hadn't burned, who had died in a bed like this one, her insides eaten by cancer.

Sadie woke. How much later? No way to know. There was no calendar or clock in the room. What there was was a man in a black suit, white shirt, black tie, and an earpiece. He was sitting in the chair, legs crossed, reading a graphic novel.

He would have a gun. He would also have a stun gun. And probably a second gun in an ankle holster.

Sadie's body was one massive bruise. She did a quick inventory and decided, yes, every single inch of her hurt. Inside and outside, she hurt.

She was on her back, head slightly elevated, a needle taped to her right arm. A clear plastic bag hung beside the bed.

Her left arm was wrapped in hard plastic sheathing, bent into a lazy L and suspended from a wire.

Something had been inserted in her urethra. It hurt, but at the same time she had the feeling it had been there for a while.

"Who are you?" she asked. It sounded perfectly clear in her head, but she had the impression it came out as a whisper.

The man's eyes flicked up from his book.

"Water," Sadie gasped, suddenly overwhelmed by the sensation of thirst.

The man rose quickly. He came to the bed and pressed a button. The door opened within seconds, and two nurses came in. No, a nurse and a doctor, one was wearing a stethoscope.

"Water," Sadie managed to say in a semicoherent voice.

"First we have to—" the doctor said.

"Water!" Sadie snapped. "First: water."

The doctor took a step back. She would not be the first or last to take that step back.

The nurse had a drinking bottle with a bent straw. She let Sadie swallow a little. A blessing.

Nurses, Sadie remembered. That's what her mother had said as she lay dying. Doctors can all go to hell; nurses go straight to heaven. Not that Birgid McLure took either heaven or hell literally.

Alone.

Sadie was alone. The realization scared her.

Just me, she thought.

She thought she might be crying, but she couldn't feel tears, only the need to shed them.

A second guy in a black suit was in the room. Older. The corporate security chief. Sadie knew him. Should remember his name, but she didn't. A third man, sleek in a very expensive striped suit, might as well have had 'lawyer' tattooed on his forehead.

The corporation was swinging into action. Lawyers, security, all of it too damned late.

She had a stupid question to ask. Stupid in that she already knew the answer. "My Dad. And Stone."

"Now isn't the time," the nurse said kindly.

"Dead," the security chief answered.

The nurse shot him a dirty look.

"She's my boss," the man said flatly. "She's McLure. She asks a question, I answer."

The doctor was busy reading the chart. The nurse peered at Sadie, as if measuring her courage. She was Jamaican, maybe, judging from the accent. Or from one of those other islands where they do cool things to the English language.

She gave a slight shrug and let Sadie take another blessed, blessed sip of water.

"I need to know how soon I can move her," the security chief said. Stern. That was his name. Something Stern. He had one of those faces that always looked as if he had just come from shaving. His tie was neat, but the collar was twisted a bit sideways around his neck. And although he was trying hard to look impassive, the corners of his mouth kept tugging downward. His eyes were red. He had cried.

"Move her?" the doctor yelped. "What are you talking about? She has a compound fracture of the ulna and radius, a concussion, internal bleeding—"

"Doctor," Stern said. "I can't keep her safe here. We have a place. Our own doctors, our own facilities. And air-tight security."

"She needs an MRI. We need to see if there's any brain damage."

"We have an MRI machine," the lawyer said, oozing confidence. A Harvard Law voice. A voice with which you were simply not allowed to argue. "I am Ms McLure's temporary legal guardian, and her attorney. And I think Ms McLure would rather have our own doctors. And frankly, you and this hospital would rather not have the media camped outside twenty-four/seven."

Stern looked at her. He was careful not to be too obvious, but Sadie intercepted the look and understood.

No, it would not do to have strangers looking inside her skull. They might see something they'd have a very hard time understanding. So, Stern knew. Useful.

"Take me home," Sadie said.

Stern nodded once. "Yes, Ms McLure. Home."

There was a park not far from Noah's home, but it was drizzling and threatened to go to full-on rain, so he and his two mates, Mohammed and Little Cora, kicked the football around in the partial shelter of two high walls.

Noah dribbled it, did an agile *pedalada*, and back-heeled it to Mohammed.

"I can, too, do a fuckin' Chilena," Little Cora insisted, referring to a bicycle kick that involved somersaulting to kick a ball out of the air. Little Cora felt no sentence was complete without the modifier "fuckin'."

"You can do it once, maybe," Mohammed insisted. "Then you fall on your head, and it's six weeks in hospital."

Little Cora charged at him, took the ball, and kicked it with impressive power and very poor aim at the nearest wall. It struck the bars on the back window of a pizza restaurant and took a wild bounce toward a motorcycle locked to the fence. The fence separated the alley from the train tracks, and just as Mohammed started berating Little Cora a train went roaring past obliterating the banter.

Noah grabbed the handlebar of the motorcycle and righted it before it could topple over. Then he went after the ball, which had rolled some distance.

A young man got there first. He stopped the ball, dribbled it a bit just to show he knew how, and kicked it away from Noah and back to his friends.

The man was Asian—Chinese, Alex guessed—and startlingly handsome. Definitely not someone from this neighborhood.

The man said, "Noah?"

And that froze Noah where he stood. His friends moved closer, slowly, protective but wary.

There was nothing threatening about the man. He didn't bare his teeth, he didn't move farther forward. He met Noah's gaze easily.

"Who's asking?"

"I'm looking for Noah Cotton."

An American accent, at least Noah thought so.

"That's me," Noah admitted with a blend of defiance and indifference. He was a city boy, Noah, bred for wariness.

The American was in his early twenties, tall, especially for someone of Chinese background, thin, immaculate. He wore a long, navy cashmere coat over a dark suit, over an expensive white shirt held at the neck not by a tie but by a sort of white floral pin.

"My name is Nijinsky," the American said. "I'm a friend of your brother."

"Nijinsky. That sounds Russian."

Nijinsky shrugged and smiled, offering a glimpse of amazingly perfect white teeth. "It's an odd name, I must admit. Most people call me Jin."

"Why are you looking for me?"

Nijinsky looked down, gathering his thoughts. Or at least acting the part of a man gathering his thoughts. Then he said, "Well, Noah, Alex asked me to look in on you if . . . if anything ever happened to him."

Noah's breathing suddenly felt labored. "Yeah?"

"Yes. Your brother was doing very important but very dangerous work. He had a special talent, you know."

"He was out of the army. Quits with all that."

"This isn't about the army."

Noah stared at him, and the man looked back with black,

almond eyes fringed by girlishly long lashes. His expression was open and frank. Like he was hiding nothing.

Nijinsky glanced meaningfully at Mohammed and Little Cora, who had strayed ever closer.

"It's all right, guys," Noah said to his friends. "Too wet out anyway. Tomorrow, eh? After school."

Little Cora had never been one to take a hint, but Mohammed was. He grabbed her arm and said, "Come on, then, LC."

"I'm taking my ball," Little Cora said belligerently, but she followed Mohammed down the alley and around the corner.

"What happened to Alex?" Noah blurted.

"You mean—"

"You know bloody well what I mean, don't you?" Noah interrupted.

The outburst brought no anger to Nijinsky's expression, just compassion. "I know that Alex suffered a sudden, complete mental breakdown. Almost overnight he went from being a normal, if perhaps intense, person to being what people might call a raving lunatic."

Now Noah's chest was pounding and he was breathing hard, too much emotion pushing out from where he'd buried it. "I saw him, you know? Twice I went to see him. Right? In that awful place. They have him chained up like a fucking dog!"

Nijinsky nodded. Nothing more.

The rain came on in a wave, rushing down the alleyway.

Nijinsky pulled an umbrella from his coat pocket and opened it seconds before the first fat drops hit. He stepped closer, to cover Noah as well, but Noah wasn't having it. He stepped back into the rain, letting it beat on his bare head and shoulders.

"He's sitting there in that place, just babbling, just, just . . ."

"What does he say? When he's babbling?"

"Nano nano nano. I know, it sounds kind of funny, doesn't it?"

"No. It doesn't, Noah. What else does he say?"

Noah shook his head. "Something about a bug man."

And there, at last, that tightening of Nijinsky's impassive eyes, that twitch of his upper lip. And the warm compassion flowing from Nijinsky was, just for a moment, a cold front.

Noah had not missed that split second of something dark. Sadness? No, although maybe that was part of it.

Fury. That was it. Fury. But quickly extinguished.

"Anything else?" Nijinsky asked. And now he wasn't bothering with the mask. He knew that Noah had seen some little bit of truth in his eyes. The bullshit was over. Truth was on its way.

"Yeah," Noah said. "This word. He started screaming it. Just screaming it like a . . . like a . . ." He couldn't talk for a moment. Too much. Too fast. He pressed his back against the wall, partly shielded from the worst of the downpour.

"Berserk," Nijinsky said quietly.

Noah's heart froze. His eyes snapped up. "What the hell does it mean? What is it? And how did you know?"

Nijinsky sighed. "What is it? It's an organization. I'm part of it. And so was Alex."

He waited and watched as Noah digested this. And as the truth dawned on Noah. "Are you here to . . ." He couldn't finish the question. It seemed absurd, and if he asked it, it would be embarrassing.

"Your brother had a very special skill. A very rare skill. Sometimes it runs in families. If you have this skill, then we may want to talk further. If not, then we will part ways and you'll hear nothing more from us."

Noah blinked water out of his eyes. "What the hell?" When Nijinsky didn't answer, Noah said, "Bug Man. Is that a real person? I mean, is he the person who did this to Alex?"

"The Bug Man is real."

"How do I . . . I mean, how do I find out if, you know, I have this thing you're talking about?"

Nijinsky drew a business card from his inner coat pocket and handed it to Noah. It was a rather odd set of handwritten instructions. Noah quickly shielded it from the rain with the arc of his body.

Nijinsky turned to walk away but then stopped at a distance and called back to Noah. "Tell me something, Noah. Which is more important: freedom or happiness?"

What was this, a game? But Nijinsky wasn't smiling.

"You can't be happy unless you're free," Noah said.

The American nodded. "Skip school tomorrow."

ARTIFACT

To: C and B Armstrong

From: S Lebowski

Division: AmericaStrong, a division of Armstrong Fancy Gifts Corporation

Status: EYES ONLY ENCRYPT Read and safe-delete

Gentlemen: You have requested occasional updates on subject Burnofsky's state of mind. We have been able to penetrate security on his computer files. The following is an extract from a video diary. Despite the fact that Burnofsky appears to be addressing someone, there is no evidence that anyone other than Burnofsky himself has viewed these files.

We assess their condition to be secure.

We make no judgments of subject Burnofsky's mental condition at this time, but note that he is a heavy drinker and opium addict.

The following is a transcript. The video itself is also available.

ENTRY FOLLOWS:

Let me tell you about the nano. Down there, down in the

nano, you see marvels, man. You think you see glory in a sunset or the shape of a tree? No, man, the genius, the creation, the architecture, the fucking complexity, the edges and the patterns and the horrors – oh yeah, because there are horrors – are down there in the meat.

You want to see God the Creator, the supreme artist? Gaze into the nano. You'll see your God, and he will scare the shit out of you.

God isn't in big things measured in miles, he's down there. Down there in a flea's antennae like a hairy tree trunk twitching for blood, and a macrophage slithering along like a shell-less snail come to eat you up, and the cells you see splitting beneath your feet, and landscapes of seething bacteria, and yeah, right there, you want to see God up close and personal?

Come with me into the nano, and I'll show you what happens when you empty a sac full of staph germs, the hard stuff, the boosted MRSA, the necrotizing fasciitis itself, the true shit, into the ocular orb, behind a man's eye. Oh, you don't know that term, that neat Latin? Does the phrase 'flesh-eating bacteria' ring any bells for you?

Cut it open – the sac – and dump it out, and it goes right to work. It eats into the eye and into the nerves and into the brain, and you haven't really seen God's true handiwork until you've seen those little staph balls, down there, down

46

in the meat – they look about as big as cats, maybe, you know? And they're fuzzy. But no eyes or face, just these soulless rugby balls covered in bumps. And man, you should see them work.

See them turn healthy cells into goo.

See them eat right through the meat, explode cells, grow; double, double toil and trouble, again and again, and eat all the while, those bumpy little balls, and by the time the guy feels the pain it's way too late.

Yeah. You want to see the face of God the Artist? Get down in the nano, watch a sea of healthy flesh overrun by those microscopic hordes, like murdering Huns.

They'll eat their way through to sunlight eventually. Through a nose, a cheek, an eye, a skull.

Praise the Lord: the Great and Crazy Artist.

END OF TRANSCRIPT

FIVE

Vincent was also visiting London, but miles away from Noah and Nijinsky.

Vincent was twentysomething, a trim, average-size guy with carefully barbered brown hair and a downturned mouth and eyes that were brown but with no sense of warmth in them. He had a slightly curved nose and nostrils that flared and a faint scar that extended half an inch above and half an inch below his lips.

He held himself like a guy who wanted to avoid attention, but he didn't have the gift of disappearing in a crowd. He had the curse of being noticed, no matter how careful he was to keep his eyes down and his face impassive. People still noticed him because there was just an air about Vincent that suggested tamped-down emotion and volatility barely disguised by his careful movements and his soft, almost inaudible voice.

He was at dinner, sitting at a dark table in a nice but not stuffy Indian restaurant on Charlotte Street, picking at a *poppadom*. The target sat across the room at one of the larger, brighter, noisier tables.

There were five people at that table and the target—Liselotte Osborne—was not the richest or most powerful, so she didn't sit at the head, she sat halfway down on one side, with her back to Vincent.

Nevertheless, Vincent had an excellent view of her eye. The left one.

A part of Vincent's mind was in the room, hearing without focusing on conversation punctuated by sudden bursts of laughter, seeing the reflection of yellow overhead lights in standard restaurant-grade wine glasses, wondering abstractedly about the choice of art on the papered walls.

Another part of Vincent's mind was across the room, perched on Liselotte Osborne's left lower eyelid. From that vantage point Vincent saw thick-trunked trees that grew in impossibly long curves from spongy, damp pink tissue. These trees had no branches; they were like rough-barked brown palm trees, bending away to disappear out of view behind him. The bark was then glopped in uneven patches by a black tarry substance, like someone had thrown big handfuls of tar at the lashes.

Eyelashes.

Eyelashes with mascara.

Vincent's spidery legs stepped over a pair of demodex, like crocodiles with the blank faces of soulless felines. Reptilian tails of demodex babies protruded from the base of the eyelash. They wiggled.

From his perch between two rough-barked, gooey, drooping eyelashes Vincent saw the vast, wet plain of white stretched out to the horizon, a sea of milk beneath a taut wet membrane. Within that milky sea were jagged red rivers. When he tuned his eyes to look close, he could make out the surge and pause, surge and pause of Frisbee-shaped red blood cells and the occasional spongy lymphocyte.

He was looking out across the white of Liselotte's eyeball—an eyeball shot through with the red capillaries of a woman who'd had too little sleep, rimmed with black tar, home to microfauna he could see and, of course, a multitude of life-forms too small even for a biot to make out.

Vincent felt a rush of wind and saw a barrier rushing toward him at terrifying speed. It was an endless, faintly curved wall of pink-gray that appeared to be maybe ten feet tall. It came rushing across the eyeball like a storm front, swift, irresistible. Jutting far out from that pink-gray wall were more of the dark brown palm trunks, curving upward and extending beyond the range of Vincent's sight. Like a wall festooned with ridiculously curved pikes.

Liselotte was blinking.

Vincent said, "Sparkling, please," in response to the waiter's question about what sort of water he would prefer.

"And are you ready to order?"

"What's the speciality of the house? Never mind—whatever it is, I'll have it. Extra spicy." He handed the menu to the waiter, who insisted on telling him the special anyway.

It did not matter to Vincent. Food generally did not matter much to Vincent. It was just one of many pleasures to which he was indifferent, although highly spicy foods created a sensation that was something related perhaps to pleasure.

Vincent—his real name was Michael Ford—suffered from a rare disorder called anhedonia, an inability to experience pleasure. It's usually a symptom of long-term drug use. Or schizophrenia. But Vincent was neither a junkie nor crazy.

Well, not crazy in the clinical sense.

Yet.

The biot with the functional and not very clever name of V2, tensed its six legs and timed the onrushing eyelid. When it was just a few dozen feet away micro-subjective or "m-sub"—less than a few millimeters macro-actual or "mack"—the biot leapt.

It flew through the air. It spread short, stubby wings that helped it avoid tumbling. It also spread its legs wide in flex position to take the shock. Then it scraped down the side of an eyelash, picked up a smear of mascara, landed, and jabbed six sharp-tipped legs into flesh. The ends of the legs split to become barbs, locking the biot in place.

Always dangerous to use the barbs because if you had the

bad luck to be too near a nerve ending the target just might feel the faintest irritation. And just might decide to scratch the itch. Which wouldn't crush the biot but could sure as hell relocate it and waste valuable time.

The fast-moving upper lid slammed violently into the lower lid. The giant lashes wobbled and vibrated overhead, a sparse forest of palm. It was an earthquake there on the eyelid, but with barbs deployed V2 was fine.

Sticky liquid squeezed up between the lids and then, when the top lid began to pull away, stretched like chewed gum until it snapped.

Tears.

Vincent had been through a crying jag on another mission and had ended up with his biot all the way down the face and trapped in running snot.

But these weren't weeping tears, just lubrication.

The upper lid receded, zooming across the icy white and then over the iris. Vincent would have found it exhilarating if he were the sort of person who did exhilaration.

There were many parts of the human body that were disturbing up close. But few more surprisingly so than a human iris. What looked like blue ice from a distance was an eye-of-Jupiter storm up close. Right at the outer edges Vincent saw blue, or at least a gray that was like blue. But it was not smooth; rather it was a twisted, fibrous mess, thousands of strands of raw muscle, all aimed inward toward the pupil, all with the job of expanding or contracting the iris to let in more or less light.

Close up—and it was impossible to get any more close up than V2, perched on the very edge of the lid—the iris looked a bit like layer upon layer of gray-and-orange worms, thinner at the outer edge of the iris, stronger at the rim of the pupil.

The pupil itself swept by below, a terrible, deep, black-in-black hole. A pit. But then if you looked straight down and caught just the right light, you could actually see to the bottom of that pit, down to the random blood vessels and the juncture that was the attachment point for the optic nerve.

Vincent did not get that image this time. Not in candlelight and soft, yellow fluorescence. He just saw the pupil as a black, circular lake, growing wider as the snake muscles of the iris shortened themselves fractionally.

The biot was 400 microns—less than half a millimeter—long and equally tall. But the m-sub feel of it—the image a biot runner experienced—how it felt to him, made it seem to be about seven feet long and almost that tall. To the twitcher it felt like something the size of a large SUV.

In mack it was the size of a healthy dust mite. But when you're a dust mite, you don't feel tiny. You feel big.

As the eyelid reached its apogee, V2 jumped off. The biot landed on the milky sea, then flattened itself down as the eyelid zoomed away, hesitated, then came sweeping back overhead like a gooey pink blanket.

Vincent thought, *Light*, and Lo! There was light. Twin phosphorescing organs on the biot's head spread ultraviolet light.

He waited for the eyelid to come back up again, ate another bite of *poppadom*, jabbed a single leg into the underside of the eyelid and let it pull it up and over the slick eyeball, and sipped his water.

It was quite a ride. And as Vincent watched the waiter refill his glass he felt a frisson, a sort of echo of what V2 felt, its back sliding along the slickery surface of the eyeball.

The trick with entering the brain by way of the eye was to reach the hole at the back of the bony eye socket. It was possible for a biot to cut through bone, but it was never quick or safe. It was the kind of thing that would start a firestorm of bodily defenses.

Reaching the hole—Vincent had forgotten the official name for it—was best done by circumnavigating the eyeball. In the m-sub it was a long walk. And all of it through the dragging wetness of tears and the vertiginous movements of the orb looking this way or that.

The two other paths to the brain—through the ear or the nose—had bigger difficulties. Earwax and the distinct possibility of a watery blockage in the one, and unimaginable filth in the other: pollen, mucus, all manner of microfauna and microflora.

This was better. For one thing, you could, if you chose, sink a probe into the optic nerve and get some macro optics—see a bit of what the target was seeing, though it was usually very rough gray scale.

The second greatest threat to a biot was getting lost. When you were the size of a mite, the human body was the equivalent of roughly five miles from end to end. So V2 dutifully made its way around the eyeball, squeezed between membranes, became a bit disoriented, before finally reaching the optic nerve just as Vincent's dinner was being placed before him.

And then, quite suddenly, he came across not the second greatest, but the single greatest threat to a biot.

They attacked with blazing speed, wheels spinning but still getting traction on the eyeball. He saw three of them immediately as they raced around from behind the redwood tree of the optic nerve.

Which answered the question of whether Professor Liselotte Osborne—leading expert on nanotechnology, consultant to MI5, the woman who could either push or derail the security agency's investigation into nanotechnology—was free or infested.

Two more nanobots were behind V2.

Five to one odds. Although if he hung around for long, more would be on the way.

Who was the twitcher? Vincent watched the way the

nanobots moved in. Too reckless. And platooned into two packs, mixing relatively benign spinners and fighters. Not an experienced hand. Not Bug Man. Not Burnofsky. Not even the new one, what was it she called herself? One-Up. Yeah. Not her, either. All of them could run five nanobots as individuals, rather than two platoons.

Vincent tasted the curry. Very hot.

He chewed carefully. It was important to chew thoroughly. It helped digestion, and digestion was often a problem during these long trips across multiple time zones.

And at the same time Vincent spun V2 toward the two nanobots he wasn't supposed to have noticed.

Vincent took no pleasure in the food, but he came as close to pleasure as he ever did when he stabbed a cutter claw into the nearest nanobot, right into its comm link, and spilled nanowire.

Vincent's phone pulsed.

Only one person could ring him and always get through.

He pulled his phone out and looked at the text. His concentration wavered, and he very nearly lost two of V2's legs to a low scythe cut from a nanobot.

Grey and Stone confirmed dead. Sadie injured/OK.

Vincent was not good at experiencing pleasure. Unfortunately he was perfectly able to experience grief, loss, and rage.

He had set aside the first news of the crash. He had stuck it in a compartment. He was on a mission, he had to focus, and from long experience he knew not to trust news reports. Maybe Grey McLure had not been on the plane. Maybe.

This, however, came from Lear. If Lear said it, it was true.

Vincent texted back, missing a couple of letters as he jammed a sharp leg into the vulnerable leg joint of the second nanobot and watched it crumple.

But more nanobots were coming. A new platoon of six.

Tgt LO infst. Engaged. Withdrfing.

If he had two biots in this, he might fight this battle and win. With three he'd be confident. But this was a losing fight.

A follow-up text from Lear: *Carthage.*

Vincent stared at the word. *No, no, no.* This was not his thing. This was not what he did.

A beam weapon cut one of his six legs. The cut didn't go all the way through, but it snapped off. It wouldn't slow him much, but it would throw off the biot's equilibrium.

This was not the time to stay and play smack-the-nanobot and maybe lose. It was time for extraction, and as quickly as possible.

Carthage. The Roman Empire's great enemy. Until the Romans conquered it; murdered or enslaved every man, woman, and child; burned every building to the ground; then sowed the earth with salt so that nothing would ever grow there again.

Carthago delenda est. It had been a slogan in Rome: Carthage must be destroyed.

Vincent wiped his mouth with his napkin.

He pushed back his chair.

V2 turned and ran from the four near and many farther-off nanobots. More were scurrying down the optic nerve. They weren't a problem: using their four legs, the nanobots were slower than a biot. Only when they had a fairly smooth surface could the nanobots switch to their single wheel and outrun a biot.

Unfortunately the eyeball was perhaps the ultimate smooth surface.

V2 motored its legs at full speed. Back around the eyeball.

Vincent made his way slowly across the room toward Liselotte Osborne.

V2 waited until two of the nanobots were close enough to open fire. Their fléchettes ate a second leg away.

Vincent felt the echo of the pain in his own leg.

V2 sprayed sulfuric acid to left and right simultaneously. It wouldn't kill the nanobots, but it would slow them, bog them down in puddles of melting flesh. And even on just four legs and dragging stumps he could maybe outrun the remaining nanobots.

Liselotte Osborne cried out suddenly.

"Oh! Oh!"

She pressed fingers over her eye.

"What is it?" one of the men asked, alarmed.

V2 was nearly crushed by the pressure, but Osborne's fingers were to the north of it now, blocking the nanobots, and V2 had a clear path ahead.

"My eye! Something is in my eye. It's rather painful."

Vincent moved smoothly forward. "I'm a doctor; it could be a stroke. We need to lay this woman down."

Funny how effective the phrase "I'm a doctor" can be.

Vincent eased Osborne from her chair and laid her flat on her back. He crouched over her, pushed her hand gently away from her face, and touched the surface of her eye with his finger.

Through V2's optics he saw the massive wall of ridged flesh descending from the sky and ran to meet it.

Vincent's free hand went into his pocket and came out, unnoticed, holding something black that might have been an expensive pen. He pressed the end of it against the base of Osborne's skull.

V2 leapt onto the finger just as two nanobots emerged in the clear from the acid cloud.

Vincent pressed the clip on the pen and springs pushed three inches of tungsten-steel blade into Osborne's medulla.

Vincent gave the blade a half-twist then pressed the clip again and withdrew what looked for all the world exactly like a nice Mont Blanc.

"This woman needs help," Vincent said.

V2 ran up the length of his finger and dug barbs into his flesh.

Vincent stood up abruptly. "I'm going to summon an ambulance." He turned and walked toward the exit.

It would be ten minutes before Liselotte Osborne's friends and coworkers realized the doctor had not summoned anyone or anything at all. And by then the pool of blood beneath her head had grown quite large, and she was no longer complaining of pain in her eye.

SIX

Vincent was already in the air on his way back to the States, Nijinsky was relaxing with a drink at his London hotel and betting that Noah would show up for testing the next day, and Burnofsky was halfway through a bottle of vodka and thinking about his pipe, by the time Bug Man arrived home and found Jessica waiting for him.

She was standing three steps up on the stoop, bouncing a little to keep warm. She was two years older than he was, eighteen, from one of those North African countries, Ethiopia or Somalia, he could never remember which.

She had possibly the longest legs he had ever seen. She was taller than he was. And all parts of her were perfect. Crazy full lips and big, light brown eyes, and skin like warm silk, and hair in sort of loose, curly dreads that dangled down over her forehead and tickled Bug Man's face when she was on top and kissing him.

"Hi, babe," Bug Man said. "You must be freezing."

"You'll warm me up," she teased, stepped down the stairs and held her arms open for him.

A kiss. A really good kiss, with steam coming from their lips and all her body heat transferring straight to his body, warming him through and through.

"You could have gone in to wait for me," he said.

"Your mother doesn't like me much," Jessica said, not complaining.

He shrugged.

The Bug Man lived with his mother and her sister, Aunt Benicia, in Park Slope, up closer to Flatbush. The neighborhood was mostly white, well-off, infested by people in what was left of the publishing business. Writers and editors and so on. People who would go out of their way to smile at the black teenager with the strangely Asian eyes and the wide smile. They wanted him to know he was welcome. Despite, you know, being a black teenager in an upscale white neighborhood.

Bug Man didn't live in one of the three-story townhomes the latte creatures spent small fortunes decorating. He and his little family had a nice three-bedroom, second floor, with too few windows and an inconvenient single bathroom. They'd lived there since moving to the States from London eight years ago. After Bug Man's father had died of a stroke.

Aunt Benicia had some style, and Bug Man's mother, Vallie Elder, had been careful investing the money from his father's life insurance. And of course Bug Man kicked in a bit from his well-paying job in the city.

He was a video-game tester for the Armstrong Fancy Gifts Corporation. That's what he told people. And how was anyone to know any different? Armstrong Fancy Gifts Corporation, you could Google it. They'd been in business since, like, the Civil War. You could go into one of their stores in malls or airport shopping areas. Bug Man could point out some of the games he had tested. There they were in the store or on the Web site.

Bug Man led Jessica inside. "It's me," he yelled. Preoccupied, his mother called back something from the direction of the kitchen. If Aunt Benicia was home, she said nothing.

"You want anything to eat?" Bug Man asked.

"Mmm-hmm," Jessica said, breathing into his neck.

Oh yeah, that worked for Bug Man. That still made his heart miss a couple of beats. It had been a lot of complicated spinner work, hundreds of hours twitching his spinner-bots, identifying and cauterizing her inhibition centers. And then implanting images of the Bug Man in her visual memory and tying them with wire or pulse transmitters to her pleasure centers.

Exhausting work, since he had had to do it all on his own time. But so worth it. The girl was his. If Bug Man was honest, he'd admit he was maybe a six or seven on the looks scale. Jessica was off the scale. People on the street would see them together, and their jaws would drop and they'd get that "Life isn't fair," look, or maybe begin to form that "Man, what has that guy got going on?" question.

That was why his mum didn't really like Jessica. She figured Jessica had to be after his money. As much as she loved her son, she knew better than to think it was his charm or his body.

Bug Man had an encrypted transmitter in his pocket, an innocuous key chain. He squeezed it and unlocked the door of his room.

With what he made at his job, the Bug Man's room could have been a high-tech haven—plasma TVs and the latest electronic toys. But Bug Man got plenty of that at work. His room was a Zen sanctuary. A simple double bed, white sheets and a white headboard, the mattress centered on an ebony platform that seemed almost to float in the center of the room.

There was a cozy seating area with two black-leather-and-chrome armchairs angled in on a small tea table.

His desk, really just a simple table of elegant proportions, bore the weight of his somewhat old-fashioned computer—he couldn't very well be completely cut off from the world—but was concealed from view by a mahogany windowpane shoji screen.

The real high tech in the room was all concealed from view. A sensor bar was imbedded in the edges of his door. It scanned the floor and doorjamb at a very high refresh rate, looking for anything at the nano level. The same technology was embedded in the window and in the walls around the electrical sockets.

The nanoscan technology wasn't very good—lots of false

positives. People who lived their whole lives in the macro didn't know a tenth of what was crawling around down there in the floor dust.

And in any case, at the nano level the walls and baseboards were like sieves. But in Bug Man's experience a twitcher would take the easy way in if possible—door, window, or riding on a biological. A biological being a human or a cat or dog, which explained why Bug Man didn't let Aunt Benicia's yappy little dog into his room.

The big weakness of nanobot technology was the need for a control station. Biots could be controlled brain to bot, but nanobots needed computer-assist and gamma-ray communication. Close and direct was best. Via repeaters if necessary, though the repeaters were notoriously glitchy.

Which meant that Bug Man took some risks being here in an insecure place. The alternative was having another twitcher running security on him day and night. That was not happening. Damned if he was letting one of those guys tap his optics and watch while he and Jessica were going at it.

Bug Man gave up enough for his job. He wasn't giving up Jessica. She was the best thing that had ever happened to him. Those legs? Those lips? The things she did?

The work he had invested in her?

No, there were limits to what he'd do for the Twins. And there were limits to what the Twins could demand, because when it came down to battle in some pumping artery or up in someone's brain, throwing down in desperate battle with Kerouac or Vincent—wait. He'd forgotten: Kerouac was out. Kind of a shame, really. Kerouac had serious game.

Well, as long as Vincent was still twitching and still undefeated, the Twins couldn't say shit to Bug Man.

So, no, the Bug Man was not going to let some other newbie nanobot handler crawl up inside him while Jessica was crawling all over him. Sorry. Not happening.

Jessica shivered a little but shed her coat.

Bug Man locked the door.

"What do you want today, baby?" Bug Man asked, pulling her toward him.

"Whatever you want," she whispered.

"Yeah. I thought you might say that."

A soft trilling sound came from behind the shoji screen. Bug Man hesitated. "No," he said.

The tone sounded again, louder.

"Hell, no," he snapped.

"Don't go," Jessica said.

"Believe me when I say I don't want to," Bug Man said. "Believe that. Don't move. I mean, you can move, but mostly in a way that involves you having less clothing on. Let me just go see what this is."

He walked a bit awkwardly from the bed to the concealed

computer. A tiny red exclamation point pulsed in the upper-right corner of the screen. Bug Man cursed again. But he sat down in the chair, popped earbuds in, and tapped in a thirty-two-character code.

He'd expected to see Burnofsky's ugly face. This was worse. Far worse. Because there on his screen were the Twins: the freak of nature comprising Charles and Benjamin Armstrong.

He masked the look of revulsion on his face. He'd met the Twins face-to-face on two occasions. This was an improvement—he couldn't see that three-legged body—but not much of one. Not so long as he had to look at the nightmare that was their heads. The image barely fit on the screen. Two heads melted or melded or something into one.

"Anthony," Charles Armstrong said. He was the one on the left. He usually did more of the talking.

"Yeah. I mean, good evening, sirs."

"We are sorry to intrude. You deserve rest and relaxation after the important work you did earlier today. Truly, we are grateful, as all of humanity will someday be grateful."

Bug Man's mouth was dry. He had long since stopped giving a damn about the Armstrong Twins and their vision for humanity, all that Nexus Humanus bullshit. He was a twitcher, not an idealist. He loved the game. He loved the power. He loved the beautiful creature in his bed. The rest was just talk. But you couldn't say that to Charles and

Benjamin Armstrong. Not unless you had a much bigger pair than Anthony Elder happened to have, because Twofer—as the Twins were called behind their back—it, or they, or whatever was the correct way to say it, scared the hell out of the Bug Man.

"It seems that Vincent is in London," Benjamin said. "As well as at least one other. We don't know who."

"Okay," Bug Man said guardedly. The earbuds were crackling. Bad connection. He pulled them out and let the voice go to speaker. It wasn't like Jessica would understand or care.

Charles smiled. When he did, the center eye—the eye they shared—swerved toward him.

Jesus. H. Christ.

"Time to press our advantage," Charles said. "We are going ahead with our great plan, Anthony. Our latest intelligence is that the main target will be in New York."

Bug Man rewarded his freak bosses with a sharp intake of breath. Jessica was suddenly forgotten. It had been all depression and frustration when word came that POTUS—the president of the United States—would skip the UN General Assembly and send the secretary of state instead.

"I thought she was Burnofsky's target," Bug Man said.

In order to shake their conjoined head Twofer had to move its, his, *their* entire upper body. The effect could have been comical. It wasn't. "No, Anthony. Burnofsky has other duties as well. And as it happens, we've, for the moment, lost the pathway to your original target."

Pathways were the macro means to a nano end. A nanobot couldn't cross long distances. They didn't fly. They didn't go very fast in macro terms. In the nano a foot was a considerable distance. So pathways had to be found—carriers, people who would, wittingly or not, carry a nanobot to its target. For the kind of targets they had in mind the pathway had several steps, each step a person who would take the nanobots one stage closer.

Bug Man stared at that massive indented forehead. Tried not to look at that eye that so should not be there. But tried to imagine what was going on inside that creepy-ass head. People whispered that Twofer actually shared a part of their brain, just like they shared that center eye and, if legend was true, at least one other part as well.

The faces were framed against night sky and the green-lit spire of the Empire State Building, in what everyone called the Tulip. The Tulip was the top five stories of the Armstrong Building, what would have been floors sixty-three through sixty-seven, except that the pinnacle of the Armstrong Building was made of a polymer nanocomposite that was transparent looking out, and rose-colored frost for those looking in. The Twins lived their entire lives within that space, high above the city, invisible to outside eyes but wide open to spires and sky.

Bug Man's original target had been the British prime minister.

It had seemed right, what with Bug Man being British by birth.

But what had happened to the pathway? They'd had a clear one to the PM.

Anthony had been studying up on Prime Minister Bowen, looking through the man's well-documented history, searching for the triggers he could pull in the old man's brain. Oh, you like horses, do you, Mr Prime Minister? And you had a bad experience with your sister's drowning? And your favorite chocolate bar is a Flake? All of that data was stored up in that wrinkly wad of goo called a brain.

A lot of wasted schoolwork, that, if someone else would be taking Bowen.

"What happened to the pathway?"

"As my brother mentioned, Vincent was in London."

"It was not done at the nano," Benjamin said, correctly guessing Bug Man's thought. "Our friend Vincent did it the old-fashioned way. He stabbed her in the brain, Anthony. You should remember that. Because these are the lunatics we are fighting." The Twins leaned forward, which put that third eye right up way too close, way too close, to the camera. The Bug Man leaned away.

"They are ruthless in a demonic cause," Benjamin said, getting heated, getting worked up. "We would unite humanity! We would create the next human, the next step in evolution: a united human race! They fight to keep humanity enslaved to division, to hatred, to the loneliness of a false individuality."

The sound of a fist pounding. The image wobbled.

"It begins as soon as you can come in," Charles said. Calmer than his brother. "There's a car waiting out front. You will come?" A simultaneous Twofer grin. "As a favor to us?"

"Yes, sirs," he said. Because Bug Man didn't want to try to guess what happened to people who refused to do 'favors' for Twofer.

Bug Man emerged, serious and shaky, from behind the screen. Jessica was waiting.

"I can't believe I'm saying this, but I've got to go. Big problem at work."

Jessica pouted, and that was about enough to break Bug Man's will, but no, he wasn't ready to keep the Twins waiting.

"But I only need you for five minutes."

The next five minutes, and all the rest of the conversation, was overheard by a single biot.

The biot—a specialized model adapted to picking up the kinds of large sound waves made by a vocal chord longer than their entire body—had spent six weeks inside Jessica's right ear. Six weeks of earwax and near misses with Q-tips the size of blimps and earbuds blasting music that was sheer vibration.

Six weeks, weakening day by day, holding on despite

everything, and now just days from death unless the biot could be taken out in a clean extraction.

In the coffee shop across the street Wilkes sat typing away on her laptop, pretending to be working on a novel, headphones on her ears.

Wilkes wasn't the best twitcher—she wasn't looking for a battle with Bug Man. But little Buggy hadn't found her, had he? He had come close a few times, close enough that she could read the serial numbers of his nanobots and clearly see his creepy exploding head logo. But she had lain low. She had frozen in place. And the nanobots that might have killed her biot and driven Wilkes to madness had gone scurrying past.

Wilkes was not a great fighter down in the nano. She was much more capable in the macro, because when pushed, Wilkes was a little rage-o-holic. She affected a tough-girl style that wasn't just style. She didn't wear those big Doc Martens to look cool, she wore them to make her kicks count when she applied them.

Wilkes had a few interesting tattoos. Her right eye had dark flames painted downward, maybe more like shark's teeth or the stylized teeth of a ripsaw. On the inside of her left arm she wore a QR-code tattoo. Shoot a picture of it with your phone and you'd be taken to a page that just had a picture of Wilkes's raised middle finger and a circular logo that showed a Photoshopped pic of Wilkes stabbing a dragon in the eye.

There was a second QR-code tattoo in a, shall we say, less public location. It led to a different sort of page altogether.

She was a troubled teen, Wilkes was. Troubled, yes. And trouble, too.

But she could be patient when she had to be. Six weeks of this coffee shop, and a crappy little basement hole-in-the-wall apartment next door to Bug Man's home.

In a weary voice Wilkes said, "Gotcha, Buggy. Got you good."

ARTIFACT

To: Lear
From: Vincent

Summary:

Wilkes's surveillance of Bug Man's girlfriend has paid off.

1) Confirmed: Bug Man was the twitcher for the McLure hit.

2) Bug Man is being given a strategic as well as tactical role. This may indicate a serious problem with Burnofsky.

3) Confirmed: AFGC plans move at UN. POTUS is target #1. Other heads of state as well.

Recommend:

1) Given our need for biot resources, especially in view of the AFGC initiative and paralysis at McLure corporate, I recommend finalizing the Violet approach.

2) Accelerated training of new recruits.

Note: I am not Scipio.

SEVEN

Inside Sadie McLure's head was a bubble. Sort of like a water balloon. Only it was the size of a grape and filled with blood.

It was thirty-three millimeters long, about an inch and a quarter. It was a brain aneurysm. Quite a large one. A place where an artery wall weakened and blood pressure formed the water balloon of death.

Because if it ever popped, blood would go gushing uncontrolled into the surrounding brain tissue. And Sadie would almost certainly die. And if not die, then lose parts of her brain, perhaps be left a vegetable.

There was an operation that could be done in some cases. But not in this case. Because the balloon inside Sadie's head was buried down deep.

She had seen the CT scans, and the MRI scans, and even the fabulously detailed, nearly artistic digital subtraction angiography. That had involved shooting dye through an artery in her groin.

Ah, good times. Good times.

If she had stayed in the hospital, they'd have done a CT looking for bleeding. Then they'd have done an MRI to get a closer look at the aneurysm.

That's when they would have noticed something unusual. A certain thickening of the tissue around the aneurysm.

So they'd have done the digital subtraction thing and then, yep, then they'd have had a pretty good picture of something that would make their hair stand up.

They'd have seen what looked like a pair of tiny little creatures, no bigger than dust mites, busily weaving and reweaving tiny strands of Teflon fiber to form a layer over the bulging, straining, grape-size water balloon.

They'd have seen Grey McLure's biots, busy at the job of keeping his daughter alive.

Sadie could see them now as Dr Chattopadhyay—Dr Chat to her patient—swiveled the screen to show her.

"There are the biots in the first image." She tapped the keyboard to change pictures. "And here they are half an hour later."

"They haven't moved."

"Yes, they are immobile. Presumably dead." Dr Chat was in her fifties, heavy, dark-skinned, skeptical of eye and immaculate in her lab coat over sari. "You know of course that I and my whole family mourn for your father and brother."

Sadie nodded. She didn't intend to be curt or dismissive.

She just couldn't hear any more condolences. She was suffocating in condolences and concern.

Over the last twenty-four hours she had absorbed the deaths. Absorbed, not coped with, accepted, gotten over, or properly mourned. Just absorbed. And somehow seeing those tiny dead biots was one step too far.

What her father had created was a revolution in medicine. It had taken him years. He had thrown more than a billion dollars into it, which had required him to buy back his own company from stockholders just so he could spend that kind of money without having to explain himself.

He had worked himself half to death, he and Sadie's mother. Then, the cancer, and he was even more desperate to finish the work, to send his tiny minions in to kill cancer cells and save his wife.

The pressure he had endured.

But the biot project was too late for Sadie and Stone's mother, Grey's wife.

For three months after Birgid McLure's death Grey was virtually invisible. He lived at work. And then . . . the miracle.

The biot. A biological creature, not a machine. A thing made of a grab bag of DNA bits and pieces. Spider, cobra, jellyfish. But above all, for the control mechanism that allowed a single mind to see through the eyes of a biot and run with a biot's legs and cut with a biot's blades, for that, human DNA.

The biot was not a robot. It was a limb. It was linked directly to the mind of its creator. It was a part of its creator.

Grey McLure's biots had been injected as close to the aneurysm as was safe. They had set up a supply chain that ran through her ear canal to shuttle in the tiny Teflon fibers. And then they began to weave, a sort of macro-actual tiny, but micro-subjective huge, basket around the aneurysm.

"You're lucky the overpressure from the explosion didn't cause a rupture," Dr Chat said. "There's some bleeding, but it seems to have stopped. Lucky."

Sadie wanted to say something mean and sarcastic about her luck—luck that had left her an orphan—but stopped herself.

"Did it do anything at all to the aneurysm?"

"It seems mostly unchanged. But as you know, the weave needs constant tending to remain strong. And in any case it was only sixty percent done. So I have to prescribe the blood pressure medications to lower your BP."

"I had an allergic reaction," Sadie said.

"There are other medications we can try. There's a whole range of—"

"Whatever," Sadie snapped. "I can read Google as well as you. I know that I already have excellent blood pressure, and that these meds won't have much effect, and they're really only there to make me feel like I'm doing something. I don't need a placebo, Doctor."

Dr Chat sighed and looked at her from under disapproving eyebrows. "You have a responsibility now, you know."

"Yeah. I know."

"This company employs almost a thousand people in six countries."

"Seven," Sadie said. "Dad opened a lab in Singapore. That's where he and Stone were headed."

Dr Chat sighed. "Is there anyone we can call to come be with you? Friends? Your grandmother?"

Sadie shot her a defiant look. "Not really, no. Not the kind of friends I want to see right now."

So the doctor left, and Sadie was alone. It was a luxurious room. The bed might be hospital style, but there was a forty-two-inch plasma screen on the wall, sleek Jasper Morrison chairs, a pad, lovely orchids in crystal vases, soft lighting, a view through a floor-to-ceiling window of the McLure Industries main New Jersey campus. And through a side door was a marble bathroom that could have graced a suite at a Ritz-Carlton.

If you had to be sick, this was the place in which to do it.

Sadie felt her gaze drawn to the image of the tiny dead biots. The last little bits of her father.

She wondered why she didn't cry more. She had cried, but in sniffles and single sobs. She had cried so long, so much for her mother. Maybe she was cried out. Maybe she had just accepted the fact that life was pain and loss.

Or maybe she was numb, waiting with calm acceptance for her own death. The last of the McLure family.

Sadie rolled out of bed. Not exactly an easy thing to do. A painful thing to do. Her arm was one long, dull ache punctuated by waves of stabbing, stabbing, stabbing that caught her breath in her throat.

The cast had been replaced with a lighter version that could hang from a shoulder strap.

The rest of her body was just one big bruise. She moved like an old woman as she made her way to the toilet. She peed a little blood, but less than last time.

She hesitated at the shower. She wanted very badly to take a shower. But it would be easier to keep her cast dry in a bath. Nurses had given her a sponge bath, but really that wasn't quite what she was looking for.

Wincing and moving with arthritic slowness, she turned on the water. There was of course a selection of Bulgari bath oils and beads. She spread the green-tea-scented salts in the water.

Getting out of the hospital gown—it was a very nice hospital gown, but still something for an invalid—took a while. Finally she stepped into the water. Then slipped and fell in all at once.

Unbelievable pain as her broken arm hit the side of the tub. The shock of hot, hot water on every square inch of her battered flesh.

But then, slowly, the heat seeped down into her muscles,

found the bruises and began to leach the clotted blood from them, soothed the twitchy nerve endings, and lulled her mind to a state that wasn't quite sleep but was close to it.

She heard a door open, but it seemed to come from far away. The voice, however, came from right next to the tub.

"Sorry to intrude."

Sadie's eyes widened to see a youngish man, maybe in his early twenties, but with a very serious mouth and emotionless brown eyes.

"What the hell?" Sadie cried. She jerked too suddenly, and her arm bounced and sent shrieking pain up from elbow to shoulder. "Damn it! Get out of here!"

"No," he said. "Not yet. We need to have a conversation."

"A what? I don't know you. Get out before security gets here and I have them beat the crap out of you."

The serious mouth very nearly twitched. As though it was thinking about a sort of smile, but not really planning to go through with it.

For Sadie's part, she refused to give in to an instinct to cover herself. That would have signaled vulnerability. And she might be naked, neck-deep in water, and half crippled, but she was nowhere close to seeing herself as vulnerable.

"My name is Vincent."

"Well, good for you. Now fuck off."

"I'm a . . . a friend . . . of your father's."

"So now you sneak in to get a good look at me naked?"

Vincent drew back fractionally. He blinked. "Yes, you're not wearing anything." Like it was the first he'd noticed. And the concerned furrowing of his brow and the way he'd kind of jerked back almost made Sadie believe it was the truth.

"What is it you want?" Sadie demanded.

"Your father and brother did not die in an accident. They were murdered. You were targeted as well. They have not given up. You will either be killed or enslaved."

Sadie stared at him. For a good long minute. She was realizing how little the word *murdered* surprised her. No one had said it to her. No one had suggested it within her hearing. But in the day and a half since the crash no one had said anything like "engine failure," or "bird strike," or even "pilot error."

"There's a robe," she said, and jerked her chin to where a thick, heavy terry-cloth robe hung. Vincent fetched it, held it open, and then turned his face away.

She climbed slowly, painfully, to her feet. Murder. Yes, that did not seem at all crazy. Her mother had taught her to listen to what wasn't said. The holes in conversation were often the most interesting parts.

Of course, if she was in danger, maybe this guy was the one bringing it.

Vincent kept his eyes averted until she had dragged the robe slowly, slowly and carefully over her broken arm and tied it with her good hand.

Then, with a sudden fluid motion, Vincent had a pen in his hand and pressed it against her heart, just beneath the breastbone.

Sadie froze. "What are you doing? Autographing me?"

Vincent shook his head. "Making a point." He drew the pen back, aimed it safely away, and squeezed it. A glittering blade shot up. "Making the point that if I were here to kill you, you'd be long dead by now."

Sadie breathed. More calmly than she had any right to do.

"Let me guess: you're here to save my life. How exactly are you going to do that?"

"For a start, like this." He touched her face and held the contact for a several seconds. There was nothing erotic in it.

"So," Sadie said flatly.

Vincent nodded. "Like I said, I knew your father."

EIGHT

The instructions Noah had been given included directions for getting to Selfridge's department store. He already knew how to get to that place. Selfridge's is on Oxford Street: it's vast, it's sleek, it's very bright yellow, it's full of things like designer bags and exotic cosmetics and oddly dressed mannequins. It glows and glitters and glistens.

It was the sort of place that instantly made Noah feel small, shabby, self-conscious, awkward, shockingly unattractive, and possibly criminal. Everything was polished and clean—and that definitely included the employees, who did a creditable job of concealing their concern that such a creature as this grubby teenager should be in, actually physically *in*, their store.

On the other hand, quite a number of those employees wore high heels and pencil skirts and taut blouses. So the environment wasn't entirely without points of interest for Noah.

He'd been instructed to go to the food department and buy a jar of sherbet pips, which cost a shocking five pounds, nearly all the money he had. Well, they'd make a gift for his mum, although she'd think him an idiot.

He was to carry the sherbet pips in a bright yellow Selfridge's bag to the cigar humidor, a walk-in sauna of sorts with hundreds of very expensive cigars on shelves and behind glass.

This was ridiculous, and Noah very nearly decided to walk away. Of course first he would try to return the pips.

But as he hovered indecisively outside the walk-in humidor, a man—Indian or Pakistani by the look of him, with an extravagant mustache—gave him a look. A look. He ushered Noah into the humidor and said, "You enjoy a good cigar?"

And Noah completed his instructions by saying the coded response, "I have your pips."

He handed the jar to the man, who looked at them and nodded and said, "Yes, I do." The mustache stretched into a smile. "You were not followed," the man said. Seeing Noah's quizzical look, he added, "We, of course, have watched you on the CCTV cameras since you left your home, and then security cameras within the store."

He was lying. No question about that—whoever these people were, they weren't that hooked in, no. They weren't police or the sort of people who could just tap CCTV at will, or even the store cameras, most likely. If they had that kind of juice, they wouldn't be doing this whole cloak-and-dagger thing.

The man eyed Noah very closely, and his eyes crinkled when

he saw Noah's suspicion. "Good. You're not a damned fool at least."

"And you don't work here."

"Clever boy. Meet me on the street in five minutes."

It was cold outside, and dark compared to the store's bright-yellow-and-chrome magnificence. It was only just noon, but the rain clouds were so low Noah could have reached up and touched them. The man materialized beside Noah and said, "Walk with me. You must not tell me your name, you have no name yet, but my name is Dr Pound."

Noah did not believe that. Maybe Chaudhry, maybe Singh, maybe a lot of things, but the man's accent did not flow from places where the last name of Pound was common.

They had left Oxford Street and now skirted Cavendish Square, one of many small, contained, melancholy parks in London. The rain started up and the umbrellas bloomed, and for a while conversation was impossible.

Then up Harley Street to one of the doors in one of the segments in the endless line of indistinguishable four-story townhomes.

There was no lift, so Noah followed Dr Pound up quite a number of steps to a brown, varnished wood door with no number or nameplate. Dr Pound came out with the key, flourishing it and grinning as though this in itself was quite an accomplishment. Dr Pound was missing two teeth together, the right canine and the one behind it. Something about the gumline spoke of a cause more traumatic than mere dentistry.

"After you," Dr Pound said.

Noah heard a *Pfft!* sound and felt a sting on the back of his neck. Then he decided it was time to lie down on the rug, time to lie down right there and then. He was conscious of the doctor's hand grabbing the back of his shirt and softening the facedown landing.

No time passed—well, none that Noah was aware of— before he woke. He was sitting in a chair. Not a comfortable chair, a very sturdily built chair that looked as if it had been bolted together out of 4 x 4 beams. Wide Velcro straps held Noah's legs to the legs of the chair, and his arms to the arms of the chair, and his back to the back of the chair.

It wouldn't have held the Incredible Hulk, but after a few experimental muscle flexes Noah decided that it would do a pretty good job of keeping him pinned down.

Both of his hands were encased in black gloves, and the gloves extruded a tangle of wires. Red, blue, green, white, black. Thin little wires that tumbled messily toward a panel that had simply been placed on the floor. It wasn't exactly elegant.

A cable ran from the panel to a Mac on a small card table.

Two moderately large TV monitors were directly ahead at eye level. They showed nothing but a creepy sort of logo, like a mechanical insect, and the word *BZRK*.

All of this had been recently moved into place. Sofa, easy chairs, and tables had been shoved aside. A rug had been rolled up. Noah was certain that this apartment had been temporarily appropriated. The owners no doubt off somewhere warmer and dryer than London, entirely unaware of what was happening at home.

"What the hell?" Noah said. His voice wasn't slurred. In fact he felt perfectly alert. He'd gone from unconscious to conscious in record time, and he wondered if it had anything to do with the head band he was wearing. Wires seemed to be coming from it as well. They tickled the back of his neck.

Dr Pound appeared. "Awake then?"

"What the fuck?" Noah said, feeling this called for something a bit stronger than a mere, "Hell."

"Sorry to have to render you unconscious, but I had to check you out at the nano level. Don't worry, you appear to be clean," Dr Pound waved a dismissive hand. The hand was holding a lit cigar that trailed putrid smoke. He also appeared to have one of the sherbet pips in his mouth. It was pink.

"From here on this will only take fifteen minutes," Pound said.

"Get me out of here," Noah said. But not like he thought it would happen. Not even like he really, really wanted it. Because he had volunteered to take some sort of test. And his brother had done it, hadn't he?

Unless this was all some sort of elaborate trick. He tested the Velcro strap around his right bicep. Yes, it was still there, and no, he was not the Hulk.

"You will play a video game," Dr Pound said. "Two games, actually. One game on the left screen is controlled by your right hand. The one on the right by your left hand."

"Games?"

"Games," Dr Pound agreed. "But you don't play for points. Points are an abstraction. On the other hand, pain is real."

As he said this he let the hand holding the cigar drift down until, as if unaware, the cigar's hot glowing tip was near Noah's arm.

"And fear of bodily injury, say the loss of a limb, is also very real."

Noah stared at his captor, looking for evidence in his liquid brown eyes that he was joking, exaggerating, fooling, or anything other than speaking the truth.

"Do you know the poet Ezra Pound?" Dr Pound asked.

"What are you doing down there?" Noah asked, wishing his voice was not quite so obviously shaky.

Dr Pound had wheeled a cart into place beside Noah's right leg. It wasn't tall, just maybe eighteen inches high, and it looked like it might be an emergency generator. Except that someone had attached a chain saw to it.

"Whoa. No, whoa. No, wait up."

Again, testing the Velcro. Again, not possessing super strength. The Velcro gave up a few gritty Velcro sounds, but that was all.

"Pound was considered perhaps the greatest poet of the twentieth century." The doctor locked the cart's wheels and swung a bracket around to affix the machine to the chair leg in such a way that the glittering chain of the saw came to within a quarter inch of the back of the chair leg.

"Okay, I've changed my mind," Noah said.

"But I've gone to all this trouble." Dr Pound winked up at him. "Unfortunately, Pound was also mentally disturbed. He was a rabid anti-Semite. And he was a supporter of Hitler."

Dr Pound had gone around to Noah's left. He picked up a wire–thicker than the others, a cable really, and ending in two small alligator clips. Pound applied one of the alligator clips to Noah's earlobe.

"Jesus!" Noah cried. "That bloody hurts!"

"Yes, and it will hurt a lot more later. I'll just apply the ground to your nose." The second clip pinched Noah's nostril.

"All right then," Pound said. "The sooner we start, the sooner we're done."

"What am I supposed to do?" The clips hurt. The presence of a chain saw was terrifying. And Noah did not want to hear about insane Nazi poets.

"Two games. One is the familiar first-person-shooter sort

of game. The second is a different game, one that requires you to traverse a complex three-dimensional structure wherein you are represented by a cute little robot called Nano."

Noah's eyes blazed at that word. His brother had babbled that word madly.

Nano nano nano.

This then was what had driven Alex mad.

"This isn't a game!" Noah cried, suddenly seeing the truth. "You're going to do what you did to my brother!"

Dr Pound raised his eyebrows in a leer. "The funny thing about Ezra Pound? He did much of his best work in a mental institution. You have thirty seconds to learn the game," Dr Pound said, walking over to his laptop. "Then we will begin."

Both video monitors came on.

On the right Noah was represented by a gun. Symbols on the right side of the screen. Weapons choices? The environment: a London street. No, not London: the taxis were yellow. New York, maybe. Animations of pedestrians walked by, cabs and cars and trucks drove by.

The graphics were impeccable. The sound was realistic.

On the left screen, the scenery was inexplicable. He was represented by a spider. The spider was atop a wavy, corrugated surface beneath a sort of Dalí cathedral of soaring buttresses.

When he flexed the left glove—no, no, they were crossed, that's right. So right glove, left screen. When he flexed, the spider moved. And the gun. Hands crossed: he would need to remember that.

Okay, a game. Focus on that. They hadn't sawed Alex's leg off. He was panicking for nothing, had to stay calm here; it was all part of that Chinese American dude's test, all about that. So foc—

"Aaaahhh!" The alligator clips sent a stab of unbelievably intense, immediate pain shooting from ear to nose. It convulsed that whole side of his face. His left eye filled with tears.

"Just so you understand the stakes," Dr Pound said. "And now: game on!"

A woman in the shooter game, just a housewife by the look of her, drew a knife and jabbed it straight for Noah's face. He twisted the glove, causing his avatar to dodge, and flicked his right finger experimentally. His gun fired. The round hit a passing car, shattering its window.

And suddenly, the unmistakable, ear-shattering noise of a chain saw. Real world. Not game.

He shot a look down, and oh my God, it was spinning, and now the teeth were just grazing the wood of the chair leg, with splinters flying and sawdust cascading.

The left! Three crudely mechanical robots, not so different from his own avatar, came rushing across the sphere, and that wasn't as important as the way a cab's window was rolling down and a gun appeared and Noah twisted his glove and fired and the shooter's very, very realistic face suddenly had a neat round hole in its forehead.

And the tiny buglike creatures in the other game, the left game, fired what looked like cute little beam weapons at—

"Goddamnit!" The electric shock again and stronger this time.

The little robots fired again and once more his face was convulsed, but now he'd missed the big man who came rushing out of an alley with an axe and swinging it and his avatar crumpling and the chain saw shrieked as it bit into the chair leg.

"Stop it!" Noah screamed, but he had no time for screaming because he had to propel his Nano avatar forward while stepping back from the axe coming down again and the little bugs spraying something at him and—

"Jesus!" as the shock seemed to blow his consciousness apart while the chain saw screeched as it bit fully into solid oak, and he could feel the splinters and feel the wind coming off it.

And then, the calm descended.

The shrill sound of the saw seemed now to come from a great distance.

Noah unsaw everything beyond the frames of the monitors.

He unfelt the fear.

He detached himself from the chair and the Velcro and the pinching of his nose and ear and unremembered his brother, and stopped feeling or thinking . . .

He leapt, came down behind the closest of the tiny robots and stabbed it with his needle-sharp leg and fired into the face of the man with the axe while racing across the sphere and flexing his spider legs and flying and pivoting to land on a bumpy gray wall that instantly attacked him with sticky fuzz balls and another shock and he kicked off a graffitied New York City wall and fired in midair and the businessman with the machine pistol never even aimed died with a bullet through his neck, arterial blood pumping.

Another shock! But it was happening to someone else. Some other Noah's cheek was twisted in spasm, and some other eye was blinded by tears.

And the chain saw had ripped its way all the way through the chair leg; it was catching on the last half an inch, but that, too, was someone else's problem.

Noah was batting away fuzz balls and pushing his way through a crowd and a spray of acid, and suddenly both monitors went blank. And up came that disturbing logo.

Noah was first aware that he could barely see for the sweat and tears in his eyes.

And then he felt the pinch of the clips, even as Dr Pound removed them.

And the silence now that the chain saw was switched off.

Noah sucked in a shaky breath. He looked down at his right leg. The saw was all the way through the chair leg, with the other three legs bearing the weight. And a red line had been drawn on the quivering muscle of his calf, not deep, just enough to draw blood.

Dr Pound moved with calm deliberation, removing the head band, ripping apart the Velcro.

"I can imagine you'd very much enjoy punching me in the face," Dr Pound said.

You have no idea, Noah thought.

But the emotion faded, pushed aside by stronger feelings and needs. Pride. Curiosity. The rush of survival.

"How did I do?" Noah asked.

Dr Pound sighed. To Noah's amazement, he laid his hand gently on Noah's sweat-matted hair. "Young man. I'm not meant to know your identity. But the family resemblance is unmistakable."

"You knew Alex?"

Dr Pound smiled wistfully. "I knew a fellow who called himself Kerouac. Who bears a resemblance to you, though he is older and more fit."

Alex.

"He was very, very good," Dr Pound said.

"Yeah?"

"But you, young nameless boy, if you are to live, you will need to be even better than he."

NINE

Sadie's arm still hurt. Now it also itched. And it chafed. Five days after it had been shattered she still couldn't use it. But the healing was much further along than it would have been for anyone else.

The McLure company clinic had skills that were not present anywhere else. Specifically, doctors who had been trained in the use of therapeutic biots. Three biots had started work almost immediately on the broken bones. Three biots carrying bladders of stem cells that were injected close to the two major breaks.

The biots were then extracted and reloaded with a second, then a third round. Then they began to shuttle titanium strands, laying them into the microscopic spaces between the two sides of the breaks, like rebar in concrete. The biots next began the tedious job of hauling bladders of what amounted to superglue. This was used to stabilize the break so that the bone could grow easily over and around the titanium and repair without enduring repeated mini-fractures.

In a few days Sadie's arm would be fully functional. In two

weeks it would be as strong as it had ever been.

The medical biot runners sat in easychairs in separate rooms to avoid any distraction. Even so they worked only three hours at a time to minimize the stress.

The stress. It seemed to be age-related; that was the preliminary conclusion: the strangeness of the nano world tended to overwhelm less flexible minds. Shorter version: it creeped people out being down in the meat.

If Sadie had stayed in the clinic, they'd have set to work in the depths of her brain. Doing the work her father had once done. Keeping her alive.

But now, Sadie was in a very different place. No longer at the campus in New Jersey. She had told Stern to let her go, and after some demurral, he had.

She'd had the McLure driver drop her at the Park Avenue apartment, but she'd gone in only to change clothing and pack a small bag.

She had heard from Vincent.

So now she was at Madison and 26th Street. Not one of the more exotic or interesting street corners in New York. There was a small square called Madison Square Park. It was a rectangle not a square, and not much of a park. But it was a place you could be at night, at midnight just to be melodramatic, without worrying too much about your safety.

She waited, by herself, with a scarf covering the bottom

third of her face and a hat pulled down over her hair.

There weren't that many pictures of Sadie in circulation—Google turned up only three. But she was, if not famous, then certainly notorious now. The sole surviving McLure. A potential focus of the needs of a media currently still obsessing over the stadium tragedy. She wanted not to be recognized. And she wouldn't be, not in an empty park at night with steam leaking through her scarf.

She was cold. It was cold and the wind made her broken arm ache and her eyes run. She stood with one hand pushed deep into her coat pocket and the other hand—gloveless because she'd forgotten she would want gloves—sticking out of a sling.

A boy came up. Handsome boy. No, a beautiful boy, and older than she, maybe eighteen, nineteen. Tall and slender, Mediterranean but with a nose and mouth and brow and expression that did not say, "descended from Spanish fishermen," but rather, "descended from the sorts of people who once upon a distant time rode around on tall horses trampling peasants."

He came to her. Raised one eyebrow and looked down at her with disappointment and said, "Are you a friend of Vincent's?"

She disliked him immediately. Not the kind of dislike that might later give way to attraction. The kind of dislike that might, with some effort, remain mere dislike and not harden into contempt.

In fact, he was Luis Aragon, the middle of three sons of a

Spanish land developer who had once been shockingly rich but was now only rich. But Luis had left his name behind in trade for the name Renfield.

"I suppose I am," she said.

"Follow me," Renfield said.

She made no move as he spun on his heel and walked away. It took him perhaps fifteen steps to realize he was walking alone. He came back at double speed. He seemed torn between bewilderment and anger.

"Hey," Sadie said, "I don't take orders. Sometimes I take requests."

Renfield blinked. He drew himself up and back, the better to turn his long, straight nose into a sort of targeting device, lining his eyes up to look down at her.

"You have a car? Or are we walking?" Sadie asked.

The boy's eyes went instinctively to a black Audi A8 idling and exuding exhaust smoke. She started walking. The boy hurried to keep up.

"What's your name?" Sadie asked.

"You must call me Renfield. In the car you will be blindfolded. And you will be prevented from removing your blindfold. If you refuse, you will remain here. These are not suggestions: these are facts."

He had an accent. Yep. A definite cultured, eliding, peasant-trampling sort of accent with too many soft *th* sounds. Also, he had rolled the *r* in Renfield. Beyond that she had no idea where the accent came from, just that he was not American born.

The urge to say GFY was overwhelming. Sadie was not in a happy or patient frame of mind. She'd gone from terror to loss to pain to this park and this arrogant snot of a human being. And if Renfield had been looking at her, he would have seen all of that, including an unpacked GFY, in her eyes.

A liveried driver climbed out to get the door. Sadie was there before him, shot him a smile, and hopped in.

Twenty dark minutes later the car stopped and the engine was turned off and the blindfold was removed and she was staring at a graffiti-tagged Dumpster. In a narrow alley courtyard, the kind of place where someone might have squeezed a couple of cars they didn't love too much.

She let the driver get the door. Climbed out. Still cold. Still New York. Sooty red brick and rusted-iron fire escapes all around and above and a smell of well-aged garbage.

Renfield thumbed a text on his phone.

"Where are we?" Sadie asked.

Renfield refused to answer. A door opened without spilling much light. "Come on," he said.

Sadie followed Renfield into a warmer interior. The door closed. Someone was standing behind her and the hair on the nape of her neck tingled.

A second door opened, and she stepped into bright lights

and white walls and a space no larger than a small walk-in closet. Renfield was not with her. No one was with her. There was a stainless steel push-door slot on one wall.

"Welcome," a disembodied voice said. "The next hour will not be very pleasant for you, I'm afraid. But it is necessary."

Noah was in a yellow cab heading from JFK International to an address in lower Manhattan.

He had never been to America. He'd never really been anywhere outside of London.

He was tired and excited. And scared. And wondering if he was caught up in some elaborate practical joke.

He'd been given an iPad with a video briefing, which he had watched on the plane. And now his head was full of horrors. But also excitement. Because his life was school and a shabby room barely bigger than a closet and a mad hero of a brother and a sad, gray wraith of a mother and a nearly invisible, beaten-down father, and a beaten-down life with nothing really on the horizon but a job he would hate and more of the same, thus and forevermore.

So maybe he was a fool to enlist with scarcely a question in some mad enterprise to stop an even madder enterprise. But the alternative was the grind that would grind on until it had ground him down.

That's why Alex had gone off to war. Because why the

hell not? His exact words when he'd told Noah he was enlisting: 'Why the hell not? Get a job in a pub or an office and have the same shit life as mum and dad? Why the hell not enlist?"

Now Noah had enlisted. Because why the hell not?

And because somewhere out there in this absurdly tall city, there was someone who called himself Bug Man. In Noah's imagination he saw himself going to see Alex again someday and telling him, "I did for the Bug Man, brother."

Noah knew that fantasy was pathetic. He didn't fool himself much, Noah; he was hard and honest with himself. He never told himself the stories other boys would, nonsense about growing up to play professional sport or winning *Britain's Got Talent* and having money and girls and toadies.

He wasn't going to university; he wasn't going to become a rich banker or whatever; he was destined, aimed, targeted like a smart bomb at a life of drudge work in a mind-numbing job and damned lucky if he could get that much and hold on to it.

He had passed Pound's test, and he had seen the greedy gleam in Pound's eye. For the first time ever, probably the last as well, Noah had something valuable.

He had five hundred nice, crisp dollars in his pocket, dollars with their obscure mystical symbolism and compact shape. He had an address on a slip of paper. And he had, by way of inheritance, a mission.

"First time, kid?" the cabbie called over his shoulder.

"First time," Noah said.

"I gotta pull over to take a whiz." The cab rolled to a stop in front of a blearily overlit store with neon beer signs and posters in the grimy, barred glass front.

The driver stepped out, leaving the meter running. Seconds later the door of the cab opened and a girl slid into the seat beside Noah. She was an odd creature, dressed in a style that might be called post-Goth or thrift-shop chic. She had a tattoo of dripping flames beneath one eye. Her features were unrefined, like any girl Noah might see back in his own neighborhood. Somehow he'd expected all New York girls to be models.

"This cab is taken," Noah said. "We haven't stopped, the driver just—"

"Yeah, the driver took a hundy to let me in. All set up in advance, blue eyes. Speaking of which, you have a little schmutz on your eye." She peered closely at him, reached across the seat, and with one finger appeared to wipe something from the corner of his eye.

"A hundy?"

"A C-note. A hundred-dollar bill. A hundy." She waited, obviously expecting something more. "You're not going to ask what schmutz is?"

"I guessed it was crumbs or something."

"Good guess, English Boy."

Noah frowned. She didn't seem the least bit threatening, but she was definitely unsettling, and he supposed, given that she was somewhat provocatively dressed and very forward, that she might be a prostitute. "Excuse my asking, but are you a tart?"

"You mean a hooker? Nah. Although . . . if I was, what would you pay?" She had a grin that was more on one side of her mouth than the other and bordered on crazy. And when she laughed it was a sound like, "Heh-heh." Not mirthful, more like a verbal placeholder for a real laugh.

Noah did not have an answer, and this widened the girl's grin.

"Relax, English. I'm all up in your eyeball checking you out. Looking for bugs, looking for bugs. You're probably safe enough, you've been watched since the other day, and you'll get the full going-over later. This is just a sort of quick peek."

"I'm completely lost," Noah said.

The driver came back, carefully avoided looking at the girl, and the cab pulled away from the curb. The girl carefully scanned the sidewalk and the empty street with a professional eye.

"You only *think* you're lost, English." Again, the sardonic nonlaugh. "Pretty soon you'll be so lost you won't even know what universe you're in."

Sadie squinted against the harsh light.

"Vincent?" she asked. The voice didn't sound quite right to be him. But neither was it Renfield. It sounded female, but low enough maybe to be a boy.

"I'm going to ask you to disrobe. And to place all of your clothing in the wall slot on your right. Then we will ask you to stand still while we run a series of scans."

"Vincent already checked me out. He put a biot on me," Sadie said.

"He also withdrew that biot, and it's been several days."

The voice was irritatingly reasonable. She kind of hated it. She shrugged and took off her scarf, coat, and boots. She pushed them through the slot.

"How far are we going here, disembodied voice?"

"Everything, please."

"I'd better not find pictures on the Internet, disembodied voice," Sadie muttered.

"You may call me Ophelia," the voice said.

"You're a girl?"

"I am," Ophelia answered. "I'll turn the voice masking off." Then she said, "Is that better?"

The voice was no longer impersonal. It was definitely female. "Yes, actually. I'm not modest, but the light in here is very unflattering."

"I'm beginning the scans now," Ophelia said. "You'll see different colors of light. You'll hear various sounds, some a bit loud. Just stand where you are."

"Okay, Ophelia."

It lasted longer than she expected. Long enough to become

boring. And long enough for her to become resentful.

The thing with Sadie was that even though she was no sort of snob, not arrogant toward other people, she had lived a life with very little discomfort. What unpleasantness she'd had to endure had been of a medical nature—the diagnosis and early attempts at treatment for her aneurysm—which just doubled her impatience now. Because everything about this felt medical in a sort of alien-abduction way.

Finally the white light returned. She flinched.

"Sorry, I should have brought the lights up slowly."

"What now?"

A door opened. A young woman stepped in. She was in her early twenties. She had black hair, long, but drawn back into an interesting knot before continuing on down her back. Her skin was dark but not from the African sun. She wore what looked like a very tiny sapphire brooch between her eyes, not a piercing but an appliqué. She had pretty eyes, but otherwise she was plain. She was carrying a handled shopping bag. She held it out to Sadie.

"Your clothing. Be careful, some of it may be hot. I microwaved it. You can get dressed now."

Ophelia. Sadie recognized the name from somewhere. Something fictional. Classical, not modern. It was just out of her grasp but she'd Google it later.

"Microwaved?"

"Microwaves aren't as much use against biots, like those I know you're familiar with. But nanobots contain tiny amounts of metal, and that makes them vulnerable to a good, old-fashioned microwave oven."

Sadie began pulling on her clothing. "Nanobots?"

Ophelia smiled. That made her prettier. It was one of those "light up the room" smiles. Sadie wished she could do that. "I've been given the job of prepping you. So I'll answer everything. Except of course about anything personal."

"Shakespeare. That's where Ophelia comes from." Sadie squirmed into her bra.

"Yes." Ophelia nodded. "From *Hamlet*. His crazy girlfriend." The smile went away. "I'm sorry about your father and brother."

"Yep," Sadie said curtly. Enough condolences.

"Nanobots," Ophelia said. "There are two branches of nanotechnology: the biological and the mechanical. Coffee?"

Sadie was dressed. "I guess a Scotch would be out of the question?"

A different smile appeared, not the room-lighting one, a more quizzical, challenging one. Ophelia could do a lot with a smile.

"Sorry. Yeah. I'm under age," Sadie admitted.

Again a new smile, this one sad, worried. "There are no children or adults with us. But I don't think we have any Scotch."

Sadie said, "It was my dad's thing. Scotch. He said it helped him to stop thinking at the end of the day. Once I came into his libratory—that was his made-up name for it because it was books and a microscope—and . . ." She stopped talking.

Right into it; she had walked into remembering and feeling, and the goddamned tears were coming. *Do not remember all of that*, she told herself. Do not remember dad in his ridiculous libratory, kicked back in his ancient leather chair with his feet up and a crystal tumbler in his hand, frowning up at his dusty old chalkboard covered in incomprehensible scribbles.

She would interrupt his concentration. To play the piano, which was also in the libratory. Or to show him a drawing. Or just to stand there because if she did, he would grab her and there would be a mock-ferocious struggle and she would end up letting him hug her.

Splattered into the concrete at the stadium. Burned in a greasy fire. And Stone with him. Her decent, funny, gentle brother.

"Coffee would be good," Sadie said.

Ophelia led the way to a kitchen. It was clearly a kitchen without a housewife or househusband. It was the kitchen of indifferent individuals who parked their tea or cookies or chips here or there. The coffee machine had a full pot, but no one had scrubbed that glass pot out probably since the day it was first purchased.

They sat at a round table. Sadie took her coffee black. Ophelia with milk and sugar. The mugs were anonymous. The coffee was bitter.

"It's called a *bindi*," Ophelia said. "The thing you're staring at."

"Okay," Sadie said. No point denying that she had been staring at the jewels that sparkled from Ophelia's forehead. "From India, right?"

"Yes. It's somewhere between a tradition and a fashion statement. It was a gift."

"It's very pretty."

Ophelia didn't seem convinced that Sadie was being sincere. "So. You know about biots. You know that Grey McLure created that technology. And he gave us access to it."

"Why?"

"Because we need it," Ophelia said. "There was a long history between your dad and a . . . well, between Grey McLure and the Armstrong Twins."

Sip. "I've heard of them. There's something wrong with them, right?"

"Clean so far." This was Renfield, coming in, pulling a chair out, and sitting a couple of feet back from the two females.

Ophelia's smile this time was pained, and a little embarrassed. "Renfield has two biots on you."

When he had blindfolded her. Of course.

"You've had biots aboard before," Renfield said. "One of them dropped a Teflon fiber on your cochlea." He shrugged. "It wouldn't cause any problems, but I'll remove it anyway."

Sadie had grown accustomed to knowing that microscopic quasi-spiders were traveling around and through her body. Her father's biots, and most recently the medicos'. But it was unpleasant thinking of this boy's eyes and ears strolling around inside her brain. The irritation was lessened somewhat by the fact that he had a bit of booger clinging precariously to one nostril. It gave Sadie an advantage over the cocky Eurotrash.

"The scans would have shown nanobots on your skin," Ophelia said. "But they can quite easily hide inside you. For that we need to take a closer look."

"Or not. If they're hiding out," Renfield said. Then he did a very strange thing. He quickly pinched off the hanging booger.

Sadie stared at him. He looked past her.

Guilty.

"You can see what I see," Sadie said. She stood up, suddenly furious. "I was focusing on your nose, and you saw it."

"A biot can sink a probe into the optic nerve, or even into the visual cortex," Ophelia said. "It's hit-and-miss. Sometimes you get a pretty complete picture. Sometimes—"

Sadie slammed her good hand down on the tabletop. It made a loud noise and caused her coffee to jump. Then she stabbed a finger at Renfield's smug face and said, "Get out of my head."

"You don't give me—"

"Do you like the feel of hot coffee on your—"

"Calm!" Ophelia cried. "Calm. Calm. Renfield? Stay out of her senses. That's not necessary to your job."

Two things were instantly clear: there was rank with these people, and Ophelia, as soft-spoken as she was, outranked Renfield.

And Renfield was conceiving a powerful dislike of Sadie. That, too, was clear.

"What else can he do in my head? Can he read my memories?"

"No," Ophelia said, still in her calm, calm, calm voice. "We can't really read memories. But we can locate them. It's like . . . Well, think of it like this: we can find it the way you can search a book for a particular word. But we can't then read the whole book. We can find the location of an idea. Then, we can spin a wire and just lay it on the surface, or we can belay off a pin that's jabbed into the brain, or we can plant a transponder."

"And what does that do?" Sadie demanded, glaring at Renfield.

"Wire or transponder, it connects two different memories or thoughts. It connects them in ways that the mind had not previously done. For example, we could locate your memories of a favorite pet. A cat, maybe. And we could link that memory to something you feared or hated."

Renfield smoothed his hair back with his hand. "And every

time you think, *kitty, kitty*, you also think, *fear, fear*."

"Enough of those connections and you can alter the way a person thinks. You can create false fears. You can rewrite memories. You can create love or hate."

Sadie, still refusing to sit down, said, "My father never would have done any of that. That's obscene."

"This isn't McLure Inc.," Renfield said. "Your father gave us the tech. He didn't run the show."

"Who does?"

"Lear."

"Who the hell is Lear?"

This now was the most subtle of Ophelia's many smiles. This one was made of respect and fear and submission. "Lear is Lear. And that's all any of us will ever know."

ARTIFACT

Statement of Charles and Benjamin Armstrong.

We are not evil men.

We do not desire power. We do not desire the subjugation of others. Our goal is freedom for the human race.

How many starve as we turn away? How many die from preventable diseases as we ignore them? How many of our fellow human beings languish in political prisons, or the prison of their own addictions? How many are without hope, when we might give them hope?

We are a freak of nature: two men joined together by an accident of nature in our mother's womb. Our brains are individual but interconnected. We cannot be separated without one of us dying.

And isn't that how all mankind should be? Shouldn't we all survive only so long as others do? Shouldn't we all be part of one great human race without hatreds, without wars, without cruelty?

We are never lonely because we are we, and not just I. Many look at us with pity or with horror. Believe us when we say that we feel the same for all of you, trapped in your eternal loneliness.

For all of human history humans have been given the opportunity to love one another. And for the most part we have failed. But this need no longer be the case. Technology offers us a way out of harsh, cold, hostile separation.

I hear you thinking, "But that is the human condition."

But why should we not seek to better the human condition? Have we not from time immemorial turned to technology to give ourselves powers that we did not naturally possess? Did we not use fire to stay warm and cook our food? Did we not use the electric light to banish the night? Did we not take to the air in balloons and airplanes and jets and thence to space itself in rockets?

Now we have the technology to banish not only the literal night, but the long, dark night of the human soul. With nanobots we can connect all people, everywhere, into one great race: the human race. No longer will some go hungry while others get fat. No longer will we turn a blind eye to cruelty, because we will feel all cruelties as our own.

Only ignorance stands between us and our goal of uniting the human race into something so much more profound than a mere social network. We can create a nexus of the entire human race.

We have in our hands the beginnings of true utopia.

Some will choose the path of evil and resist this glorious future.

We will mourn them.

Charles and Benjamin Armstrong

ARTIFACT

KING LEAR

Dost thou know me, fellow?

KENT

No, sir; but you have that in your countenance
Which I would fain call master.

KING LEAR

What's that?

KENT

Authority.

King Lear, William Shakespeare

TEN

Vincent contemplated the China Bone and watched—from the Asian grocery across the street—as Karl Burnofsky shuffled inside.

Burnofsky was flanked, at a discreet distance, by two TFDs—Tourists from Denver. Two of the usual AmericaStrong security men from Armstrong Fancy Gifts. One was a woman, actually, but that was beside the point.

The Armstrong Fancy Gifts Corporation might be run by a mad, twisted creature, but its outward face was relentlessly low-key. Their AmericaStrong men didn't walk around trying to look like Secret Service or extras from a Hollywood muscle flick. They dressed in LL Bean and Land's End. They wore pima-cotton polo shirts and down jackets. So that in New York City they always looked like those most invisible and easily forgotten of creatures: tourists.

TFDs—Tourists from Denver.

Burnofsky went inside to find that elevator. The two TFDs stayed outside, waiting and chatting and stamping their feet against the cold until a car drove up to offer them warmth and shelter.

The China Bone: no sign, of course—discreet, always discreet. It had been here in Chinatown since 1880, though within Chinatown it had moved maybe a half dozen times. The people who needed to find it, found it. In the old days it had been just the better class of opium smokers. All Chinese at first, largely sailors. Then some of the artsier, more adventurous Victorian-age white men.

The China Bone had grown more refined and exclusive by the 1920s. It expanded from opium and marijuana during Prohibition to include alcohol as well. The style, as Vincent had once seen through the right eye of a waiter, was very upscale. Think Ritz-Carlton for wealthy drug addicts; that was the modern China Bone. A little too gilt and plush for Vincent's austere taste, but he supposed if you were going to be an opium addict—and Burnofsky certainly wasn't about to stop—this was the place to indulge.

Vincent had caught a glimpse of Burnofsky then, through the waiter's eye, as the brilliant drunk and addict—and God knew what else—slid into one of the many alcoves, there to await the pipe.

It had been fascinating to Vincent. Burnofsky was a genius. Not the sort of man one thought of wasting hours in drug-induced fever dreams. And inevitably perhaps, Vincent wondered whether the drug could give him what he had never experienced: pleasure.

Vincent had come no closer to Burnofsky then. And he had very nearly lost his biot when the waiter decided on a sudden trip to Mexico with some friends.

The disadvantage of the biot: unlike the nanobot, the biot had to be retrieved.

Vincent paid for the organic Thai rub and the green chilis he'd picked up. A few spicy things, not so that he would enjoy the food he made, but so that he could at least acknowledge it.

Something.

He'd been twelve when he was diagnosed with the anhedonia. Anhedonia commonly had a psychiatric cause, usually drugs. So they thought then, anyway, and so his mortified parents had assumed. Little Michael using so many drugs he'd lost the capacity for pleasure, oh my God, what have we done to cause this?

It was a long two years of virtual house arrest before they got around to taking a look at possible *physical* causes. Then they found the lesions on his nucleus accumbens as well as the inadequate production of dopamine.

Vincent stepped out of the direct neon and fluorescent glare and into the cold night, holding his little plastic bag. He had happened across the shop while trailing Burnofsky many months ago. He'd continued to shop here; it was a very well-appointed store. But he had also become fascinated by the China Bone, by what it represented: a need for pleasure so terrible it drove people to self-destruction.

His actual mission was at a hotel bar just a block away. That's where he would find the woman.

Anya Violet. Not her birth name. She had been born Anya Ulyanov. Russian. When her father had moved the family from Samara to New York, he'd changed the surname to something a wee bit less . . . problematic. Ulyanov had been the original surname of Lenin. A lot of weight to carry around, that name. So. Bye-bye Ulyanov, hello Violet, which at first had been pronounced Wee-o-lett. Now Violet. Like violent without the "n."

Anya's mother had always liked the flowers. Violets.

Dr Anya Violet, current employment in a secret section of McLure Industries. Even her friends and family didn't know that her work was with biots. Vincent did only because BZRK had long had full access to McLure's secure computers.

Who the hell was Lear that he'd been able to get such total support from Grey McLure? And how many times had Vincent asked himself that question? And how many times had he stopped himself from pursuing it, because while Lear might be anyone and had become a nearly mythical creature, Caligula was very real, and Vincent had a definite impression that if he ever did penetrate Lear's secret, Caligula would stab, shoot, garrote, drown, or otherwise end Vincent's life.

That was Caligula's . . . contribution . . . to the cause.

Vincent thought of the note he had appended to his report. "I am not Scipio."

Scipio was the Roman general who had finally destroyed Carthage.

Would Lear accept this push back? Would he or she allow Vincent to refuse Carthage commands in the future? Or would Lear know that in the end Vincent would do what Lear needed him to do?

Tonight would be the third time Vincent accidentally ran into Anya at this bar. Anya lived nearby. Vincent didn't, but he had an apartment a block away that looked exactly as if he lived in it. In case.

The hotel was not fashionable. It was dark and smelled like soy sauce and peanut oil. The bar was even darker, but it smelled of beer and fried wontons. There were just four small tables and an equal number of stools at the bar, and no one was there but Anya.

Vincent saw her before she saw him. He noted with quiet satisfaction that she had dressed for the occasion. This was their first planned meeting. Well, the first that Anya knew to be planned. A date. Previously she'd worn the comfortable work-casual clothing she wore in her lab. Previously she'd come here for her after-shift drink precisely because there was zero chance of being hit on and she could just have a fruity drink or two and chill, relax, mellow, slough off the brain-draining activity that defined her work.

That had changed when she met Vincent. For one thing Vincent was an attractive younger man. Anya was ten years older than Vincent. Anya was lovely. Tall, with near-perfect legs and just a little poochy-pooch at her waist that hardly anyone would notice, and her skin still looked very good, and so did her reddish-brown—do they call that auburn?—hair.

A good face. A face with character, which in this case meant that she had the echo of eastern invasions from the steppes.

And Vincent. Ah, once he confessed to the whole anhedonia thing there wasn't a woman worth her tight skirt and her generous display of cleavage and the expensive scent steaming from her neck who wasn't interested.

Unable to experience pleasure.

We'll see about that.

That's what they thought. And he would find a way to explain that he still knew how to *give* pleasure. That was game, set, and match, as one might say if one were talking about tennis.

Anya's working theory was that Vincent had probably dated nothing but bimbos his own age or younger. All very pretty, no doubt, but what did a girl that age really know?

"Vincent!" Anya said, lighting up, swiveling on her stool so that he would catch just a bit more inner thigh than was strictly necessary. Kiss kiss, cheek cheek, all very New York. But Vincent slid back just a bit slower than he might and let his cheek linger a little too long, and yeah, she responded.

He drew back at last, and now in addition to seeing her flushed face he saw through two sets of biot sensors.

V1 was headed toward the eye, running through a deep valley filed with tumbled crystalline boulders of makeup. Expensive makeup—finer grained—had a tendency to stick to biot legs, a bit like mud.

V3 confronted a landscape Vincent could not at first make sense of. He was on a long, gently curved plain of dimpled, spongy flesh. But in the distance, perhaps half a centimeter mack, was a huge pillar as big around as a redwood tree. It was vertical to the fleshy plain. V3 was sideways, which meant that actually the thick pillar was roughly horizontal.

Vincent's actual eyes, the big, brown, real ones, flicked toward Anya's ear. Of course: an earring. Maybe white gold or platinum. Through the eyes of the biot it looked flaked and corrugated, like an old muzzle-loading cannon. And when the biot got closer, Vincent had a view of the hole, the puncture through which the metal passed.

In the macro Vincent saw the diamond that hung below the lobe. He'd never seen a diamond from biot level. It might be interesting. But this wasn't a sightseeing trip.

One in the eye, one in the ear.

"I just stopped off to get a few things," Vincent said, holding up the bag as proof. "I was early. But I didn't want to be rude and show up early."

Maybe he could have just trusted her. Maybe he could have told her what he needed. Maybe he could have brought her into BZRK. That had been his original plan, to recruit her, to have a back door into the McLure labs.

But he couldn't afford a maybe anymore. He needed a yes. He needed what she could give to the cause, and he needed it immediately.

Ticktock. It was all a matter of necessity, and didn't necessity justify everything?

"It would have been okay. I was early, too."

They shared a conspiratorial "We like each other" smile. Vincent assumed she was planning on sleeping with him. He certainly hoped so: he needed time to do his work.

He needed time with Anya. And, too, there was attraction. Vincent was anhedonic; he wasn't asexual. Need was one thing, the pleasure one took from satisfying a need was a different matter.

Damn it. She'd been swimming. Or maybe just showering. Either way V3, in her ear, had just run smack up against a wall of water. Probably no more than a few milliliters, but it was held in place by surface tension, so rather than forming a lake he could run across, it was more like a giant water balloon he would have to swim through.

Unless he broke the surface tension. In which case V3 would go for a sort of flume ride, probably out into the outer ear. But also possibly into a hastily raised napkin and from there to a lap or the bar counter.

"I'll have what she's having," Vincent said to the bartender.

Anya put her hand on his arm and laughed. "No, no, this is awful, really. No self-respecting man should drink this. Too sweet." She was so confident in interrupting. He noticed. Older woman, accomplished woman, advanced degrees and a responsible position.

"We'll have two shots of vodka, very cold, neat," Anya said. She winked. "My Russian blood, you know."

"Are you trying to get me drunk?" Vincent flirted.

"If that's what it takes," Anya said, voice husky as Vincent sent V1 gingerly through the mascara line, stepping over what looked like a recently deceased demodex—interesting—onto the eye, and down below the lower lid.

He withdrew V3 from the ear. Vincent had been caught in a folded napkin once before. It was hell trying to find your way out. Vincent could probably find his way out of a larynx quicker than he could a napkin.

They did their shots.

An hour and ten minutes later they were in Anya's apartment.

Some time later still she had fallen asleep in his arms.

Vincent was by that point fairly convinced that Anya was clean of nanobots.

And he'd already begun to use V1 and V3 with reinforcement from V2—still recovering from two leg breaks on its earlier mission—to stretch the neuronic fibers from her pleasure centers to her images of him. She may only like him now. Or maybe not even that. But over the next few hours, while she slept and he did not, her affection for him would grow. Soon the mere thought of him would release endorphins into her bloodstream. And her natural caution and reserve would be degraded. She would like him; she would trust him.

Vincent vowed that he would remove it all once he had what he needed. That, he told himself, was the difference between BZRK and the Armstrong Twins. Vincent did only what he had to do. He would minimize the betrayal. As much as he could.

"Because we're the good guys," he whispered to himself even as, unasked for, the memories of murder in a small restaurant in London bubbled to the surface of his mind.

Burnofsky didn't have the kind of money or juice (or entourage) that the music producer (who shall remain nameless), or the overexposed industrialist (who shall, likewise, remain nameless) had, so he didn't get one of the larger, deeper alcoves at the China Bone.

They didn't know Burnofsky's name, not his real one, just the name he gave them: John Musselwhite. Did the management know it was a fake name? Probably. Most likely they'd have been horrified if he gave a real name.

It was a loft, this room, vast, but not a wide-open space. There was a sort of catwalk that went around the room, but it had been nicely done, industrial, yes, but well lit, cinematic almost. There were security guys but ever so discreet, dressed in loose-fitting black trousers and white shirts, like something you'd see Jackie Chan wear in one of his movies. Generic Asian chic. If they had guns, then the guns were concealed, and the security men smiled. Smiles, smiles. In two of the corners were tall dancing platforms, essentially open hydraulic elevators that raised the dancers up or down, like slow-motion pistons. The girls were varied and swapped out often enough that neither they nor the patrons would become bored.

The music was softer than you might expect from a den of iniquity. It was not, Burnofsky thanked God, the music of the aging rocker he had just seen the back of. In fact he'd never heard music quite like it anywhere else. It was a soft pulsation with a repetitive melody and had a quality of perpetualness about it. A bit like house dance music, although no one but the professional dancers would be expected to dance.

Beneath the catwalk were the alcoves. They were mocked up to look a bit like an Eastern bazaar, as though they were tents, so what you saw looking across the room were tent flaps or beaded curtains or, in the case of some who enjoyed flaunting their vice, canvas drapes pulled back to reveal and invite.

The center of the room was a rectangular bar, all lacquered ebony with tasteful red and gold highlights. They served alcohol of course, and food as well, though few people ate the dumplings. It was more that some of the patrons didn't like staying inside their alcoves but enjoyed mingling and chatting, often with the bartenders. And then, some people liked a vodka with their pipe.

Burnofsky entered his narrow alcove, no bigger than a good-size department-store dressing room, with just a pair of easychairs and a small table, a dim lamp, and an old-fashioned rotary phone. Burnofsky knew the drill. He lifted the receiver and waited until a voice answered.

"Yes, sir. How may I be of service?" A man's voice, kind, understanding, nonjudgmental.

"Ah-pen-yen," Burnofsky said, the China Bone's preferred term.

The voice said, "Very good, sir. Shall we make all preparations, or would you prefer to do your own?"

"You prep it." Burnofsky smiled. "I trust you."

He hung up and relaxed back into the chair. From the alcove to his left came the spicy-sweet smell he loved. From the other side a sudden explosion of laughter, quickly stifled.

He'd been looking forward to this all day. The day had included a long face-to-face with the Twins. That was never a good thing. Especially when the heart of the meeting was to tell Burnofsky that Bug Man would be taking the lead on the UN job.

He hadn't argued much. Bug Man's tactics were sound. But he was arrogant, and Burnofsky could see too many ways things could go wrong. Burnofsky didn't like the sense of plans being rushed. There would be another UN General Assembly in a year. Another year's planning and they'd be in a much stronger position.

Right now AFGC had a grand total of twenty-seven qualified twitchers, counting himself. Twenty-seven. To target and control six major heads of state while maintaining all their existing projects? The logistics were staggering.

Infest the prime ministers of Britain, India, and Japan, the chancellor of Germany, and the presidents of China and the United States? That was six teams in six cities, spinning away inside the brains of four men and two women who were among the most-watched, most-observed people in the human race?

Bad wiring had a tendency to cause seizures. Seizures in an average person were manageable, but in a head of state? The POTUS just had to twitch to have an elite team of doctors probing her ten different ways. And what then? What happened when the doctors at Bethesda found a head full of nanobots?

Panic, that's what. Phone calls to the FBI, the CIA, the NSA, every foreign intel outfit. The rumors were already out there. A Google search would turn up the paranoids—some with surprisingly accurate information.

If the FBI suddenly had proof? Physical proof?

AFGC might control the deputy director of the FBI, but he alone would never be able to contain something like that.

Twenty-seven twitchers. And of those maybe five who could fight half as well as they spun. That's what the kid didn't get. Bug Man didn't understand that twenty-seven was really closer to seven who could fight. And maybe three who could fight and win against the very best.

A waitress appeared. She was carrying a silver tray. She bowed slightly, set the tray down, and backed out of the alcove.

The tray was covered with a thick, white cloth, and on that cloth rested a narrow glass tray of long matches and an ornate Cloisonné water pipe with a long, bent bronze neck and a tiny bowl.

Burnofsky closed his eyes and smiled. When he opened them again, his worries and troubles were already starting to recede because rescue was at hand.

Troubling visions of failure, discovery, capture followed by twenty years cold turkey in a federal prison, would disappear soon enough.

But not just yet. A sweaty, nervous man was standing in the

entrance, pushing aside the drape, diffident, bobbing like he was halfway to a bow.

Burnofsky had forgotten. There was business to be conducted before pleasure was to be savored. He didn't stand up. He did offer his hand.

"Lord Elfangor?" the man whispered, practically wetting himself. "I'm Aidan Bailey." The accent was Australian or New Zealand, one of those. A UN employee, of course.

Burnofsky sighed. Of course. This would be One-Up's work. And as usual she had taken the most dramatic route. He squinted up at the man, trying to recall the exact nature of his wiring. He was a Scientologist, which meant he was already prepared to buy into alien mythology. A bit of a change from the usual giddy idealists churned up by Nexus Humanus and delivered to AFGC.

Burnofsky wondered how One-Up had inserted that "Lord Elfangor" bullshit. Had she actually gone to the trouble of tapping phonemes to invent a name? Unlikely. More likely she'd cauterized some critical thinking—there couldn't have been much there to begin with—wired the man's religious indoctrination to some bit of TV trivia or movie lore and come up with the name, then tied it to a pic of Burnofsky.

She tried too hard, One-Up. Occam's razor: find the simplest solution.

"I am Lord Elfangor," Burnofsky said. "Thank you for coming."

"I . . ." The man laughed, sudden, surprised. "I don't even know why I'm here, really. I just knew . . ."

"You knew you had to be here," Burnofsky said, doing his best not to glance at the pipe, willing himself to play out the role. "As though a force greater than yourself, a mind much deeper than your own—"

"Yes! That's it!"

"Mr Bailey, very rare are those who can hear the summons. Rarer still those with the wisdom to heed the words of the Masters."

He was making it up as he went along. He'd seen One-Up's report, skimmed it, but hadn't memorized all the details.

"What you do here today will save the human race," Burnofsky said solemnly. "You have something for me."

Bailey nodded. He was believing. But he was troubled that he was believing. He sensed something wrong. A part of him knew. A part of him was fighting it, even as his hand went slowly to the inner pocket of his jacket.

"You are feeling enturbulated. You are concerned that you do not have your ethics in," Burnofsky said, and held his breath. Had he said it right? He had a near-perfect memory, and he'd read about Scientology—

"Yes," Bailey said, and laughed with relief.

Burnofsky winked. "When we are done, you will feel clear." He watched the man closely. It was dangerous to be playing with unfamiliar cult terminology. It was too easy to make a revealing misstep.

Bailey drew his hand from his pocket and placed a flash drive in Burnofsky's palm.

"Thank you," Burnofsky said. "You have done well."

Bailey breathed a huge sigh of relief.

"You can go," Burnofsky said. "And, oh, um, if you happen to meet a young woman with the unusual name of One-Up, give her a message for me."

Burnofsky looked him in the eye. He was sure that One-Up's nanobots were tapping the optic nerve, or perhaps even listening. He scribbled a few words on the pad of paper, tore off a sheet, and held it up so Bailey could see it.

"'Make it clean, and far from here,'" Bailey read the words aloud. "I don't understand."

Burnofsky waved a hand to shoo the doomed man away. The last thing they could afford was this fool talking to his Scientology auditor and sending those loons into a frenzy.

So at a safe distance from the China Bone, an artery in Bailey's head would burst.

Burnofsky wondered why he had given the kill order to One-Up. She didn't need it. She knew a wire job this rough and ready, this tenuous, needed to be terminated.

It occurred to him that he wanted to take the burden of guilt on himself. That he often did that. Maybe if One-Up were older . . . But a seventeen-year-old girl should have some deniability for murder.

How in hell had it come to this?

Burnofsky remembered—how many years ago had it been—when he and young Grey McLure had worked together. Back in the day. Now Grey was dead. And Burnofsky had made it happen, even if it was Bug Man who had done the actual deed.

He slipped the flash drive containing security codes—CCTV access, computer access, door passes for the United Nations Building—into his pocket.

He raised the pipe and lit a match.

Twenty-seven twitchers to take over the world. Half of them nothing but messed-up children.

Yeah. Well. What . . .

Oh! Oh, yes.

Oh, yeah . . .

Burnofsky lay back, forgetting the pipe still dangling from his hand, and laughed softly, happily to himself.

ELEVEN

"Who are you?" Sadie asked.

Noah shrugged. "They said not to tell anyone my name."

They looked at each other across the shabby room. The walls were a water-stained green. The ceiling was pressed tin with a repeating wreath pattern that wrapped around the place where a light fixture must once have hung. The couch was cracked brown leather, and there was a rectangular glass coffee table decorated with rings left by cups and mugs. A disappointingly empty bag of hot-and-spicy Doritos sat next to an equally empty soda can.

There was a TV. CNN was on, but muted.

There was a computer. Someone had left it on a game site.

There were cameras, but neither Sadie nor Noah saw those because they were no more than nail holes in the crown molding.

Sadie was seated in a deep, badly upholstered Morris chair. Noah had just walked in and looked a bit lost. She had a mug of green tea. He had a camouflage backpack that he pushed against the wall so as not to trip anyone.

Sadie was sharply alert, despite not having slept at all, and Noah was blinking too much and breathing too hard as a result of not having slept enough.

Morning had cast a gray shadow behind the pulled-down blinds in the tall windows.

Sadie saw the inexpensive luggage, the jacket that had definitely not come from any of the shops on Fifth Avenue, the sneakers, the arguably cute and definitely authentic bed head, the tentative mouth, the alarmingly blue eyes.

She had noted the English accent. She knew—from her mother, from her mother's British friends, from several visits to London—that English accents came in a wide range of types, from, "My ancestors cleaned out stables," all the way up to, "Your ancestors cleaned my ancestors' stables." Noah was definitely on the stable-cleaning end of the spectrum.

That made her inclined to like him. Or at least to think that it might be possible to like him.

For his part Noah saw a girl doing her best not to look like the sort of girl who was probably comfortable ordering around grown men and women. A girl with servants, he thought, you could see it in her look. Not haughty. Not a bitch. But also not even a little bit shy about looking him in the eye and allowing her judgment to show clearly.

She thought he might have some potential. She also expected to be disappointed.

He thought she would never agree to go out with him.

She liked his eyes.

He liked her freckles.

She thought that he probably thought she looked a little startled.

He thought she could probably smell his "I slept on a plane" breath from clear across the room.

Nijinsky and Ophelia came in together. Renfield just behind them. He took up a post leaning against the corner of two walls.

Noah looked at Nijinsky with some surprise. He had last seen him in London and somehow identified him with that city, despite him being an American.

Nijinsky smiled. He had a warm, quizzical expression, and Noah thought, hoped anyway, that Nijinsky might not be a bad person.

Noah watched the way Nijinsky took in the physical setting. Weary familiarity and disdain. Nijinsky was not a young man who would ever approve of water-stained green walls or coffee rings on tables. He was casually dressed in a blazer and slacks and collared shirt that taken all together must have cost—by Noah's estimate—a hell of a lot.

Noah had not met Ophelia, Sadie had not met Nijinsky, but of course no one wanted real names spoken, so neither Noah nor Sadie were introduced.

It was frankly starting to annoy Sadie. She was quite

confident that Nijinsky knew who she was. Obviously Ophelia did. They all did. Except maybe the boy. The one with the startled look on his face and the eyes that kept going back to her again and again.

As for Noah, he knew that Nijinsky knew who he was, but beyond that there was no reason anyone should know him.

Ophelia sat on the couch, close to Sadie, and patted the space beside her while smiling at Noah. Noah obeyed and sat.

Nijinsky looked around, a little desperate for a seating solution, and finally lowered himself with minimal physical contact onto an armless chair. He flicked his blazer expertly so that it draped just the right way. His trouser legs stayed where they should and did not reveal above-sock flesh.

"We've never had two new people at once before, so procedures are a bit ad hoc," Nijinsky said.

"But very glad to have you both," Ophelia said. She had two smiles, one right after the other. The one for Sadie was sisterly. The one for Noah was cordial, and also included the information that she was too old for him, nothing personal, but he was not to flirt with her.

Noah hadn't been considering flirting with her. He was in fact desperately trying to avoid looking at the sprinkling of freckles across Sadie's nose and cheeks, and he was trying not to feel the sadness that throbbed through her tough-girl expression, because, well, there was no because, really. He just wanted to look at her. And he knew he shouldn't. But he did look at her and then looked away and did this possibly twenty times. And bit his lip, which didn't help.

"You've both been given some basic information," Nijinsky said. "You know why you're here. Your motivations are your own. You just need to know that you've already crossed the line. Sorry if that wasn't obvious, but you are in. *In*. And there is no out for either of you."

He didn't smile, so it wasn't a joke. He leaned forward, elbows on knees, signaling that this was serious.

"You are part of us now. You'll get orders. And you'll obey them." Nijinsky's eyes slid over Noah to rest quite deliberately on Sadie. Noah used the excuse to steal his own look, and boy, you did not want to be the guy who was on the wrong end of the defiance in Sadie's eyes. It wasn't a put-on; it came from all the way down deep. From reptilian brain and spine and fist.

Noah looked away and rested his own gaze on Nijinsky. Was it racist of him to think that Asian eyes showed less expression? Whether it was or not, Nijinsky was hard to read. And then, just a glint of amusement. Nijinsky liked Sadie. Not *that* way, but he liked her.

"We all get orders," Ophelia said.

"Yes, we do," Nijinsky agreed.

"We all understand."

"Yes."

"The stuff that matters . . ." Ophelia finished the sentence with a shrug.

"We've all lost people," Nijinsky said.

Ophelia nodded. No smile. The skin of her face was brittle, stretched, concealing memories. It was hard now to imagine that face ever smiling. And yet she had, hadn't she?

"We don't want to lose any more," Nijinsky said. "We put our lives on the line. And those who run biots risk their sanity. We do this of our own free will. We do it so that we and the rest of the human race will continue to *have* free will. So that people will be able to choose: right or wrong, good or evil. The other side claims to want universal happiness, and I'll tell you: they aren't lying."

He let that sink in for a moment, a self-consciously dramatic pause.

"They would use technology to make the human race into a sort of insect society. To make us all one mind, united. No unhappiness, no stress, no rage or jealousy. But we choose a different world. We choose the right to unhappiness."

"We're fighting for unhappiness?" Noah asked skeptically. "It sounds a bit crazy when you put it that way."

Nijinsky laughed, delighted. "Oh, it is." Then, serious again, he said, "We fight for the right to be what we choose, to feel what we choose. Even if what we choose seems crazy to others."

"If it's all the same to you, I'll fight for revenge," Sadie said.

Nijinsky's eyes glittered. "Oh, yes. That's fine with me."

A look passed between him and Ophelia. Ophelia looked satisfied, almost an "I told you so" look. They were pleased, Nijinsky and Ophelia, pleased with their new recruits.

"We leave our old names behind, and choose a new name," Nijinsky went on. "From the start it became a . . . let's say a custom . . . to choose the name of someone, real or fictional, who had slipped the surly bonds of sanity." He made a wry smile.

Ophelia said, "Vincent for Vincent van Gogh, Nijinsky, Hamlet's Ophelia, Stephen King's Annie Wilkes, Caligula." She blinked when she said that name. "Kerouac, Renfield here—a character from *Dracula* no less—and, of course, Lear."

Sadie, who missed very little in life said, "Who's Caligula? That's a pretty heavy name."

Ophelia used her eyes to direct the question to Nijinsky. Nijinsky closed his blazer and buttoned it. "This isn't the Girl Scouts. We can't allow betrayal."

Sadie smirked. "Caligula is your enforcer."

"What is this?" Noah asked. The sound of his own voice surprised him. He hadn't intended to speak. "You came to me. You told me and—" He glanced at Sadie, realized he wasn't supposed to be indiscreet, blushed, and picked up the dropped thread of his thought. "You came to me. Then that fucking test. And I was, like, okay then. Now you're saying what? What are you saying?" His mouth didn't look tentative now. There was a curl in the upper lip that made it seem just a little bit as if there was someone harder hiding behind the blue Bambi eyes and the diffident manner.

Nijinsky nodded slightly to himself. "I'm telling you that if you betray BZRK, you will get a visit from Caligula. And I want you to understand this, boy." He stabbed his manicured finger at Noah, not angry, but like, "Hear me, remember this, or God help you," and said, "No matter who tells you they can keep you safe from Caligula, they're lying. No one can keep you safe from Caligula."

Sadie looked at him, the blue-eyed boy. Never a blink. No flinch. "I wrote a paper on Sylvia Plath. She was a poet. She was thirty when she stuck her head into the oven. Turned on the gas. Breathed it until she was dead. Her children were in the next room." She blinked once, a slow, deliberate move. "Is that crazy enough for you?"

Nijinsky drew back, almost like he feared contamination.

Noah looked at her in absolute wonder and he thought, *She's already crazy*. And at the same time thought he would fall asleep that night only after lying awake a long time and thinking of her.

"Sylvia, then?" Nijinsky asked.

A slight headshake. "Plath."

It had a religious feel, that moment. No one smiled or

laughed or winked or, Noah was sure, even considered doing any of those things.

"How about you, kid?" Nijinsky asked, still looking at Sadie. At *Plath*.

"I don't . . . know . . ." Noah said. "I mean . . . I wrote an essay on Nelson Mandela once. But he wasn't crazy."

That did earn a smile from Ophelia, an unambiguously sweet one. Renfield looked puzzled and a little offended to find himself puzzled. He had no idea who this Nelson Mandela was.

Noah wasn't sure how to read Plath's look. Sizing up. That was as close as he could get to defining it. She wasn't quite judging him, just assessing him. Measuring him. Like she might do if she was picking up a screwdriver and wondering, Is this the right size?

Ophelia said, "If we're to have a Plath, perhaps we should have a Keats. Also a great poet. Plath was American; Keats was British. He was also depressive and an opium addict. And like Plath, he died very young. In his twenties."

"Two poets in one day," Nijinsky said. He stood up, moving with just a little less grace than he'd shown sitting down. "This may seem silly. Making you take new names. But it has a point."

"It's not . . ." the newly named Keats began to say.

"The point," Nijinsky said, eyes seeking theirs, each in turn, "Is that you must right now, here, without pause for further consideration, and without later regret, accept that you are in a fight with a deadly enemy. From here forward your lives are in danger. From here forward you surrender any claim to privacy. From here forward there are only two outcomes for you: death or madness."

His phone rang.

He drew it out, looked at the caller, turned abruptly, and walked away.

"Or victory," Ophelia said quietly, when she was sure Nijinsky would not overhear.

TWELVE

"They're in," Nijinsky said into his phone. "Plath and Keats."

"Dr Violet is wired," said Vincent into his. "She'll give us what we need. Tonight. It should be safe enough to bring the two young poets."

"Are you going to equip them both? Plath hasn't even been tested."

Vincent hesitated. "Do you laugh at the idea of instinct, Nijinsky?"

"Yours? Never."

"I'm going to equip them both. Instinct. And need. Time is short. She'll do."

At the same time miles away, in another location, Burnofsky dropped the flash drive from the China Bone in front of Bug Man.

And Ophelia wrote an e-mail to her brother back in Mumbai. She told him about her studies at Columbia. She invented some problem with one of the professors. She attached a picture of herself and a girl she didn't really know, standing in front of Low Memorial Library, both of them making peace signs at the camera.

And Renfield showed Plath to her room and Keats to his. They were adjoining but not connected.

Plath's room looked like a miserable, run-down hotel where a drunk might spend his last days. Keats's room looked not unlike his room at home, except that it could do with an England poster. The rooms were identical.

"How long do we stay here?" Plath asked.

"There is usually a period of observation and training," Renfield said. He was looking her up and down in a way that implied it didn't need to be a lonely time for her.

"What is there to observe?" she asked. "I'm sure you have biots on me."

Renfield did a sort of aristocratic nod, not exactly a bow, but an acknowledgment. "Not me, personally, at the moment," he said.

"They can read my thoughts?" Plath asked. Asked and answered, but she wasn't convinced.

"No."

"See what I see?"

"Yes. And hear what you hear, depending on where they are

placed and whether they are equipped for hearing large sound waves."

Plath struggled a bit with that. Keats blushed.

Renfield actually seemed to experience a moment of fellow feeling. "You get used to it."

And he was, at that moment, seeing the grainy, gray-scale images he was getting from a rather bad connection in Keats's eyes. His biots were running yet another check for nanobots: couldn't be too careful.

He was seeing his own proud expression as Keats looked at him. Then Keats's quick glance at Plath's chest. Then the refocus on her face. The quick glance away when Plath looked toward Keats. And then a bit longer than necessary on Plath's neck, cheek, ear.

Yes, the young prodigy there was smitten with Plath. Or at least checking out the possibilities. Renfield considered resenting the fact. After all, if anyone was going to be spending quality time with the prickly young thing, it should be Renfield himself. It's not as if he was exclusive with his other friend.

But then he remembered that Keats was Kerouac's brother. There was a great debt there. Renfield would honor that debt by looking out for the youngster. But in a way that didn't allow Keats to have . . . quality time . . . with Plath.

There were limits even to debts of honor.

*

147

A few minutes later, Keats lay on his cot, staring up at the ceiling. He should be afraid. Instead he was overwhelmed by the thought of her. Just a wall separating them.

Could they read his thoughts?

Maybe not. But they might be looking through his eyes and that was close enough. What about when he went to the toilet? Jesus.

Had Alex gone through all this?

And more, obviously.

But Alex was a soldier, tough as they came, and Noah was not. Noah was a kid whose only training was in video games, footie, and the arcane art of barely scraping by on schoolwork. He had been in three fights in his life, the first when he was nine and an older boy had called his mother a MILF. That had cost Noah a black eye and a torn ear. The other two had involved eruptions on the football field and had ended when teammates pulled him back.

War? That was Alex, not Noah.

Not Noah: Keats. He supposed he'd have to look the poet up. Three poets suddenly in his life: Pound, Plath, and Keats. Did poetry drive people mad, was that it? And Kerouac. Not a poet, but another writer.

What a strange way to be following in Alex's footsteps.

Would his brother notice when Noah missed his scheduled visit? Would some part of him guess where Noah had gone?

Would he be proud? Or would he yank on his chains and shriek a mad warning about the nano and Bug Man and BZRK?

At some point jet lag reached for him and dragged him down hard and fast and he fell asleep.

Plath, pacing her room, did not.

Could they read her thoughts? She tended to believe they could not. But that didn't mean they weren't watching her pace.

If they were reading her thoughts like a Facebook page, these would be the status updates:

I am completely alone. I feel scared, also liberated.

Renfield is an asshole.

Ophelia and Renfield are playing Good Cop/Bad Cop to gain my trust.

I chose 'Plath' for myself so they chose 'Keats' for the boy with the blue eyes. That was deliberate: they want us to be a team.

My arm hurts like hell, can I get an Advil or six?

What next?

Across town, in the Tulip, Charles and Benjamin Armstrong used very old-fashioned tools to organize their thoughts: 3 x 5 cards.

Coordination, fine motor skills—and gross motor skills,

too, for that matter—had always been difficult for them. Each had an eye. But a single eye does not allow for depth perception.

Each had an arm. But writing sometimes requires two arms, one to hold the paper in place.

The Twins had struggled to master writing. Keyboards and pads were easier. But Charles and Benjamin valued the pain of overcoming difficulty. Life had always been hard for them. Anything physical had been difficult and sometimes humiliating. On the day many years earlier when the seventeen-year-old Twins had smothered their grandfather with a pillow, they'd had great difficulty coordinating the action.

Old Arthur Armstrong had raised the boys on a diet of paranoia and reckless self-indulgence. They had loved him in a way, and he had been proud of them.

He had asked them to end his pain-wracked life, and they had agreed, but only on condition that they immediately inherit Armstrong Fancy Gifts Corporation.

Arthur had beamed with pride. He had raised them right: if they were to kill him then, by God, they had a right to demand a payment.

Still, when the time had come, it had been hard to manage. The old man was near death, but still some panicky instinct drove his body to spend its last energy struggling. And with two uncoordinated hands, it wasn't easy to hold the pillow down long enough, hard enough, to complete the suffocation.

The cards now before them bore carefully handwritten notes in felt-tip block letters:

POTUS
PM of UK
PM of Japan
Chancellor of Germany
President of China
PM of India

It would be a global strike. The six most powerful political leaders on Earth. Taken together they ruled half the human population. Three quarters of the world's wealth. Virtually all of the world's technology.

An argument could be made for including Russia, France, and South Korea. Indeed those three cards were set aside for future use.

"Ambitious," Charles said.

"Too ambitious?" Benjamin asked.

"Burnofsky made good arguments for a more incremental approach," Charles said. "And with McLure dead maybe he is right. BZRK will be crippled without access to McLure money and facilities. Perhaps we have more time."

Twin monitors moved on robotic arms, keyed to their movement. Each monitor had its own camera, and each camera focused on one side of that too-broad face. It allowed them to see each other's face, to speak not just beside each other, but to each other—eye to eye to eye.

The surface of the desk was a touch screen with identical menus to left and right. From here they could call up cameras everywhere. The fifty-ninth floor, where the twitchers worked. The twelve floors of laboratories, the testing facilities on the twentieth and twenty-first, the business offices on the lower floors, the model gift shop at ground level, the subterranean garage, the dedicated elevators that serviced the Tulip.

They could also call up sight and sound from the main offices of Nexus Humanus in Hollywood, and the satellite offices in Washington, London, Berlin, Moscow, Buenos Aires, and just blocks away in Manhattan.

And, too, they could see the hundreds of Armstrong Fancy Gift shops in airports and train stations and on tourist streets around much of the world.

And they could watch the homes of key employees, see who came to visit, observe their families, watch as they fought or showered or cooked dinner or made love.

Their empire came to them through a thousand hidden cameras, a system for them and for them alone. Charles and Benjamin Armstrong, who could not go out into the world, watched unseen and unsuspected.

But for now they watched each other. Watching his twin's

eye, Benjamin could see that Charles was not very serious, that he was playing devil's advocate. Benjamin smiled tolerantly.

"The longer we wait, the greater the chance of discovery," Benjamin said, walking back through their decision making. Reiterating. Like it was a liturgy. It was reassuring. "We've had several close calls."

"At any moment the technology might be discovered," Charles agreed.

"We know the FBI had possession of a nanobot. What if we had not managed to retrieve it?"

"And we know that MI5 is actively investigating."

"There have been repeated efforts by Anonymous to penetrate our AFGC networks as well as Nexus Humanus," Benjamin said.

"Oh yes, the hackers are after us."

"The FBI is thwarted for now. But MI5 persists."

"Indications of Mossad interest."

"An attempt by Swedish intelligence to penetrate Nexus."

"Too many eyes are turning toward us, brother."

That image troubled both men. They watched: they were not themselves watched.

"BZRK is weakened by McLure's death, but not defeated," Benjamin cautioned.

"Fuck BZRK," Charles snapped.

"Fanatics."

"A death cult."

There followed a long silence, during which both men looked down at the cards, and the third eye wandered lazily. Beneath the cards the table screen showed a lab worker entering data.

"Time is short."

"The time is now."

"If we are to succeed, brother."

Another long silence.

"Six targets," Benjamin said with a deep sigh. When he sighed, it stretched the flesh between their heads, slightly distorting Charles's mouth. "Four men, two women, all surrounded and watched. Each requires a fully resourced team, a main twitcher, a relief twitcher, housekeeping, security . . . a minimum of ten people per team. And each is a potential target; each presents the possibility of discovery."

Charles sighed. "Bug Man. Kim. One-Up. Alfredo. Dietrich." Pursed lips. "Burnofsky. Six at the top level."

"Average age, what, seventeen, if you leave out Burnofsky?"

"Twitchers," Charles said, and made a snorting sound. "Young and arrogant, intelligent, and unstable by definition."

"Twenty-two more at the second level. Seventy-one at third level."

"Risky and useless respectively, for this kind of work."

They looked down, all three eyes now, at the cards.

Benjamin placed his finger on the one that read "Chancellor of Germany". And pushed it to the side. "He's likely to lose in the next election. A waste of resources."

"Five, then," Charles agreed. "US, China, Japan, India, and the UK."

"Five."

"Not later, but now."

"Now," Benjamin agreed with finality.

Their dog, a beagle, came trotting across the polished wood floor and rubbed against Benjamin's leg. Charles took a treat from a jar on the desk and dropped it into the animal's mouth.

"There you go, Maisie," Charles cooed. "Good girl."

"That dog of yours," Benjamin muttered. "Why does she always rub against me?"

They went then to take their shower but were interrupted by news, brought to them by their body servant, Hardy, who was an old man with a wonderful ability to resist flinching when he looked at his two charges.

Hardy handed them a pad, open to a message. They read it as Hardy helped them out of their tailor-made clothing with the unusual zippers and openings.

"The trap," Benjamin said.

"The Vincent flytrap," Charles said, and that *bon mot* gave them both a hearty laugh.

ARTIFACT

To: Vincent
From: Lear

Proceed to equip Plath and Keats.

Note: The UN General Assembly attack must be stopped. No one's life or sense of morality is more important than that goal.

Follow orders, Vincent. It will be your salvation.

ARTIFACT

To: C and B Armstrong
From: AmericaStrong, a division of Armstrong Fancy Gifts
Corporation
Status: EYES ONLY ENCRYPT Read and safe-delete

A recent Wikipedia edit included information prejudicial to
our interests (see paragraph #3 below). That paragraph
has now been deleted and was online for only twelve
minutes. We suspect source material from KSI, Swedish
Intelligence.

Project MKULTRA
From Wikipedia, the free encyclopedia
"MKULTRA' redirects here. For other uses, see MKULTRA
(disambiguation).

Project MKULTRA, or **MK-ULTRA**, was the code name
for a covert, illegal CIA human research program, run by
the Office of Scientific Intelligence. This official U.S.
government program began in the early 1950s, continuing
at least through the late 1960s, and it used U.S. and
Canadian citizens as its test subjects. [1][2][3][4]

The published evidence indicates that Project MKULTRA involved the use of many methodologies to manipulate individual mental states and alter brain functions, including the surreptitious administration of drugs and other chemicals, sensory deprivation, isolation, and verbal and sexual abuse.

Recent evidence suggests that MK-ULTRA also experimented with early versions of nanotechnology. When those efforts were frustrated by congressional budget cuts, the research was handed off to the Armstrong Fancy Gifts Corporation and their weapons research division. All records of AFGC's involvement have been expunged. A number of individuals involved have died under suspicious circumstances.

THIRTEEN

A knock.

Sadie—she hadn't begun to think of herself as Plath, not yet—said, "Who is it?"

"Vincent."

Vincent. Sadie hadn't seen him since he appeared suddenly in her bathroom. He looked the same. Twentysomething going on a thousand.

The boy with the blue eyes, Keats, was with him. Keats looked like he'd just been roused from bed. Of course, she probably did, too, considering that she had just been roused from bed.

Renfield was a few feet back in the shadows. He had struck an arms-akimbo pose, like a soldier on guard. She saw the wariness with which he looked at Vincent. Vincent didn't seem to do anything to cause this reaction, he wasn't angry or domineering. He was quiet and self-contained and looked a little sad in his dark raincoat. But Sadie had to admit that she felt a bit of Vincent-awe herself: she remembered the blade of his pen.

It was night outside. She had slept the sleep of exhaustion, all through the day.

"Things are moving a bit quicker than we'd like," Vincent said. "Usually there would be time to teach you. Prepare you. But we have an opportunity tonight."

Why was it absolutely impossible for Sadie even to imagine saying no to him?

Her eyes widened. Had they done something to her? In her brain?

As if he'd read her mind Vincent said, "Both of you are alone. Keats: Renfield retrieved his biots while you were asleep. And Ophelia's are back with her, Plath."

Plath.

"How do I know that?" Sadie demanded.

Renfield looked about ready to say something but stopped himself and took half a step back.

Vincent said, "Listen to me, Plath. You, too, Keats."

He knew her real name. But he wasn't using it. She had a feeling he would never slip and call her Sadie. Might not even think it.

Plath. It took some thinking about.

"I need you both to trust me," Vincent said. "I don't mean that I'd *like* you to trust me. I mean that I *need* you to trust me. For that reason, I will never lie to you. If you were ever to catch me in a lie, you would never fully trust me again. So I will never lie."

Sadie glanced at Keats. His suspicion was an echo of her own. "Okay, then," she said. "What are we doing?"

"We are going to make your biots."

Her breath caught. "Now?"

Renfield led the way. Not the way they had come into the building, not through that alley, but down a steep, narrow set of steps, and then a broader set of steps, and then through a door, and a room that was obviously the dry-storage space of a restaurant. Cans of chili sauce. Big plastic tubs of mayonnaise. Pickles. Ketchup. A surprisingly tall stack of boxes of canned soup. Canned sodas and bottled water.

Sadie smelled grease, vinegar, and urine.

Renfield opened a second door, and they stepped out into a dark and regrettably fragrant hallway with a door labeled "Men" and another "Ladies", and at the open end of the hallway a side view of a lunch counter.

The restaurant was narrow. New York narrow. Smeared mirrors and a six-inch-wide counter on one side, five stools with cracked plastic seats on the other, a low counter decorated with chrome napkin dispensers and stained plastic menus. Behind the counter a mess of mismatched refrigeration units, a grill, a drinks cooler, and to top it all off a cash register covered with age-curled clippings of cartoons from newspapers and magazines.

A very old man with white whiskers sat hunched in a

too-large jacket eating a grilled cheese sandwich. The only employee was a guy who might be in his late twenties, with a near-eastern complexion, sleepy eyes, and an apron. He was scraping the grill.

He did not look up though the four of them appeared as if by magic from the direction of the restrooms.

"This is the only time we'll ever travel together like this," Vincent said when they stepped out onto the cold, windy street.

They walked two blocks in silence to a hotel with a cab stand. The taxi ride took ten minutes—there was a lot of road repair on Sixth Avenue.

Vincent had the cab drop them two blocks from where Sadie suspected they were going. The McLure Industries downtown building. The headquarters, in theory at least, though the main campus was over in Jersey.

"They'll recognize me," she said tersely to Vincent. "And there are cameras."

Vincent nodded approvingly. "Good thinking. But you don't need to worry." They stopped on the street across from McLure Industries. The lobby was dimmed, but Sadie could clearly see two security men at the desk, even at this hour.

They crossed, passed by the lobby door, and went around the corner to the loading-dock gate. Vincent pulled out his phone and thumbed in a code. Peeking over his shoulder Sadie saw grainy security-camera footage of the loading dock.

The view shifted. And again. He had access to McLure security.

Then Vincent sent a second message. The steel door began clanking up. As soon as it was head high, Vincent led them inside and the door lowered again.

The loading-dock area was clear and as cold as the outside.

Sadie spotted a security camera overhead. The red light was off. Vincent sent a significant look to Renfield, who nodded tersely. For a heart-stopping moment Sadie thought Renfield was carrying a gun. But then he smirked and held up a Taser for her to see.

"Don't worry, it shouldn't be necessary," Vincent said. "I've been here many times. But there is no video of me, and no one but . . ." He hesitated. "No one but one man has seen me here. Just the one man whom I dealt with. Unfortunately that man is no longer with us. But I still need to get to a certain facility."

"Yes." She said it, and somehow it knocked the wind out of her. Her father. He was the man Vincent had seen. He was the man "no longer with us."

A freight elevator carried them up two dozen floors.

As it rose Vincent said, "We're going to meet a woman named Anya. She's a scientist. A friend of mine. She will most likely do what we ask of her. But there is a chance she won't. I haven't had time to prepare her as thoroughly as I would like."

Prepare her.

Sadie found the words chilling. She would be meeting a

woman who had been *prepared*. She noticed Keats's reaction, a brief look of disgust that came and was quickly suppressed.

Yes. Interesting. Maybe there was more going on with blue eyes than she'd thought at first. And he looked like he had a nice body underneath the layers. And he was very definitely interested in her; she'd noticed that right away. He wasn't subtle.

Why on earth was she thinking about any of that? It disgusted her. She disgusted herself. But a part of her brain knew the answer: *Because of all the things you have to think about, Sadie, my dear, Keats is the only one that isn't terribly sad or terribly frightening. So think about what his bare arms and shoulders would look like, because the alternatives . . . oh, Sadie, you don't want to think about any of those things.*

Vincent had a swipe card that let them walk through various locked doors. There were cameras everywhere. And everywhere the little red indicator lights went dark.

A final door.

Vincent hesitated, seemed to gather himself, and knocked.

A very attractive woman, at least a decade older than Vincent, opened the door. She and Vincent did the kiss-kiss, but with a bit more than "just friends" emphasis.

Sadie was instantly certain she and Vincent were sleeping together. And it occurred to her that during that brief contact Vincent had quite possibly transferred biots to her.

Down the rabbit hole into paranoia.

"Thank you, Anya, for helping us," Vincent said. He held her two hands while he said this. "These are John, Sylvia, and R.M."

Hands were shaken. *Sylvia*, Sadie thought to herself. Okay. And John must be the poet Keats's first name. As for Renfield, she was going to have to Google that. Was it R. M. Renfield?

"The tragedy has disrupted things," Vincent said. "Your help is vital, Anya. John and Sylvia both have very serious medical problems, and you'll be helping them, and me, tremendously."

Anya's eyes had stayed on Sadie a bit too long. She recognized her, or thought she did. And a line had appeared just above the bridge of her nose, a frown, a doubt.

"Get the goddamned signal repeater back up!" Bug Man shouted. "Goddamn it! God*damn* it!"

Signal was in and out. One second he had a clear, almost HD-quality view of the people in the room, and the next second he was looking at static.

One thing was for sure: that was Vincent he'd seen leaning in for a kiss. AFGC owned some bad video of Vincent, junk, but good enough that Bug Man had spent hours watching it on a loop, trying to suss out his opponent. Trying to see what the dude was about. The video showed Vincent walking to a taxi. That was all of it, but Bug Man had watched it probably fifty times.

Now he leaned forward in the twitcher chair, muscles straining, teeth gritted. Vincent. Right there, now. Real and big as life. And Bug Man with a crap repeater killing his communication.

Burnofsky was at his elbow. "They're working on it, Anthony."

"It'll take three minutes just to patch in a replacement unit," Bug Man raged. "You'd better damned well hope Vincent takes his time."

"You have visual again," Burnofsky remarked.

He could watch the screen over Bug Man's shoulder. He saw what Bug Man saw, and so he didn't need to be told that this was low-res video, glitchy as hell.

"Yeah, I'm going to take Vincent on with this," Bug Man said with savage frustration. "I'm pulling back out of range."

"First thing he'll do is check on his wire," Burnofsky predicted.

"He won't find anything wrong there," Bug Man said. But in his head he was going over it all again. His nanobots were well away from Vincent's elegant web of wires and transponders. But Vincent had something eerily close to psychic ability when it came to sensing an enemy. It would take so little to alert him.

Bug Man executed a simple reverse. It would move all twenty-four of his nanobots—fighters all, no spinners—in a precise move-by-move reversal, back down into the woman's brain. It wasn't the best way to move, but with lousy com-municaions it was the best he could do.

The screen split into twenty-four smaller screens. Three of them were totally dark—probably optics that had been blocked by fungus. Fungus was always an issue, little mushrooms that were unfortunately sticky. Or maybe one of them had picked up a macrophage along the way.

Bug Man enlarged one of the best-quality visuals. He saw images of half a dozen nanobots walking backward, retracing their steps. Back along the optic nerve, like daddy longlegs in a tunnel. He switched to rear-facing views. Even lower res, and he didn't dare burn up battery by switching on all twenty-four light arrays to clear things up.

Right now Vincent could take his handicapped army apart. This repeater issue had to be solved. In a couple of days he'd be inside the brain of the president of the United bloody States, and he didn't want to be watching visuals more degraded than a beat-up Game Boy.

"Just got news. It's going to be a while," Burnofsky announced. "They don't have a backup on-site. It's on its way, but it'll be twenty minutes. Not three."

"Twenty minutes?" Bug Man felt the blood drain from his face. No, this was not possible. He was not going to get his butt handed to him by Vincent. "Get some macro force in there," Bug Man said.

"At McLure headquarters?" Burnofsky laughed. "If you have to lose some nanobots, lose them, Anthony. It's not the end of the world."

Bug Man pulled off his gloves, pulled off his helmet, and unwound himself from the chair. The nanobots would continue automatically returning to their earlier start point. They didn't need him to do that.

"Oh, temper, temper, Anthony," Burnofsky said. He was laughing.

"You want to get your balls cut off by Vincent, be my guest." Bug Man jabbed his finger at the old man. "I don't play this game in order to lose. When communication is up, ninety percent minimum, give me a call. Maybe I'll still be hanging around."

"I'll need to take a few cells," Anya said.

They were in a lab, Noah—Keats, had to remember that—supposed it was a lab, anyway. He'd never been in a lab before and didn't know what they looked like except from films. But Dr Violet was wearing a white coat. And most of the equipment was white and chrome. And the floor was stainless steel, as were the walls.

So: a lab. Or maybe just a steel room with some unfathomable pieces of equipment, the only familiar part of which was the syringe in Dr Violet's hand.

It had a tiny little hook on the end of the needle. Wait, that couldn't be right. And there was no plunger, just a needle, really and—"Ow!"

She had stabbed it into the pale part of his arm, and now there was a tiny gobbet of his own meat stuck to the end of the needle and a small but enthusiastic bleeder.

"That's the only part that isn't automated," she said with a distant smile. "Also the only part that hurts." She handed Keats a Band-Aid.

Dr Violet set the syringe on a small stainless steel holder. She then took a windowed plastic bag from a drawer, tore it open, and withdrew something rectangular, the size of a phone, or a little smaller. It was white, smooth, sleek with rounded edges. It looked like something from an Apple store.

She pressed the only button, and the rectangle opened like a blooming flower. A light came from within.

"It's called a crèche," Vincent said. "Each crèche holds two biots. Or will, once they've grown."

Dr Violet deposited the piece of human flesh within the petals, pressed the button again, and it closed.

Plath did not cry out in pain when it was her turn. But she'd had warning, unlike Keats.

He wondered what her real name was. He wondered if he'd ever know. Susan? Jennifer? Alison? He had the feeling everyone but him knew it.

She was looking around the room with some expression other than fear or nervousness. More like regret or loss, maybe.

Keats was good at reading expressions. Girls always told him he understood them. It had worked for him, that ability to actually pay attention to girls' emotions. It seemed that looking at their faces occasionally, and not just at their breasts or bums or legs worked wonders. Occasional glances at eyes and mouth and forehead, that was the ticket.

Which was not to say that he wasn't aware of the curve of Plath's breasts as she leaned over to take the Band-Aid.

The crèches slid into what looked very much like ancient CD drives.

"There are many unique aspects to the biot process," Anya said. "Gene splicing, of course. The basics of that are well established. But intra-species splicing at these speeds is new and unique to McLure. And very closely guarded."

"Why not get it out there?" Keats asked. "I mean, look, secrecy is the *problem*, isn't it? If everyone just knew that this was possible . . ."

Similar looks from Dr Violet and Vincent silenced him.

"It's illegal," Plath said. Not like she was guessing, or like she was just realizing it. But like this fact had long been known to her. "If the government ever learned that we . . . that they . . . were recombining DNA to make whole new life-forms? This place would be swarming with FBI, everyone involved would be in prison, and the company would be bankrupted."

Keats started to ask something else, but a flicker, just a slight, unspoken *No* from Vincent stopped him.

What he'd been about to ask was this: Why doesn't the other side, the bad guys, why don't *they* tell the FBI?

But the answer was clear enough, when he thought about it. It was a pact of silence. Both sides had incriminating evidence on the other. If one side went public, so would the other. If that happened, both sides would be hauled off to prison. And the technology would die.

Except: no.

No, that was wrong, wasn't it? It wouldn't die. It would be taken over by the government, weaponized even more than it already was.

And what government could resist the opportunity to engage in a bit of nanowar with whatever enemies arose? Even if those enemies were their own people?

Keats noticed Plath watching him. She knew all this. She was watching the thoughts revealed on his face. Timing him. Wondering how long it would take for him to put it all together.

She seemed moderately impressed by what she saw.

And I just realized who you must be, too, Keats thought. *Oh my God: you're the* daughter. *The surviving McLure.*

He sat back in his chair. He'd been leering at a billionaire. That couldn't possibly work out well.

Still. They were just a wall apart back at the . . . what was it supposed to be called? BZRK headquarters? That sounded a bit melodramatic for a dump above a greasy deli.

And she didn't seem the snobbish—

Keats put his hand to his forehead. Suddenly the room was spinning. He put his other hand on his chair, afraid he was going to be tilted out of it.

"Do you have a bedpan or something?" Vincent asked Dr Violet.

She nodded, stood up, drew two enamel kidney-shaped pans from a drawer, and handed one each to Keats and Plath.

Plath was actually the first to vomit.

Keats found that fairly revolting, but a small triumph. A very small triumph since he hurled ten seconds later.

The world was spinning around, and he was a scrap of nothing caught in a whirlpool.

"What you're experiencing now is normal," Vincent said.

It didn't feel normal. Keats heaved again and this time missed the bowl. He fell forward. Vincent caught him before he could hit the floor.

Renfield stepped in to do the same for Plath, who was cursing in between retching sounds, a very unhappy-sounding girl.

"We call it childbirth," Vincent said. His voice was matter-of-fact, calm, not like he was trying to soothe Noah's panic but doing it anyway. "It's a kind of inside joke. Because what's happening is that your biots are quickening. Becoming alive. You're feeling the disorientation of being in your own bodies while simultaneously being somewhere else."

Keats had a sudden flash of a dark, flat plain stretching out beyond view.

A flash of lightning.

A series of flashbulb pops. *Pop!Pop!Pop!*

An elephant. Crippled.

No, a spider. Legs forming. But as big as an elephant.

Forming as he watched. Writhing. Almost as if it was in pain. Crying out with the writhing of still-forming limbs since it lacked a mouth to scream.

Beams of brilliant green light.

A spray of mist.

And suddenly a different view. A close-up in a flash of grainy light: a second creature, like the first, jerky movements, legs that ended in lobster claws, thrashing.

Then, "Oh, God!" Plath cried. "I saw its face."

She tried to bolt from her seat, but Renfield held her in place with hands on her shoulders.

"Biots often have a sort of eerie resemblance to the donor of their human DNA," Dr Violet said. "Each of you has two biots growing. You're seeing one of them through the still-forming eyes of the other."

"Okay, okay, I don't . . ." Keats said, and then whatever he'd been about to say was blown away by an image in flashing strobe light of the monstrous spider, turning, turning, and oh, God, oh, God, he was seeing through both sets of eyes, seeing himself seeing himself seeing himself as a sort of vile spider with no, no, noooo! Eyes! Blue eyes like his own eyes, oh God.

"It can be disturbing," Vincent said from a million miles away.

What were they doing to him?

Keats saw his brother, shackled, screaming, screaming, and now his own head was filled with lunatic visions.

He whimpered. He didn't care that he whimpered.

He didn't care that he was crying aloud, howling like a mad thing. Howling. Like his poor, mad brother.

Vincent felt sick inside. This was a dirty trick he was playing. They'd had no preparation. No training. He at least had seen films; he had seen micrographs. He'd been shown what to expect. By that cold bastard Caligula, yes, but shown anyway. Better than the nightmare Keats and Plath were entering.

These two, these straining, shrieking, sobbing teenagers were taking it all in one awful jolt of disorientation.

He hadn't just thrown them off the deep end and told them to swim. He'd thrown them into the ocean and told them to outswim the sharks.

He closed his eyes, and the memories came rushing back. The violent nausea. The feeling of being twisted out of reality, like the hand of some malicious god had reached down to rip him out of the fabric of time and space.

And they still had no idea. No *idea*. No way to understand that this transformation was permanent. No way to really understand that they had just bet their sanity. Their lives.

But Lear needed them. Lear was right. No time for the usual niceties; here you are, kids: welcome to the asylum.

Wait till they see the demodex. Wait until they see their first mite. Wait until they see the blood cells rushing around them like Frisbees.

Wait until they stare out through another man's eye.

And wait . . . Vincent froze.

All the while, V1 and V2 had been making their way along Dr Violet's optic nerve.

Something. What was it? He'd seen something, something that made the hairs on the back of his head stand up, twitched by tiny muscles, a signal of fear. What did he have to fear?

He backed V1 up.

Sent V2 ahead cautiously.

What had he seen and not seen?

And there it was. Just a few cells torn from the optic nerve when someone disconnected too quickly.

Trap.

FOURTEEN

"They've got the new repeater in place, Anthony."

Bug Man glared at Burnofsky, enjoying watching him sweat. Bloody old fart. He looked like that aging rocker who had just died. The old junkie. Bug Man would hate ever to have to infest Burnofsky, see that wrinkled old parchment skin up close, probably crawling with parasites with all his natural defenses weak. Those bushy eyebrows would be alive with vermin.

"Is it looped in?"

"Dammit, get back in there, Bug, or I'll do the job for you," Burnofsky snapped.

"And have you end up wasting two dozen of my branded nanobots? Have Vincent think he took me down?" Bug Man stormed back into the playroom.

He slipped on the gloves and slid back into the seat. Burnofsky watched over his shoulder as he tested the communications. Twenty-one of the twenty-four screens lit up. Most showed other nanobots. Some had views of the brain fold where they were hiding. Down in the meat.

Brain mapping was off for the moment.

"Now bugger off, old man, you can watch from the other room."

"Macro is on its way."

"The fuck?" Bug Man raged. "I thought you said there was no way!"

Burnofsky shrugged. "I ran your suggestion by the Twins. They agreed with you: they thought it was worth the risk to go macro as well. So I guess if you want credit for the kill, you'd best hurry, because it may be a bullet not a nanobot that does the job."

Bug Man quickly formed the nanobots into four platoons of six each. Not even the Bug Man could handle twenty-four individual nanobots. The platoons would perform identically, which sometimes ended up with the tiny robots getting in one another's way, but there were techniques to minimize that. If you had the skills.

He would send them in waves, a platoon at a time. The first group would locate Vincent's biots. If Vincent spotted them, they'd engage immediately. If not, they'd wait while the remaining forces were moved up. Then, bam! Waves of four, maybe ten or twenty seconds apart. Boom, boom, boom, and down goes Vincent.

Bug Man had a fantasy: he wanted to take one of Vincent's biots alive and haul it out into the macro.

Keep it alive and play with it for a while. As Vincent went slowly mad.

Plath pushed Renfield's hands off her shoulders. She wasn't going to freak out, but she didn't want to be touched.

The pain in her healing arm helped keep her focused. And maybe Vincent's soothing tone, but not being touched; and then she slipped to her knees, bent her face forward, and retched again on the floor.

What was that she was seeing? Some nightmarish beast, and another beside it. Standing on tall, clean, pyramidal spider legs on a long field of bumpy, grainy material that made her think of leather.

Vincent's voice, urgent, no longer soothing, said, "It's a trap."

And he was on his feet, grabbing Anya Violet as she turned to run, snatching her trailed arm. She almost got away, wriggling out of her lab coat. But Vincent caught her and yanked her violently toward him and locked her neck between his forearms.

She squirmed but could not get away.

"Is she—" Renfield snapped.

"Nanobot sign," Vincent said. "No contact yet, but any second now. Contact Caligula. We have a problem."

Renfield tapped his phone. "You should kill her," he said, not looking at Vincent, not meeting anyone's eyes. "Snap her neck and retrieve your biots. Let AFGC come and do cleanup.

Let Plath and Keats grab their babies—they're viable by now in their crèches. Then we get out of here."

Plath stared at Vincent. She and Keats just stood there, helpless, not really knowing what was happening, not knowing what was coming, sick in stomach and heart, minds swimming.

Was she going to see a murder? Right here in front of her? Was she going to see Vincent snap the woman's neck?

"Get their biots," Vincent said to Renfield. "We're getting out of here. We'll take Dr Violet with us."

"Let go of me," Anya cried. "Get off me!"

"And have them track their nanobots?" Renfield drew a gun from the back of his belt. Not the Taser he'd shown before. This was the real, very real, thing.

Vincent said something that sounded like, "I'm not Scipio," which meant nothing to Sadie and not much to Renfield or Noah, judging by the blank expressions. "Unless you're taking over here, Renfield, get their crèches."

Renfield looked shocked by the suggestion that he was taking over. He licked his lips, nervous.

He pushed Keats aside to punch commands into the console. The drawers that had slid open to take the crèches now slid open to release them.

Renfield glanced at them, read the labels, and handed them to Plath and Keats respectively. "I'd hold on to these real carefully if—"

"I'm under attack," Vincent said.

And there they were, zooming into Vincent's split field of vision, four . . . five . . .

At that moment Vincent was seeing three different realities.

There were Keats and Plath staggering from the mind warp that was the biot quickening. And Renfield with a gun dangling in one hand while he passed the crèches to the two teenagers. And Anya's hair, right in his face, and the smell of her, and the surge of her blood pushing to squeeze past the pressure of his strong forearms.

And in the micro, two visuals, V1 and V2. Color-enhanced to full. The true view in the nano was gray scale—cells had color only in large numbers and seen from a distance. But with enhanced color the nano world became vivid: greens, reds, eerie yellows, and startling pinks.

The only way to fight a battle: Technicolor.

The nanobot twitcher must have realized that he'd been spotted by Vincent's biots. Now they were wheels down and zooming toward him along the cable of nerve, their daddy longlegs arms trailing as stabilizers.

Vincent pushed Anya away, spun her around, set his biot legs to grip, and punched her hard in the eye. Hard enough to cause her to drop to her knees.

In the micro it was two impacts. The first, the punch, was

much the harder. Hard enough that even after it was absorbed by the skull bones and the giant gooey mass of the eyeball, it still hit like a magnitude-nine earthquake.

The nanobots, caught off guard, toppled off their unstable unicycle wheels. Two crashed together. A leg went flying. A sensor array twisted.

V1 and V2 shot forward, six legs each, powering ahead, measuring the seconds before the next impact.

The easiest kill on a nanobot was the sensor array: the little robots weren't much good without eyes. The array was two triangular visual sensors, plus UV emitters, and what was believed to be a sort of microwave sonar.

This entire mass sat slightly elevated on a short, thick mast. Breaking the mast, snapping it off, was almost impossible. But it had a weakness that allowed it to be twisted.

The second-easiest kill was to jam the leg gear. A nanobot had a single motor that ran all its functions, but it was well shielded. On each side were three articulated legs, all attached to a single hub.

The single wheel was in the center. It extended below the belly of the tiny robot and would make contact whenever the legs lowered the body.

Down in the micro they looked big, of course, as big as tanks. Giant spiders made of strangely pebbly steel. With their legs trailing and wheels spinning, they moved at what seemed like freeway speeds.

Wheel-up and running, they were still very quick, but slower than a biot.

To Vincent's inner eye there were two visual screens showing the nanobot attack from the target position, and separately from an off angle.

He had one, maybe two seconds before Anya's knees hit the floor and there would be a second impact.

Both Vincent's biots zoomed forward, legs a blur. They hit the two crashed nanobots.

V1 stabbed a cutting blade into the leg joint of one.

Leap! And V2 landed, all legs joined to form a single point of impact on the second.

And there! A flash of color betrayed a crudely drawn logo on the side panel of one nanobot. It was a grinning face with an insect exploding from its head: Bug Man.

Vincent's biots gripped nerve again, and the second impact came, gentler than the first, just enough to make an onrushing nanobot swerve.

It zoomed past, and Vincent tripped its trailing legs. It spun, and as it spun Vincent fired his saddle-back beam weapon. It hit the only thing it could kill: the nanobot's sensor array.

Three down and two to . . .

And then, the swarm was coming up from both sides, a rushing torrent of nanobots.

"Could use some help," Vincent said.

"Left or right?" Renfield replied, and touched his finger to his ear, picking up his biots.

"Right," Vincent said.

Renfield grabbed Anya's face. He stuck a finger into her right eye as she yelled and kicked at him and cursed furiously.

But Dr Violet was irrelevant now. She was no longer a person—she was a battlefield.

"I've got you, Vincent, got you so good," Bug Man said.

The impact—that had been clever, Vincent must have punched the host body, playing the macro as well as the nano. And that had cost Bug Man three nanobots.

So forget the wave upon wave, time to swarm for a quick kill. He sent the three intact platoons down the side of the nerve, walking on the vertical—gravity didn't mean much down in the meat.

Now Bug Man saw nineteen screens, all filled with the two enemy creatures. From one nanobot he had a nice, clean, close-up of one of Vincent's biots. Almost handshake close, it seemed. Close enough to see the face, with its insect compound eyes huge above the smeared brown mockery of its pseudo-human eyes.

The close-up view cost him: with superhuman speed Vincent's

biot leapt sideways, charged, and ripped the nanobot open.

Another screen dark. But it didn't matter. It may have been a kill, it may have been a blinding, but Bug Man was playing his troops as four platoons now, and even blind nanobots could still follow directions.

Swarm, Bug Man thought, and saw his screen fill with the desperate biots as his entire force charged, following four variations on that core instruction.

He saw Vincent's two biots spin, stab, leap. Goddamn, he was good. A bloody ninja, he was! Two more nanobots were crippled.

So fast!

Not fast enough, though. Not this time.

Nanobots ripped an arm from one of the biots. It waved on Bug Man's screen as it flew away, and he laughed.

Two legs gone from one of Vincent's children, so now it wasn't moving nearly as fast, firing that little popgun laser and missing, and burning stripes into the nerve tissue.

Bug Man understood: Vincent was drawing the immune response. They would sense the damage and send macrophages oozing up to kill the invaders.

Stupid and desperate. The macrophages were a hindrance to nanobots, but they could actually kill a biot—if they managed somehow to glom on.

What was Vincent playing at?

What did he know?

For just a few seconds, Bug Man hesitated.

"My eyes!" Anya Violet cried.

"I've got two on—' Renfield shouted.

BOOM!

The door of the lab blew inward.

Not from impact like a battering ram, but from explosives.

The concussion knocked everyone flat. Ears ringing.

Plath screamed. No one heard.

Keats shouted, grabbed his head with both hands as blood gushed from his nose.

Men in Land's End khaki and polo shirts under LL Bean down jackets came rushing in, guns drawn, a swarm of thugs in colors called jonquil, bright leaf, and lavender ice.

Down in the meat the swarm of nanobots and the two biots were rocked. The hit wasn't as hard as the punch, but Vincent wasn't prepared this time. V2 snapped two legs, caught, and twisted in the first arriving macrophages.

Lymphocytes—white blood cells—came in various shapes and sizes, and these were called macrophages. They looked like squashed sea sponges, all rough and bumpy. They were the size of flattened roadkill raccoons. They oozed and squirmed along the nerve highway like slow, stupid attack dogs.

The crippled V2 struggled with one leg to get free, but two of the phages had grips and were enveloping a stump, making purposeful movement all but impossible.

V1 had been sent tumbling into a jumbled pile of nanobots.

Platooned, Vincent realized as they reacted en masse, six acting as one. This close in, unprepared, he had the edge over them, and stabbed and cut in a frenzy, even as he felt, felt it as though they were on his own legs, the macrophages. And now men with guns shouting, "Don't move! Freeze! Down on the floor!"

Then a McLure security guard, blood all over his chest and gray uniform, gun drawn, lurched into the doorway and *BAM! BAM! BAM!*

One of the TFDs went down. And then the back of the McLure man's head exploded.

Vincent felt the macrophages reach his body, tendrils of Silly Putty that tried to draw him in as if he was a gigantic bacterium.

He felt the stabs and rips of the pile of platooned nanobots, random, stabbing and cutting each other too in their frenzy, but hitting him again and again, and now his vision was blurring as Anya screamed, and Keats staggered, and Renfield raised his gun, took aim at the TFDs and *BAM! BAM!*

Explosions everywhere, like being inside a drum, gunfire at close quarters, and Renfield was down like a brick, a hole in his chest pumping like a fountain, and a TFD was on one knee feeling around with bloody hands in the area of his own groin and Plath—out of nowhere—with Renfield's gun and *BAM! BAM!*

More McLure security, a definite step up from the usual rent-a-cop because they were standing there in a gun battle and giving as much as they took, cursing, screaming, shooting, the stink of gunpowder and blood, machinery holed.

Vincent was on his face, on the floor, deaf to everything but the loudest noises.

And there, amid the crazy, he saw Keats. Keats with hands trembling and yet doing the exact right thing, somehow knowing, picking up the Taser that had fallen from Renfield's hand as Renfield fell, and now Keats looking right at Vincent and Vincent nodding and the Taser jolt hitting Anya's body.

Light traveled from the Taser's firing points to Vincent's eyes and he sent his biots leaping clear as a split second later the Taser's charge sent the nerves beneath his spider legs into spasm.

Nerve fibers twitched, yanked the legs from nanobots, hurled others into flesh walls. What seemed like meters m-sub became mere centimeters m-sub as the spasm contracted nerve and wracked muscle.

Vincent sent both his biots, half-crippled, but not dead just yet, no definitely not dead, straight into the confused mass of nanobots, plowed bodily into them with all the speed they could manage and kept thrashing ahead, dragging the macrophages with them, scraping them off in the tangle of thrashing titanium.

The biots erupted through the platoons of nanobots that now added the goo of macrophages to their difficulty unraveling themselves.

Aftershocks, spasms, as Anya's nerves tried to gain control.

V1 was down. Legless now. Immobile.

Vincent saw it, turned V2 to grab it with his pincers and kicked backward, hauling V1 after it, macrophages eating into it still.

Bug Man stared in horror. He was down to twelve active visuals. Maybe three or four of the blind nanobots were still functioning, but he had a choice now: take a few seconds to replatoon them or just send them all pell-mell after the retreating Vincent.

The tectonic shock—Bug Man still had no idea what had caused it—had made a mess of his forces.

"Looking a little rough there, Anthony," Burnofsky drawled. "Maybe time for a little macro help of our own, eh?"

That decided it. No way Bug Man could let Vincent escape. He'd started with a twenty-four-to-two edge. He would never live it down if he lost now.

Mass attack, Bug Man ordered. A banzai charge. A solid wall of nanobots. They surged toward the retreating biots.

But they'd have to leg it. The cleverness of summoning the macrophages was clear now: the spongy, brainless monsters made it impossible for him to switch to wheels.

Race on: wounded biot, pulling its twin away, versus nanobots.

Bug Man knew he would win the race, would eventually catch up, even without wheels. But how many of his nanobots were still functioning? How many would be tripped up? Was this a banzai charge or a kamikaze attack?

"Tell them to shoot Vincent," Bug Man said, grinding out the words.

"You tell them, boy genius. You give the kill order." He held a phone to Bug Man's ear.

Macrophages ate into Vincent's biot flesh as he motored backward, dragging his other biot. The nanobots would catch him. He was moving too slowly. If he dropped V1 . . .

And if he didn't . . .

Renfield's biots would turn the tide. Where were they? What the hell was keeping Renfield?

Vincent turned to see, and there was Renfield, on his back, arms splayed wide, head lolled to one side. Vincent could see him. Renfield would not be rescuing anyone.

There was a shoe blocking Vincent's field of view.

Then a gun jabbed his ear. Cold steel.

"Freeze, motherfucker," a stressed voice said. "And I mean all the way down in the meat. Or die."

Plath still had the gun in her hand. She had never fired one before. The noise—so much louder than in the movies—and the kick—so much more satisfying than she'd have guessed—had surprised her.

And the horrifying fact that it had worked.

She had aimed, squeezed the trigger, and sent a lead projectile through the air to smash flesh and bone.

The man she had shot now sat in a pool of blood flowing from his groin. She had made that happen.

And yet even as she stared in horror her head was filled with the nightmarish vision of awful, lurching, spiderlike monsters, grainy and gray, and tumbling madly around on a plain that had tilted up without warning.

Vincent was facedown. A man in a blood-splattered parka held a gun to his head.

Keats took her arm, squeezed hard, and propelled her toward the door.

Renfield lay in a dark-red lake.

Dead and dying men sagged against equipment. Smoke filled the air. Anya Violet was crawling through blood.

Then, in the doorway, a man.

He was smallish, maybe five feet eight. He was stocky but

not fat, and dressed with great care in a deep-purple velvet blazer, collared shirt, sage slacks, black leather boots. On his head was a top hat. The hat was a sort of faded version of the blazer, with a wide gold band and a jaunty feather.

He was craggy, tan, sardonic, and amused, and his eyes were black at the bottom of deep valleys. He might be forty or he might be sixty, and he carried something with him, a feeling, an aura, a dark truth that swirled, invisible but felt, and undeniable.

Sadie knew without being told.

Caligula.

FIFTEEN

He had a pistol in his left hand. In his right was a short-handled axe. The axe looked strangely like a child's notion of a Native American tomahawk: it had a painted handle with what looked like leather strands hanging from it. The blade was liquid red.

There were three surviving TFDs when Caligula walked in.

The first spun, raised his weapon, and fell backward with a hole through his forehead. The sound came afterward. A huge bang.

A second AFGC man had a bullet through his windpipe and the third, attempting a belated and futile escape, stopped when the axe appeared as if by magic in his back. The down and nylon poofed out around it.

Caligula stood in front of Anya so she couldn't crawl any farther.

"No," Vincent gasped. "Not her."

Caligula looked around and said, "Anyone else?" He pushed Anya with his foot so that she fell onto her side.

He went to look down at Renfield. "Shame," Caligula said. "I liked him."

He pulled the axe from the spine of the gibbering, terrified TFD whose legs had stopped working altogether. And shot the man in the head.

Then with four powerful chops he hacked through Renfield's neck. No evidence of biots could be left behind.

Plath would have thrown up again, but her belly was empty.

Caligula pulled a black plastic trash bag from his pocket, dropped Renfield's head into it, tied it off, and handed it to Keats. "Carry this. Don't drop it."

"What the hell—" Keats demanded.

Caligula looked at him with amused disbelief. "New kid, huh? Well, new kid, you don't question the man who's saving your life." Caligula knelt in front of Vincent. "What's with you?"

"Two in her head." He indicated Anya Violet. "Ambush. I'm in trouble. Renfield . . ."

"Renfield won't be helping," Caligula said. He stood up, turned now to Plath, looked at the crotch-shot man, still moaning in terrible pain. "Never aim for the balls. Aim for the center of mass. Unless you ever get good enough for head shots."

"I didn't . . . I didn't mean to, to aim there, I just . . ."

"Well, you might as well finish him off."

Plath shook her head violently. She held the gun away from her as if she would drop it on the floor. But she didn't drop it.

Instead her gaze was drawn to it, she held it up and looked at it.

Caligula laughed. "They are seductive, aren't they?" Without needing to look he pointed his gun at the injured man and fired once. "See? There you go. You can tell yourself it wasn't you that killed him."

Caligula went around the smoky room picking up loose firearms. He checked each one, popped an empty clip and found a replacement inside blood-soaked clothing.

He handed one handgun to Keats and the other to Vincent.

"We're probably going to have a bit of a fighting withdrawal here," Caligula said, kneeling now to look at Anya. "Now, listen to me, whoever the hell you are. Vincent over there doesn't want me to kill you. But if I have the slightest trouble with you—any trouble at all—I will ignore young Vincent and shoot you. I don't know if you've been wired or not. If so, it's going to take all your focus and concentration. Try. Try very hard."

He stood up, wiped his bloody axe on a body, and said, "All right then. Follow me."

The elevator was playing a cover of Lady Gaga's 'Poker Face.'

The buttons were bright. The walls were mirrored. Plath saw herself. Pale. Freckles on the bridge of her nose. Hair matted with sweat.

It was Keats and her. Caligula had summoned the first elevator and boarded with Vincent and Anya. "You two come out ready for a fight," he'd advised them. "And listen: don't accidentally shoot me. Right? I will resent it."

It had taken a while for a second elevator to come. Plath and Keats, waiting, staring at the call button, both self-conscious with their pistols, both with heads swirling with images of tumbling monsters.

"Oh shit!" Keats cried at one point. "I just saw color. The thing. Just like a flash of color."

"Still gray scale here," Plath said.

Keats looked at the crèche still in his hand, shook his head, irritated at his own stupidity, and slid the thing into the back of his jeans, where it should be safe so long as he didn't sit down. Or get shot in the rear.

The elevator had come, and Plath had punched the button for the lobby.

"What do we do when the door opens?" Keats wondered aloud.

Plath had no answer. Or rather, she had one, but she didn't want to say it. The gun weighed a hundred pounds. The grip was slick with sweat.

They passed the tenth floor.

The seventh.

"I take this side, you take that side," Keats said. "I'll go first. As soon as the door is wide enough."

Plath nodded curtly, not trusting herself to speak, and not

minding, for once in her life, that someone had basically told her what to do.

Third floor.

The elevator slowed.

Took a slight bounce.

Through the doors came the sound of a gunshot.

Plath wondered if she had wet herself. Wondered why it mattered, and the door opened and Keats shoved through and *BAM!*

And she stumbled after him.

Caligula stood there; Vincent and Anya leaned against a massive marble pillar.

"What the hell are you shooting at?" Caligula asked. Not angry, just curious.

"I . . ." Keats said.

The lobby lights were low, but still plenty of light to see two McLure security guards dead. Someone had shot them and dragged them out of the line of sight from the sidewalk outside. They were behind a stand-up billboard for an event at the Museum of Modern Art, sponsored by McLure Industries.

As Plath emerged all the way from the elevator she saw two other bodies in the one Caligula had taken.

"Cops are on the way. Bad guys are on the street outside."

"Is that them?" Plath nodded at an SUV and a compact car steaming exhaust out at the curb.

"Yes. We're going to go and take the little car." With a fluid motion Caligula grabbed Vincent, held him at arm's length, and put a gun to his head. "Let's go."

Caligula marched Vincent like a prisoner through the glass doors, out onto the sidewalk, leaving Plath and Keats behind with a panting, shattered-looking Anya glancing around wildly, wondering if there was an escape, any escape.

Anya was, Plath realized, almost old enough to be her mother. And Plath, and a boy she'd never known before, were suddenly in the position of having to shoot the woman if she tried to run.

Vincent's biots dragged themselves away.

Bug Man's nanobots were in pursuit.

The chase was long, but now it was reaching a desperate point. Now V1 and V2 were stepping onto the eye. He had stayed on muscle fiber as long as he could because there he was at par in terms of speed.

But the time was up. Now he had no choice but to back onto the orb itself, and when the nanobots followed they'd be beyond the macrophages, out onto a slick, smooth surface—as slick as anything in the human body. They would drop to their wheels and trail their legs and outrun Vincent in a matter of seconds.

Vincent felt Caligula's gun pressed against his ear.

"I'm going to lose," Vincent whispered.

"Can't help you down there in the meat," Caligula said, his voice grating, then rising to yell, "Hey! Assholes! This is Vincent. You want him? I'll trade you for free passage outta here!"

The window in the SUV lowered.

Vincent saw a man talking on a phone. Tense. Waiting for some kind of answer.

The small car lowered a window as well. A muzzle emerged, aimed at them.

Something appeared in the air. An object the size of a baseball, but dull steel. It flew from Caligula's hand, right through the window of the SUV.

Caligula pivoted, fired, *BAMBAMBAM!*

A cry from inside the small car.

A shout of panic from inside the SUV.

Caligula yanked Vincent down with him as he dropped to the pavement.

The grenade exploded inside the SUV.

Nanobots had their wheels in contact with the eye, and V2's legs were slipping, and the windows blew out of the SUV, and the doors exploded outward, and three nanobots were on Vincent's crippled biot, stabbing and stabbing, and Vincent felt it as if each stab was in his own guts.

He cried out and Caligula fired again at the small car and yelled, "Get out here, now!" and waved his arm and Vincent saw Keats and Plath and Anya all running, and a fourth person, too.

A fourth person.

A Goth street girl with a weird tattoo on her eye.

Keats missed a step as he recognized her: the girl from the cab.

"The woman!" Caligula yelled to the newcomer as Vincent felt a terrible pain deep inside himself and Keats yelled, "Right eye, right eye!" and the Goth girl, Wilkes, jabbed a finger hard into Anya Violet's right eye, and Anya cried out in pain and tried to bat the girl away.

V2 leapt over the ripped and dismembered body of V1, reckless, heedless, not giving a damn now, because this was the end, so all in, Vincent knew, all in.

The biot killed two nanobots before losing its legs. Both of Vincent's biots were now almost immobile. Two of their total twelve legs were still attached.

Nothing left but the stingers in their tails and the tiny beam weapons. But without legs neither was of much use.

Eight nanobots surrounded the two dying biots.

"Can I get a withdrawal? Can I get a withdrawal?" Bug Man yelled. "What's happening in the macro?"

"A bunch of dead people is what's happening," Burnofsky reported.

"Tell me!" If he could get a withdrawal—if someone, *anyone*, could be there to offer Bug Man a way to climb off the woman—then he could drag one of Vincent's biots with him. Maybe both.

It would be unequaled game play.

Unequaled!

"What the hell are you doing?" It was Jindal bursting in. "The Twins are seeing all this! Quit screwing around. Kill him off! Kill him off!"

Bug Man felt as if he'd been kicked in the chest. In all this time it had never occurred to him that his video was also being watched live by the Armstrong Twins.

He turned sickly eyes on Burnofsky.

Burnofsky laughed. "Yeah, there's that."

Bug Man gritted his teeth and surged his nanobots ahead.

"Caligula," Vincent said. He sat hunched forward in the backseat, looking like he might throw up. Plath was beside him and a girl she'd never seen before. Anya was jammed in the passenger seat with Keats. Six of them in a car made for five at most. A car with one window gone and blood all over the dashboard.

Caligula drove with the same compact precision he did everything. Police cars went screeching past, heading for the massacre at McLure headquarters.

"Caligula," Vincent said again, and the killer in the front seat sighed and answered.

"Madness or death," Vincent said. "Make it death."

"You don't give that order, Vincent," Caligula said calmly. "Only Lear gives that order."

"Shut the hell up: no one's giving that order," Wilkes said. "I'm the cavalry. Yee-hah."

A ghost of a smile on Vincent's face.

SIXTEEN

"He'll be okay. Vincent, I mean. He'll be okay." Nijinsky looked somewhat the worse for wear. His hair was short of perfect, and his collar was limp. He almost flopped into the chair.

Plath had showered. The water had run red and she'd stayed in there quite a while, crying where the others couldn't see her.

She sat now beside a solemn, shell-shocked Keats. He still had blood splatter on his face. He still smelled of gunpowder.

Anya was . . . somewhere . . . with Ophelia. Caligula had disappeared. Wilkes sat a little apart, noisily devouring a bag of spicy Doritos.

Renfield's head in the plastic bag had been taken away to be incinerated, obliterating any evidence of nanotechnology.

"Two of Vincent's four biots are injured and lame for the time being," Nijinsky said. "They're back in crèche; they'll likely recover. Wilkes's biots also were roughed up. But she went two against eight with the Bug Man. Saved Vincent and made it out alive."

Nijinsky made a little salute, which Wilkes saw but did not

acknowledge. She ate mechanically, stuffing the chips in her mouth, eyes looking at nothing.

"You both got thrown in the deep end tonight," Nijinsky said, not quite apologizing. "It must have been tough."

"It was a bloody nightmare," Keats shot back. He blinked. Drew a little further into that diffidence of his and added, more quietly, "Still is."

"Yes, and more to come," Nijinsky said.

"Not tonight," Plath snapped, and was gratified that Keats nodded in support of her.

"Got that right," he said.

Nijinsky waited, letting the silence calm them both down. Plath felt like someone had rubbed her entire body with sandpaper. Like she'd been shot up with speed. Like a screaming rant was at the tip of her tongue just waiting to be released.

Ophelia came in. "She's under control," she said without elaboration. She was carrying a bottle and a tray of mismatched and not-very-clean glasses. She set them down in front of Nijinsky. He poured a whiskey for himself and for Ophelia. He looked speculatively at Wilkes, Keats, and Plath.

Plath accepted a glass. Following her lead, so did Keats. Wilkes joined last. She snatched the glass angrily.

"To Renfield," Nijinsky said.

Five glasses tapped and five shots went down with varying degrees of gasping and coughing. The liquid fire spread through

Sadie's stomach and radiated out through her body.

"I hope he is with his God," Ophelia said.

Wilkes shook her head, but still said, "He wasn't all bad. Just kind of a dick."

But something was off about her cynicism. A false note. And Plath saw her turn away quickly to hide some emotion.

"Now," Nijinsky said briskly, "as bad as this has been, we have big things to deal with. With Vincent at half strength we need you two trained and ready. Your biots are being kept dark and cold. Below a certain temperature they become dormant. You may still experience flashes, but you should be able to sleep. So. Go do that. Sleep for a few hours. Then training starts."

"What if we don't want to train?" Plath demanded. "What if we just want the hell out of this asylum?"

Wilkes made a sardonic sound. "Honey, you are already all the way in. There is no out for you."

Nijinsky did not dispute that. He said, "Go. Sleep."

Plath wanted to sleep. It was dark in the room. The window was too dirty to see through, and even though she guessed it must be morning out there, somewhere, only a faint gray penetrated to highlight peeling paint on the high ceiling.

She could feel her biots, still, as a sort of nagging presence in her brain. Like a child crying in another room. But at least she was no longer looking out through their eyes.

She felt numb, almost dead inside, and raw and angry outside. She wanted to smash her fist into the wall. She wanted to sleep. She wanted to throw open the door and just run, run right the hell out of this horrible place. And she wanted more of the whiskey.

She wanted her mother. And her dad. And her brother.

And she wanted the boy in the next room, because even if her mother and dad and brother were still alive, they would never be able to understand what had happened to her.

But he would. Maybe. Keats.

They had set it up this way, of course, Vincent and Jin. Probably not through some grand conspiracy, they had just known that two terrorized teenagers given poets' names would reach out to each other.

She wondered if his door was locked.

She wondered if she tapped, just softly on the wall, would he hear her? So softly it wasn't even a tap. So softly she could deny it?

She barely touched knuckles to wall.

A louder but still quiet tap at her own door.

He had come. Instantly. He'd been lying awake, too. He'd been waiting for her summons.

But still, she could just . . . not. She could just not respond. And he would go away, because he wasn't a guy who would push at her, was he? How could she know? She'd known him a few hours and barely spoken.

But she knew.

Sadie got up and went to the door. She composed her face and opened it.

Keats stood in sweatpants, bare feet, and a T-shirt. "I'd like to talk to someone," he said. "I'd like to talk to you, I mean."

Again, she liked him, because what he had done was pretend she hadn't tapped on the wall. He was letting her deny that neediness if she chose to.

"Come in. I'd show you around, but there isn't much to see."

He took the sole chair. She sat on the edge of her bed. She was in a long man's T-shirt, legs bare, socks on her feet. He was probably seeing too much—the T-shirt was white aside from a faded logo. And he was noticing, but she didn't care.

"What have we got ourselves into?" he asked.

We.

Ourselves.

Sadie had no answer. Words seemed too small.

"I guess we're not supposed to tell our real names," Keats said.

She shook her head. No.

"I'm from London."

"I love London."

"You've been?" He smiled shyly, delighted to find something they had in common.

"My mother was English." She watched to see if he noted the past tense. He did.

"Wish we were there?" he asked.

She let go of a small, abrupt laugh. "God, yes. Or anywhere."

"Euro Disney?"

The suggestion was so perfectly absurd she started giggling. And that brought a smile, a real one, to his lips, and his blue eyes lit up even brighter than before.

"Really, any of the major theme parks," she said through laughter. "I'd go see the giant ball of twine in Kansas."

"Is that real?" he asked.

Suddenly serious she said, "Dude, I no longer feel qualified to say what's real and what isn't."

He looked down. "Dude. Well, my America visit is complete. I've been called 'dude'."

She took up the bantering tone. "How have you liked America so far?"

"Oh, it's about what I expected," he said.

That unleashed an almost hysterical burst of laughter from both of them.

"You suppose they're watching us?" Keats asked, looking up at the ceiling.

"I hope so. That way they'll be able to see this." She held

up the middle finger on both her hands and stuck them in the air.

"So," he said, faltering a little, "would you go out with me sometime?"

"That depends. What did you have in mind?"

"We get something to eat. See a movie."

"I shot that man." The words were out before she knew they were coming. A sob escaped behind them. And quiet tears.

"Yes."

Neither had anything to say for a long time after that. Both sat in the dark, perched awkwardly on the edge of chair and bed.

Finally Plath yawned. "If I asked you to stay with me tonight . . . I mean, if I said I wanted you to lie next to me and sleep. Could it be just that? Could it just be that we—' Her voice broke and she couldn't speak.

"You mean could we just be here together because we're both scared to death? And hurt? And don't have anyone else?"

She nodded. "Yes. That."

She lay back on her narrow bed. He came and lay down beside her. Only their shoulders and thighs touched. For a while they lay staring up at peeling paint. And then, finally, sleep took them both away to terrifying dreams but also to a degree of oblivion.

In Brooklyn, a similar scene.

Though Jessica did her programmed best, the Bug Man just lay in his bed staring at the ceiling.

He had beaten Vincent. That much he owned. No matter how Burnofsky sneered. No matter how much the Twins may have raged—at least in Bug Man's imagination, because they didn't call.

He had beaten Vincent.

He had.

Would have finished him off, too, except for stuff that happened in the macro. Which was not Bug Man's fault.

The reports that came in from the lone survivor of the McLure building massacre mentioned a Taser. That's what had kept Bug Man from finishing Vincent.

Macro stuff. Up *there*. Not down in the meat. Down in the meat Bug Man had taken Vincent down.

Damn right.

Whatever Burnofsky had to say.

Within a millimeter of dragging a still-living biot off the field. God, that would have made Burnofsky depressed to the point of suicide. And the Twins? They would have kissed his butt with their nasty freak mouths.

He could have messed with a captured biot until Vincent admitted that Bug Man ruled the nano.

Ruler of the nano.

So cool.

That would have been . . .

He heard sounds coming from outside his room. His mother getting up to go to work. His aunt would sleep another hour.

Bug Man rolled out of bed and pulled on his clothes.

"What's the matter, baby?" Jessica asked.

"Nothing."

"Come on, sweetheart, I can—"

"Shut up," he snapped. Then in a gentler voice, "Look, just leave me alone, okay? Just . . ." He left her and went to the kitchen.

Bug Man's mother was a mother-looking woman. She was overweight; she didn't dress fancy; her hair was done once a week at a salon run by another black woman from Britain, although she was from somewhere to the north, Newcastle or whatever.

His mother was watching the coffee brew. Just standing there.

"Hey, Mum," Bug Man said.

She looked at him with a critical eye. "You got in late last night."

The small TV on the counter was tuned to a cable-news channel. The sound was off. The picture was some jittery new bit of video from the stadium. It showed the plane hitting the stands. Still. Even now.

"Yeah. There was a . . . you know, screw-up. A thing that happened."

"You didn't get fired, did you?"

"No, no, nothing like that." He reached past her to snag a mug and filled it with coffee though the pot wasn't fully done. He added milk and sugar, lots of sugar. "They actually love me at work. I think I'm, like, their best guy. Tester. You know?"

His mother shook her head slowly, not to what he'd said, but to what she'd seen on the TV. "Kind of person who would do something like that. Savages."

For a moment—but just for a fleeting moment—Bug Man almost connected that word *savage* to himself. Almost made a link between the horror on the screen and his own actions. But it passed and left no trace.

"No, they love me at work," he repeated, hoping she would hear it this time.

"Just make sure you remember how lucky you are to have that job. So many people out of work."

"Yeah. Well, I'm good at it. That's why they have me. Because I'm the best."

The toast popped up.

On the screen a man ran trailing fire and smoke, tripped and fell, and died.

"If you're having toast, I'll put some in."

Bug Man sipped his coffee.

He had beaten Vincent. Yeah, he owned that.

Next time he'd finish it.

He took his sweetened coffee back to his room, sent Jessica packing, and despite the caffeine, fell asleep.

Bug Man woke suddenly, knowing he was not alone.

Four men stood around his bed. They were strong men, all dressed in casual clothing, innocuous pinks and tans and teals.

"What?" He sat up but only made it part of the way before powerful hands grabbed his biceps and his ankles. They flipped him over onto his belly.

"What the hell?" he cried.

"No one's home," one of the men said. "Yell all you like."

A phone was thrust into his face. A video image appeared. To his horror it was the faces of Charles and Benjamin Armstrong.

"Anthony," Charles said in a calm, measured voice. "We are not about ego. We are about peace and unity, bringing all humans together, so that all men are brothers and husbands, all women sisters and wives."

"Listen, I'm sorry about—"

But the video was still running. It wasn't live; it was recorded. It was a message.

A sentence.

"Your pride cost us a victory in that battle, Anthony. Your *pride*."

"Let me go!"

"We love you, Anthony," Benjamin said.

They held him, one set of powerful hands for each limb, but then the man holding his left ankle must have managed to have a hand free, mustn't he? Because that man had a club in his hand. Bug Man could see it, glancing frantically down over his shoulder, a thick, round, polished, dark piece of wood.

"But punishment is demanded in this case," Benjamin continued.

"However much we regret it."

"What the hell?" Bug Man cried, and the club smashed down on the back of his thighs.

The pain was incredible. Unimaginable.

"We do love you, Anthony."

And a second blow landed. He cried out in agony and fear.

And a third blow and every muscle in his body was twanging tight as he screamed into his pillow and one of the men holding his arms bent low, brought his ugly yellowed eyes close to Bug Man's tear-streaming, strained face, and said, "That was from the bosses. But we lost good men last night, you little Limey piece of shit. So this last one's from us."

The club came down hard and for a moment Bug Man's brain just shut down.

He felt their hands release.

He heard them leave the room and close his door.

SEVENTEEN

Plath did not dream of the night's violence. She dreamed about her brother. In her dream he had grown up. He had a family. Two little girls and Sadie—not Plath, Sadie—was coming over for dinner, and it was all strangely televisionish, not real. The girls were perfectly pretty. Eating a cereal in a bright box: Kellogg's Nanobots.

At first that didn't seem strange to dream-Sadie as she walked through the scene.

The kitchen was middle American, with a refrigerator covered in children's drawings and pictures and report cards with straight As! Yay! written in red pen.

It was nothing like the home Stone would probably have had. In the dream he had a more prosaic life than he'd have had if he had lived and taken over McLure Industries.

The cereal was coming out of the box now, crawling in a swarm toward the little girls' bowls, refilling as they spooned up the crunchy nuggets.

"I didn't feel a thing," Stone said.

"You must have been afraid," dream-Sadie argued.

And behind him, back where Stone couldn't see but Sadie could, the nanobots were crawling up over the little girls' white arms and over their colorful dresses and up their necks and all the while the girls smiled.

"Bang and it was over," Stone said, nodding like it was true and like he remembered it and like there was nothing at all strange about his commenting on the circumstances of his own death.

The cereal nanobots were disappearing into little pink ears and noses and eyes.

She woke up.

A knock at the door.

Someone in her bed, a chest her head lay upon. She yanked back.

"I'll get it," Keats said. He worked his arm, the one she'd been sleeping on, like it was numb, which it probably was. He opened the door.

It was Ophelia. If she was surprised to find them both in the same room, she didn't show it. She had two Starbucks, two bottles of water, and a brown bag with some kind of pastry, all in one of those corrugated carriers.

"Need you both in about twenty minutes," Ophelia announced. She even had a smile that said, That's an order, not a request.

In the bag they found muffins. One looked like blueberry, the other might have been raspberry.

"I'll take the blueberry," Plath said. The cups were both lattes. They drained the water bottles, sipped the coffee, and wolfed down the muffins, no time for talk.

Keats reached over and brushed a crumb from Plath's mouth.

"Probably shouldn't . . ." Plath said. She meant that they probably shouldn't do that. The touching thing that was the prelude to more. That's what the smart part of her was saying, while a completely different part of her was wondering why he hadn't touched her in the night as they lay side by side.

Keats looked up sharply. He nodded once, a regretful expression. Then, "What do you think is on for this morning?"

"Something disturbing," Plath said.

Keats smiled. "Thanks for taking care of me last night."

"I thought it was the other way around."

Keats shook his head and looked down at the floor. "I was a mess."

Plath said, "Yeah, you're right. Me? I was fine."

A small laugh. "I wish I didn't have to call you Plath. I don't want to think of you as a poet who gassed herself."

She was so close to telling him. Sadie. That's my name. But with an effort she stopped herself. "They want us close. But they don't ever want us to forget."

Ophelia showed them to a room they had not seen before.

It was up a ridiculously narrow interior staircase. It was like a shabby parody of the lab from McLure. Someone had hammered together a plywood table shoved against narrow, greasy windows that let in the gray gloom of New York. On the table a couple of mismatched microscopes, something that looked like a very expensive Crock-Pot, a small stainless steel freezer.

But the focal point of the room was a massive piece of glowing, white machinery with which Plath was all too familiar.

"Is that an MRI machine?"

Ophelia nodded. "With some very customized add-ons. Yes. I'm told it's worth about five million dollars. So don't put your coffee cups on it."

It was a bizarre anomaly. It was possible to accept the junky attic lab or the massive, humming hulk of technology, but the two didn't seem as if they should share the same reality.

"We usually take more time with training," Ophelia said. "But time is short. The enemy is planning a major strike. It's a winning move if they pull it off. So we have to stop them."

"What is the plan?" Keats asked.

"United Nations General Assembly. Most of the world's heads of state—our President Morales, your Prime Minister Bowen, Keats. AFGC is going to try to place nanobots in them and others. China. Japan. India. Maybe more."

Keats shot a look at Plath.

"AFGC. What is that anyway?" Plath asked.

"The Armstrong Fancy Gifts Corporation."

"That doesn't sound like an evil organization setting out to dominate the world," Plath said.

"That's the idea," Ophelia said. "If you try telling someone the Armstrong Fancy Gifts Corporation is taking over the world, they'll think you're crazy."

"Would they be wrong?" Keats muttered under his breath.

Ophelia leaned close to him. She had a smile for this occasion, too, and it was solid steel. "It's good to have a sense of humor, Keats. But don't be flip. Don't make the mistake of thinking this is a game."

"No, miss," he said, because Ophelia suddenly seemed much older than he.

Ophelia tapped an oblong plastic case on the cluttered table. "Your babies are in here. They're warming to room temperature. When I open this box, they'll see light, which means you'll see through their eyes."

Both Sadie and Keats looked nervously at the box.

"Each of you has two biots. Each of those biots has two types of eye. A compound insect eye that is very good at detecting motion, and a quasi-human eye that is somewhat better at color and definition. But the human brain is not well suited for making sense of these disparate visuals. So each of you has been altered."

"Say what?" Keats snapped.

"When we sent our biots in, we brought a package of altered stem cells and planted them in your visual cortexes. It's not strictly necessary—a biot runner can see without them—but they'll see the actual, not the enhanced, visuals. See, down at the nano level there's no real color. Pigmentation is too spread out, not sufficiently concentrated to be seen. So with bare visual you'll see shapes and edges, but all gray scale. With enhanced visual you get color as well."

"Do we want to see what's down there in color?" Plath asked.

"In a battle it's very, very helpful."

"I guess we'll just move right past the fact that you have no right to be planting anything in our brains," Plath snapped.

"Yes, we will," Ophelia said. "We don't have a lot of time. So let's get to it, shall we? We're going to activate one biot for each of you, and then place them. Down in the meat, as we say. I'll have one of my own biots accompany yours, Keats. A guide."

"Wait. What? Now?" Keats asked.

"Plath, you have the simpler task. Yours is a simple tour. But our friend Keats here is needed to take on an important job almost immediately."

"Important job? What job?" Keats demanded, as Plath tried to avoid feeling like she was being slighted.

"Plath," Ophelia said. "I have three biots working at the site of your aneurysm. The Teflon weave was dangerously weakened by multiple traumas last night. I'm like the boy in the story, the little Dutch boy with his finger in the dike. I'm holding it together, but I have other duties. And we need someone who can remain close to you."

Plath hated the look of shocked concern on Keats's face. It looked a lot like pity.

"And Wilkes will walk you through your own tour, Plath," Ophelia said. "If she ever gets here."

"I'm here." Wilkes climbed out from a dark corner, rubbed sleep from her eyes, did a simultaneous smile and yawn, stretched and said, "Just have to pee first." They heard her clattering down the stairs.

"Now listen to me, both of you," Ophelia said, leaning into them, clasping her hands like she was considering a prayer. "You're going into a very, very strange world. What you see can be quite disturbing."

"I'm already disturbed," Plath said. "I can feel that . . . that thing . . . in my head again." Then seeing that Keats had misinterpreted her, she snapped, "No, not the damned aneurysm. The biot. Mine. My biot."

As though Sadie had said nothing, Ophelia continued. "We all have this view of ourselves as a body and a mind. We think of our mind as a sort of thing outside ourselves, like a soul, a sort of essence of us. What it is, is a computer made out of synapses. A staggeringly sophisticated computer, but still in the end just a few pounds of slimy pink-and-gray tissue kept alive by oxygen and nitrogen carried there by superhighways of pumping blood."

"You don't believe in a soul?" Keats asked.

"I believe science is in this hand," she held out her right, palm up, "and religion is in this hand." She held out her left, but curled it to conceal the palm.

"I've seen too many MRIs of my brain to doubt that it's just an organ," Plath said.

"The greater surprise is the rest of the body," Ophelia said. "We think of it as a body. A singular thing. Skin over organs and bones, but all of it *ours*. Human." She shook her head slowly, dark brown eyes glowing. "We are not *all* human. We are closer to being an ecosystem. Like the rain forest. We are the home to thousands of life-forms. They live in us and on us. Like jaguars and frogs in the rain forest. In the human ecosystem there are viruses, bacteria, fungi, parasites.

"And we, even our human parts, the things that are us, often appear as if they are separate living things: and they are. Each blood cell is alive, independent of the rest of the ecosystem, at least somewhat. You'll understand when you see a cell splitting right beneath your feet. Or some day if you end up in an artery, God forbid, when you see antibodies—they'll look no bigger than pieces of gravel to you—flying to attach to a bacteria."

"Lovely," Keats said.

"Actually, it is lovely. Your body is under constant attack from microscopic enemies, and your—"

"Tell them about the mites," Wilkes said. They hadn't heard her come back in. To Plath and Keats, in a conspiratorial tone, she said, "Ophelia loves the cells. Loves her some enzymes. But that's not what will give you nightmares."

Wilkes sat on the table of the MRI machine and crossed her legs. This would have afforded an uncomfortable view but for the fact that beneath her skirt Wilkes had on bright green tights. "Yeah, see, you don't go down into the blood highway unless you have screwed up bad. If you do, say to escape from nanobots, find yourself a teeny, tiny capillary to drill in, because a vein or an artery? That's like diving into a crazy rockslide or something. That's an avalanche, there. And who knows when or if you get back out. But. But that's not the daily meat."

"She's right," Ophelia said. "We spend our time in eyes and ears, in the brain itself. In order to reach those targets we travel through hair, across faces, eyebrows, and eyelashes. And along the way—"

"It's like crossing a desert drawn by Dr Seuss or Salvador Dalí," Wilkes interrupted. "Wrinkles and crevices and hairs the size of trees."

"And parasites. The two you'll encounter with some frequency are mites—dust mites and demodex. Dust mites are about the size of your biots, but taller. They'll look quite large to you in m-sub. Micro-subjective. Demodex are smaller. They'll look like alligators crawling."

"Jesus. Are they dangerous?" Keats asked.

"Naw," Wilkes said, and waved that suggestion off. "They eat dead skin cells. They aren't lions. Or tigers. Or bears. Oh, my. Pretty fucking creepy, though." The fact seemed to delight her.

"The thing you need to understand is that you are visiting what might as well be an alien planet." Ophelia tried out an encouraging smile. It didn't work. So she sighed. "Plath, you and Wilkes will go walkies around Keats's face and eye, and maybe the ear."

"I'm tired of ears," Wilkes pouted.

"Keats, you and I will do a little of that, and then we'll go all the way in."

Sadie said, "I don't understand why I can't be the one to take care of my own brain. Why is it everyone else's job? Why does he have to do it?"

"Plath, think about it. If the aneurysm ever does rupture, as your brain is dying and you're wracked with migraines, hallucinating in all probability, who is going to run your biots in to fix the leak?" She leaned forward and took Plath's hand in hers, held it until Plath had forced herself to relax into the touch. "You're important to us. You have resources we will need, when you're able to access them. And this boy . . . this young man . . . is going to keep you alive."

EIGHTEEN

Plath placed her finger in the open flower of the crèche.

It was the hand of God descending from the sky. Huge. Like someone stabbing a pink blimp into the pinkish soil of the culture medium.

She saw her finger, both small and large, both a part of her hand and a giant pillar disappearing up into the sky.

Both were in her head.

She gasped.

"Now make your biot move toward it," Wilkes said.

"How?"

They sat in chairs next to each other. Two rickety chairs placed side by side but pointing in opposite directions so that Sadie was face-to-face with Wilkes.

A similar setup on the other side of the MRI machine. Sadie could see Keats's eyes. Her destination. Insane.

"Think it," Wilkes said with a shrug.

She thought it. And yes, she could see the dimpled spongy surface of the medium flowing by beneath her as she ran.

Hah-hah! It worked.

"You have six legs," Wilkes said. "Plus two arms."

"Uh-huh." Sadie wasn't really listening. She was focusing on the sheer speed with which that window inside her brain was moving toward the finger. Zoom.

She saw the swirls of fingerprint now. An object the size of a skyscraper, but curved, and covered in amazing whorls that soared up and away into the sky. It looked strangely like some stucco walls that are finished with a toothed trowel.

But as she ran—as her biot ran—the giant became even more detailed, and close up the fingerprints began to look like farmland seen from an airplane, the prints like furrowed fields but where each row stood five or six feet high. And there, strangely atop the rows rather than down inside, were what might be holes drilled at regular distances.

The flesh became less smooth and now seemed more like a desert of dry, baked earth.

Anxiety hit her in a wave. She was meant to climb up onto that alien surface. Her finger twitched, scooted wildly across the surface, almost riding over the biot.

"Aaaah!" Sadie cried.

"Don't worry, you can't crush it. Too small. You know how hard it is to squash a flea?"

"It's . . . It's leaking! My . . . the . . . my finger!"

And indeed from the holes a glistening liquid began to seep.

A liquid that sat atop but did not soften the baked soil terrain. Little droplets that just sort of stayed there.

"Sweat. You're jumpy so your skin starts to sweat."

Plath stopped. The curve of the fingertip made what had seemed like a vertical pillar into a descending roof of dried, tilled soil now intermittently oozing small droplets of liquid. The drops should fall like rain, but they didn't. It clung to the cracked, furrowed surface.

"Freaky, huh?" Wilkes asked with a smirk.

"I'm supposed to get up there?"

"Yep. Jump. You can jump probably ten times your own body length. You jump up and grab on. Don't worry about gravity. Gravity is nothing to the likes of us!"

Plath held her breath, trying to calm her heart. She closed her eyes—her macro eyes—and leapt.

The biot twisted expertly in midair and landed upside down. Her legs gripped, and she hung there like a fly on the ceiling; but it was no longer a ceiling, it was a vast farm field spread out before her. Vertical and horizontal had lost their usual definite meanings.

"Hah!" Plath cried.

"Yeah, hah!" Wilkes agreed. "Definitely: hah."

"I'm on my own finger."

"Heh-heh-heh," Wilkes cackled. "Better than 'shrooms."

Plath wasn't quite sure what that meant, but she was

feeling the rush of this adventure now. She was freaking Spider-Man.

"Now what?" Plath asked.

"Now you stay put in the nano, and you go over and poke your boyfriend in the eye in the macro."

"He's not my boyfriend," Plath said automatically.

"That's good, because what you'll see of him will probably deep-freeze your girl parts. If you know what I mean."

Wilkes was a strange girl, with her creepy, eye-dripping tattoo and her clothing that somehow split the difference between dominatrix and thrift-shop emo. But Wilkes was her Yoda on this trip, so Plath was inclined to be tolerant.

Plath focused on the task of walking toward Keats. The boy's face had an expression of mixed amazement and fear that was probably a pretty close facsimile of her own.

They met at the foot of the MRI. Ophelia stood beside him. Her smile now was all about mystery and memory. She was remembering when she'd done this same thing, felt these same trembling fears.

"You first, Keats," Ophelia ordered. "You just put the tip of your finger as close to the eyeball as you can get without touching it. Then you hop off."

Keats's finger trembled close to Plath's eye. She couldn't help herself blinking as he touched her.

"Ahh!" he cried, and jerked back.

"Eyeballs!" Wilkes said, and laughed her heh-heh-heh laugh. "They're a trip."

Plath's turn. She tried to touch his eye. She saw the vast white orb beneath her, like she was in orbit on an alien farm planet above an Earth of red-rivered ice and a distant . . .

She jumped.

But the eyeball, that sky-filling planet, drew suddenly away.

"Sorry!" Keats said.

There was nothing beneath Plath's biot feet. She was falling.

"Don't move, moron!" Wilkes yelled at Keats.

Plath fell, twisting. The "ground" zoomed past below her. Like she was flying a supersonic jet just inches off the ground. She saw no detail, not at this speed, not twisting madly like this.

Sick fear welled up in her.

"Grab anything you can grab!" Wilkes shouted. "Shit!"

The ground was falling away, like she'd been flying low over a mesa and had the ground suddenly dip.

Then she saw something gigantic on the horizon. It appeared first as a sort of ridgeline, a swelling rise stabbed with leafless tree trunks, each traumatized by something that had chopped it crudely off. Like someone had clear-cut a sparse forest of redwood trees.

Then she was flying over those trees and seeing a huge chasm, like the Grand Canyon opening beneath/beside her biot as it fell. And within that terrifying dark canyon stood massive slabs of grainy, pearlescent—

"I'm passing his mouth!" Plath cried out.

Then she hit something she hadn't even seen coming. An amazingly tall tree that sprouted from the flaked-flesh landscape below, rose high in the air, then veered away toward what was either down or ahead.

The biot bounced away from this tree and now was falling through a forest of them, impossibly long palm trunks. One rushed up toward her and she twisted, extended her six legs, hit it—with strangely little impact—and grabbed on tight.

In the macro she panted, almost doubled over from the nauseating sensation of falling miles through the air.

"I'm in . . . like trees."

"Short stubby trees or great big long ones?"

"Really long ones!" She was shouting for no reason. Wilkes and Keats and Ophelia were all standing right there. "They look pink."

"That's color enhancement. If you think about it, you can actually change the color." Wilkes laughed her heh-heh-heh and added, "Of course maybe that's another time. Let's just get you back where you belong."

"I'm holding on to the tree. It looks like dead leaves down there on the ground."

"Dead skin cells. Some folks think they look like fallen leaves.

Other people think they look like shredded cardboard. Anyway, doesn't matter. You're down in your boyfriend's stupid pseudo-beard. No offense, Keats."

Keats reflexively stroked the sparse hair on his chin.

"It's dark!" Plath yelled. "Stop that," she snapped at Keats.

"Okay, well, this is unexpected," Wilkes said. "We're going to need to get some coffee or tea or whatever."

"Coffee?"

"Yeah, honey, you got a long walk ahead of you. Up the chin, around the mouth, bypass the nostrils—you do not want to go in there—and meet me up by the eye. As slow as you'll be, probably half an hour before we even get to go eye-skating."

Wilkes waited, grinning. When Plath just stared blankly, she said, "Eye-skating. Ice-skating. Right?" Then she sighed. "We're BZRK, it doesn't mean we have to have no sense of humor."

So they sipped coffee.

And Keats and Ophelia had some, too.

And from time to time Keats would stare at Plath as if she was a monster. He was inside her. Ophelia had led him through her eye and into her brain.

From time to time Plath would look at Keats, needing reassurance that he was actually, still, a human being.

At one point Wilkes grabbed a powerful magnifying glass and scanned Keats's face. The light she used was like a break in clouds that lets streaming sunlight through. "There you are. Either you or a wandering mite. No, it's you. You're just under his left eye."

Plath had been told about the demodex. Warned about the demodex. But still she screamed.

Like some awful crocodile mated with a dinosaur. It was smaller than she was, but not small enough. It was long, tapered from the front where its six legs stuck out, stubby, more like paddles than legs.

Plath stopped breathing.

Then breathed again, too hard, too fast. The demodex was moving. A tiny insect mouth seemed to be questing toward her.

She reared back.

"Are you sure it won't . . . It's like . . ." She didn't say what it was like. Because it was not like anything she had ever seen or experienced. A living thing, its deformed baby legs motoring slowly and inefficiently. It was chewing a fallen leaf. No, a dead skin cell. Eating it contentedly.

And yet it was impossible not to imagine it as a predator. A reptile, a monster from another planet.

It was too small to see with a human eye. Too small even for a magnifying glass, smaller than a dust mite, smaller than her biot.

But size alone did not reassure. A wild boar is small, a mad dog is small.

"Aww, isn't he cute?"

She heard Wilkes's voice and realized that somehow she was seeing what Plath was seeing. Which could only mean . . .

Plath's biot eyes looked up and saw a creature far more terrifying than the demodex.

It towered over the skin-eating monster. Spiky antenna from a smooth, green head. A long, narrow body with three tall legs on each side. The head was topped by a pair of compound eyes that wrapped down the side of the head like Princess Leia's buns.

Where the mouth should be was a sort of proboscis, a tube, hollow and with something viscous dripping from the end, like mucus from a cold sufferer.

It had arms like a mantis. Dangerous and powerful. They ended in small asymmetric claws that had one short and one long pincer.

But it was the eyes . . .

The human eyes, smeared across that insect face, staring soulless from beneath the compound insect eyes. That was what finally obliterated Plath's careful self-control and let her scream.

And scream.

And there, suddenly, a hand on her shoulder, Nijinsky standing behind her.

Nijinsky looked at Wilkes. "Is she seeing you?"

Wilkes nodded.

"You should have warned her."

"Is that what my biot looks like?" Plath gasped. "Does it . . . does it have my eyes?"

Wilkes grinned. "Beware, Plath," she said, mocking, and not in the jokey way she'd been before, but with an edge of aggression and anger. "It's a weird world down there in the meat. And the weirdest thing of all is us."

"It wasn't me," Burnofsky said, first thing, first words out of his mouth when he next saw Bug Man. He grabbed the kid and pulled him into a side room, out of sight, out of sound, and looked him in the eye and said, "I don't like you, Anthony, but it wasn't me."

He smelled of booze. His pupils were the size of pinheads. So drunk *and* high. Nasty old geezer.

"This isn't a game to the Twins, kid." He slurred it.

"Yeah, well, as long as they keep you in dope, right?"

Burnofsky made a small laugh. Then he leaned in, too close, and said, "Yeah. Exactly. That's my price. And yours is thinking you're a big man, and that piece of ass you go home to every night. And Jindal? He's an actual true believer, a true hive mind, Nexus Humanus sucker. And One-Up? More like you. More about ego. We all have a drug."

"And Twofer? I guess they're the dealers."

"See, you're not so stupid," Burnofsky said.

The back of Bug Man's legs hurt. The bruises made it hard for him to walk without limping. He had cried for the first time in . . . how long? A long time. Oh, definitely, he had cried. Anthony Elder had cried into his pillow and told Jessica to stay away.

They had lain him out like a little punk and whacked his ass.

Now here he was planning to take down the biggest target in the world. Final briefing. Final prep. And instead of getting what was his due, to swagger in as big as an elephant's balls and have everyone kiss his ass, he'd had to hobble in like a cripple.

"Two ways forward now, Anthony," Burnofsky said. "Rebel or excel."

"What the hell are you babbling about?"

"You turn against them. Or you show them your true worth."

"Rebel? You'd like that wouldn't you? AmericaStrong thugs would be down on me and really fuck me up. Maybe kill me."

"Not maybe, Anthony."

He was so sure that it made Bug Man take a step back. It was true. He saw it in the old man's rheumy eyes. The Twins would kill him. And Burnofsky knew this with absolute certainty.

Because.

Because he'd seen it happen.

"Who'd they kill?" Bug Man pressed. "Somebody stood up against them? Who? You tell me. You tell me who it was."

"She was as good as you."

"Who's this 'she'?"

"It runs in families, this talent we have, Anthony. This girl, Carla, yeah, lousy name to stick on a girl. Named after her father."

Burnofsky's pale, whiskered face was ghostly. And yes, right then, with the scientist's face too close and the stink of booze sweat coming off him, and drilling into Anthony with those needle-hole pupils, yes right then Bug Man remembered that Burnofsky's first name was Karl.

"Stood up to them, see, when she realized what was going on, what the real game was." Tears were leaking out of Burnofsky's eyes. "About your age. Like most twitchers. Gamer kid. They had her lace some juicy bacteria. The Twins had a grudge, see. A woman named Heidi Zulle, a shrink. You've heard rumors about the Doll Ship?"

"Some kind of . . ." Bug Man didn't have the right word for it.

"A floating house of horrors, and Zulle was in charge of using drugs and so-called therapy to keep the victims in line. She had a change of heart that coincidentally came after the Twins had her . . . well, suffice to say, something much worse than they did to you, kid. She tried to give the Doll Ship's location up to an intelligence agent. She failed, and then she ran, so, no more Heidi Zulle."

"The Twins took her out?"

"They had Carla do the job. But they didn't tell her what she was doing, what she was delivering. And I was there, too, and I didn't know. Flesh-eating bacteria, a sac of it. And, well, that was too much for Carla."

"Christ."

"You think you've seen some shit down in the meat, Bug Man? You've never seen that, or anything close." Burnofsky shuddered. "Carla was a twitcher. Like you. But see, Anthony, she was still a human being. Unlike you. You? You don't even know how many died in the stadium, do you? Doesn't matter to you, because you're a bloodless, amoral little piece of shit. All that matters to you is that you got spanked."

The truth dawned on Bug Man. The truth of what Burnofsky was telling them. And the why of it.

"They want you to tell me this," Bug Man said, and his voice cracked. "You're threatening me."

Burnofsky laughed delightedly. "Like I said: you're a smart kid."

"They killed your daughter. And you're still their bitch?"

"Everyone dies," Burnofsky said. "Some die clawing at their eyes in agony as the bacteria eat their brains and eyes from the inside out. Others . . . others die happy, floating on waves of soft, warm pleasure. That second death? That's what Carla had. That was my price. That's what her loving father got for her."

"And you lecturing me about the dead. You should kill yourself, old man. You should kill *yourself.*"

"What makes you think I'm not?" Burnofsky asked dully.

They stared at each other until Bug Man could not look into those eyes any longer.

"Now. I believe we have a meeting to attend, Anthony."

NINETEEN

On the screen was a diagram.

Across the top of the diagram were five boxes containing the names MORALES, TS'AI, HAYASHI, BOWEN, and CHAUKSEY.

Bug Man knew these were respectively the leaders of the United States, China, Japan, the United Kingdom, and India.

His first thought was that the Twins had pulled back a little. No Germany, France, or South Korea. It bothered him just a bit, because the plan had been to take down every head of state whose country had serious nanotech. This was a pullback. A pullback meant nervousness, and nervousness in others had a way of making Bug Man nervous.

Helen Falkenhym Morales. President of the United States.

Beneath the box with her name was a line of attack. A pathway. The trick as always was to get from point A to point Z. Fortunately there weren't that many letters. "A" was the deputy director of the FBI, who was already an asset. "B" was a Secret Service agent who was not on the presidential protection detail but was a friend of the FBI guy. They played a weekly game of squash.

Easy transfer, there.

"B" led in turn to his Secret Service mentor, "C," who was definitely on the presidential detail and would be in New York with the president.

"C" might be enough. He might make physical contact with POTUS at some point. But the more reliable path was from "C" to "D."

"D" was the president's "body man," although in this case it was a "body woman." Her name was Liz Law, a name that should have made her some kind of superhero. She was the first person to see Morales in the morning and the last to see her at night.

To reach Liz Law was to reach the president, period.

A,B,C,D.

E.

Four jumps.

Some of the others had it tougher. The path to the Chinese president was seven steps. Some had it easier. The path to the British PM was three steps. Someone had quickly replaced the dead Liselotte Osborne in that pathway.

Bug Man blinked, defocused the chart, and looked around at the room. Jindal was the briefer. He was standing at the ready, twirling a laser pointer nervously in his hand.

The various lead twitchers were around the table.

Kim. An Asperger's case if ever there was one. Skinny Korean kid, looked about twelve, although he was probably seventeen. He tended to avoid eye contact. And any physical contact. And would occasionally interrupt the conversation with some totally off-topic remark. A good twitcher, methodical, careful.

Dietrich. He was maybe twenty-five, a German with hair so thin and light it seemed to float on a breeze of its own, a sort of thinning blond halo. Behind his back people called him Riff-Raff, after the butler from *The Rocky Horror Picture Show*. An Armstrong Twins true believer. Dude had totally drunk the Nexus Humanus Kool-Aid and licked the bottom of the glass. He was barely good enough as a twitcher, and Bug Man would not have wanted Dietrich covering his ass down in the meat.

Alfredo, now he had potential. He came from some tiny island in the middle of the ocean. The Azores, whatever those were. His family had raised bulls for the street bullfights they had there. He had made a name for himself in online games, where he had a tendency to reach the top level in half the time it took anyone else. A pretty good twitcher, Alfredo, but volatile, capable of losing it entirely when someone crossed him.

And then, there was One-Up. She was sixteen, a white girl from some Oklahoma suburb. She could have been a beauty but meth had destroyed her teeth, and now that she was clean she had a bad set of veneers. It gave her a startling, too-white, too-bright shark smile.

One-Up was tough and fearless and dangerous. All the love and energy she had once put into finding meth to smoke and deal she now devoted to the game. She was weird, obsessive, as thin as a classroom skeleton, and probably clinically insane. But Bug Man had fought alongside her once, going up against Kerouac and someone they didn't know, and bottom line? The girl had game. She had taken over the Bowen target during the reshuffling when Burnofsky got bumped off the POTUS.

There was one other person in the room. She was sitting in a corner, wearing khaki slacks and a pink pima-cotton shirt. She had blonde hair—a bit stiff—one leg crossed over the other, hands on the arms of her chair. She was a white woman with a pert little nose and sculpted eyebrows. Sugar Lebowski, operational head of AmericaStrong, AFGC's tough-guy division. Some called her the Little Lebowski, although there was nothing laid back or cool about her.

She hadn't been there for Bug Man's beating. But she had sent the order and chosen the men, and sat there with her pink-lipsticked mouth smiling pertly as they reported what had gone down.

Bug Man nodded at One-Up and ignored the others.

Feeling self-conscious, he took the seat at the head of the

table while Burnofsky took what was either the other head or the tail of the table.

Kim had the Indian PM; Alfredo was on the Japanese; Burnofsky had the Chinese now; and Dietrich, who had been warming up to go after the German, was now prepping to fill in for anyone who pulled up sick or failed.

The pain of sitting was excruciating. The bruises ached and burned. The muscles twanged.

Jindal started to give a rundown, using his laser pointer. And listening with half his brain, Bug Man began to stew. Things were not quite what they had seemed. Yes, the POTUS was a slightly bigger target than the Chinese president, but the path to the Chinese dude was seven jumps. So while the Twins had given Bug Man the honor of the prime target, they had given Burnofsky the harder job, at least in terms of navigating the pathway.

Jindal started the briefing. It was all very official sounding. Very Defense Department. But these weren't colonels and generals listening. One-Up was playing a game on her phone. Dietrich was acting way too enthusiastic. Alfredo seemed to be catching up on his Facebook messages.

Burnofsky seemed about to fall asleep, nodding off, catching himself.

Bug Man played his role. He stared with great focus at Jindal. But his mind was on the pain in his legs. It was also on what

Burnofsky had told him. Was it a warning? Yes. But what kind of warning? He was trying to manipulate the Bug Man, but to what end?

What was it the man wanted in the end? Did Burnofsky want Bug Man to go rogue and end up as dead as his own daughter?

Beneath all of that was the raw emotion. The humiliation. Bug Man wondered how many of the people sitting at the table knew that he had been smacked down by the Twins.

Were they all secretly smirking at imagined image of his crying? The first one who gave him a wrong look . . .

It was time to put them in their places. Time to remind them who he was.

"You done talking, Jindal?"

Jindal stopped in midpoint, started to say something, decided to say something else, which was, "I'm all done."

"All right then," Bug Man said. "Everyone's already heard I came real close to taking Vincent out. The only reason I didn't was stuff up in the macro." He glared at them, daring them to argue. One-Up might have smirked a little. Maybe. And then, with an effort, he forced himself to meet the gaze of Sugar Lebowski.

"Yeah. That's right, Sugar, a fuckup in the macro." He spit the words at her, defiant.

She looked back at him like she was looking at one of her rumored three ex-husbands.

"Seems like none of Sugar's boys can handle the Top Hat Man, the BZRK macro hitter," Bug Man said.

Would she argue?

No. She would not. Because in the end she was replaceable. And the people in this room—especially Bug Man—were not. The world was full of thugs. But a great twitcher?

"Point is," Bug Man allowed generously, "I probably still could have made a kill on Vincent. I had him. But I wasn't focused. I wasn't on my game, right?"

Yeah, they were looking at him with respect. Yes, they were. All except Burnofsky, because Burnofsky knew what had gone down. And Sugar, whose complexion was darkening toward angry red.

Well, time would take care of Burnofsky, time and the opium or the booze. Or maybe Bug Man would take care of him one day. And Sugar? He'd get in her head some fine day and wire her up. Maybe make her think she was itching night and day. Make her shred her own skin.

Bug Man stood up because his legs hurt too much to keep sitting on this poorly padded chair. All eyes were on him, even Burnofsky, who seemed sleepily amused.

"We all come from gaming, right? Every kind of platform. Games. So then we get the chance to play the ultimate game. Anybody here ever played anything half as good as twitching? Ever remember any game environment half as cool as being down in the meat?"

Nods of agreement moderated by indifference and distraction, about as much close attention as you were ever going to get from this crowd.

"Someone told me I needed to stop thinking about all the stuff up on that board like it's just a game. It's all serious now, all heavyweight. Real."

He looked right at Burnofsky, leaving no doubt who he was talking about. "Yeah, that's all bullshit. We all came for the game. We win by remembering *it's a game*. What happens up in the macro? Who gives a shit about that unless it gets in the way of the game?"

He pointed at the board. "See that? It's a game plan. *Game*, my brothers and sisters. Just a game." He paused for dramatic effect. "But it's one hell of a game. And we're going to win it."

Plath washed herself very carefully. With a washcloth and a bar of soap while standing at a sink in the narrow, unpleasant little bathroom that had been designated for her and Keats.

The eyes that stared back at her were crawling with vermin.

Footballs of pollen, all bright as Skittles, and eerie green fungi clung to hairs that grew from a fallen-leaf forest floor of dead skin.

She knew because she had seen all of that on *him*. On his face, his mouth, his eyes. She had seen him for what he was and knew that he had seen her in the same way.

Up in the macro he might have a hard, smooth chest and strong shoulders. Up in the macro she might be able to imagine touching him in those places. Up in the macro she could imagine kissing lips that down there, down in the nano, looked like aged sepia-toned waxed paper, like a wall of yellow-tinged—

She shuddered and closed her eyes, closed the lid tight, Oh, good, visiting time for demodex.

"Aaaahhhhh," she cried, and scrubbed with the washcloth. She scrubbed at her eyelashes, scrubbed her face, couldn't even really think about the rest of her body because God only knew what monsters crawled and clanked around the rest of her square miles of dead-surfaced flesh.

Think of yourself as an ecosystem.

You're a rain forest.

You're an environment. A world. A planet inhabited by life-forms more alien than anything invented in science fiction.

She threw the washcloth down and had to resist the urge to use her fingernails to scrape every inch of her skin.

It wouldn't help. It would just create some new horror, ripping the trees from the soil, piling the dead skin in clumps, revealing blood-tinged undersoil, exciting the rise of lympho-cytes rushing to close off contamination while bacteria propagated and viruses—thankfully they were too small to be seen even down at the nano—rushed to squeeze inside her, spread through her blood, and eat her alive.

She was panting, holding on to the sink with both hands and then wondering what the hell was growing on that sink. How would the cracked porcelain look down there, up close?

They'd retrieved her biot and put it back in cold storage. But she felt it still. Felt them both. Tiny windows would open in her field of vision, and she would see groggy biots barely moving, slowed by cold, on the pink plain of sterile medium.

She would have thrown up, but the thought of what might come out of her mouth . . .

Plath left the bathroom, shaky, mind turning back again and again and again, drawn back and never escaping the memories and the reality.

She opened the door to her room. Her cell.

She sat on the edge of her bed and tears came. She wanted to cry without thinking of giant waterfalls splashing over crawling demodex, of the tears briefly refreshing dead skin, carrying fungi and pollen and bacteria and—

"Just cry, Goddamnit!" she told herself.

Cry for this miserable room.

Cry for the trap she'd stepped into.

Cry for the loss of simplicity, the loss of the simple notion that a boy's blue eyes were blue because the sky wanted to be reflected in them, and not colorless and not a million miles deep through a dark tunnel ringed with spasming fibers and—

"Stop it!"

Suddenly she slapped herself. Hard. The fact that it hurt was almost a surprise. The giant hand with its agricultural furrows and bright beads of sweat had hurtled through the air to land on the surface of her face, and the result was a sting.

Sensations shooting through nerve endings, twitch-twitch-twitch, and hello, there: brain says someone slapped us in the face.

A knock. The door.

She knew it was him. She didn't want to see him. But she couldn't say no. How did you say no to someone who had spent the day crawling through the folds of your brain?

She opened the door. She didn't try to hide the fact that she had been crying.

He didn't try to hide the fact that he'd seen things he would never be able to get out of his mind. The eyes were too wide, the mouth too shocked. Hours had passed, and he still looked like a near-miss victim in a horror movie.

For a moment both of them seemed to forget that they had the power of speech. They just shared their trauma with a look.

And then something simply irresistible took hold of Plath, and she grabbed his head and pulled him to her. Waxed-paper lips on waxed-paper lips. Eyes closed. Fierce. Breathing onto each other's face. Who knew what horrors on tongues that found each other within a Carlsbad of mouth, a vast, dark cave guarded by tombstone teeth.

And for a time measured only in seconds, they both forgot.

Their hearts accelerated. The blood surged through arteries, delivering it to parts where it might be needed. Diaphragms tightened. Hormones flooded. Fingers searched through hair without thinking of mites or of Seussian forests.

For those few seconds they forgot.

And then, with a shock they were apart.

They stood now with several feet between them. Panting. Staring at each other. Amazed. Bodies still telling them to take a step, to close that space again, to wrap an arm, touch, stroke, taste, stiffen, and open.

Still they said nothing. Way beyond words, the words would only confuse what they both knew at that moment. They had found the way to shut out the horror, at least for a time. A few seconds of time that might be stretched into minutes.

It was Plath who finally broke the silence once her heart was back to something like a normal human rhythm. "How are we supposed to do this?"

He might have made a leering joke of it, but that was not Keats. No, he wasn't that guy. Not someone to miss a huge and terrifying truth or hide it behind evasions.

"I've been inside your brain," he said. "But I still don't know you. And now here we are."

"Suddenly you're all I have," Plath said. "My family. My whole life. And now here we are."

"What are we to each other?"

Plath shrugged. She shook her head, breaking contact with the gesture. She sat back down on her bed. Keats remained standing. "I'm probably not supposed to tell you this, but right now I don't really give a damn. My whole family is dead. My mom from the usual: cancer. But my dad and my big brother, murdered. By them. By the other side."

Keats nodded. "I figured that out. I figured out who you are. I think I know your real name, even, I heard it on TV. But I'll call you Plath anyway. I don't want to slip up."

She looked at him. Her eyes were dry. The demodex could stop trying to swim. The tears were being absorbed into dry flesh and evaporated into dry air.

"It's a reaction to trauma," she said. "What just happened between us."

"We've just been yanked way out of reality. Away from our homes . . . violence . . . blood everywhere and scared pissless. And this. Things in my head, I feel them still, even when they're supposedly asleep, I know they're there."

She nodded.

"And Jin says that's it, they'll be in our thoughts from now on," Keats said.

"Our little six-legged children."

That brought a completely unexpected laugh from him. She smiled in response.

"They die, and we go mad," Keats said. "Maybe . . . Maybe I'm not supposed to tell you, but like you said, I don't give a damn: my big brother is in a madhouse right now. Chained. Raving."

Plath narrowed her eyes. "He was part of this?"

"They tell me he was very good. I imagine he was. He was the strong one. The brave one. Me, I was . . ." He trailed off, sighed, and sat down beside her.

Their shoulders touched. That was all, but she wanted so badly to lean her head against him. This boy she didn't really know.

"I'm not a vulnerable person," Plath said.

"Everyone's vulnerable. I've seen that up close."

"I don't make friends that often," Plath said. "I think I'm kind of a bitch."

He smiled and looked down in an unsuccessful effort to hide the smile from her. "I think that's maybe not a bad thing when you're with this crowd. In this situation."

"Listen to me," she said. She looked straight at him until he returned the gaze. Their lips were inches apart. "I don't fall in love. So don't expect that."

"I guess I do. I have that inside me, I mean, falling in love. I've never been. But I feel it inside me. So I guess you'd better expect that from me."

She remembered his lips on hers, and they were not tea-stained wax paper. That memory was somewhere else, still there, but this was a new memory and even more real.

He moved closer and she let him. He surprised her then, because his kiss was not the urgent, charged kiss of before. It was tender and infinitely gentle. He pulled away before she was ready for him to do so.

Keats stood up. "The idea is not to hope. They want us to be focused. Under control. Maybe Jin and Vincent and the rest are good people. Maybe they're trying to do what's right. But they aren't me, and they aren't you. And maybe they can press us into this war of theirs, but they can't tell us how to feel."

She locked eyes with him. And as if they were making a sacred pact, they nodded, and smiled sheepishly, and Keats left.

ARTIFACT

Just hacked Swedish intel. Expected data on blondes in saunas, hah. Mostly looks like unencrypted junk. But there was something weird. I saw a posting by TinyTIMPO2 last week on nanotech and thought this might be interesting.

So it's this fragment. It was saved unencrypted then they must have noticed and encrypted it and wiped the original. This fragment survived. Ran it through a Swedish-English translation program. The source is definitely MUST Militära underrättelse-och säkerhetstjänsten, and it's def an internal memo.

. . . *scenario first advanced by Eric Dexler, a nanotech pioneer. Nanobots capable of self-replication could, due to a simple error in programming, in theory obliterate all life on the Earth.*

Nanotech creatures could be programmed to clean up a chemical spill, perhaps an organic compound like benzene. But benzene contains carbon. All living things likewise contain carbon. An error in programming, even a slight one, could cause nanobots to begin consuming any and all carbon.

The problem becomes acute if nanobots are built to self-replicate. If you began with your Adam and Eve nanobot reproducing themselves in one minute, and their progeny doing the same in another minute, and so on, the population of nanobots would increase geometrically at an astounding rate. In a matter of hours there would be billions. In days, trillions, enough nanobots to consume all carbon within Sweden, killing every living thing.

Within a week the nanobots could obliterate all life on Earth.

Dexler calls this phenomenon, "The gray goo." It is no more elegant a phrase in English than in Swedish. Obviously this is an unlikely scenario, but given our recent –

Anyone interested?

ArmandtheGimp

TWENTY

There followed days of training for Plath and Keats. Days in which they did not kiss, but thought about it, and did not make love, but thought about that, too.

To no one's great surprise Keats was the quicker study with biots. With his two uninjured biots Vincent took him down in the meat to stage mock battles. Vincent taught him how meaningless gravity could be, how to avoid immune responses, how to think in three dimensions not two, how to leap, stab, cut, carry weapons, and when all else failed, run away.

And when Vincent was done with Keats, Ophelia took over and showed him the patient job of hauling Teflon fibers into place and weaving them into the basketwork around Plath's pulsing aneurysm.

Plath was not a prodigy, but Nijinsky allowed that she was really not bad, not bad at all. And in one area she beat Keats hands down. She was a born spinner. She easily learned to read the 3D holographic brain maps, to stab the probe and light up the far-flung connections of memory. To make sense of what she saw there.

Those memories played as video loops, or still photos in Plath's mind. Sometimes both more and less than that: not an image of anything real but a monster or a saint, glowing figures built by the mind itself to represent feelings.

There was a core template of the brain that was a sort of overview, showing in general terms which parts had certain functions. She quickly became familiar with the centers of vision, hearing, smell, touch. She knew where to find the controls for hands and feet, fingers and toes, the centers of speech. Those were roughly the same in any human brain.

But the essential job of a spinner was to rig connections between parts of the brain not normally connected. A spinner had to know how to find a visual image, or a scent, or a sound, or a face, and wire it to a memory that would evoke a certain emotion.

Pleasure. Pain. Fear. Hatred. They all had their locations. Wire—actually a filament much more complex than simple wire—oozed, spiderlike from the biot's pseudo-proboscis. Electronic signals that might have found their way slowly from point A to point B along neurons, jumping synapses, now zoomed along the superhighway of the wire.

"How much difference does it make if every time I see a face I also feel angry?" she asked Nijinsky.

"The first time? Not much. But brains adapt and add new layers. So if you draw a connection between a face and, let's say, desire, the brain begins to absorb that. The first connection is by wire, and the next hundred, maybe. But soon the brain builds reinforcing structures. Backup pathways. So soon, you can't see that face without also feeling desire."

"You can make someone want someone."

Nijinsky nodded. "We can make someone want someone."

"It's . . . Never mind."

"You think it's wrong."

"It is wrong."

Nijinsky nodded. "Yes. It's wrong. We're doing a very bad thing in what we believe is a very good cause."

"And the other side?"

He made a face that acknowledged the truth of it. "Yes, they think exactly the same thing. That they are doing bad things in a good cause. At least many of them do."

"Can we undo what we do?"

Nijinsky thought about it. He stood with his arms crossed, perfectly clean and pressed as always, the only perfectly neat object in that miserable building. "We can undo some of it. Most of it, if we do it right away. Over time it becomes basically impossible to undo. Although we can layer a whole new connection and alter the brain's path."

"What are you doing to Anya Violet?"

The question caught Nijinsky off guard, as she'd meant it to. He gave her an approving smile. "I don't know. She's . . . Well, Vincent has responsibility for her."

"He got to her first," Plath said. "Right? But somehow the other side guessed his move and they were waiting."

"We don't think she's been wired by them, if that's what you're asking. She was just infested. Vincent—we—got careless."

"He's wiring her now, isn't he?"

Nijinsky said, "Let's get back to your training."

So she trained. She sent word to Stern, the McLure security chief, that she was safe, that she was in Switzerland at a mental health spa where she was getting help with grief counseling.

Did Stern believe that? Probably not. But she was *the* McLure. And as Stern had said, he did what the McLure asked of him, even when it meant pretending to believe a lie.

The day would come when she would have to meet with the lawyers and hear the will read out, and discover what her father had planned for the unlikely reality that had now occurred: Plath . . . no, *Sadie* . . . alone in the world.

But of course Vincent had plans for handling that. "Not time to worry about that now," he had told her. "We have the biggest fight in the war ahead of us. We got lucky the other night, thanks to Caligula and Wilkes, and we know what the other side is up to. We have to deal with that. We have to stop them. Then we'll have time to deal with your future."

"I don't enjoy being treated like a piece of some big puzzle I'm not allowed to see," Plath told him. "I'm not the dumb chick who needs to be kept in the dark."

"No one thinks you're the dumb chick," Vincent had said in his grave, sincere way. "But we compartmentalize information. We set up roadblocks, so that if they take one of us, break one of us, manage to turn one of us, the damage can be limited."

"Just tell me this. We're not all there is, right? It's not just you and Jin, Ophelia, Wilkes, me, and Keats. It's not six people, right? Seven if you count Caligula. Because then I'm really just a fool."

Vincent nodded, taking the question seriously. "It's not just us. No. There are people above us. Lear. And there are other cells. In other places. Some will be coming soon to help us with this battle."

That had reassured Plath. A little, anyway. And she slept better that night. Okay, she told herself before she fell asleep, we're not alone in this. I'm not one of seven lunatics. I'm one of maybe hundreds of lunatics.

She'd wished Keats was with her so she could say that to him and make him laugh. And for a while she'd lain there in her bed picturing him just a thin wall away, wondering what he was doing. What he was thinking. Wondering if when he saw her in his mind's eye, he saw the bulging aneurysm deep in her brain and felt some mixture of pity and disgust.

Or whether he thought of her lips, up in the macro, the pink, soft lips, not the nanovision of tea-colored parchment.

She wondered if he knew the color of her eyes. She knew his. Even after seeing the truth down in the nano she saw his eyes as blue, blue, blue.

In her entire life Sadie had never thought this much about a boy. In fact, add up all the boys she'd ever thought about and it didn't equal the time she spent in just one night thinking about Keats.

When she analyzed this fact, it made little sense. Keats was far from being the most handsome. Sadie had gone out with some extraordinarily attractive boys. And yet, remembering them, flipping through them like an iTunes rack, she wanted none of them here, now. She wanted none of them to knock on her door. Not the way she wanted Keats to knock, right now.

You're messed up, she reminded herself. You've gone through hell. You lost your father and brother while almost dying yourself. You saw people burning. You were hurt. Your brain was messed with. You were attached to your own little hideous, deadly, creepy insect children.

You shot a man and watched him bleed.

And you went where only a handful of people have ever been. You saw things no one needed to see.

You've been down in the meat.

The boy next door spends part of his day inside your brain,

weaving Teflon reeds into a basket to keep you from dying.

None of this leads to a wise, considered decision. All of this leads to rash and stupid and desperately needy decisions. All of this pain and death and fear leads to your needing to be held, needing to be lifted out of it all. It leads to fantasies of Keats and his hands and his lips and his body.

Was he thinking the same things about her? Right now, this minute?

She could imagine the pictures, the fantasies in his head. He was a boy, after all, so yeah, he thought about her. In some very specific ways no doubt. Which was fine, so long as whatever he thought of her, however she looked, whatever he imagined her doing, it had nothing to do with dangerous human-eyed mutant insects down—

Footsteps. Loud, not concerned with nighttime.

A loud knock—a banging, really—on her door.

"Up. Now. Up and dressed."

She recognized the voice. Caligula.

She rolled out of bed, stumbled to her clothing, dressed with shaking hands, and stepped into the hallway. Keats was there before her.

"What's happening?"

He shook his head, mystified. They found Vincent and Wilkes in the common room. Anya Violet sat in a corner, meek, wary, diminished.

Caligula said, "Is this everyone?"

Vincent said, "Ophelia is visiting family. Jin is out."

Caligula smirked. "Yeah, he's quite the party boy, isn't he?"

"What's going on?" Vincent asked, impatient. Plath noticed the way he avoided looking at Anya. And she noticed that Anya's lipstick was smeared a little, and that some of it, a trace, was left on Vincent's cheek.

"The Beijing cell was just hit," Caligula said. "Two escaped, everyone else dead. The Delhi cell barely escaped a team that went after them, three dead there. Armstrong is coming after us. Trying to take us out before the main event."

"Do they know *this* location?" Vincent demanded. He was on his feet. All business now.

"Let's not wait around to find out," Caligula said. "Grab your bugs, leave everything else. You have two minutes."

"All of you, get your biots." Vincent ordered.

Plath and Keats ran, along with Wilkes, to the upstairs lab.

"Grab any crèches up there," Vincent shouted after them.

It wasn't two minutes but closer to five before they were ready. Plath had her groggy biots crawling into the safety of her own ear, walking through pollen and dust and around tiny hairs the size of bamboo.

In her pocket she had a crèche—two of Ophelia's dormant biots.

"Well, that was kind of like two minutes," Caligula said

dryly. "Now, we don't know what's outside. I've got a car waiting. But we don't know. So here." He handed a gun to Plath. "You did okay with one of these last time."

"I don't want—"

"I don't give a goddamn what you want," Caligula said. He noted the gun in Vincent's hand. "Rule number one: no one accidentally shoots me. I will resent it."

In the end there were no AmericaStrong TFDs waiting out in the New York City night. They crammed in the back of a long black limo and drove out of the city toward Long Island.

Caligula sat in the front next to the driver. Vincent tapped on the separating glass and said to Caligula, "I've contacted Ophelia. You want to pick her up?"

Caligula considered. With his hat off for the drive Sadie could see that his long hair was a fringe, and that the bald spot on top was split by a livid, jagged scar running back to front.

"She have a car?" Caligula asked.

"Yes."

"Tell her to get on the nearest highway. Doesn't matter what direction. Just tell her to keep moving until we can reach her."

"Don't you have anyone you can send to bring her in?" Vincent asked.

Caligula turned in his seat. His smile was incredulous. "I'm not Five-O, Vincent. I can't just send Danny and a squad car. Anything from pretty boy?"

Vincent shook his head curtly. The glass partition rose again.

"So, having fun so far?" Wilkes asked Keats.

He managed a faint smile. Then he turned his head and looked out of the window. They drove through darkened Brooklyn.

No one seemed to want to talk except Wilkes.

"Anyone else hungry? Doughnut places are open. We could buy a dozen assorted."

No one answered.

"Raised doughnuts, not the cake ones," Wilkes said. "I don't really like cake doughnuts, although I will eat them. But for one thing, in a cake doughnut the hole is all crunched up. I believe a doughnut should have a true hole."

She let that sit for a moment, smiling at Keats. Then said, "I like to stick my tongue in the hole."

Keats looked a little panicky.

"How about you, blue eyes?" Wilkes asked innocently. "Do you like to stick your tongue in the hole?"

"I'm not hungry," Keats said defensively.

Wilkes blinked theatrically, doing a double take. "Is that true, Plath? You should know him well enough by now to know whether he likes to stick his—"

"Wilkes," Vincent said wearily.

"What? If he doesn't, I'd be happy to train him," she said, and laughed her odd heh-heh-heh laugh, cracking herself up.

Then she looked out of the window and began digging a sharp thumbnail into the flesh of her arm. Repositioning and doing it again. And again.

Plath met Keats's eyes and saw that he had noticed it, too.

Each of them living with the fear in their own way. Anya Violet practically defining a separate space as she refused even the slightest acknowledgment of the others. And Vincent tapping into his phone, face blank, eyes glittering, the corners of his mouth tugged downward even more than usual.

"Is it much farther?" Keats asked Vincent.

"At least an hour," Vincent said. "If you can sleep, do it."

Keats nodded and closed his eyes.

It didn't fool Plath. Or at least she didn't think it was real until Keats started snoring softly. Her immediate reaction was outrage that he could sleep at a time like this.

"I like your boyfriend," Wilkes said.

"He's not . . . Whatever," Plath said wearily. "You have one? A boyfriend, I mean?"

"Not a boyfriend," Wilkes said. "There was this guy I would occasionally share a sweaty hour with. It was just sex. Comfort. Not love. That's over."

"What happened?"

"Got shot. I guess he, uh . . ." Wilkes shook her head angrily as her voice choked. "I guess he bled out. Because some stupid bitch ratted him out to the Armstrong Twins."

She stared pure hatred at Anya. And Sadie recoiled in shock as she understood. Renfield and Wilkes? No way. The arrogant young aristocrat and the tattooed tough chick?

Comfort. Someone to reach out and touch when night and fear closed in around you.

Wilkes dug her thumbnail again, and this time drew blood.

Ophelia drove Interstate 84 between Waterbury and Hartford. She had a gun on the seat beside her. She had two of her biots in her brain, sitting, doing nothing. She had to hope that the other two of her "children" were cared for.

She had to hope that the house of her grandfather, which she had just left, much to his surprise and concern, was safe from attack.

She had to hope Vincent and the others were well.

She had to hope that car pulling up parallel to her was not a problem. She had no illusion that she could somehow win a gunfight with a carload of TFDs.

"Na hanyate hanyamane sarire," Ophelia said. It meant, roughly, that consciousness was eternal, not vanquished with the death of the body.

Which was no doubt very comforting to very enlightened people. For her part Ophelia did not feel particularly enlightened. She felt cold fear.

*

Nijinsky had danced hard and drunk hard, and now he was considering the possibilities among the three guys who had made serious efforts to hit on him. Well, the three who were even in the game. More had taken a run at him, various twinks, bears, muscle pups. But none of them were his type.

Nijinsky liked guys with an edge. With something dangerous about them. Punks. Anarchists. Homothugs.

He checked his BlackBerry then remembered the battery had died. It needed replacing, it wasn't holding charge as well as it used to. Well, BZRK could survive without him for a night.

Now, back to the possibilities. One was at the bar, one was dancing, one was falling down as his legs buckled. Now on his butt on the floor, down amid knees and feet, he was clawing at his chest, at the two Taser prongs that had whizzed past Nijinsky.

The music was more than loud enough to deaden the zapping sound. Where the hell? Nijinsky crouched instinctively and spun like a parody of a guy trying to look ninja.

Something hit him hard in the back of the head. Hard enough to send him staggering forward. A woman, not big, just a woman who looked like a suburban housewife, strode right through the dancers who, when they spotted the gun in her hand, backed away fast.

Nijinsky felt dizzy. There was no pain yet, just something like the echo of a massive blow. A club or one hell of a big fist. He was stunned. Unable to comprehend.

He leaned back against the bar, knocking over a stool in the process. A pair of very tough bikers made to rush the blonde woman. She swung the gun toward them with an 'I wouldn't if I were you' look.

The music died. Now Nijinsky heard cries and shouts and voices yelling that someone should call the cops.

"My name is Sugar," the woman said to Nijinsky. She pushed the muzzle of her gun directly against his temple. "If you even come close to touching me, I'll blow your head off. Don't want your nasty little bugs in my brain. Now walk."

He walked. Staggered. Out the back door. There he was clubbed again on the back of his neck. It was a hard blow, and it should have knocked him unconscious. It didn't, but he saw the opportunity and slumped, eyes closed, head lolling.

Rough hands grabbed him under the arms and tossed him into the backseat of a car. They handcuffed him.

"You sure it's safe to touch him?"

"As long as he's unconscious he can't do anything with his biots." Sugar, in the front seat. Nijinsky kept his eyes shut. His head on his chest. Regulated his breathing. No signs of consciousness.

"I've seen this guy somewhere before," one of the men said.

"Billboards," Sugar said. "He's the model they use for Mountain Dew Extra."

"Hey, yeah. I'll be damned. The MDE guy. Huh."

Nijinsky's biots were already on the move, emerging from his eyeball to race down his cheek. A part of him thought: *this powder I'm wearing has an interesting variety of shapes*. It was probably basically talcum, although it came with an expensive name brand. It was strangely like rock flakes. All jagged and irregular. His biots clambered over a landscape of the weirdly sharp boulders.

Maybe next time skip the powder.

The car sped through the night. The biots sped across his skin to his lips. Here would be the tricky part. His head was swimming as the pain in his neck and head hit him full-on. Damage had been done to skin, muscle, and bone.

Oh, yes, pain. Oh yeah, oh *shit*. Don't show it, Shane, don't show any sign of consciousness.

The biots clambered down over his upper lip. And again, he regretted the goo of lip gloss. It was sticky and slowed his boys down. But now they reached the barrier between skin and mucous membrane.

Time for tongue.

He'd seen a tongue down at the nano once before. It wasn't his favorite thing to see. Carefully, slowly he stuck the tip of his tongue to touch his lip.

Through his biots he saw a dark mass coming down out of the sky.

Imagine a tight-packed army of hooded men. They are so close together the bottoms of their hoods almost touch. And the hoods themselves are pink. Sharp at the top. Cones of waxy pink flesh.

Imagine within those tight-packed, rough, waxy-pink cones there are things that look like tiny Styrofoam noodles, the floats you might use in a swimming pool. And alongside those segments of tube are short strings of beads. Mardi Gras down amid a serried rank of pink-hooded Klansmen.

And those noodles and beads are the bacteria that make their home on the tongue.

It took an effort of will for Nijinsky to send the biots rushing to leap aboard that alien landscape.

A stab of pain and Nijinsky couldn't hold in the groan.

He drew his tongue quickly into his mouth, and his biots were flooded with a gush of pearlescent saliva. The tongue curled at the sides, warping the landscape.

"He's awake!"

"Don't let him touch you!"

Nijinsky drew in breath and spit. It was a hurricane-force blast that picked up saliva and biots with it.

The spittle flew the two and a half feet from Nijinsky's forward-thrust mouth to Sugar's stiff blonde hair.

He felt the biots land as if it were his own legs absorbing the impact.

"No!" Sugar cried. She began beating at the back of her head.

The impact actually helped by pressing tall, rough-textured hair trees down toward the scalp.

"What did you do?" she demanded, turning to rage at Nijinsky.

"Did it get on you?" one of the thugs cried.

The smart move, Nijinsky knew, the winning move for them was to shoot him right here, right now. They didn't do that. Which meant that something was stopping them.

They didn't want him dead; they had some other idea in mind, and that knowledge gave him power.

His biots were racing across the dead leaves of Sugar's scalp, scurrying through a sort of birch-tree forest.

Ears, eyes, nose. Which way? The nose was the easiest in terms of direct route, but the most dangerous: a sneeze could be deadly. And indeed Sugar now tried to force a sneeze, blew air out of her nose frantically.

"Pull over. Pull over," she cried. She pointed to an all-night Duane Reade. "The drugstore. You. Go in there. Get me . . . um . . . um, bug spray. And Purelle. Q-tips. Hurry!"

She kept beating at her head, and indeed the forest was having unusual weather as the trees slammed down, flattened, sprang up again. Then she started scraping at her scalp with her fingernails.

This was dangerous.

Nijinsky kept his biots close together. He wanted a single field of view to deal with.

The trees parted and suddenly, moving with impossible speed, was a fingernail. Sugar kept hers moderately long so that only the fingernail and not the fingertip now tore through spongy scalp skin.

The nail was a wall of ridged, dead cells, flakes held together by the rough glue of keratin, and over that a translucent layer of clear nail polish that from his perspective seemed as thick as a sheet of ice.

The edge of the fingernail was like a monstrous plow. It ripped up dead, fallen skin cells as it raced toward the biots. Jump right! The massive plow roared past. But now she was scratching her head like a madwoman. Fingernails everywhere, leaving oozing blood behind, platelets coming up out of the ground and resting in shallow furrows dug by huge claws.

Nijinsky saw a clearing ahead: the edge of her hairline. She hadn't started scratching her face, at least not yet, so N1 and N2 bounded along through the last of the hair and out onto her forehead.

Then: luck!

A huge bead of sweat, ten times their own height, a tsunami, a crazy bead of liquid containing as much water as a swimming pool oozed up through her skin, shone in the dashboard lights, a drop, poised, quivering, like a skinless grape or a water balloon.

It would roll. And when it did it would move faster than any biot.

Nijinsky sent his biots racing toward the sweat drop, and then, rushing down, a second drop was already on the move! It would hit the first drop and join with it and then . . . almost too late!

N1 and N2 leapt, hit the side of the mass of water just as surface tension broke and the drop began rushing like a mountain river down toward Sugar's eyeball.

Biots spun like socks in the spin cycle.

"Knock him out!" Sugar yelled, realizing belatedly that it was her only move.

The butt of a gun smashed into Nijinsky's head, and with his last draining ounce of consciousness he saw the sweat surf spin his biots through the eyelashes and drop into the familiar comfort of an eyeball.

A blink and he was both unconscious and safe.

TWENTY-ONE

Plath was almost there before she clicked. She looked at Vincent. "Are we going where I think we're going?"

He barely spared a second from texting and scrolling through news sites, or whatever it was he was doing. "Yes."

Montauk had already shut down for the season. Kids were all back in school. At this time of year it was only the few bargain-hunting old people still around, and they didn't keep the restaurants open this late.

The house itself was past what town there was. Down a winding private road. Gray shingles and black shakes on the roof, and pane windows, two full stories and rooms up there under the dramatically steep roof. A rich person's house, no question about that. The nearest neighbors were out of sight behind a bluff. The ocean was right there down a path through grass-tufted dunes. You could hear it sighing and sweeping, and you could smell the salt.

Plath knew the house, having spent many weeks there growing up. Not every summer, but most of them. And the occasional spring or fall jaunt to take advantage of a sunny weekend.

Vincent had a key, but some sense of decorum caused him to hand it to Plath. She opened the door.

"Do you know the security code?" Vincent asked her.

She punched it into the keypad.

All of this was of course observed by Keats and Wilkes.

"Now can we just call her Sadie?" Wilkes asked.

"No," Vincent snapped. He didn't like this. He didn't like what all of this was doing to his carefully constructed secrecy. "Get inside. This is a safe house. We'll be here until we figure out whether it's okay to return to the city."

"Lock up behind me. Two people awake at all times." This was from Caligula, who didn't sound as if he thought that was a mere suggestion. He went back out to the car and came back with a shotgun slung over each shoulder. He tossed one to Vincent. He handed the other to Wilkes.

"What about me?" Keats asked.

Caligula made a wry smile. "I only have two with me. And I know Vincent will pull a trigger." He cast a sidelong look at Vincent and said, "Vincent is a regular Scipio. And I know this little bitch," indicating Wilkes, "is nuts. You, sonny? We'll see about you."

Vincent pulled Caligula aside, actually grabbing his arm. A hush fell as something very dangerous, a soft, slow danger, like a purring tiger, passed between the two men. Vincent let go of Caligula's arm.

"There's a police report of an abduction at a club in Tribeca where Nijinsky goes sometimes," Vincent said.

Caligula nodded. "Does he know this location?"

"No. This is on my list, not on his."

"That's good."

"What are you going to do?"

"I'm going to bring the dot-head chick in. Nijinsky won't be coming."

"We're not abandoning Jin."

"Yes. We are," Caligula said, and walked away.

"Fuck that!" Wilkes yelled after him. But the door closed and he was gone. She turned to Vincent. "We're not leaving Jin to those people."

"We're doing what—"

"We're not leaving Jin just because some killer in a goddamned velvet hat says to!"

Sadie wondered whether now, finally, Vincent would lose his cool. No. "Do you know where they have him, Wilkes? Because I don't. Maybe if I did? But I don't."

"Get hold of Lear, tell him—"

"He knows." Vincent waited to hear anything else Wilkes might have to say. But she had apparently used up all her outrage. "Find rooms. Wilkes, you and I will take the first watch. Keats? There's a small basement room. Take Dr Violet down there. Lock the door. Bring me the key."

Plath's choice of room was easy: her own. Getting there was the hard part because she had to walk by the master suite, where her parents had been back, back so long ago.

And Stone's room was next door.

Plath did not allow herself to open the door to see and hear the emptiness of her parents' bedroom. But she did open the door to Stone's room and stood there, leaning in slightly without letting her feet cross the threshold.

It was professionally decorated with Montauk-appropriate themes of sailboats and dunes, sandals and kites. Only the faintest sense of Stone as an individual showed: a Frisbee on the desk, a huge stuffed white rabbit wearing a woot! T-shirt, a single framed picture of Stone and . . . and Sadie, definitely not Plath, when he was maybe nine and she was a sadly dorky-looking seven. The picture had been taken right here on the beach. On the wall was a framed replica of an old-style gold record: the Rolling Stones' *Beast of Burden*. It was an inside joke between them, the idea that Stone as the heir apparent was the beast of burden.

"I don't know what room to go to." Keats, just a foot away. He'd come up unnoticed. How long had he been standing there? How long had she?

"My room," she said. "I can't sleep there alone."

277

She crossed the hallway to her own room. She snapped on the light and did not see what she expected. Her room was just as she'd left it when she'd last been here. Was it two summers ago? No, not that long. And somehow, it was all unchanged. But if she had changed, how could her room still be the same?

Her bed was made. Her window shades were open to the sea. Posters of Against Me and the Methadones. Books, actual old-style, physical books, filled a couple of small shelves. Knickknacks. Beach kitsch, all displayed to achieve maximum ironic effect. A basket with half a dozen bathing suits, mix-and-match tops and bottoms. A framed, autographed picture of Christopher Hitchens hung next to a framed, autographed picture of Tim Armstrong. A Ramones beach towel. That made her smile.

Keats stepped in and looked carefully around, noting details, nodding to himself every now and then.

"Well?" she asked him.

"You used to be Wilkes," he said.

The observation was so surprising her jaw actually dropped open. She looked around, saw it as he was seeing it, and laughed. "Huh. I was just thinking how alien it all feels."

"Yeah. Well, things changed, didn't they? All this craziness, it has a way of, I guess, pushing everything in a different direction. Maybe before all this started happening Wilkes was some little Catholic schoolgirl wearing a plaid frock with her hair in pigtails."

"Somehow I doubt that," Plath said.

"That's a big bed."

"I thrash in my sleep."

"I noticed. The other night. But on that narrow bed the thrashing potential was limited. One could thrash in this bed."

"Are we talking about having sex?" Plath asked.

"I don't know," he admitted wearily.

"You want to," she said flatly.

"I thought I had you fooled."

"There are certain signs . . ."

"It seems weird not to, I guess. Have sex, I mean. I've been inside your brain. You've been inside mine. It's not as if there's anyone to yell 'For shame!' at us."

"No," she agreed. "The only thing stopping me . . ." She fell silent, not sure how to explain.

"You don't want to do it just because you're scared and we're thrown together. You don't want your first time to be—"

"How do you know it would be my first time?" she snapped.

He shrugged. "Just a feeling, I guess."

She mirrored his shrug. "Yeah, well . . . I guess I was hoping for something more than a desperate terror-grope. For my first time."

"So, you're a romantic," he deadpanned.

She smiled, and liked him a great deal right then. "That's me, a romantic." She went to her bookshelves and tilted her head to look through the titles. Then, realizing he wasn't buying that distracted act, leaned back against the little student desk and said, "To tell you the truth, Keats, I am seriously messed up. I don't think I'm showing it. I know I'm not letting myself feel it. I'm kind of just crushing it down inside me. But it doesn't feel good. It feels like I'm ignoring a tumor or something. Like I'm just pretending and looking away. And . . ."

She ran out of words then.

Keats nodded slowly, taking time to put all of that away in his memory. Then he said, "Well, you're certainly not going to get me to have sex with you now."

"Rain check?" she asked.

"Let's get some sleep."

They turned off the lights and lay together again. This time the bed was wide enough that they did not need to touch. But their hands reached out, and their fingers twined together.

"Keats?"

"Yeah."

"Are you inside me?"

"Well, that's not a question any boy wants a girl to ask."

"Keats."

He was quiet for a bit, then said, "Yes. Little K2 is currently checking on his basket-weaving work."

"Okay. Thanks. But shut him down and go to sleep." And then, still later. "But that's all right? You wouldn't ever . . .

I mean, I know what Vincent said. You aren't wiring me. That's not why I feel this way, right?"

"On the lives of everyone I love: no."

But after that their hands did not touch.

Nijinsky woke up no longer in the limo. He woke up in two places at once. One was a garage. Not one of those big, underground garages, a standard two-car garage of the sort you might find in any upscale suburb. There was only space for one car, actually, because the other half was filled with children's bikes, boxes of Christmas ornaments, power tools.

The other place Nijinsky woke was just under an eyelid. He recognized the terrain. It was not his first time squeezed between eyelid and eye.

Nijinsky was seated. He had no choice in the matter. He was tied, hands behind his back stretched around a wooden dining room chair, ankles tied to the legs.

Sugar Lebowski stood before him, dripping wet, wearing different clothes than she'd had on before. This was her home, Nijinsky realized, somewhere out on Long Island or in Jersey. Which meant that he was not going to leave this place alive. Or at least not without a brain filled with wire.

There was a twitching station too. More primitive than what he would have expected. It wasn't the high-tech marvel BZRK had been led to expect of AFGC, more like an Aeron chair with a clunky computer parked alongside; wires, a pair of gloves attached to the chair with bungee cord, and a forty-two-inch monitor propped atop a rickety occasional table.

Obviously a jury-rigged portable model.

The two thugs were not there. But a young man with fly-away blond hair was. He must have been in his early twenties. European, Nijinsky concluded, assessing the clothing brands and choices.

Sugar didn't waste any time. She grabbed a rusty golf club, a nine iron, and swung it level, straight into Nijinsky's shoulder. Which hurt like hell. Almost made him forget the throbbing at the back of his neck and the goose egg growing under his hairline.

It was an interesting choice. A shoulder hit like that.

Nijinsky sent his biots racing.

"What's your name?" Lebowski asked. Before he had a chance to answer she swung downward and smashed the golf club into his thigh.

Which nearly made Nijinsky swoon from pain.

But was also an interesting choice.

"Tell me your name!"

"Santino Corleone," he answered.

"That's very cute. Funny, you don't look Italian."

"You're very observant."

She smashed the club down on his shoulder again. It hurt,

but it had started to go numb from the earlier blow.

"Careful, you don't want to hit my face," he gasped. "You've got very strict instructions not to hurt my face."

Sugar Lebowski laughed, not a pretty sound. "Yeah, I'll admit: that's quick of you. Very quick. What are you, Chinese? Korean?"

"I thought I was Italian."

"You know what won't mess up your pretty face?"

She hauled a child's red wagon with an electrical charging unit inside into position in front of him. She ostentatiously plugged it into the wall. The dial lit up and a voltmeter needle jerked.

A set of jumper cables ran from the transformer and Sugar lifted them carefully. She was ready, Sugar was. Ready and just a little eager.

The blond man spoke then. His accent was German, Nijinsky was pretty sure of that. "This is unnecessary. I can be—"

"Seriously? A squeamish Kraut?" Sugar snapped at him.

The German waved a hand at her and Nijinsky both. "Why am I here in the middle of the night? To watch you play games? Let me touch him, please, so I can begin my work." He made a vague gesture toward the twitching chair.

So, he was indeed a twitcher. Sent here to wire Nijinsky, turn him around, and use him as a Trojan horse. Nijinsky looked at him with interest. Older than a lot of twitchers. He wondered how many bugs he had on board. Not that there was much Nijinsky could do if the twitcher unloaded onto him. He had only one biot still on board. The other two were nearing the medial rectus, one of the major muscles controlling the movement of Sugar Lebowski's eye.

From where he sat the muscle looked a bit like one of the massive cables used to hold up a suspension bridge. It attached to the eye in a way that suggested an unsuccessful attempt to fuse steel wires into bloody ice.

"Looks like you washed very carefully, lady," Nijinsky said.

"Call me Sugar," she said, and stabbed at his chest with the clamps of the electrical charger. Nijinsky's body jumped as far as it was able to without snapping ropes.

He sagged, and it seemed to take a few seconds at the very least for his brain to begin to make sense of the world.

"Okay, Sugar," Nijinsky said. "That pissed me off. I'm releasing a bit of sulphuric acid onto the muscle that holds your right eye steady laterally. You know, side to—"

"What?" She turned a horrified look on the German. "That's a bluff." It wasn't quite a statement, and it wasn't quite a question.

The twitcher shrugged. "Some biots are equipped with—"

Sugar pulled a gun and held it to Nijinsky's head. "Stop it, right fucking now!"

"It's too late for the medial," Nijinsky said. "You'll probably start blurring pretty soon."

"I can feel it!" She cried, and slapped her free hand to her face.

"Let me get him out of there," the twitcher said, and moved toward her.

"You want to put your filthy little bugs inside me?" she demanded of the German.

"It's not so bad being cross-eyed," Nijinsky offered.

He saw the acid working. It didn't take much to melt through the first few strands of taut muscle. He used the tail spur of his biot to add a few more drops. The biot would eventually secrete more, but the acid bladder was quite small, and only a small amount could be used at any time.

Of course Sugar wouldn't know that. The twitcher might not, either.

"I can feel it. It's burning!"

"Stupid woman, get out of my way." The German slid his hand into one of the gloves at the makeshift station, drew Sugar to him with the other, and as she wriggled away, cursing, he brushed his free hand against her face.

Then he slid the second glove into place and sat staring intently at the monitor.

"Get out of me or I'll shoot you now," Sugar snarled at Nijinsky, doing her damp best to intimidate him. He had no doubt she meant it. It made him sad.

The feeling surprised him a little. He'd never really expected to survive this war. But he'd always pictured his final moments as one of terror and defiance. Sadness, though. That was the feeling. So many things he would miss out on.

The German's nanobots were an unseen swarm, presumably heading into and eventually around Sugar's right eye.

And then, suddenly, the cable snapped. One second the muscles of Lebowski's eye were stretched overhead, and the next second they were gone and only acid-melted stump ends were left.

In the macro, Nijinsky saw Sugar's eye jerk inward.

Her *left* eye.

The twitcher saw it, too. "You stupid woman, he's in the other eye!"

"But I felt it!"

Nijinsky shrugged as well as he could. "Power of suggestion. And just so you know: what happens next you won't feel at all because strangely enough the brain itself does not feel pain."

"What are you doing to me?" Cold terror now. Good. He was glad he could at least make her afraid. It seemed fair enough, since she would almost certainly make him dead.

"That depends. You call off your boys outside and let me walk out of here, and nothing. Otherwise I dump all the acid I have deep inside your brain, where it will eat through until—"

She jabbed the gun hard against him.

"You have orders not to kill me, don't you?" Stalling. No

doubt she'd been ordered to deliver him wired. But she could always claim she had no choice. And she wasn't looking as if rational calculation was dominating her thinking.

She tried to manage the jumper cables with just her free hand, but it sent up a shower of sparks, so she set the gun down in the wagon.

Well, Nijinsky thought: *better than a bullet.*

She jabbed the cables against the bare flesh of his neck.

The pain was awful. But brief. There was a popping sound and the garage went dark.

Typical suburban homes are really not wired for performing electrical torture. A breaker had blown.

Nijinsky had worked one leg free of the rope. He kicked it straight out. With all his strength. And he felt the satisfying impact with Lebowski's knee.

She fell into him. He wrapped his one free leg around her and held her tight, willing himself to get his face close enough to hers to retrieve his biots, who were already far from the center of her brain, having left no dripping acid behind there, and were rushing to—

The lights came back on.

And at the same time Nijinsky saw something far worse than the enraged face of Sugar Lebowski. There, waiting for him, just off her lower eyelid, as though they had anticipated his every move, were two dozen nanobots.

The German had read the bluff.

Whatever fragile moment Nijinsky had had was over now. Lebowski wormed free.

His biots waited as the nanobots encircled them.

"Now, I believe we shall do this my way, yes?" The German said. "Our Berserk friend here will cause you no further harm, *Fraulein* Lebowski."

"How does it look?" she asked the German, and spread her eyelids apart with one hand so he could see the eye that now very definitely looked inward at her surgically perfected nose.

"Not so bad. It can be fixed," he soothed.

Then when she turned away, the German quickly, silently, slid out of the chair, freed his hands, picked up the golf club, and swung it hard against the back of her neck. She sank like a sack of wet gravel.

Nijinsky felt the blow through his biots. He stared. At the German. At the nanobots surrounding his biots on the fallen woman's face.

"My name is Dietrich," the German said in an urgent whisper, and a great deal less accent. "And I will tell you that saving you was *not* an order from Lear. Which means I may soon be visited by Caligula unless you and I cook up some story that does not involve me blowing my cover to save your life."

TWENTY-TWO

Bug Man had to fly down to Washington to put some of his troops aboard the deputy director of the FBI. That part was easy. The FBI guy was owned.

He had already installed Jessica at the Sofitel Hotel, where she sat pouting prettily, ordering room service, and watching movies. A TFD had been sent down with Bug Man to act as his "adult." Bug Man might rule the twitcherverse but still a sixteen-year-old black kid—even one with an English accent—checking into a hotel with a stunningly beautiful young lady didn't happen without a responsible adult.

The next transfer was quite easy. Again, the FBI guy—his name might have been Patrick, Bug Man could never remember—was following instructions, after all. It took place during a squash game at the University Club. An accidental bump, a tumble to the polished floor, a jab of knuckle in the ear, hold for three seconds, and ta-da!

Bug Man had decided on an ear entry after seeing that the Secret Service agent target—whose name, he believed, was an implausible John Smith—wore soft contact lenses. It wasn't that lenses were a major obstacle but rather that people who wore them were forever dropping in waterfalls of saline, or suddenly having to take out a wrinkled lens. Bug Man did not want to find his boys trapped inside a dark contact-lens holder.

So in through the ear it was.

Ears were iffy. If someone had been swimming or showering or, worse yet, had an inner-ear infection, there was no getting through. But if you knew the way and the ear canal was clear, you could make it.

The ear canal was like a cave filled with stalactites and stalagmites and whatever you would call something that grew horizontally. The hairs came from every direction: up, down and in between. They were tiny compared to eyelashes.

The cave felt quite large down at the nano. Earwax was a constant issue, with clumps of it along the "floor" and other bits of it hanging from above. And the entire cave was pockmarked here and there with holes like a sort of tiny, slow-motion geyser. Like the holes in Yellowstone that would burp up a glob of hot mud. Only in this case the hot mud was earwax.

Up in the macro, Bug Man was installed in a van parked just around the corner on M Street. No repeater necessary, straight signal.

He moved twenty-four fighter nanobots and four spinner-bots into the ear canal, marched them over the earwax down to the eardrum. An eardrum at the nano was a hell of a thing to see. Kind of like the skin of a bass drum if that bass drum was five stories tall m-sub, and anchored not by a fitted ring but by a tiny bone behind.

Bug Man waited until the squash game was over because the effect of that squash ball hitting the wall at high speed, that *thwock!* sound, hit the eardrum like a rock drummer smashing it with a stick.

The whole damned thing, that five-story-tall disk of what looked a bit like bleached, translucent liver, vibrated, and down in the nano that vibration was huge.

So he waited until John Smith—could that possibly be his real name?—was done smacking hard rubber balls. But next would come a shower, and that was potentially hazardous. He picked a relatively quiet moment and sent his nanobots scurrying beneath the now-moderately vibrating membrane.

Here at least they were safe.

But the next bit of the trip would involve climbing up the back side of the eardrum—something best done when the agent was asleep.

The van would be moved to just outside the Secret Service man's Fairfax home. And during the night Bug Man would enter his brain and put his spinners to work.

Somewhere in that man's brain was a picture of his mentor and friend, agent Francine Petrash, attached to the presidential detail. It would be a tough wire job. Bug Man would have to convince John Smith to touch Agent Petrash's face. He had some ideas about that. But it would mean an all-night wire job.

So, for now, Bug Man headed back to the Sofitel for some sleep.

Roughly three hundred miles away Dr Anya Violet looked at Vincent and said, "I know you're doing something to me."

At that moment Vincent was sitting with his feet up on the windowsill. He was gazing out over a gray, overcast Atlantic. Down on the beach, his two new recruits were walking and talking. Obviously relaxed in each other's company. Leaving footprints on pristine, damp sand.

"I'm just watching the waves," Vincent said.

"I feel differently about you," Anya said.

"Do you?"

"Goddamnit it, Vincent. I didn't betray you. I was used. I was set up. They must have guessed you'd come through me. They knew you'd need access to the lab."

"That's right," Vincent said. He was half listening. Watching Plath and Keats down on the beach. Thinking that Nijinsky had told him only part of a story, that Jin didn't trust Vincent—or want to burden him—with more.

Vincent and Wilkes and Ophelia, the three of them, had swarmed over Jin's brain. There was no sign of nanobot infestation. No wire. They had checked eyes, ears, even nose. They had sent biots crawling across his skin and deep into his brain and found nothing at all.

Nijinsky was clean.

But he wasn't telling the whole truth about his encounter with Sugar Lebowski. He was telling only what he had to tell. Concealing something.

And all the while, Vincent's two injured biots were stringing wire deep inside Anya's brain. It would be some time before they were capable of battle. His two healthy biots were in his own head. Waiting.

"I know you're wiring me," Anya said. The sound of her voice was a stab in the heart because it was her voice, but no longer entirely her own tone or emotion. She was speaking as someone would to a loved one. There was a sense of hurt. Of betrayal. Like you'd feel if someone you cared about was treating you badly.

Wire. It stretched from her memories of him to memories of everything she cared for, believed in, admired. Loved. Already Vincent was entwined with her mother, with her sister, with her favorite sushi restaurant, with her childhood teacher—who had told her she had a special ability—to her favorite scents.

She was being hard-wired to trust Vincent.

And maybe more than trust.

But she was still doubtful. Suspicious, because she was a very smart woman, and very self-aware, and he liked that in her. And soon he would wire all of that suspicion away.

"I do what I do because I have no choice," Vincent whispered.

I am not Scipio. I do not slaughter women and children and boast of it before the Roman Senate.

I will save your life, Anya, he thought. *You don't understand: Lear will send the Carthage message unless I make you one of us.*

I will save your life, Anya, by destroying your will.

"I want you to make love to me," Anya said. Her voice cracked with need.

"This isn't the night for—"

She rose, came to him, knelt, took his legs down from the sill, and touched him.

Vincent pushed her away, gently but decisively. "No, Anya. I'll do what I have to do to save your life. But I won't let you lower yourself."

Vincent knew about Bug Man and Jessica, the beauty he had turned into a living slave. He was not Bug Man.

Anya's eyes flashed furiously. "You make me need you and then give me nothing? That's your act of charity, Vincent? Wire me to be hungry and then let me starve?"

"I have to live with myself," he said. He stood up and she followed him as he rose, still very close, so close they touched and where they didn't touch they wanted to.

"You want me," she said. "You may not take any pleasure

from it, but you want me: your body betrays you. And whether or not it's real, Vincent, whether it's my true desires or something you've done to me, in the end there's no difference."

"There is to me," he said.

He pushed past her, his throat tight, blood pounding through him.

I am not Scipio. And I am not Bug Man.

So many things I'm not, he thought bitterly. *And so few things I am.*

Later Keats and Plath cooked pasta. It wasn't an old family recipe, just some sauce from a jar. Plath used the massive pot her mother had once used to boil crabs, right here, right absolutely here in this very kitchen in a very different world.

And they had a dinner, all of them, Vincent and Anya, Nijinsky, Ophelia, Wilkes, Keats and Plath. They drank a nice Barolo. They passed around the freshly grated Parmesan. And it was normal if by normal you meant a horrible parody of normality.

Nijinsky had somehow found enough clothing of Plath's father to look quite modelish again. And Wilkes kept her sudden digressions into hostility under control. And Anya looked at Vincent with loving eyes while he ate mechanically. And Ophelia somehow found her repertoire of smiles that made them all feel better.

And still it was the most desperately sad meal Plath had ever had.

It was Keats who broke the code of silence and asked Vincent, "When does it start?"

"Tomorrow," Vincent said. "Our British cousins are in the city. They'll be taking—defending—their prime minister. We have our president. And . . ." He paused, glanced at Anya as though not sure whether he could speak freely in her presence. Something reassured him, and in accepting reassurance, Plath thought something inside Vincent twisted and writhed a little bit, too, and he said, "And we have a little surprise for the Armstrong Twins."

Every fork except Wilkes's stopped moving.

"I won't lie: they hit us pretty hard. We believe now that AFGC have targeted our president, Keats's prime minister, the Chinese president, the Japanese and Indian prime ministers. Five targets. But the Armstrong Twins hit our Chinese and Indian cells very hard. So we're probably going to have to give them up. And that's very bad."

"The Japanese cell is very tight, and they don't seem to have been hit. So we'll leave the Japanese PM to them. Same with our British cousins."

"God save the king, eh?" Wilkes said to Keats.

"Or at least the prime minister. Even if he is a Tory," Keats answered.

"Nijinsky and I are the first team on President Morales. Wilkes and Ophelia run counterforce for that," Vincent went on.

"What's counterforce?" Plath asked.

"There are three ways to stop a twitcher," Ophelia explained. "You can beat him down in the nano. You can incapacitate him in the macro: in other words, kill him. Or you can wire him. Wilkes and I will be looking for the twitchers. They'll use multiple locations near the UN Building to avoid having to use signal repeaters."

"Their repeaters are junk," Nijinsky interjected.

"We have word from Lear—possibly from a mole inside AFGC—that one of the locations will be inside the UN."

"Inside the building? What, inside the UN itself?" Plath asked.

"Armstrong Fancy Gifts Corporation," Ophelia said. "They still run more than four-hundred gift shops in airports, in train stations in Europe, and in places like museums. And in the basement of the UN."

"You've got to be kidding," Keats said.

"That's what we think," Vincent confirmed. "So Ophelia and Wilkes are going to see if we can't at least disrupt them there. Maybe expose them so they have to withdraw."

"What about Keats and me?" Plath asked.

Vincent glanced guiltily at Nijinsky.

Nijinsky frowned, sensing that something bad was coming. He said, "They aren't ready for—"

But Vincent cut him off.

"Lear has ordered . . . and I agree . . . that we need a counterattack. Something to throw them off. It has to be something real, with a real chance of success. The other side isn't stupid—we can't just wave our hands in the air and distract them."

Nijinsky put down his wineglass with a little more force than necessary. "What are you sending them into?" He was seated directly across from Vincent.

Vincent took a sip of wine, stalling. Then, with no more emotion than he might have in announcing that tomorrow's weather would be rainy, he said, "We're going after the Twins directly."

"May I speak to you in private, Vincent?" Nijinsky said through gritted teeth.

"My friend Jin thinks I'm sending you two on a suicide mission," Vincent said, staring hard at Nijinsky, who glared back.

"Are you?" Plath asked.

Vincent nodded slightly. "Probably."

"What if we say no?" Plath demanded.

Vincent turned from Nijinsky and met her gaze. "You won't."

"What makes you so sure?" Plath said. "Have you done something to me, is that it?"

"I told you I would never—"

"Then how the hell are you so sure we're going along with this suicide mission?"

"Because they murdered your father and your brother. And they damned-near killed you," Vincent said. "And when I mention that to you, your eyes blaze and your teeth start to show, and you aren't a person who lets her family be wiped out without fighting back."

"This is how we repay her father?" Nijinsky demanded. "By getting her killed?"

Vincent slammed the side of his fist down on the table. Every dish jumped. No one breathed. "Do you think I like this, Shane?"

Almost as shocking as Vincent showing emotion was Vincent using the name "Shane" instead of Nijinsky.

"You don't *like* anything, Vincent. That's why Lear has you running this cell. A man without pleasure is a man without any idea what life is about." Nijinsky pointed at Plath. "She's sixteen, for Christ's sake. She's barely trained. And him, young Mr Hormone there, he's already in love with her. If she goes, he'll go."

Nijinsky was shaking with emotion. Vincent had already brought his under control.

"Yes. That's what I figured," Vincent said. He stood up carefully, pushed his chair back, said, "I've had enough. Enjoy your dinner," and carried his plate to the kitchen.

TWENTY-THREE

"You think maybe the time has come to tell me how the hell we're going to do this, Vincent?" Nijinsky said.

Vincent answered. "Lear made it very clear that the plan stays with me until there is no other choice."

The two of them were walking down Third Avenue past the British Consulate, a building of no particular interest once you had noted the Union Jack flying alongside the Stars and Stripes.

"British Embassy?" Nijinsky asked, eyebrow raised.

"We're heading over to Lex. Over to the W Hotel. We're meeting someone."

"I suppose I shouldn't ask who?"

"You may recognize her. Tatiana Featherstonehaugh."

Nijinsky looked at him tolerantly. "It's pronounced 'Fanshaw'."

Vincent frowned. "Really? All that to get Fanshaw?"

"The English," Nijinksy said, and shrugged as though that explained it. "She's a society type. What is she doing involved in this?"

"Ours not to reason why," Vincent said. "She'll be at a reception at the Hilton over by the UN shortly, right after we meet her. That's where the POTUS is staying. It's just a meet and greet with Morales and Bowen and various Anglophiles before they both head to the General Assembly for their speeches. A society thing. She's helping us, courtesy of our London friends."

"You're sure the president's going to be there?"

"That's never guaranteed," Vincent said. "Presidential security makes every other kind of security look lazy. If the Secret Service even smells anything . . . But if he is there, we're in."

"And meanwhile?" Nijinsky asked.

Vincent stopped, retreated beneath an overhang as a light rain began to fall. "There's a very good chance none of us come out of this alive, Jin. That's just the reality."

"The two kids, though . . ." He didn't really have a conclusion to that sentence.

"It's not just them. Wilkes and Ophelia, too. All of them. All of us. If it makes you feel any better, I argued with Lear."

"Did you?" Nijinsky believed him; he just wondered how you argued via text.

"I reminded Lear of their value. Keats as a twitcher, Plath as the connection to McLure money and technology. Maybe if the Armstrongs hadn't hit us so hard in China and India. Maybe then we could hold something back. But this is it. This is the fight we can't lose, and yet AFGC will probably be able to wire the heads of the two most populous nations on earth. We start the day off with a disaster, Jin. Do you get that? We've already lost half the battle. We can't lose it all."

It was still raining, but Vincent was done talking. Nijinsky followed, troubled but silent.

They pushed through the revolving doors and into the lobby of the W Hotel. Nijinsky had been there before, Vincent had not.

"Where is she meeting us?"

"Penthouse." Vincent had a swipe key, and they took the elevator to the top floor. A capably tough-looking man with an Israeli accent opened the door.

He led them through a hall and into a beautifully decorated suite.

Tatiana Featherstonehaugh was what an older generation would have called a knockout. Her last name was English by way of her husband, but her skin was a few shades too dark, her mouth too wide and lips too full, to be from a cold, dark country. She had begun life in the less-desirable neighborhoods of Seville, Spain, but had spent her early childhood always on the move with her widowed father, a Romanian by birth, as he chased scarce jobs through Argentina, Uruguay, and Panama.

Tatiana wore a casually elegant outfit of which Nijinsky approved. Jewelry was of the understated yet very expensive variety, with platinum and diamonds and Peruvian opals to set off her eyes and not a cubic zirconium in the bunch.

She looked at first glance to be a rich man's trophy wife—her husband was in fact older and very rich—but there were lines in her face that spoke of pain, a determination in the set of her jaw, and a degree of focused attention that made you feel as if you'd been stripped down to your component parts.

Possibly she had had a trivial thought once in her life, but it had not happened often.

"You would be Vincent," she said, and held out her hand.

"And this is Nijinsky," Vincent said.

That brought a smile from Tatiana. "Interesting name."

"Thank you," Nijinsky said.

"I was just having tea," Tatiana said. "I've picked up a few habits from my husband: tea with milk, and a love of horses."

She served from an elegant china set that had not been supplied by the hotel but had to have been brought in.

"I would rather not have you crawling around in my eyes or brain," Tatiana said.

"That's . . . understandable," Vincent said.

"I don't want to have to poke myself in the eye before I shake hands with the president."

"No," Nijinsky agreed.

"So I've thought of an alternative. I've already had a manicure. My nails are very clean. I can signal you when it's time, by allowing my fingernail to touch the president's wrist as we shake hands."

Vincent and Nijinsky sipped tea and exchanged a look.

"That would work," Vincent said. "If we were quick."

"I have some of our British friends on this finger." She held up her right hand, index finger. "I thought you might take the middle finger."

"We often do," Nijinsky deadpanned.

Tatiana smiled and said, "Can I ask you both something?"

"Of course, ma'am," Vincent said. "Why are we doing this?"

"Really? I'm a 'ma'am,' am I?" She mocked Vincent gently. She waved that question away. "No, I understand well enough the why of it. I've . . . met . . . the Armstrong Twins." There was definitely a memory hovering just out of sight and giving her lilting enunciation sharp teeth. "No, I wanted to ask what it's like. Down there? Is it very horrible?"

Vincent deflected the question to Nijinsky.

Nijinsky thought for a moment, finding his words. "No. It's not horrible. I mean, at first, yes. And for some people, yes, they never come to . . . to love it."

"But you do love it?"

"It's . . . I've seen a lot of planet Earth," Nijinsky said. "I've traveled a lot. And sometimes you might almost start getting bored with it. You might start thinking, *Is that all there is?* And then you go down in the meat."

"Is that what you call it?"

Nijinsky nodded, a little embarrassed. "It's like, the world, the planet, suddenly got so much bigger."

"Not smaller?"

"No. By going down there, seeing what's down there, it's like you've spent your whole life just seeing surfaces. Like you've seen the covers of books and never seen the words inside. It's vast down there. It's a universe. It's more universes than you can even imagine, because what I've seen is just a few parts of *Homo sapiens* at the nano. How many millions of other things are there to see? What's the surface of a frog like? What's it like to be down in the meat on a jellyfish? How about a cactus? A stalactite? A rattlesnake? It's . . . You could never possibly run out of things to see."

He sipped tea, which was now almost cold.

"I suppose it's possible to enjoy it," Tatiana said doubtfully.

"Some become addicted," Vincent said, gloomy, no echo of Nijinsky's enthusiasm. "Others are driven over the edge. They can't handle it. It's too much. They can't unsee it."

For a few moments they sat in silence, digesting each other's words and nibbling at tea cakes.

"I know what happened in Shanghai and Mumbai," Tatiana said. "It's very important that neither you nor my British friends fail. We will likely lose Ts'ai and Chauksey. Do you know what this will mean?" Neither of them answered, so she did it herself. "The Armstrongs will be free to operate in China and in India. They'll facilitate the spread of Nexus Humanus into those countries, allowing them to identify and recruit talent. They'll gain access to resources—technology and money. They will be immeasurably stronger."

"Yes," Vincent said, narrowing his eyes curiously. He had expected a contact. He had not expected a lecture. This woman, he realized, was connected to Lear.

Might even be Lear herself. Only a blind man could fail to see the knife-edged intellect behind the beauty-queen eyes.

The thought knocked him off-balance. He had walked into the room sure that he was in charge. He no longer felt that way as he sat listening to Tatiana Featherstonehaugh lay out the strategic picture in a way that Lear never bothered to do.

"If you are able to keep President Morales safe, and if Mr Bowen and Mrs Hayashi are also kept safe, we at least have the possibility of reaching out to agencies within China and India and warning them. We can at least cut off any attempts to enlist the UN itself in the Armstrong cause."

"Yes, ma'am," Nijinsky said.

"Don't fail," Tatiana Featherstonehaugh said, and there was nothing of the socialite or the trophy wife in that tone; that was pure, confident authority speaking. It was an order.

"No, ma'am," they both said, despite having been warned off that title.

"How shall we do this then?" Tatiana asked, brightening and lightening at once.

"I'll touch my finger to yours," Vincent said. "And then Nijinsky will do the same."

Tatiana held her hand out, palm up. "Don't get yourselves killed. Some day when this is all over, I'd love to invite Mr Nijinsky here to a dinner party. You, Vincent, don't strike me as the party type."

"No," Vincent said, and looked just a little forlorn.

Dog fur at the nano level is less like a palm tree and more like a sort of limp asparagus. That was Plath's first observation.

She wanted to focus on the fur, which was an overgrown forest of thick hairs, all pressed down around her so that it was dark down there, down there beneath the eerie forest on the German shepherd's muzzle. She wanted to focus on anything that wasn't one of her own biots with their smeared Sadie eyes and compound bug eyes atop that, and the drooling spinneret mouth, and the bug legs and the mantis claws and . . .

She walked beside Keats, a hundred yards away from their biots on the dog. They were pretending to be young lovers because that was a good cover, two teenagers with their arms interlocked, occasionally bumping together deliberately and smiling, and maybe a butt grab here or there, the way a young couple might do walking through Central Park on a cold but clear fall morning.

But she was also down on that dog's muzzle, the one being walked by the girl with the strange black-flame tattoo beneath one eye.

The dog in question was on a choke collar, and yet Wilkes could barely hold him. He was a dog rescued from a dog-fighting ring. He had not yet been resocialized. He was still savage and vicious and looking for prey.

Plath and Keats, two biots each, were side by side in the thicket just above the animal's upper gumline.

The target was a beagle being walked by two TFDs, with two more TFDs scowling at passersby. One wore a plastic bag over his hand, ready to pick up the beagle's poop should the beagle decide to go.

They formed a loose triangle: Wilkes with the tugging, snarling German shepherd; and the AmericaStrong TFDs with the beagle; and the two young lovers enjoying the unlikely sunshine.

They saw it and felt it at the same time. Saw Wilkes accidentally drop the dog's collar. And felt in their biot legs the sudden lurch as the beast went tearing across the grass.

And then.

"Fuck!" Plath yelled, not because of anything up in the normal world.

A huge, armor-plated monster, as big as an elephant, had just dropped out of the sky.

"Jesus!" Keats echoed at the same instant.

It rested on four articulated legs although it may have had more. It was a dinosaur, a clanking science-fiction monster, a nightmare. The hind legs vibrated with pent-up energy.

It was narrow, as though it came presquashed. Like a football with most of the air let out. The body seemed made of armor plates with rapier-like hairs directed toward the rear. The head was the true nightmare: a helmet with two blank eyes that did not turn or look or even seem to notice the biots that must have been themselves no bigger than dogs to the towering, mighty, indestructible flea.

It was impossible to believe the sense of energy contained within that prehistoric monster. It made the biots vibrate.

It was, in every way, the physical embodiment of something evil.

"It won't bother us," Keats said. "Just . . . Just . . . Oh my God!"

The German shepherd hurtled toward the clueless beagle.

The flea knelt down as if in some pagan prayer, until its mouthparts touched the dog's flesh. And then, like bent, distorted scimitars, began sawing—not stabbing but sawing—into dog flesh.

"Don't look at it," Plath said, not following her own advice because the lovey-dovey act up in the macro could not be sustained while their biots were in the shadow of this grotesque, quivering thing.

"We need to be ready," Keats said. "We'll only have a few seconds."

And then the blood began to flow. Tiny red cough drops oozed from the hole the flea had made. It was a slow geyser of red marbles, red Frisbees, red that should be a liquid but seemed more like wet gravel as the flea sucked it up, and it was almost impossible to look away or to prepare for the fact that—

Impact!

The German shepherd hit the beagle like a ton of bricks.

"Now, now, now!" Plath cried, and she would have been seen and heard by the TFDs except that they suddenly had a dog fight on their hands.

The German shepherd's huge mouth clamped onto the rolling, howling, terrified beagle, and the flea was almost forgotten as the impact jolted the four biots.

"Go, go, go, go!" Plath said, and her two biots, with Keats's right behind, raced toward the gumline, which had been a sort of ashen ridge just beyond the edge of the forest of fur and was now something apocalyptic. The black gums writhed madly, as if they were watching a magma field in a terrible earthquake.

And that ridge of flesh was now shoved into a whole hair planet, a writhing hallucination of close-packed hair and huge comets of saliva, and then, for no reason, the flea leapt! It flew up and out of sight with such incredible speed that it was if it had been shot out of a cannon.

"Jump!" Plath urged.

They jumped.

But to their shock, gravity wasn't where they thought it would be. The German shepherd had rolled the beagle all the way over, and the biots were falling but the ground was rolling around them, a twisting madness of slobber and dog lips and hair, and suddenly they landed, grabbed desperately, falling through hair like skydiving without a parachute into the rain forest.

Wilkes was running to retrieve her dog.

The dogs separated for a split second and *BAM!*

The gunshot was loud, too loud for a public park, and the German shepherd squealed and stumbled and the beagle cowered and Wilkes screamed as a good dog owner would when someone's just shot her dog.

"What did you do? What did you do?" she screamed, and rushed to the dying animal.

One of the TFDs pulled out a wallet, peeled off a couple of bills, and let them drop on the dead dog. Another gathered up the beagle, and all together they beat a hasty retreat.

It was not until then that Plath and Keats were sure they were on the right dog.

Like any two concerned passersby might, they trotted over to

Wilkes even as they ran their biots fearfully into the beagle's fur.

"You okay?" Keats asked Wilkes.

She held up two one-hundred-dollar bills. "I'm fine. But Hitler Hound here is looking a bit out of it."

"Hitler Hound?" Keats asked.

Wilkes shrugged. "It seemed like a good name for him. I'm sorry for him, but damn, he was a crazy-ass dog. He tried to bite me. And C-notes are always welcome."

Plath was disgusted. "Yeah, you can get something else tattooed."

"Drop dead, sweetie," Wilkes said with a derisive look. "I don't happen to be a billionaire. And you two need to start walking toward the AFGC building. You don't want to be out of range."

They left Wilkes to deal with the dead animal and walked the block and a half to the Starbucks nearest the AFGC building.

"Do you see that?" Plath asked as they sat with lattes and muffins.

"What?"

"It's a bite. Where the other dog . . . I think you're too far away, I don't see you, but it's almost . . . awe-inspiring. The flesh, it's like it was peeled back. Like the edge of a meteor crater or something. The hairs are all twisted. There are pools of spit, I guess that's what it is. And things swimming in the spit. And the blood . . . It's, I . . ."

She was looking straight at him, but beyond him, too, and he was likewise looking through her and seeing not the wound but what looked like a far-distant mountain that he hoped was the beagle's nose.

"We probably shouldn't be talking. It sounds crazy," Keats said.

"This is New York. Crazy doesn't draw much attention. I need to get away from the wound. They'll dump disinfectant all over it."

She sipped her coffee. "What if I can't find you? It's like looking for someone in a hundred acres of woods."

"Just remember the hair points to the back end of the dog. We want the front."

Keats sent one of his biots to thread its way, like a monkey going hand over hand, up through the flattened hair, up into the light.

Biots did not have long-distance vision. At least not what would pass for long distance in the macro. They could see distant patterns of light and dark and some limited color, but not the detail of a face.

What Keats could see from his fur-top perch was an endless, undulating sea of fur, each individual hair clearly visible within the immediate circle but with distance turning spiny, horizontal hairs into a smear of brown and white. Twisting his biot around, he could form the picture—through insect and humanoid eyes—of a promontory, a peninsula, that ended in a massive black rock the size of Mount Rushmore.

The nose.

Their target.

"I'm on the head," Keats said across the table. "I can see the wound. It looks like something plowed through the fur. If you can see the wound, you're not far from where I am. Just walk against the direction of the fur."

He looked up, into what felt to him like the sky. What he saw was a pale green cloud, larger than any object he had ever seen in real life. And it seemed to wrap itself around the forest of fur, but in one place ceased to be green and became a brown color. It enveloped the entire horizon.

"I think we're being carried by the black one. The black TFD in the green shirt," Keats said. "I can't really see. Just shapes and colors. It doesn't make much sense."

Sounds were too large somehow to make much sense of either. Like earthquake rumblings, but too confused to decipher.

Then, a single sound, audible to both of them. Like a gong being struck way off in orbit.

"Elevator?" Plath wondered.

"Maybe."

Far-off thunder that might have been voices. But the sound waves vibrating up from human throats were too big to be decipherable by biots not specifically equipped.

"Your first biots are basic models," Vincent had explained. "Fully capable in battle, fully capable for spinning wire. But there are tweaks and add-ons—both biological and technological—that come later. Each time we add a level of capability, we add a layer of complexity. At first, you want to keep it simple."

And they'd been grateful for that, because "simple" was all the complexity they could handle.

And yet now they both really wished they had every conceivable upgrade.

They would have to operate on instinct. They would have to guess when some giant hand belonged to the Armstrong Twins.

If they guessed wrong, they could end up anywhere.

"How do we take our biots back?" Keats asked.

"You're just thinking of this now?" Plath asked him as she swirled the cup to mix foam and coffee.

"If we can't recover them . . ." It was a question.

"I don't know," she said.

"It's too late to stop now."

"Do you feel that? Vibration?"

"Maybe his tail is wagging." Keats suggested.

"Do you really think we lose our sanity if . . ."

"I've seen it."

"That's a new shape," Plath said.

"Yeah."

"Is it him? Them?"

"Might just be a vet." Keats closed his eyes, trying to focus. "I see fingers."

"Someone is staring at us."

It took Keats a moment to figure out what version of reality Plath was talking about. His eyes popped open. "Who?"

"Girl at the counter. Picking up a drink. The creepy one with the fake teeth. The one who looks like a shark," Plath said.

"Just ignore her, she's just—"

"No," Plath said. Her eyes were narrowed. It was like a beam of energy connected her to the girl. "She's texting someone. Let's get out of here."

Plath stood up, and Keats jumped to follow her.

Then the girl with the shark teeth turned toward them, too fast, too predatory. Too knowing.

Too determined.

She reached for Plath.

The girl, who called herself One-Up, just wanted to touch them.

TWENTY-FOUR

Wilkes was already arriving at the UN. She had a prepurchased ticket for the tour—good thing, there was a crowd waiting. Mostly they were school kids, a happily rambunctious bunch of middle schoolers from some school in Harlem that favored maroon uniforms. And there were tourists, and thankfully there was Ophelia.

"How did it go?"

"I made two hundred bucks," Wilkes said. She tried to pull off a swagger, but it didn't go anywhere.

"This is the last tour group before they shut the place down for security," Ophelia chided. "You barely made it."

"Don't sweat it," Wilkes said. "Vincent has it all planned out."

"I have a lot of faith in Vincent," Ophelia said. "But he's not perfect."

Wilkes laughed. "How come you never show anyone else but me this gloomy side of your personality?"

Ophelia didn't answer, just made a slight harrumphing

sound and then shared one of her resigned-looking smiles.

They moved through the main lobby like obedient tourist sheep, threading through an art display of children's pictures of some terrible conflict. Wilkes hadn't kept up on current terrible conflicts, having enough to keep her busy with her own. But the pictures were not encouraging. They did not exactly counter her sense of impending doom.

She looked up at soaring windows, at old Sputnik hanging there like a misplaced Christmas-tree ball. She had done a report on Sputnik. When was that? Fourth grade?

She saw a memory image of herself carrying her threefold cardboard display into class, setting it up, trying to act cool even then. But also feeling it would be nice if she got an A.

How had all that been just one life? How could she have ever been that little girl?

"You ever hit on Vincent?" Wilkes asked.

"I don't hit on boys," Ophelia said with an edge of disapproval.

At the security line they emptied their pockets into the tray and passed their purses through the scanner. Scanners did not detect the presence of biots.

The trick was to look entirely normal and average, something that was easier for Ophelia than Wilkes.

They saw the famous Chagall stained glass, a beautiful blue full of floating images of peace. Angels or whatever they were.

They saw the General Assembly room, a surprisingly

intimate space, despite the fact that it was supposed to be a gathering place for the entire world. It reminded Wilkes of the planetarium her class had visited in what, eighth grade? Is that where she had let Arkady touch her boob?

And they followed meekly along when it was time to go downstairs to the bathrooms, the special UN post office, the café, and the gift shop.

They moved away from the group then. It was safe to do so now.

They sat together eating veggie burritos UN style—not very good, really—and drinking coffee and getting their nerve up.

The gift shop was just next door. It was not called Armstrong Fancy Gifts—unlike the ones in airports—it was just called the UN Gift Shop. Very imaginative. But it had the trademark AFGC products: supposedly homemade cookies in cellophane twists, the books selection that included a prominent display of the bestseller *Nexus Humanus: The Next Step in Human Evolution*, and the clever, throwaway handheld games that sold for three dollars and included accelerometers and multiplay and inline upgrades that made them the cheap impulse equivalent of expensive pads.

"So a lousy burrito is my final meal," Wilkes said.

Ophelia looked at her, serious. They didn't talk often, the two of them. Wilkes was more or less the diametric opposite of the graceful, reserved Ophelia.

"Are you afraid, Wilkes?"

"Hell, yes, I'm afraid," Wilkes said, talking around melted cheese and a dropped bean. "You know what's weird, though. I'm afraid of never getting down in the meat again. That is weird, right?"

"You like it down there?"

"Better than up here sometimes," Wilkes said. "Are we bonding like true BZRK sisters?"

Ophelia put her fork down and pushed her food away. "I don't seem to have much appetite."

"Hey, the condemned person is supposed to have a choice of meal. Right? Like guys on death row? They always order a steak."

"I don't think they grill steaks here."

The light, that's what was so desperate about the scene. The glaring fluorescent light that turned their flesh to some color between bathroom grout and paper pulp. And the wobbly round tables and the terminally bored cafeteria workers.

A hell of a place to get your nerve up for a suicide mission.

"I always wanted to go to one of those fancy steak places," Wilkes said. "It's not about loving the steak all that much. It's just you see those places in movies, and you think, wow, that must be kind of cool—to be one of those people who don't really give a damn about anything but a fat, juicy steak. Maybe a martini, even, you know. Or those other ones? I forget their name?"

"Margaritas?"

"No, I know margaritas," Wilkes said, suddenly cranky.

Ophelia smiled tolerantly. "I don't eat meat. But I would join you in a margarita."

"You're a vegetarian? I tried that for a while. It didn't take. Is it a Hindu thing?"

Ophelia shrugged. "For some of us. For me it's more of a health thing. Also my parents are vegetarians. I don't want to disappoint them."

"Me, I worry I'll disappoint Vincent. That's stupid, isn't it? Why the hell should I care? He's not offering me heaven and a bunch of hot guy virgins, or whatever. That's what you guys get in heaven, right?"

"No."

"Are you sure?"

"I would remember that. I'm Hindu: we just get reborn. Although I think I like your idea better."

"A couple girls, too, maybe, just because life is short and try everything, right?"

Ophelia chose not to answer that directly. "Vincent does generate a certain degree of loyalty, doesn't he?"

Wilkes looked at her, very serious, eye to eye, or at least eye to eye-dripping-with-tattoo-ink, and said, "I'd die for him. I don't think he even likes me, and I would totally fucking die for him."

Ophelia said, "And I will die because Charles and Benjamin Armstrong are a disease."

There was venom behind those words. No smile. Anger, quickly covered up, but Wilkes saw it and grinned at it.

"You're not telling me something," Wilkes said.

"No time. And this isn't the place," Ophelia said, turning stern.

"If we come out of this?"

Ophelia nodded, and surrendered what might be the last of her smiles, a wistful creation tinged with loss. "If we survive, we can play twenty questions, Wilkes."

"Time to go?" Wilkes asked, and to her intense irritation there was a quiver in her voice.

Ophelia didn't answer. She reached up and peeled the bindi from her forehead and slid it into the coin pocket of her jeans. Then she stood up and walked out the cafeteria door and into the gift shop.

Plath snatched a just-delivered triple-grande skim cappuccino off the Starbucks counter and smashed it into One-Up's face.

"Ahhhh!"

"Run!" Plath hissed.

They ran from the Starbucks. The Starbucks that was the closest one to the AFGC building.

A stupid error, Plath saw that now. *Stupid!* Of course AFGC people would go there, of course they would. They would go there and another twitcher—another person who knew what it was like to be in two places at once—would notice the faraway eyes, the gaze that looked at things unseen in the macro, and intuit what you were.

They'd been sitting there in Starbucks, staring past each other, eyes flitting here and there, not looking at each other though they were face-to-face. The shark-toothed girl had *felt* what they were.

They pelted out the front door onto the street, glanced wildly in both directions. "Follow me," Plath yelled.

"It's your city," Keats panted.

And there was One-Up tearing after them, her jacket trailing streams of coffee and foam. She was young and fit and fast, but not fast enough to easily close the distance, especially when she was dialing as she ran.

"She'll warn them!" Keats yelled.

As they ran, pushing through indifferent pedestrians, slipping on dropped hot dogs, running blind despite Plath acting like she had a plan, they were each seeing the huge fingers touching the distant wounds on the beagle's back.

"That's not a vet!" Keats panted. "He's stroking, not examining a wound."

"It's *them*," Plath said.

They aimed their biots toward the wound, toward the

God-fingers that reached down from a misty, vaguely detailed sky.

They raced across the fur, not descending back to the skin but racing hair to hair, leaping from horizontal asparagus shaft to asparagus shaft, grabbing and kicking and oh, wow, it would have been exhilarating except that up in the macro there was a thick crowd of people clogging the intersection ahead of them.

One-Up had only to touch them. Neither had biots on board. Neither had a defense. A single touch and a rush of nanobots would be on them, then inside them.

Race tree trunk to tree trunk!

They skirted the crowd and for a minute they thought they had gained some ground, but there was One-Up rushing, halving the distance. They tried to cross the street, but it was a steady stream of yellow cabs. The only way out was to take One-Up down.

It was a game of tag. All she had to do was get a hand on them. She was yelling into the phone, "Get a twitcher on my frequency! Now now now!"

Plath heard her clearly. Their eyes met. One touch and whoever was no doubt rushing now to take over One-Up's nanobots would send the deadly little robots onto Plath or Keats. Nanobots would rush into Plath's eyes or ears and into her brain and pull the plug on the aneurysm, or maybe just get to work wiring her brain.

Yeah, well: screw that.

Plath grabbed a woman and spun her into One-Up's path. The woman went down hard, but One-Up leapt over her like an Olympian. Then she landed on something wet and slipped.

The lights changed and cabs screeched to a halt and Keats and Plath were in the midst of those crossing the street, hurrying, pushing, and the goddamned God-fingers were stroking the fur now, no longer exploring the wound, a hand that blotted out the sun, an entire storm front made of ridged farmland held improbably upside down.

"Jump!" Plath yelled, and Keats at first misunderstood and jumped in the crosswalk.

Plath kicked her two biots up, twisted in midair like a cat, or a fly, and gripped onto farmland dotted with pearls of oozing sweat.

The hand went shooting past, and Keats was swept away beneath her or up in the sky or whatever the hell direction it was now.

"Keats!"

His biots jumped and missed and fell away, back onto the beagle, and Plath yelled. She spotted a man leaning on a cane. He didn't look as if he needed it as badly as she did, so she snatched it from him, turned and ran straight at the on-rushing One-Up.

She didn't swing the cane, she jabbed it. The rubber tip

caught One-Up in the chest, and she said, "Ooof," like in a comic book; you could practically see the word balloon.

Plath hit her again, another jab, then gripped the cane, a nice wooden cane, and swung it down hard on One-Up's protective up-raised arm.

One-Up cried out in pain, and Plath hit her again and again and again all the while screaming, "Fuck you, bitch!"

Then, with One-Up on the pavement bleeding, Plath knocked the cell phone from her hand and sent it skittering across the sidewalk.

After that Keats and Plath ran, because New York wasn't a place where you could just beat someone up without cops coming.

Eventually.

Keats grabbed her hand and pulled her away.

"We're separated," Keats said breathlessly.

"I know. I know," Plath said.

Her biots ran blindly across a human palm, no idea where to go or what to do. And no better idea, really, up in the macro.

"This jacket is hot. I think I'll wear a summer dress. Something sleeveless." The voice was not recognizable, not even through the sensors of the two nanobots specially modified to detect sound waves. Even with the best "Big Ears" a nanobot rendered every voice into a high-pitched whine.

But the droll sense of humor was that of the president of the United States.

"That would certainly draw the media, Madam President." The second voice was Liz Law, the president's body woman, who at that moment unwittingly carried a small but potent army.

"In April I had the honor of meeting with the queen. Goddamnit. In April I had the honor of meeting with Her Majesty the queen." The president was practicing her toast. "Her Majesty. Her Majesty the queen."

In the end, it had been easy for Bug Man.

He had made all the jumps along the pathway. Down in Washington, and then back in New York. Like a passenger plane making multiple stops, or a flea hopping from dog to dog. Now all his boys—twenty-four fighters, four spinners—were ready and primed and quivering with readiness on Law's finger.

Nanobot optics had strengths and weaknesses. Biots saw in greater resolution; it was one of their strengths. Biots were insanely quick at detecting movement and had a connection between sight and mind and action that made them superior to nanobot fighters one-on-one.

But nanobots were machines, and had the advantages of machines. For one thing their visual data could be combined to form macro images. Line a dozen or so nanobots up in a row, point their optics in the same direction, and the computer at the base station could form those smaller images into a larger one. Nanobots produced digital data, and digital data was, as always, wonderfully manipulable.

It was complicated, using the optics that way, and doing it meant keeping a large percentage of his force stationary, which Bug Man did not like. No twitcher did. But sometimes it was worth it.

Worth it now as he saw the actual face, the familiar jowly chin all the comics joked about, the sleepy/smart eyes, the stiff, brown hairdo, the slightly too-hip earrings, all of it. Probably the most recognizable face on Earth.

It was only a flash, that image, because Liz Law's fingers were moving, fussing about. So Bug Man saw a dish and a desk and a sleeve and a cloth used to wipe something from that sleeve, and the presidential face again, then a window . . .

"In April I had the honor of meeting with Her Majesty the queen. When my good friend, Prime Minister Bowen, joined us, Her Majesty pointed out . . . What is it, Tom?"

A new voice, male, too far away to be understood. It spoke briefly. "That's good news," the president replied. "Good work, Tom. Tell the Speaker that seven percent is fine."

Bug Man was in a storefront dental office directly across First Avenue from the UN. On the outside the office looked a lot like a tavern. On the inside it looked a lot like a tavern after an epic drinking contest, because the dentist, receptionist, hygienist, and two unlucky patients were stacked like firewood against a back wall, passed out after being shot full of a narcotic that would guarantee a nice, long sleep.

A sign on the front door pleaded illness and asked patients to call to reschedule.

AmericaStrong techs had moved the twitching gear into the two examination rooms, and now monitors hung from bungee cords above the dental chairs, and wire, gathered by Velcro ties, spooled onto the immaculate floors. Bug Man sat in the chair in Exam Room A while Burnofsky sat in Exam Room B.

Somewhat to Bug Man's irritation, Burnofsky had also made it along his pathway and was now positioned aboard the Chinese leader's assistant/girlfriend.

The president was at the Hilton Manhattan East hotel, barely a block from the dental office that was itself just a block from the UN. Bug Man would have direct linkage all the way through, from the reception at the hotel to the UN.

By the time the woman reached the podium he expected to be busy wiring her brain.

The Chinese UN mission was farther away, up 40th Street in a sleek new office tower built by the Chinese as a statement of their ambition to be seen as the world's *other* superpower. At that distance Burnofsky had to use signal repeaters. Bug Man wished him nothing but static.

It would not be enough for Bug Man to succeed; Burnofsky

must also fail. Then Bug Man would stand unequalled atop the twitcherverse.

The POTUS had moved to a smaller room. The picture swirled dizzyingly as Liz Law's finger swung by her side and then soared up into space to take something.

Bug Man saw a sky of fibers, each like a bridge cable.

A garment.

Was it the president's? Was it time?

But then the fibers zoomed away, off into the distance where they rested on the presidential shoulders.

"Just let me get that, Madam President," Liz Law said.

Bug Man could see the president's face clearly in the serried ranks of nanobot optics. Had he missed his moment? Fear swelled within him. What would the Twins do if—

But no, now the hand was rushing toward the president, touching, smoothing, and *now, now, now!*

Bug Man's army raced across fingertips and leapt. He could see the picture of two dozen nanobots falling, like an insect army platoon jumping out of an airplane.

The ground—those same fibers—rushed up at him.

With twenty-eight tiny impacts Bug Man's forces landed on the lapel of the president of the United States.

TWENTY-FIVE

Ophelia went straight up to the gift-store clerk and asked, "Do you take Mastercard? I mean, I know you have to take Visa, right? Because it's the UN? Visa? Get it?"

While Ophelia distracted the clerk, Wilkes went to the book rack, bent back the pages of several paperbacks, pulled out a lighter, and set fire to as many of them as she could get to before the clerk yelled, "Hey, what are you doing! What are you doing?"

Wilkes smiled, and Ophelia turned, walked quickly to a shelf of stuffed toys and kid's books, and deployed her own lighter.

"Oh my God, what are you doing?" the clerk cried, waving her hands as if frantic fingers would solve the problem. And now the handful of other patrons in the store had to choose between screaming, running, screaming and running, or trying to corral the obviously crazy woman and girl.

Wilkes reached under her skirt, up into the waistband of her tights, and pulled out something that looked exactly like a pistol. In fact it was plastic and therefore had gone through security without a problem. And if the patrons who now raised their hands and said things like, "Whoa, whoa, take it easy," and backpedaled, had taken the time to examine the gun, they'd have spotted it as a fake.

But when a crazy person is waving a gun at you, sometimes you don't search for serial numbers.

Ophelia set fire to a bunch of glossy commemorative picture books, and a nice oily smoke was coiling up to the ceiling.

Alarms began jangling.

Sprinklers came on fitfully, spitting and then spraying water over all the tacky merchandise.

To her credit the clerk did not flee, so Ophelia reluctantly smashed a snow globe against the back of her head, and she and Wilkes pushed around the counter, into the back room, and through the door that led to the storage area. It was a fairly compact space full of flimsy cardboard boxes, most with Chinese as well as English markings.

The obvious back door opened onto a blank, overlit hallway that presumably went on to find a loading dock or freight elevator somewhere.

"That's not it," Ophelia said.

"It has to be here. Has to be," Wilkes said. "Otherwise we're just going to jail for arson."

"And assault," Ophelia added, still holding the snow globe.

They raced around the perimeter of the small storeroom, pushing boxes away, knocking things over. Out in the shop

332

there was yelling, and an authoritative voice saying, "What's going on here?"

"Two crazy women!"

"Where did they go?"

And the sound of a walkie-talkie and the UN guard calling for backup and ordering the loading dock closed down.

"Here!" Ophelia hissed. There was a space not blocked by boxes, where the wall was covered by a suspiciously large poster of former UN chief Ban Ki-moon.

"No one cares that much about Ban Ki-moon," Wilkes agreed. She tore the poster down, revealing a very ordinary door protected by a very unordinary passkey system.

They had been briefed on this. And they'd been told that if all they did was start a fire and draw cops and firemen, that would probably be enough.

"That would be a C-plus," Vincent had told them.

But now with the adrenaline pumping, neither of them wanted to take a C-plus.

Wilkes banged loudly on the door.

Nothing.

She kicked it with her boot, and out in the shop a second guard must have arrived because there was a worried, conspiratorial conversation.

They had seconds left.

Then, a muffled voice through the door. "Who is it?"

Ophelia glanced at Wilkes, who deepened her voice and said, "It's Bug Man. Open up."

"He's English," Ophelia whispered.

"It's fooking Bug Man, open the bloody door, I have to use the loo!" Wilkes yelled.

"Use your swipe card," the muffled voice answered.

"I lost the bloody thing, didn't I? Now open up, you tosser!" She sounded a bit like Rupert Grint. Or at least an American's version of Ron Weasley.

To their mutual amazement, the door opened, revealing a TFD in characteristic polo shirt and chinos.

Wilkes jammed her fake gun under his chin and pushed him back.

Ophelia slammed the door closed behind them. Then, as the TFD was just beginning to notice that the so-called gun didn't feel as though it was made of steel, Ophelia smashed him in the face with the snow globe, which broke and sent fake snow and plastic representations of the UN Building tumbling down his front.

It didn't knock the TFD out and he was recovering fast and realizing he was in trouble and the gun wasn't real and that he had maybe just forfeited his own life, so he came back swinging hard, wild, and half blind.

Wilkes gave him a Doc Marten testicular adjustment, punched him, and Ophelia punched him and it was a melee.

The TFD went down on his back but with his hands around Ophelia's throat, so Wilkes just started kicking him in the side of the head. *Crump! Crump! Crump!* Again and again.

Ophelia was able to pry his hands off her neck, but Wilkes never stopped, not until the side of the man's head was red and bits of bone were showing.

"Enough, enough," Ophelia gasped.

Wilkes buried a boot into him once more, a sort of final "And stay down" move.

Wilkes, Ophelia decided, was a girl with some issues.

Ophelia searched the semiconscious and definitely-not-going-anywhere TFD and came up with a Taser, a walkie-talkie, and a gun.

She handed the gun to Wilkes, who tossed her toy away and said, "I think this one's real." Then, "I think I broke my big toe."

They looked around and saw that they were in a room with nothing but a chair and two more doors. One was easily opened and turned out to be a bathroom. The other was swipe card-protected, and a further search was needed to turn up the guard's card.

"Well," Ophelia said. "We shouldn't have made it this far."

"No, I don't think Vincent expected us to. I think we already moved from C-plus to a solid B."

"I'd say it was lucky, but now we're really in it."

"Distract and disrupt," Wilkes said. "Right?"

Ophelia drew a shaky breath. "If there are twitchers on the other side, they're the target. Shoot them or infest them and get the hell out."

"A little of both?" Wilkes said.

"Bang-bang, jab-jab, run like hell."

"Let's rock it, sister."

Keats was marooned on the beagle's fur. The hand was gone, and Plath's biots with it.

"Don't worry about me," Keats urged. "Go!"

Plath sent her biots racing across the farmland of the palm. A biot leg brushed a sweat blossom and popped it like a water balloon.

"I don't know if it's him. Them."

They were panting in a freezing, filthy alley, Keats holding both her arms. She leaned back against graffiti-scrawled bricks. They breathed the steam of each other's mouth.

"Keep moving. Toward the light. That'll probably take you to the head. The head is the target."

"What about you?"

"I'll find another way," Keats said.

Sirens. Maybe not about them at all. This was New York, after all, and sirens weren't exactly rare.

"We can't go too far, but we can't stay here, either. They'll have Armstrong people on the streets, and cops, too," Keats said, feeling and sounding desperate. "Where can we go?"

"There," Plath said, pointing at the yellow sign of a car rental agency across the street.

"What?"

"Rent a car. Drive around the block."

"Yeah," he said. "Okay. Okay. Wait. We're too young."

"Goddamnit," Plath cried as her biots ran from palm prints to land where the ground, deeply creased with valleys, rose up all around her, warping, buckling. The hand was closing, and her biots were in darkness, running around a circular landscape, going where? Going where?

"There," Keats said. He pointed at a Dumpster. He pulled Plath along with him. He lifted her with hands at the waist, feeling too much contact and at a really inappropriate moment as her behind went so close to his face. He piled in after her. It was dry at least, as most of the tossed-out Chinese food had frozen stiff during the cold night. That would change as their body heat thawed the worst of the garbage. But the smell wasn't as bad as it might be.

Keats pulled the lid over them, and they lay huddled together in the filth.

"Maybe he'll pet the dog again," Plath said.

"Maybe," Keats answered.

They were spooning in garbage. Their biots were a few hundred yards and a universe away.

From the sky came hands. Keats saw the fingers again, reaching down toward the raked forest where the wound was. Fingers. Then, floating down from the sky, a huge tubular opening, like the world's biggest fire hose. Like the water pipe they buried under the street.

An eruption of crystalline goo vomited from the tube and landed in wondrous spirals on the injury.

"They're working on the dog," Keats said. "Now I'm seeing a bandage. Like a white blanket the size of a city block."

"I'm off the hand. Up the arm," Plath reported.

"I want to get to you," Keats said. "I don't want you doing this alone."

"Don't get hurt," Plath said. His arms were around her and she felt his warmth and she was afraid, and she could hardly swallow her throat was so dry. How could it be that she was here, needing him to be with her not just here but there as well, needing him not just in the macro but down in the meat?

Plath's biots raced through a sparse forest of arm hairs. Then beneath a sleeve, a sky made of woven ropes. Was it even the correct arm? Was it one of *them*? Or was she racing up the arm of some minor player, some guard or secretary?

"I'm going to tap the dog's eye," Keats said. And he sent his biot racing across the alien forest's treetops.

"I don't want to lose my mind in a Dumpster, Keats."

"My name's not Keats," he said.

"Don't tell me your name," she whispered.

"I know yours."

"My name is Plath," she said, sounding more determined than she felt.

"I'm passing the bandage. It's like a circus tent! Tape pulling at hairs. It's . . ."

"You think we'd have liked each other if it wasn't like this?" she asked.

"We wouldn't have met," he answered.

The Dumpster top opened. Hearts in their throats.

A McDonald's bag dropped in, and the top closed again.

They heard street sounds, alley sounds. Conversation, shouts and laughs and normality, and none of that helped because they were a million miles away from normal.

"I'm at the head. Shorter hairs," Keats said. "Here's hoping this dog doesn't have fleas or lice or . . . Eyelid. I'm there. Demodex. I hate demodex. These are different, though. Jesus."

Her neck was in his face. It smelled of French fries. And he could not resist the urge to kiss that neck as he raced toward the slow-blinking eyelid and the dark pool of a whiteless eye.

She felt his lips on her neck and sighed and did not resist as she raced at full speed, two biots, two windows open in her head, one seeing the other biot pull ahead, a bug that was somehow her. She was there, there in those creatures even as she shivered from his touch.

"I won't let you go crazy, Keats," she said.

"Too late," he said. "We're already crazy."

She twisted around and kissed him as she recognized the shift from thin, wispy body hair to the chopped, torn stubble of a shaved face.

Was she on the face of the Armstrong Twins?

And if she was, what was she going to do about it?

She kissed Keats, and felt her body respond, and wondered whether she would commit murder.

And suddenly, there it was. A room, dimly lit, and two twitcher stations with two twitchers in place, gloved, reclining, helmeted, with screens hanging, showing nanobot armies on the march.

Half a dozen faces turned to stare at Wilkes and Ophelia. The twitchers didn't notice them at first, but others did, and the reaction was quick but not as quick as Wilkes, who started shooting *BAM! BAM! BAM!*

"Fucking die!" Wilkes shouted, and fired at men and women and screens and walls.

Ophelia ran at the nearest twitcher, a boy or young man, couldn't see his face, but she jammed her hand up under the mask and her two biots leapt onto a pimple like Vesuvius, an angry red mound.

The twitcher turned and ripped off his helmet and a Taser hit Ophelia, dropped her to her knees as a shoe swung hard and knocked her onto her back.

"Ophelia!" Wilkes cried, and fired and fired until the slide on the gun stuck in the open-and-empty position, and then she threw it at the nearest monitor.

Someone very large knocked her back into the wall.

Well, she thought, *that was at least an A-minus.*

Tatiana's fingernail, a vast curve of scaly keratin, touched the bamboo-in-crusty-dirt skin of the president.

"Touchdown," Nijinsky said.

"Go," Vincent said.

They were in the crowd that had gathered at the UN Plaza. A crowd of people who were there in vain hopes of seeing someone important, or of panhandling, or there to shout a slogan and wave a sign.

A large percentage of this particular crowd seemed to be very upset about something going on in Gabon, a country Nijinsky placed vaguely in Africa. In any case they were chanting with great enthusiasm and in a complex, catchy rhythm.

A smaller group was irate about global warming, and a third bunch was in a party mood and evidently about half in the bag. They had come to protest the closing down of nude beaches in France.

Nijinsky had no strong opinion on Gabon and not much interest in global warming, either, but he'd seen a few nude beaches, and given the types of people who liked to take their clothes off on the beach, he thought he might be with the French government on this issue.

The crowd provided anonymity. And twitching proximity to both the Hilton down the street and the UN itself.

The downside was that they'd both had to go through security to stand here, and that meant no weapons. That probably didn't matter too much since their weapons were at this moment launching themselves onto the president's hand.

Two biots each, racing along a very famous arm, zooming through thin hair, high-stepping over dead skin cells. Nijinsky had a sudden vision of being hauled in front of a congressional committee someday to explain just what the hell he thought he was doing scurrying across the presidential flesh.

The NYPD, who managed the crowd, were old hands at demonstrations, and they stood casually at ease, watchful but not paranoid. But both Vincent and Nijinsky assumed this crowd was about half made up of various security people: Secret Service and intelligence services from basically every other nation on Earth that could afford spies. In fact it was entirely possible that there was not a single actual civilian in the crowd.

So caution, Vincent had warned. Don't think we aren't being overheard. Don't think just because the guy standing next to you is wearing a daishiki or flowing robes or a fishnet thong with an anarchist's *A* tattooed on his bare chest he's not actually MI6 or Russian SVR or Mossad.

"I hear sirens," Vincent said.

Nijinsky was taller; he could see over the crowd. Fire engines. A lot of them. And they were definitely turning into the UN.

"Fire," Nijinsky said. He noted Vincent's tight nod. They both had a good idea why fire engines might be rushing toward the UN headquarters.

"They're both tough," Vincent said.

Nijinsky said nothing but wished he believed in someone who listened to prayers. Ophelia was irreplaceable. And Wilkes? She was a mess. Even by BZRK standards, she was a mess. But she was their mess.

"You prefer left or right?" Nijinsky asked Vincent.

"Left."

"What do you think this is? Shoulder?"

Vincent glanced at a woman who was looking at him a little too closely. The woman was chanting along with something or other and her voice was into it, but her eyes were not.

"Yeah. Shoulder," Vincent said. "Jin, take my hand."

"Oh, how I've waited for this moment," Nijinsky snarked. But he understood. He took Vincent's hand and they smiled at each other in a very friendly way that caused the suspicious agent's eyes to slide away to some more likely target.

"Mite," Nijinsky said, gazing into Vincent's eyes.

"I see it. I'm feeling the vertical. Neck."

"Yeah."

A few hundred yards away, four biots might determine the fate of the human race. And here, in the macro, Nijinsky began to realize he needed a bathroom.

More fire engines. It was an all-out five alarm, with ladder trucks and ambulances, and it was possible to feel the tension in the crowd. Something had clearly happened, and the demonstrators and tourists and spies all wondered what the hell it was.

Word started to move through the crowd. *"Fire. Some kind of a fire."*

"Is it terrorism?"

"Just fire trucks so far."

The NYPD were definitely interested, and a police captain talked into his walkie-talkie. Nijinsky saw worry in his eyes. And he could swear he saw the man's lips form the words, "Shots fired."

The ripple of information moved through the cops, who were suddenly no longer taking an easy shift of crowd control and were beginning to realize something bad was happening.

"Jaw," Vincent said.

Vincent's phone lit up with a message. He let Nijinsky read it over his shoulder: *Presumed terrorist incident at UN bookstore.*

So much for presidential speeches at the UN, Nijinsky thought. No way would the Secret Service let the POTUS near the UN Building now. He had no idea what the hell Wilkes and Ophelia had managed to do, but it was something rather more dramatic than merely drawing security to the hidden twitcher room in the UN basement.

He glanced at Vincent and saw a tight-mouthed half smile.

"Ear," Vincent said. "Time to split."

"She could use a little electrolysis," Nijinsky said.

At the best of times Vincent had not much sense of humor, and none now. He did not answer.

Both men aimed their biots up and headed for the presidential eyeballs.

ARTIFACT

Partial text of speech by Grey McLure prepared for delivery at an MIT seminar on the dangers of nanotechnology. His wife's illness forced him to cancel the trip, and McLure never spoke publicly on the subject.

Begin with a square sheet of tofu perhaps eighteen inches on each side. Now carefully lift that fragile, gooey mess up and begin folding it. Soon you have a handful of wrinkled tofu, a sort of slimy ball of the stuff. That is the cerebrum. The part of the brain that makes a human human.

It rests atop a sort of upside-down leek. That's the brain stem. And stuck up underneath the tofu and resting behind the brain stem is the cerebellum. The cerebellum looks a bit like a wad of cooked but sticky spaghetti squished into a clump.

But this map is nothing, not even a bare beginning. It's the equivalent of having a world map that only names continents. You won't find your way around with a map that just says, "Asia."

No, there are countries down there. There are barriers and borders, individual nations called Wernicke or Thalamus or Broca. Hundreds of them, and each has a unique character.

But you still don't know your way around. Your map shows you how to find Mexico and France and Azerbaijan. And that's better than just knowing the continents, but it won't get you to a particular city or house.

The complexity is as great as that of Earth itself. Three pounds of goo stuffed into an elliptical bone cage. Within that goo are arteries pumping oxygen — far more than to any other organ. And massive bundles of nerves running from nose and ears, from fingers and toes, from your stomach and your heart, and above all from your eyes.

Those nerves are a fire hose of data. Millions of databits. All of it pouring into what may be as many as ninety billion synapses. Those nerves are the oceans, the ports, the airspace of the brain. And each synapse is like a one or zero in a binary computer. These are the roads, the streets, the alleyways of our map.

But we haven't begun to see the complexity. Because those billions of synapses generate as many as a quadrillion connections.

And you see now that we have gone from continents to countries to the oceans and rivers and then down to the roads and alleyways and down there, down there if you see the map in its ultimate detail, you see a planet with a quadrillion — a thousand trillion — people.

Imagine a large beach. Huntington Beach or Waikiki.

Imagine the grains of sand on that beach. You may approach a quadrillion grains of sand.

So how do we begin to imagine that we can map out the human brain with sufficient accuracy as to allow manipulation at the physical level?

Because we don't need the quadrillion. Or even the billions. We don't need to see all the detail. The brain itself will find what we need. It will show us synaptic networks.

Memory is elusive because it is spread across so much of the brain. Go back to that sheet of tofu. Stab eight pins into it. Draw lines between them. There's your memory of your mother's face, each pin a piece.

But as you look at the pattern you notice something. All those connections passed through the hippocampus. The hippocampus is the router. Tap the router and you can light up the networks of memory.

It's not much to look at, the hippocampus. They say it looks like a cross between a slug and a seahorse. Just a couple of inches long, one on each side of the brain.

But for wiring the human brain? It's the user interface. It's the betrayer. The Judas of the brain.

It is theoretically possible for nanotechnology to tap the hippocampus to, in effect, "light up" the locations of a specific memory. It might even be possible then for this theoretical nanotechnology to shut down areas of memory.

Or even to augment them, or alter their import.

One could imagine a world in which a nanotechnology robot could run an artificial neural fiber between two different memories, or between a memory and areas of the brain associated with specific emotions.

Of course such a thing would be a criminal misuse of a promising technology, and I think it falls into the category of scare story rather than genuine threat.

TWENTY-SIX

Wilkes and Ophelia lay on the floor beneath billowing smoke drawn in from the gift store, where the fire had spread despite the sprinklers.

They were down, but Ophelia's biots were not out, not yet, they were rushing to find refuge down in the meat of one of the twitchers.

Panic reigned in the room. The two twitchers—the young Asian boy and a pimply white kid with a lot of wavy brown hair—yanked off their helmets, TFDs kept screaming, "Stay down, stay down," although neither of the bruised women were likely to get up.

And now came the shouts of, "Drop your weapons, *now*!" And those were not TFDs, those were UN security, and not the rent-a-cops either, but serious hard guys in body-armor and helmets, armed with assault weapons.

Some part of Ophelia's mind saw what would happen next. The AFGC operation here was blown wide open. There was no way, none, to cover this up. The Armstrongs had made a terrible mistake, and now everything would be exposed.

They couldn't let that happen. Which meant . . .

"They're going to blow the room!" a man's voice cried.

"No!"

The twitchers leapt from their seats; TFDs bolted, shoving them aside. The UN security, believing they were being charged, fired.

Ophelia grabbed Wilkes's collar and dragged her toward the door and the security guys yelled at her to freeze and in one second he was going to squeeze that trigger and—

"They're going to—" Ophelia yelled.

And then the explosion.

It was an incendiary placed in a suitcase. It was detonated remotely by Sugar Lebowski who had seen it all on-screen in her command post on the fifty-eighth floor.

Jindal had come down from the fifty-ninth, feeling more comfortable with security than up on the empty twitcher floor. His face was the color of cigarette ash. He turned horrified eyes on her.

"No alternative," she whispered.

The only way with the whole operation exposed. Close off avenues to exposure. Damage control.

First she'd lost Nijinsky. Now this.

Jesus.

Disaster.

On the monitor she had seen a flash of white followed by nothing. She stood there willing a picture to return, but of course, no, that wasn't happening.

Sugar knew that after the initial explosion there would be choking smoke and a fire that would burn so hot nothing would be left in the room. Not a wire, not a fingerprint, not even the metal in filled teeth. And definitely no nanobots.

She was shaking. Her hands trembled.

No choice. None at all. Not once the fire department and UN security got there, and coming right behind them, the SWAT teams and the FBI and the whole alphabet soup of investigatory agencies. They would have found everything.

Now they would find a few bones and little else.

Which might also be all anyone would find of Sugar Lebowski. Her mouth tasted like vomit. Her heart was hammering away so loud she almost couldn't hear Jindal.

"Are they all dead?" Jindal asked. He sounded like a little kid asking his mommy.

"They're fucking charcoal," Sugar said harshly.

There was a camera mounted openly on the wall of the AFGC control room. Of course she knew the Twins had other cameras as well. Up there, a hundred feet above her, they would be watching. She could feel it.

It was clear to Sugar at that moment that she would be very

lucky to live out the day. Letting Nijinsky escape would have been enough to infuriate the Twins. Yes, she'd been attacked, taken by surprise, and yes, Dietrich should share some of the blame, but they weren't understanding, forgiving people, those two. But that paled to insignificance compared to this.

Was she so valuable to the company, to Charles and Benjamin, that they would have to keep her alive? Would she ever make it home to see her daughter?

Sugar turned to face the camera. "That's just two twitchers," she said. "We still have Bug Man, Burnofsky, One-Up, and Dietrich. One-Up is running late but she's reliable. When she gets to the location with Dietrich, we can repurpose either Kim's or Alfredo's nanobots to him at the hotel location. If you choose, we can also shift One-Up from her current target."

There was of course no answer.

Her insides twisted. She glanced at the link to the hotel location. It showed Dietrich already suiting up as the spare twitcher. She peered past him. The camera angle wasn't good. One-Up's chair was on the other side of a bed that had been pushed out of the way, and light was coming in through the window that blinded the camera a little.

But peering hard she could see that the far chair was still empty. She'd just reassured Twofer that One-Up was reliable. She was a prima donna, but she always showed up. But this was no time for her bullshit.

"Where the hell is One-Up?" Sugar yelled, losing her cool a bit as she considered her own likely demise.

He jumped. Others in the room jumped as well. They were all staring at her with accusing eyes. She was the one who had ordered the bomb.

"She . . ." Jindal began. "You know she always has to have a Starbucks. She went out and . . ." He shrugged and looked around helplessly. "It's a thing with her. It's a superstition. You know that! Half these twitchers have OCD. They're all nuts."

Sugar's phone rang. It made her jump. It had to be them. It had to be the Twins.

Sick with dread she looked at the number. It was not a recognized number. She pushed the answer button and held it to her ear.

"Who is this?" she asked.

"It's me, it's me, I've been trying to get through!"

One-Up.

"Slow down," Sugar said with all the authority she could manage. "Explain yourself."

Sugar listened. And she glanced at the camera and imagined those two freak faces, imagined those three awful eyes boring into her.

She would never survive this day. Sugar saw her house. Her daughter. Her husband, whom she didn't like very much, but he was good cover.

The Twins were going to have her killed. By one of her own men. She glanced quickly at the angry faces around her. *One of you*, she thought. *One of you.*

She wished she could cry. But if there was any way out of this, it was by dealing with this new threat.

There was an opportunity here, a desperate opportunity.

She turned away from the monitor to her deputy, a beefy but smart former cop named Paul Johntz.

"Paul. We've been penetrated. There are at least two BZRK twitchers. They'll have to stay within range of the building to run biots. Get every piece of muscle we have and follow me."

"I'm tapping optics," Plath said. She'd been shown how to do it. But only once. She sank the probe. It was a rigid little spear on the end of a piece of nanowire. She had to use her mantis arm to do it, and it was awkward. Like throwing a harpoon with a lobster claw.

The probe sank and . . . And nothing.

She reeled it back in. Stabbed it deeper into the nerve. And suddenly, "Ahh!" she said.

"Shh," Keats said. "People."

There was movement near the Dumpster. Plath fell silent. A new visual had opened up. So strange. Like a window inside a window. Like picture in picture on a TV, except that this picture was black-and-white and grainy, as if the pixels were all an inch on a side.

Then she remembered: the raw feed from the optic nerve was upside down. She reversed it mentally, as well as she could anyway, but still it made no sense.

She drew back the probe. Twice more she stabbed, and then she had it. Not clear, still grainy, but wider in scope, less like she was looking at the world through a straw.

She was seeing an eye. The very eye she was looking through.

She was looking in a mirror, that was it.

Her stomach was tied in knots. Yeah, it was a mirror, or the high-tech equivalent of a mirror, and now the eye swept across the mirror, no longer looking at itself. Looking at a face.

A face like no other.

"It's them," she whispered voicelessly.

Keats held her close.

Bug Man and Burnofsky got the same message on their monitors at the same time.

One-Up missing. Kim and Alfredo dead. UN locked down.

You must take your targets.

CBA

CBA. Charles and Benjamin Armstrong.

Bug Man and Burnofsky.

Both had reached their targets.

Two armies of nanobots were in place. One on the Chinese leader, one on the American.

Kim's nanobots were in place on the Indian, Chauksey. Alfredo's little army was still two jumps away from Prime Minister Hayashi. Those forces were immobilized for now, until they could be repurposed to a new twitcher. That would take time.

Dietrich wasn't good enough to reach the Japanese in Bug Man's estimation. But assuming One-Up was on track, they might still take the American, the Brit, and the Chinese.

Bug Man took a gamble. Time to make it clear he was more than just a twitcher. His game could extend into the macro. He keyed a message to Twofer.

Suggest: take Dietrich off Jap give him Indian.

No reply. But that was okay.

Victory was still within reach. The unknown was whether any of the targets were defended. In a fight One-Up could handle herself, and so could Burnofsky.

Even if only Bug Man and Burnofsky prevailed, the world's two greatest powers would be subtly but inexorably bent to serving the wills of Charles and Benjamin Armstrong. Whatever had happened or was still to happen to the others, it wouldn't matter, not if he and Burnofsky succeeded.

Of course in a perfect world, Bug Man thought, *in a* perfect *world, Burnofsky and all the rest would fail and only the Bug Man would triumph.*

But that was an ambitious dream.

Time to begin the wiring of the president of the United States.

He laughed out loud at the thought.

The Twins would kiss his ass this time. They would bow down before him.

Then, Bug Man saw.

Two biots were rushing along in his wake, racing up behind him as his army pelted down along the optic chiasm.

Oh, yes.

Oh, hell yes.

Is that you, Vincent? Please, God, let it be.

No macro interference to mess anything up this time. The ultimate battle for the ultimate prize.

"I hope you're watching, Mr Charles and Mr Benjamin. Because this . . . will be epic."

The cops were beginning to move the crowd away from the UN Plaza. There was a very serious mood in the air. Something very bad had happened, and New York's finest were not in the mood to take backtalk from anyone.

Helicopters were overhead. Sirens were still wailing as more and more security flooded the blocks around the UN.

One thing was sure: Wilkes and Ophelia had provided one hell of a diversion.

Then, Vincent saw. He was all the way down in the optic chiasm when he spotted the nanobot army racing away.

"Bug Man," Vincent said.

"I'm on my way!" Nijinsky replied.

Bug Man's nanobots stopped moving away. Six platoons turned, one then the next, to face the biots. The exploding head logo was faint but unmistakable in the phosphorescent light.

Vincent smiled at Nijinsky. A real smile.

"It'll be over by the time you get there, Jin."

The Twins were watching the windows open on their table.

They saw the blank screen that had been focused on the UN station. It was an ominous rectangle of static now.

They saw the scene outside the UN Building, a carnival of flashing lights as every fire or police vehicle in New York gathered.

They saw Dietrich acquiring control of Kim's nanobots, already in position, hidden for the moment in the Indian prime minister's dark hair. That had been a good suggestion from Bug Man, although of course Benjamin had thought of it first.

They puzzled at the sight of One-Up, looking battered and bloody, being hustled into the chair beyond Dietrich. They didn't have the audio on, but they could see her rage. She kicked a trash can as she passed and punched the air. Furious.

They also saw what Burnofsky saw inside the brain of the Chinese premier.

And what Bug Man saw as he turned to face his nemesis.

The rods and cones in their retinas fired tiny electrical signals down the optic nerve.

At the very back of their brains their visual cortex translated those signals into images.

But neither Charles's eye, nor Benjamin's eye, nor the eye that stared out from between them, could turn inward and see the two biots that had at last reached the hippocampus.

Neither of them could know that Sadie McLure, who now called herself Plath, lay curled in a young man's arms, contemplating their murder.

The TFDs had a twelve-block area in which the BZRK twitchers might be hiding. Each block packed with tall buildings, with hundreds of offices each. And the fact was that even that cordon was an estimate, a best guess. No one knew the exact limits of a BZRK twitcher's reach. But as a practical matter, if they extended the cordon any farther it would have to include Grand Central, not to mention the subway stations.

At ground level there were something like a dozen coffee shops, twice that many restaurants, fast-food joints, pizza parlors, copy shops, dry cleaners, office-supply stores, shoe shops, tourist-junk shops, florists . . .

It was an impossible search. Sugar Lebowski had eleven guys. But she had the advantage of knowing whom she was looking for: Sadie McLure. And some guy, but the smart play was to look for Sadie.

Cars. Parking lots. Driving around in a cab. Inside about a thousand offices. They could be any of a million places, and she had to find them. With eleven guys.

Two street people were arguing loudly over who had rights to the cans in a bin. Sugar went up to them and said, "Shut up, assholes." She held up a hundred-dollar bill, and that got their attention even through the haze of booze and schizophrenia. "A hundred bucks if you find me this girl." She had a picture on her phone and gave them a five-second look. "Find her in the next ten minutes and you can drink for a week. Go!"

To her men she said, "One-Up said they were sitting in a coffee shop, so they are probably still at street level. If they had an office, they'd have been there to begin with. So get every hobo, bike messenger, street vendor, cabdriver, doorman, and building security guy. Offer them a hundred. If that doesn't work, offer them a thousand. Get me that little bitch."

The explosion threw Wilkes clear into the shop. She slammed into a stand of T-shirts. She was burning, tights curling, hair crisping, blouse smoking. She slapped at the fire on her legs and yelled, "Ophelia! Ophelia!"

There were bodies everywhere, some moving, some not. Choking, oily black smoke filled the shop, a thousand times deeper and more intense than what had resulted from her own little exercise in pyromania. The smoke was like a falling ceiling, pressing down, squeezing the air into eighteen inches near the floor.

Wilkes lay flat, rolled over to put out any remaining flames on her body and crawled like a demodex, worming her way across the floor. She swarmed over debris, over bodies, yelling, "Ophelia!" with less and less breath. The choking started then, the coughing that ripped at her throat and sent her into chest-wracking spasms.

She found two stumps burning like torches and knew, just knew, it was Ophelia. Her feet were gone. Her legs were the wicks of candles.

Wilkes gagged on smoke, vomited, wept, grabbed at UN souvenir T-shirts and pressed them over burning flesh that smelled like gyro meat on a spit.

She crawled to Ophelia's head. Ophelia's eyes were open, wide, indifferent to the smoke, staring in horror. That look, those staring, terrified eyes were worse than the burning limbs.

"They're dead!" Ophelia wailed. The smoke pressed down

so low over her face that the exhalation of her horror formed spirals and eddies.

"Get . . ." Wilkes said, but that was the limit of her powers of speech, her throat was swelling, her stomach was retching again.

"Dead! Gods, no. No! Nooooo!" Ophelia screamed.

Wilkes knew she wasn't talking about the people who had just died.

"Ah! Hah-hah!" Ophelia raved. She made a barking sound. Like a seal. And then she started thrashing, flailing her arms, kicking her mutilated legs, screaming and screaming until finally the smoke choked her down to guttural, coughing grunts.

Wilkes gave up then.

Enough.

A terrible sadness swallowed her up. Goddamn it, Ophelia deserved to live.

Then through slitted, weeping eyes she saw the toes of boots, black-and-yellow rubber legs, and down through the smoke like a demon god came alien bug eyes and a black helmet with a red shield and the blessed initials FDNY.

TWENTY-SEVEN

Keats had heard Vincent loud and clear on the stupidity, the futility, of any decision just to send biots running around blindly.

Biots didn't have the speed or the senses to go careening off on their own. There had to be a pathway.

He was on a dog's nose. In a room that almost certainly held the Armstrong Twins, but others as well. He couldn't see anything but shapes as huge and as distant as the clouds.

He could hear vague voices like distant thunder.

That was what he had to go on. Clouds and thunder as he rode around on a dog's nose that looked like some alien, dry lake bed of parched mud.

No way to do anything useful. No way to save himself or Sadie.

And then he spotted the flea. That clanking, armored, Transformer-eyed monster. No time to think.

He raced his two biots toward it, tearing back along the dog's snout, full out, as fast as they would run. The flea didn't notice him. The flea didn't give a damn. The flea had no predators in its life aside from some distant dog collar. It was intent on finding the red-red kroovy, as they said in *Clockwork Orange*: blood. Only blood. And the biots weren't a source.

He ran up to the side of the flea as it tapped a slow spurt of corpuscles, sucking them up into its mouthparts, and the biots leapt.

They hit spiky legs and clambered madly up, their own legs thrashing, up over the powerful, spring-loaded haunches and *Slam!*

The flea's legs fired, and the jolt was so powerful it snapped one of K1's legs and impaled K2 on a flea spike.

Keats cried out in pain, feeling it almost as much as his biots did.

"What is it?" Plath whispered.

"Muscle twinge," Keats lied, and, oh God, he could barely manage that, because the power of that jump was staggering and impossible. The flea accelerated like a bullet from a gun. It tumbled as it flew, somersaulted at jet-fighter speeds, but was almost instantly slowed by the pressure of air rushing past like a tornado. It landed by falling and twisting through a forest of trees to hit rough dog skin again.

The whole jump had lasted maybe a second. It was almost impossible to process.

Keats knew he had to get off the dog. He also knew the flea

would jump toward the smell of more blood. Unless a way could be found to cause it to jump randomly, in a flight response.

The key had to be the spiky sensory hairs.

Each biot grabbed two of the spikes and yanked.

A second explosion and the flea hurtled upward, twisting and tumbling, and this time when it landed it didn't kneel to feed. It trembled slightly. It was bothered by the stimulation of the hairs.

Keats could feel it quivering, already gathering strength for another jump.

He yanked madly at the hairs, and this time the flea shot upward as before, but when it came down, it missed its grip. The flea rolled down the side of the dog like a tiny boulder.

Spinning, biots hitting hair, air, hair, air, hair, air—until suddenly it was all air and the flea was falling free of the dog.

The flea hit the floor and bounced, not dead but slow to right itself. Keats jumped his biots clear of the tiny monster and landed on an endless plain of Swiss cheese that seemed trapped beneath two feet of rippling, translucent glass.

It took Keats a while to decide he was on a wood floor. The wood itself—beneath the transparent protective coating—was like a honeycomb, with millions of smaller, roughly rectangular holes, and here and there, larger holes like cut arteries. At the nano it was a desecrated graveyard—a living thing that had been sawed open and imprisoned beneath polyurethane. It was impossible not to believe the glassy sheet would open and he would fall into those holes.

The flea was upright behind him. A vast shape was moving away, a wobbly mountain. The dog probably. Maybe.

Plath was talking to him. In the macro. For a moment he'd lost contact. He'd forgotten the girl in his arms.

"People are coming," she whispered.

And suddenly there were voices right next to the Dumpster, hands touching, fumbling at the lid and a hard voice saying, "We find her we split it, right?"

And Keats knew right then, knew what he had to do. "Don't argue," he said, and rolled over swiftly atop Plath, pushed her rudely down into the trash, bucked back upward, rising like some vengeful swamp creature, just as the cover on the Dumpster flew back.

"Aaarrrrggh!" Keats yelled.

Two startled faces, bearded, filthy, gaped as Keats kicked off, cleared the edge of the Dumpster and fell more than jumped onto the two men. The three of them went down hard, and Keats was the first up.

He panted, bent over, winded by the sudden violent movement. The two street people stared in amazement.

"Looking for me?" Keats gasped.

"It's the bitch we want," one said.

"She's gone," Keats said.

"The woman said there were two of them," the first street person reasoned. The second one was apparently not talkative. "Get him!"

Keats set off at a run. The day had not come when he couldn't outrun a pair of unhealthy old dudes in ill-fitting sneakers.

He tore down the alley toward the street. One of his pursuers, the talky one, was pushing a shopping cart piled high with cans and assorted junk.

No problem staying ahead of them, he just had to make sure they didn't give up and go back to check the Dumpster. At the same time he was scanning the honeycomb floor and spotting something absurdly tall, a vast, dark shape on the horizon. It reached up to heaven.

Keats burst out onto the street as both biots raced toward that tall distant object. As soon as he hit the sidewalk he knew he had made a mistake. Two men in khaki slacks and down jackets spotted him, spun, and took off in pursuit. They were a hell of a lot healthier than the street people.

Keats ran on two surfaces. On concrete blocked by bodies. On a sheet of ripply glass over honeycomb. He felt like he was flying. He felt like he was racing against himself. He covered meters and micrometers, saw skyscrapers ahead, one measured in hundreds of feet, and one likely no more than three.

He plowed straight through two guys walking side by side

and looking down at their BlackBerries. He kicked through an A-frame sign advertising a Chinese menu. He could hear his pursuers panting into headsets, "It's the male, it's the male! Heading west down Forty-third!"

And that was not good because it meant there were others playing the game of Catch-a-Keats.

A body to his right, crossing the street, practically hurdling the cabs as they blurred past.

It's the test, he realized with a shock of recognition. Dr Pound's test. Only he had no weapons.

Wham!

Keats went flying into a wall, bounced, hit the ground face first, skinned hands and knees and cheek and they buried him in bodies, knees in his back, arms twisting behind him, plastic handcuff ties cinching his wrists.

An SUV screeched to a halt, bumped up onto the curb, its wheel inches from his face.

"Let me go! Let me go! Get off me! Police! Police!" Keats yelled, but then a rubber ball was forced into his mouth. Duct tape went swiftly around his head locking the gag in place.

They picked him up and threw him roughly into the backseat.

The crowd at the UN was going to be run through security, that much was definite. What looked like a major terrorist strike at the UN? That meant everyone on the plaza was getting ID'd and eyeballed by suspicious cops. Already Nijinsky was hearing people mutter about 9/11.

Mounted police were moving in, ready to chase down any runners. The horses *clip-clopped* and snorted. Tall-seated men with visored eyes looked down at Vincent and Nijinsky and the various demonstrators—and security people pretending to be demonstrators.

That wasn't good. Both BZRKers had fake IDs—good ones that would pass casual scrutiny and even make it through a superficial computer check. But a deeper check would reveal them as fake. And that would be trouble.

But nothing like the trouble down in the nano.

The president of the United States, Helen Falkenhym Morales, was a battleground.

The Secret Service, upon learning of the situation at the UN, had moved her out of the reception into a safe room at the same hotel. An entire wing of rooms, as well as the rooms below and above the president's safe place had been emptied.

Plainclothes agents with pistols were joined by armored agents with submachine guns, nerves all a-twang, and God help the chambermaid who wandered inadvertently into that perimeter.

But it didn't matter.

The cluster of nanobots, platooned, was right ahead. Bug Man had sent his spinners scurrying away to relative safety. If he lost his spinners he lost, period.

"Banzai," Vincent said, just loudly enough for Nijinsky to hear, and sent his biots rushing into the nanobots.

The nanobots were spreading to left and right in the vast chamber of the chiasm. The fluid environment slowed V3 and V4 a little, like running into a headwind. But it also meant Bug Man couldn't drop wheels and ramp up his speed, which left the biots the faster of the two.

Bug Man would try a pincer. He would pull back the center and send the wings around like the claws of a crab.

Vincent wasn't having it. He charged until he was at the midpoint between the scurrying wings, noted that the nanobots on the right were slipping and sliding, gaining weak purchase on tight, slick terrain, and pivoted toward them.

V3 and V4 each stabbed a nanobot in the com-stack. That was better than ripping them open: it was faster and it would leave Bug Man wasting time trying to restore visuals.

The biots clambered right up over the two blinded nanobots and sat atop them. The biots were longer, so their tails and heads hung off fore and aft, which meant two useful things: Bug Man would have to climb up over the legs of his own blind nanobots to get at Vincent—a notoriously difficult move, especially if you were platooning.

And by climbing atop the useless nanobots, Bug Man's visuals would be confused. Nanobot sensors would have a hard time making sense of the tall pile of arms and torsos.

But that wasn't slowing the Bug Man down. He had a move of his own. Two nanobots ran up and stopped just out of reach of Vincent's stabbing and cutting arms. Then two other nanobots used the stopped nanobots the way a gymnast uses a mini-trampoline to vault.

Two nanobots came soaring down at V3 and V4, lances out.

"Heh," Vincent said to no one. "Nice."

The police had formed a cordon and were now passing people through a small gap. Get your IDs out. Get your stories straight.

Sure enough, three supposed demonstrators flashed what had to be NYPD or FBI IDs and were passed through to stand with the officers and point out the suspicious.

One of them pointed at Nijinsky.

"Shit," Nijinsky said.

Vincent collapsed the legs on the left of V3 and the right of V4 and rolled the biots over the legs of the blinded nanobots.

Bug Man's aerial attack missed, and he slammed into the blinded nanobots, stabbing his own creatures.

A net wash: two of Bug Man's boys dead, but time wasted and time was not his friend.

Time to swim.

He pushed off into the transparent fluid. Biots were not good swimmers—their legs could motor away, but the result was more of a churn than a swim. Twisting the claws with each stroke could give it some additional forward momentum, but not much. The only comfort was that nanobots were even worse.

The biots floated just above the massed nanobot army.

"You look familiar," a cop said to Nijinsky. And just in time Nijinsky's fingers slid from the fake passport in his inner coat pocket to the real one.

"Well, I do some modeling," he told the officer, a short, powerfully built woman.

The male officers scowled.

"Where have I seen you?"

Nijinsky shrugged. His biots were racing to catch up to the battle raging deep within the president's brain. He was not Vincent—experiences on multiple levels at once tended to make him a bit slow and distracted.

"You mean . . ." he said, as his biots dodged around a sticky cluster of macrophages.

"Like what do you model?" she asked, getting less friendly by the second. She flipped open his passport while Vincent waited with seeming calm and a slightly puzzled expression behind him. "Simple question, Mr Hwang. What do you model?"

"Oh. Well, I guess most people recognize me from the Mountain Dew billboards."

The cop shook her head. "No, that's not it."

"Armani underwear?"

She crinkled her forehead at him, comparing face to photo. "Were you ever in a movie?"

Yes, he had been in a movie. But he wasn't happy about it. And the cop had been playing with him because she was grinning, and he could see that she was anticipating enlightening her fellow officers.

"Yes, Officer," he said, "I—"

"It's sergeant," she corrected, and pointed at the stripes on her sleeve.

"Sergeant," he corrected tersely. "I was in the last *Saw* movie."

"What happened to you in that movie?" Now the other cops were grinning, knowing there was a funny coming.

Nijinsky sighed. "I was castrated by a chain saw."

"Ouch," one of the men said.

"Must have been after you did the underwear ad, huh?" the woman asked, enjoying the moment immensely, although to her credit she avoided guffawing.

"I'm so glad I can be comic relief. Sergeant," Nijinsky said as his biots dug through the meninges of the president and pushed their way into the brain itself.

"Did you see anything suspicious, Mr Hwang?"

He shrugged. "There were a bunch of sirens, we looked around, and someone said there was a fire."

"And why did you come to the UN today?"

Time to take a chance on getting Vincent out with him. "I'm actually on a date. My friend here," he indicated Vincent, "is a big fan of President Morales. I told him we wouldn't be able to see anything. But . . ." Nijinsky shrugged.

Vincent carefully led a floating nanobot and fired the fléchette gun this biot carried. The pellets were slowed instantly, but with extraordinary luck they might jam a joint on the nanobot.

The cops checked Vincent's ID and asked him the same question, but then the sergeant said, "Go on, Mr Hwang. You've suffered enough."

"Ouch," a second officer said.

Vincent sliced a badly positioned nanobot open and grinned, as though sharing Nijinsky's discomfort.

TWENTY-EIGHT

Plath lay in the garbage.

And she walked through the deep folds of a human brain. It was a long trek to the hippocampus. It was buried deep in the crumpled tofu. Wilkes had taught her the way, the long way down and under, to find the brain stem, that stalk a hundred times as thick as the largest sequoia.

"Then just go north," Wilkes had said.

"North?"

"Up."

"How do you tell which way is up?"

"Blow a bubble, see which direction it floats," Wilkes had said, then she had added, "Of course, biots can't blow bubbles."

Then Wilkes had relented. "If it seems like the stem is getting smaller, you're going south. If you run into spaghetti the size of a subway train, you're heading north."

Plath had found the cerebellum, the spaghetti bowl. She'd pressed on beneath, lost but maybe not, going in the right direction or not. Someday maybe to emerge. Or not, and if not then to leave her own sanity down here, down in the meat.

Maybe Keats had escaped. Surely. Maybe he was free, but they might have him. She wished she was still tapped into the eye so she could see if Keats was suddenly dragged before the Armstrong Twins. And because then she would be within reach of light and air and escape.

Was there something unique about the brain upon which Plath's biots walked?

This was a brain that had ordered kidnappings, beatings, and murders.

This was the brain that had turned a silly cult into a tool for recruiting an army.

This was the brain that dared to plot a new course for evolution itself. That desired the end of all human freedom. That might by action, or by error, unleash upon the world the catastrophe of self-replicating nanobots.

This brain, those firing neurons, those crackling synapses, this mass of pink cells floating in organic soup, had ambitions that dwarfed those of history's great monsters.

This brain had murdered her family.

And yet, to look at it, down here, it was no different than Keats's brain. No different than her own.

Where in this organ was the evil?

That was what needed to be killed, Plath knew.

And she knew that, at the instant she decided that she had to change this brain, had to deprive it of its free will, her own brain would give no outward sign of having set out on a course of deliberate destruction.

Was this, at last, the goal? Was she on the hippocampus? By the light of the biots' dim phosphorescing organs it looked like Keats's. It matched the memories of maps in her own brain.

There was no time for a careful, cautious rewiring. Not even time to ensure that she was in the right place.

There was only time for mayhem.

Each of Plath's biots began to extrude wire. She attached one end to a slightly protruding thumb of neurons and raced off to attach the other end . . . well, wherever she happened to.

Charles and Benjamin Armstrong watched with avid, fanatical attention as the battle within the president raged.

It seemed Bug Man had lost three nanobots.

It also seemed one of Vincent's biots had lost two legs on one side.

It was all here, right here, right now, right before their eyes. If Bug Man succeeded, then victory was theirs, despite everything. The deaths of Kim and Alfredo would mean nothing.

There had been delay as Dietrich marshaled Kim's biots. The eyebrow of the Indian prime minister, Madhuri Chauksey, filled the monitor as Dietrich sent his nanobots toward an eyelid entry.

"If we get Morales, Ts'ai, Chauksey, Bowen . . ." Benjamin said through gritted teeth.

"Despite it all, we are only down by the Japanese."

"The British . . ."

"Watch. One-Up is very good, you know. She lacks discipline, but she plays the game well."

One hand and then the other would tap the menu bars. One screen and then another would open, close, shift, focus, pull back. The Twins had their own game, and this was it: the assimilation of data from a flurry of inputs.

"If we get the president . . ."

"All we really need," Benjamin reassured his brother. "Morales. If we take her alone, we have victory."

"We'll take them all," Charles declaimed loudly.

On one screen, biots churned through brain as a dozen nanobots swam lazily toward them. It had a slow-motion, balletic feel. Pellets were fired but went harmlessly past. Beam weapons would be useless.

Suddenly there was a full-face view of one of the biots. Eerie, semi-human brown eyes seemed to be looking at them. Vincent's eyes. As if he could see them watching him.

The twins sat back fractionally.

And for some reason Benjamin said, "Arabella."

"What?"

"The . . . that was the name of the horse. Grandfather's mare."

Charles glanced at him, curious, waiting for the significance of this remark. But Benjamin's eye seemed to be looking at things not present.

The stress of excitement, Charles thought.

Vincent's biot grappled with a nanobot. Stabbed at the nanobot's optics but missed. A second nanobot tried to latch on but lost its grip and floated away minus a leg.

Charles shot a glance at Burnofsky's screen.

He had reached the brain of the Chinese leader. His nanobots, all in neatly ordered ranks, were tearing along, well on their way to begin the slow, cautious wiring of the second most powerful leader on Earth.

And One-Up? Bless the girl, she had recovered quickly from whatever had so enraged her earlier.

"Hah-hah!" Charles exulted.

"They tried to make us read *Tale of Two Cities*. Remember?"

"What has that to do with this?" Charles demanded, frustrated. He'd only ever had one person to celebrate victory with, and his brother seemed indifferent and distracted.

"What?" Benjamin asked.

"*Tale of Two Cities*?"

"What about it?" Benjamin demanded. "Incontinence. It's spelled e-n-c-e. Like 'influence'. Not like 'ambulance'."

Charles stared at the mirror monitor, at the reflection of his brother's eye. And suddenly Hardy was rushing toward them, a man who never rushed, whom the Twins would have thought lacked the capacity to rush.

"Sirs!" Hardy said, but already the cause of the interruption was clear. The Twins twisted their body to see Sugar Lebowski and four of her men carrying the squirming, kicking, gagged body of a boy.

They threw the body onto the Oriental carpet.

"What the hell?" Charles bellowed. No one entered the Tulip without a specific invitation. They might have been indisposed! They might have been unprepared!

It was outrageous. No: sacrilegious.

But clearly that was not at the top of Sugar Lebowski's mind at the moment. The Twins had seen Sugar furious, scared, sarcastic. They'd watched her cook with her daughter, shave her armpits, and make love to her husband. But they had never seen anything like the look of disordered panic on her face.

Sugar patted her disordered hair into place. She was red in the face, her newly made lazy eye staring at the bridge of her nose. She was panting.

Scared.

Of them, of Charles and Benjamin.

"What is this?" Benjamin demanded, furious.

The dog came waddling over to investigate the boy.

"There's been a . . . a . . . a breach," Sugar managed to get out.

"A what?" Charles snarled even as he watched a killed, split-open nanobot twisting slowly inside the president's brain.

Sugar gathered her wits, took a steadying breath, and said, "One-Up was in an altercation at a coffee shop. The one across the street. She spotted what she believed were two BZRK twitchers. They attacked her and escaped."

"That's why she was late?" Charles demanded. "I thought it was because of traffic disruptions caused by the UN debacle."

"No, sir. But she had a hard time getting through because the UN matter flooded the local cell-phone service. As you saw, I was busy coping with the UN situation. As soon as One-Up got through to me I—"

"I'm sad," Benjamin said. "I wanted to ride Arabella."

That stalled conversation for several seconds.

"We believe one of the two was Sadie McLure," Sugar said. "This is the other one." She kicked Keats's leg but without much conviction.

Charles tried to stand, but Benjamin lagged behind and the effort failed. Then he stood, too, but now Charles was off-balance.

This was something that never happened to them. Not since they were children.

"What the hell is the matter with you?" Charles demanded sharply.

"Remember the Morgenstein twins?" Benjamin asked.

Something like a look of panic crossed Charles's face. The twins had long since learned to move in synch. This kind of disconnect was humiliating. And Benjamin's distraction was nothing short of bizarre.

The slow-motion battle inside the president's brain had turned into vicious three-on-one combat as nanobots ripped at a wounded biot. Pieces of the biot were coming loose—legs, bits of body, twirling slowly away, joined by shreds of cut-up nanobot.

Charles stared at Sugar Lebowski. "You let . . . Are you suggesting . . ." Charles's face could grow red without having the same effect on Benjamin. But it meant the heart they shared beating harder and faster, and this in itself caused Benjamin's eyes to grow wide with confusion.

"They may be here," Sugar said in a ragged half whisper. "I mean, *right* here."

To which Benjamin said, "Remember the GI Joes we got for Christmas?"

The wire was formed by spinnerets derived from spider DNA. A cluster of tiny retractable spigots extruded strands of fiber that then were twisted into cable.

Of course the result was not spider silk but a more complex structure that adhered like silk but conducted the minute electrical charges of the brain along a superconducting element.

The wire could be simply stuck to the surface of a brain structure, or it could be pinned. Pinning was just what it sounded like—a pin (a biot could carry a dozen) with numerous barbs was stabbed into the brain matter like a piton holding a climbing rope. Each pin would contact a different neuron or cluster of neurons.

In a careful, cautious wiring each pin would then be sampled to get an idea of what memory or function was involved.

Plath didn't have time for that. No time to sample, no time to refer to brain maps or to pass the data through computer analysis.

She had time only to stab and rappel with the wire and stab again. She had planted fourteen pins and strung seven wires so far.

She had scattered her transponders. And she had also strung some random surface wire. There was no way to know what effect it was having, if any, because it was exactly what you didn't do if you wanted the subject to be unaware of what was happening. There was no subtlety or art involved. This wasn't wiring as Vincent or Bug Man might do it: this was amateur work. Panicked, terrified amateur work. Her biots were racing without a clue or a plan.

P1 stabbed a pin deep and lit up all barbs. It attached wire and scampered away as fast as its spinnerets could produce wire. Stopped and stabbed again.

And then it occurred to her: Why just A to B lines? Why not keep the wire running from pin to pin to pin? Like a cat's cradle.

So now, from her fragrant Dumpster hiding place, she stabbed and crisscrossed wire, with both biots nearly drained of fluid. Soon she would have to stop and wait for the silk glands to reload.

But for now she ran and leapt and stabbed and listened to the sounds of running feet in the alleyway and shouted voices as far too many people searched for her.

Vincent said, "V4 is in bad shape."

"I'm almost there, Vincent, pull back if you can." Nijinsky was hustling them down the street, putting distance between them and the security magnet of the UN.

"Later they'll remember us," Vincent said. "You need to look to your macro security, Jin. They'll find you."

"Goddamnit, Vincent, focus on keeping your biots alive."

Vincent shuddered. Nijinsky saw it, a sort of spasm that twisted the impassive features into a human expression of fear.

Nijinsky was sick inside. His biots were running so fast he was in danger of getting lost. His light organs couldn't glow far enough ahead. It was like driving at a hundred miles an hour on a dark, back-country road with dim headlights.

Vincent stopped moving.

"Oh, Jesus Christ!" Vincent cried. "Oh, oh, oh."

The hollowed-out look in Vincent's face told Nijinsky all he needed to know.

"No, no, no," Nijinsky cried, and put his arms protectively around Vincent as Vincent's eyes filled with tears and he began a low, soft moaning.

TWENTY-NINE

"Yeah, fuck you! Fuck you! Fuck you!" Bug Man cried.

The dead biot—so very dead, split into two barely connected pieces, dead, and floating legless, dead, through the fluid—was a miracle.

He had lost half his force doing it, and the chiasmic chamber was dotted with legs and sensors and wheels and unidentifiable pieces of circuit and metal skin. The Bug Man logo floated by one of his screens, but none of that a mattered: he had killed one of Vincent's biots.

It froze him for a moment.

No one had ever killed one of Vincent's boys.

No one! Only him. Only Bug Man.

"Oh, fuck yeah."

He could take his time now, minimize risk, because unless Vincent was Clark Kent, he was sucking wind right now and more distracted than he had ever been before.

Bug Man quickly took stock. He had eleven active fighters. All his spinners were safe.

Eleven to one, and the twitcher, the mighty Vincent, was somewhere gasping and wheezing like he'd been gutshot.

Vincent's remaining biot had managed to propel itself to the upper surface. It was hanging from a neuron bundle, staring down at the eleven nanobots that now rose slowly through the goo.

"I'll be gentle, bitch!" Bug Man exulted. "Hah-hah!"

He would form a perimeter on the surface first. Keep four of his nanobots floating, just in case Vincent launched off again.

He had him surrounded.

Hell yes, he had Vincent surrounded. And Vincent's biot seemed almost helpless. It stared with its insect eyes and with its human eyes, and it did nothing, not a damned thing, as Bug Man's nanobots closed the ring.

Keats's biots tore across the cellular floor toward something towering and dark.

As it happened he was facedown now on that very floor, though to him it was smoothly polished wood—very, very different in the macro than what he saw in the nano.

In fact he was bleeding on that floor. Blood flowed from his nose and formed a pool that oozed around his cheek and the side of his mouth. Each time he breathed out through his mouth a red bubble formed. He saw a reflection of his eye in the dark pool. The eye looked scared.

"My brother is . . . he's not feeling well," Charles said.

Keats could not see his biots, of course. But he looked in every direction, trying to match up what he saw with his eyes and what he saw in his brain.

Nothing.

Well, not nothing exactly. He saw three legs beneath the desk. Three legs wearing identical shoes. One left, one right, one . . . neither. The leg in the middle was thinner, but it wore not only the identical shoe in a smaller size but an identical sock and identical trouser leg.

He couldn't see anything above the knee. And he doubted that he wanted to.

"Egg scramble, bamble!" Benjamin yelped suddenly. "What . . . what did I just do?"

Plath's biots were somewhere in Benjamin's brain, that much was instantly clear to Keats. And in a second or two the Twins would realize what had happened. A few seconds after that they would begin to torture him to find out where Plath was.

Or maybe kill him, if they concluded he was the twitcher.

And they would bring in their own twitcher with nanobots to go in after Plath's biots.

He had to get to her. Had to. But his biots were racing toward what might be a table leg for all he knew.

More men were coming in now. He could hear them in the

macro. And far more important, he could feel the vibration in the nano. The vibrations. Coming from his right, from the door.

Which meant . . . which meant the biots were moving toward the Twins. Or toward Sugar. Or toward any of the forest of legs that now rushed past him, over him, security guys, guns in hand.

"We don't need more of your thugs, Sugar, we need a goddamned twitcher!" Charles bellowed. The three feet pressed against the floor. The chair was pushed back. This time the Twins rose successfully.

The biots were close now, close to a wall a hundred feet tall, a wall with a long, horizontal cave beneath it.

It had to be a shoe. Or a table leg. No, a shoe.

"We have Army Pete in the building," Sugar said, desperately. "He's downstairs. We need to get him up here to place his nanobots and then—"

"He's a third-rate hack!" Benjamin snarled.

"Our best guys are—"

"Get him!" Charles said.

"You, you, and you: get Army Pete. Drag his ass up here and make sure he's loaded up," Sugar said, relieved to be snapping orders again.

"The army was filled with communists in those days!" Benjamin ranted.

The biots were in the open-sided cave formed by the shoe.

Had to be that. Had to be a shoe, didn't it?

The ceiling above K1 and K2 was creepy in its normality. It looked like a vast quilt—plastic fibers woven together as if by a million tiny seamstresses. It had the look of basketwork, almost uniform, weird in its unnatural uniformity.

And suddenly that ceiling was coming down fast. Keats made his biots leap and twist. Biot legs clutched strands of neoprene and scampered upside down toward light at the end of the toe.

The shoe flattened as the Twins walked. It seemed as if the biots must be crushed, but there was a pattern in the sole and Keats sent his creatures diving into a long, straight channel, then forward again.

He couldn't help but stare as Charles and Benjamin walked. Left. Right. Drag a nearly limp middle leg. Left. Right. Drag.

The center leg had some movement, but it was as if it was numb. It moved in a jerky sequence all its own, out of synch and thus hauled along, scraping toe across the floor.

They were coming to Keats.

The left foot stepped in Keats's blood. Corpuscles surged up and around the biots, finding them even in the depths of the channel. The biots powered on through their creator's own blood, red Frisbees clinging to spiky feet and clustering on biot bellies.

"Make him sit up," Charles ordered. "Remove the gag."

Instantly, rough hands grabbed Keats and hauled him almost to his feet before slamming him on his butt.

The feet were immobile. The biots rushed over and through blood to the end of the channel and turned the corner onto the toe, and Benjamin said, "I don't feel right, brother."

Keats stared up into the faces of the Twins.

He knew better than to be horrified by mere deformity. He'd had a teacher once with paddle arms no more than twelve inches long, a birth defect, and so he knew not to stare, and he certainly knew better than to shudder and pull back and lose for a moment his ability to take a breath.

But this was something out of a nightmare. This was no mere deformity. This was Satan playing with DNA.

Charles's eye glared pure hatred at him. Benjamin's eye was filling with tears. And the third eye, soulless, dead, devoid of spark, wandered before at last focusing on him. He saw the brown iris contract.

"You'll tell me now where the girl is," Charles said in a low voice.

Keats should have said something pithy and defiant. He didn't. His mouth wasn't working.

"You're a handsome one, aren't you?" Charles asked. "My brother and I have not had that particular advantage in life. Tell me, boy: What's it like to have that face? What's it like to have women look at you and admire you?"

"Speak up!" Sugar said. Her voice betrayed her own fear. And someone, Keats didn't see who, buried a toe in his kidney and made him cry out in pain.

"Do you have a knife, Ms Lebowski?" Charles asked.

"A knife? I . . . No, sir."

"I do," a male voice said. There came the snicker-snack sound of a Swiss Army knife opening.

"Promote this one; I like a man who is prepared," Charles said to Sugar. "Give the knife to Ms Lebowski. Ms Lebowski, what part of a man's face attracts you?"

"I . . . the . . . the eyes," Sugar stammered.

Biots were on top of the shoe now. Too far. They would never climb that towering body in time to do any good.

"No, we can't take his eyes, Ms Lebowski. How would he be able to appreciate what had happened to his face if we took his eyes?" The faces, the eyes, scanned the surface of Keats's face and focused at last on his nose.

"Will the girls think he's pretty with his nose cut off, Ms Lebowski?"

"Jesus . . . I," she said.

"Let him feel the blade," Charles said, his voice guttural now.

Sugar pressed the blade against the side of Keats's nose. He could see it. He could feel it. His heart hammered in terror. He tried to twist away but powerful hands imprisoned his skull.

"No, no, don't do it, miss," Keats begged.

"Then tell me where to find the McLure," Charles grated.

The knife would slice through flesh. It would cut his nose and hesitate at the cartilage but it would cut and cut away and his nose would fall to the floor, a useless piece of dead flesh and he would forever—

"Now!" Charles roared. "Tell me now!"

"I don't know where—"

"Cut off his nose! Cut him! Do it!"

"I—" Sugar said.

"Cut off his nose or you'll lose your own!"

"He's a kid!" Sugar begged.

"I don't know where she is!" Keats pleaded.

"Don't hit me, Granddad!" Benjamin cried.

"Shut your mouth, brother! Cut him now!"

But even as Charles bellowed, his body was jerked away. The Twins stumbled back, and through eyes filled with tears, Keats saw Benjamin flailing madly, swatting at something no one but he could see.

"Brother!" Charles cried.

It was a lunatic dance, two halves of the joined body struggling, staggering, slipping in the blood.

The Twins stumbled back into the desk, which scooted away so that they fell hard on their behind, and Keats felt the impact through his biots and the blade slid away from his Keats's nose and Benjamin, in a child's voice, kept saying, "Communists!"

Then Charles roared in frustration. He swatted at his brother's head but couldn't reach. He swatted with arms too short to reach across the width of his own body and shouted, "Control yourself! Control yourself!" as he lost the last of his own control and now flailed, tried to pull himself up and ended in knocking the whole desk over.

Pens and phone and dog treats and a soft-drink bottle all slid to the floor. The touch-screen desk lay on its side, still displaying the battle inside the president.

Charles got his hand on the drink bottle, holding it awkwardly by the fat end, and jabbed it now, hit his brother's face with it, and blood gushed suddenly from Benjamin's mouth even as he kept yelling, "Communists! Communists!"

"Shut up! Shut up! Shut up!"

Charles bashed his brother's mouth. A tooth bent inward and gushed blood. The lips were jagged and red.

"He's going to hurt Benjamin," Sugar said. "We have to stop it."

She moved fast, whipped out plastic ties, the same as the ones that held Keats, grabbed Charles's hammering hand and using her full weight, pushed it down.

"Get off me, you cow!"

"Standing orders, sir: we step into a fight between you two. Your own orders."

"He's let them take him. They're inside him, and he's let them do it. He's weak! He's always been weak!"

She put her knee on the hand, yanked the chair close, and fastened Charles's hand to the crossbar.

"Following your own orders, sir," Sugar pleaded, but she didn't look as if she believed it. She was darting glances at the door, like she was counting steps, like the elevator door a hundred feet away was the doorway to paradise.

Benjamin was weeping now, blubbering like a baby.

"He's here!" one of the TFDs yelled, and Army Pete, a teenaged boy wearing a droopy army surplus jacket, was practically hurled into the room.

Sugar said, "What the hell took so long? You, twitcher! You're going in."

Army Pete was a mediocre twitcher and a first-rate smart-ass. But he knew enough as he surveyed the scene—the bloody boy on the floor and, far worse, the terrifying spectacle of a handcuffed Charles still trying to beat a raving Benjamin—to avoid favoring everyone with his wit.

"Got a twitcher chair? I can't do shit without my gear."

"Damn!" Sugar yelled. "Get a chair up here. Now!"

Army Pete started to object, but no one heard him for the rush of TFDs racing to comply. Or at least racing to get the hell out of the Tulip.

THIRTY

"I'm with you, Vincent," Nijinsky said.

With him on the street, holding his friend, propping him against a wall.

And with him now as his two fresh, undamaged biots ran to the rescue.

"Too late," Vincent whispered.

Nijinsky stared across a half centimeter of space that felt like a city block, at Bug Man's forces. Two of the nanobots were slowly, maliciously dismembering Vincent's biot.

Nijinsky felt each ripped limb through the shuddering form of his friend.

Eleven of Bug Man's nanobots.

Two of Nijinsky's biots.

Maybe. Maybe. But Nijinsky was not Vincent. He would almost certainly lose, and if he lost, then he would be where Vincent was now: a shattered man, helpless and vulnerable.

Bug Man did not attack. Bug Man did not want this battle,

either. He didn't need it. By now his spinners would be deep within the president's brain.

The two of them stared at each other through alien eyes, Bug Man and Nijinsky.

Nijinsky made his lead biot open its arms in supplication.

Bug Man's nanobots stood still for a long minute, doing nothing at all.

Then they lifted the body of Vincent's second biot and shoved it through the fluid. It floated on the current, and Nijinsky was able to grab what was left.

Carrying the legless, eyeless, mutilated body, he turned and ran away.

Up in the world of streets and skyscrapers, Vincent said, "Jin . . . Jin . . ."

"Yes, Vincent."

"Take me to Anya."

When they found her, Plath had two pins left, and no more than a single long strand of wire.

She had built a cat's cradle of pins and wires in Benjamin's brain. It extended across roughly one square centimeter of the hippocampus. It would take an experienced nanobot twitcher no time to find her, but quite a while to actually reach her.

But in the macro her time was up. Someone had finally had the sense to question the two bums who had flushed Keats.

And some bright AmericaStrong thug had decided it was time to take a closer look at the Dumpster.

The lid flew open and powerful hands dug down into the trash until one of those hands closed over an ankle.

Then there were loud cries and warnings, and Plath was hauled bodily up and out, dropped on to the ground, and kicked once very hard in the stomach.

In the elevator going up to the Tulip they decided she needed roughing up. She took a backhand to the face that split her lip. They didn't want the bosses thinking they had gone soft.

The elevator door opened onto a scene of wild contrasts. Within the soaring heights of the Tulip the Twins had built a world. Offset layers of platforms hung overhead—bedrooms, bathrooms, display rooms—each connected by a short, double-width escalator. The ground floor was thirty-six thousand square feet, most of it sunk in gloom. But she had glances of amazing things back in the unlit distance: what could only be a tank, an entire carousel, a Predator drone hanging from wires, large animal cages, a firing range.

But the space directly before her, the corner of the cavernous room, was what fascinated. Half a dozen TFDs. A woman who looked as if she had just stepped out of the J. Crew catalog by way of a spa. A massive desk that had been overturned so that she could see the screens built into its surface, and see a nano battle raging, and an entire Christmas tree of police and fire department lights at the UN, and other things she didn't recognize.

She saw them, the Armstrong Twins, as broad as two men, tall, powerfully built, but fused together in a way that made the mind rebel.

TFDs were manhandling a massive chair, like the world's highest-tech La-Z-Boy. Others were hauling monitors, trailing wire, searching for an electrical outlet.

Keats sat on the floor. The beagle sniffed at the pool of his blood.

The TFDs threw her down beside Keats.

"You didn't have to bring the chair up here," a kid in an army jacket objected. "I could have run it from downstairs."

"What?" the J. Crew woman demanded.

Army Pete shrugged. "Dude, I just needed someone to act as a pathway. One of your guys could have come downstairs; I could have put my boys on him, right? And then—"

He fell silent in the face of Sugar's blazing fury. "You could have told me."

"I figured you understood how—"

"Communists," Benjamin wept as if it was the saddest word in the world.

Keats, sitting in his own blood just a few inches from Plath, held her gaze, and then looked over his shoulder. Plath followed the direction of his eyes. She saw his hands, bound as hers were with a plastic tie.

His wrists were red. He was using the gruesome lubrication to work his hands free. Plath saw cuts. The meat of one thumb was lacerated deeply. But his hands were almost free.

Charles yanked at his own captured arm and almost hit himself with the chair. "You can let me up now, Ms Lebowski," he said. "I have control of myself. I won't harm my brother."

Sugar Lebowski, Plath realized. Nijinsky had briefed them all on her. She almost smiled now recalling his description of: "a bleached, Botoxed, boob-jobbed suburban mommy with a stick up her ass and a gun in her purse."

"Yes, sir," Sugar said. But Plath heard hesitation.

Keats saw her. He tried to show nothing, but Keats didn't have a poker face. He was afraid for her. He was sad to have failed in his brave effort to save her.

She wanted to tell him that she would rather be here with him than alone. She wanted to tell him that she would share his fate. That she was no more afraid than he was.

But the truth was that she was sick with fear. Her limbs were stiff. She couldn't stop blinking. Her lungs were unable to draw enough breath, as though she were being squeezed in a vice. The corners of her mouth were weighted, her tongue was a foreign object, her hands trembled.

She saw then the livid bruising and battered lips of the right half of the Armstrong Twins. Benjamin. She remembered that. He was the right half.

He was shaking. He was yanking the shared head. His eye was wild, not with rage but with some unreadable emotion.

Charles was straining to look complaisant, to seem normal. It was a sort of Janus mask, and like that mythical, two-faced Roman god, Charles and Benjamin were striving to look in different directions. They were facing the same way but seeing very different things.

So she was in Benjamin's brain.

She had twisted enough circuits to push him to malfunction. She had knocked him off the rails. Her biots were like a computer virus, disrupting and confusing, firing off synaptic signals that went to the wrong places.

That knowledge did not make her less afraid.

Charles looked past Sugar and her hesitation and saw Plath. "You would be Sadie," he purred.

Every eye turned. Except for Benjamin.

"It will be a great pleasure to welcome you to our great work," Charles said.

"Never," Sadie managed to whisper. Then finding her voice, she said with more force. "Never."

Charles smiled. "Soon many of the world's most powerful leaders will join our cause. Do you imagine that you will resist?

No, no, little girl, we'll manage to change the way you think about things."

An almost imperceptible nod from Keats.

Deep inside Benjamin's brain, P1 and P2 held their last pins. Plath stabbed deep with the first pin.

Benjamin's whole body shuddered. He cried out, "No, Charles! No! No! Stop it!"

Charles looked as if he'd been the one stabbed. His eye widened, and his brow shot up.

On the screen a biot was being dismembered.

Plath played out the last of her wire, ran with it and the final pin. Her biots leapt across wires already laid, and each time they did the new filament touched and signals flew and Benjamin cried out, "I'm pushing as hard as I can, as hard as I can, he's still breathing!"

"Someone silence him!" Charles demanded. "Ms Lebowski, you silence my brother!"

The wire played out. The spinnerets failed. Plath wrapped the frayed end around the final pin.

"Die, old man! Die!" Benjamin raved.

And Plath sank the last pin.

Benjamin's body arched in a seizure so powerful that his legs smashed the bottom of the desk. The screens went dark. His arm shot out into the air, hand clenched into a claw.

Plath heard the sound of bone cracking.

She pulled the pin out.

"We're walking out of here," she said.

Paul Johntz stepped behind her and pressed a gun muzzle against the top of her head. "He spazzes out again, you take a bullet."

"I'm the one doing it," Keats said. "Leave her alone." It was heroic, but also unconvincing.

A gasping Benjamin wept with a child's sobs.

Charles, aghast, stared in horror at Plath.

"Which is faster?" Plath asked. "The bullet? Or the biot?"

"Listen to me," Charles grated. "Mr Johntz, you are now head of AmericaStrong. Here is what you will do: order your men to arrest Ms Lebowski. Then you will—"

Plath stabbed the pin into Benjamin's brain and again came the seizure, choking off Charles's speech as the shared face strained and the shared neck twisted and the single spine seemed almost to form a C.

Benjamin's teeth cracked.

Sugar Lebowski said, "I can get you out of here. But it will cost you."

"A million?" Plath asked.

"Twenty," Sugar said. "I have kids. Disappearing isn't cheap."

"Done," Plath said.

"No one is going anywhere," Johntz snapped.

Keats kicked with his bound legs and all the force he could command. His feet hit Johntz's ankle. The fall wasn't immediate; the man took a stagger step to the side and Sugar Lebowski was up like a cat. She drew the belt from her skirt and whipped it around Johntz's neck from behind, all the while yelling, "Everyone back, everyone back, stay out of it!" to the remaining TFDs.

But Johntz was too big to go down. He was straining to turn the pistol to point at Sugar, who grunted like an animal as she put all her slim weight into choking.

Keats levered himself up and hopped, splashing through blood, grabbed the TFD's gun hand and twisted it to aim the muzzle at the man's head.

For several terrible seconds they fought. Sugar slowly choking the strength out of her deputy, Keats twisting as he tried to stay on his feet. Then, a loud explosion.

Johntz had a quizzical look on three quarters of his face, and a gaping hole for the rest. He dropped instantly.

The other TFDs had stood by, paralyzed, not knowing who was in charge. Army Pete said, "Damn." He held his hands up in a "Not me" gesture and backed toward the door.

Keats held on to the pistol as the man fell.

Sugar Lebowski had part of Johntz's brain in her blonde hair. She unwrapped her belt from the dead man's neck and with shaking fingers threaded it back into her skirt.

"We need to get our bugs," Keats said. The gun was still in his hand. It felt good, not bad in his grip. It felt like safety.

"It will take me ten minutes to get back out of them," Plath said. "Do I leave them like that?"

"Like that" meant sweat pouring off the Twins, who were held in the grip of Benjamin's seizure. No one could live for very long under that strain.

Plath was asking Keats if she should kill Benjamin Armstrong—and most likely his brother, too, because it was impossible to imagine how one could die and not the other.

"We're not them," Keats said. Then, doubting his own words, said, "Are we?"

Plath went to stand over the helpless monsters. Monsters? What other word could be used?

Monsters from birth. Feared and hated by all who saw them.

Feared and hated now by her, too, and for good reason.

The skin between the two faces, the place where the flesh had been glued together in the womb, was raw. The force of the seizure had nearly made Benjamin tear his head away from his brother.

She pulled the pin.

ARTIFACT

To: Lear
From: Nijinsky

Wilkes is alive and back with us.

Ophelia is alive despite the loss of both legs below the knee.

Keats and Plath are both well and performed magnificently.

Vincent is suffering from a deep depression following the loss of one biot. The second biot was badly injured but is recovering. Vincent is being cared for, outcome very uncertain.

We failed in our main objective.

We await instructions.

Visit

WWW.GOBZRK.COM

to discover a ground-breaking interactive digital transmedia
experience that extends and expands the world of

BZRK

far beyond the pages of this book.

EGMONT PRESS: ETHICAL PUBLISHING

Egmont Press is about turning writers into successful authors and children into passionate readers – producing books that enrich and entertain. As a responsible children's publisher, we go even further, considering the world in which our consumers are growing up.

Safety First
Naturally, all of our books meet legal safety requirements. But we go further than this; every book with play value is tested to the highest standards – if it fails, it's back to the drawing-board.

Made Fairly
We are working to ensure that the workers involved in our supply chain – the people that make our books – are treated with fairness and respect.

Responsible Forestry
We are committed to ensuring all our papers come from environmentally and socially responsible forest sources.

**For more information, please visit our website at
www.egmont.co.uk/ethical**